THE SPLENDID OUTCAST

The African Stories of
Beryl Markham

By the Same Author

West with the Night

THE SPLENDID OUTCAST

The African Stories of
Beryl Markham

Compiled and Introduced by Mary S. Lovell

HUTCHINSON
London   Melbourne   Auckland   Johannesburg

First published in 1987 in Great Britain by Hutchinson Ltd, an imprint of
Century Hutchinson Ltd, Brookmount House,
62–65 Chandos Place, London WC2N 4NW

Century Hutchinson Australia Pty Ltd,
PO Box 496, 16–22 Church Street, Hawthorn, Victoria 3122, Australia

Century Hutchinson New Zealand Limited,
PO Box 40-086, Glenfield, Auckland 10, New Zealand

Century Hutchinson South Africa Pty Ltd
PO Box 337, Bergvlei, 2012 South Africa

Printed and bound in Great Britain by
Butler and Tanner Ltd, Frome and London

British Library Cataloguing in Publication Data

Markham, Beryl
  The Splendid Outcast: the African Stories of Beryl Markham
  1. Title   2. Lovell, Mary
  1823'.914[F]
  PR 6063.A642/

ISBN 0 09 172604 2

For Beryl's granddaughters
Fleur and Valery
In memory of their father
Gervase Markham

Contents

Introduction

Beryl Markham had an extraordinary life. Her parentage and her birthplace ought to have guaranteed her a life within the comfortable constraints of Edwardian "county" society, a life in which she would have received a formal education of English literature, French grammar, painting, and needlework taught by governesses. Dressed in restricting crinoline and pantaloons, Beryl might have sat gazing dreamily out of schoolroom windows onto the Leicestershire countryside, or played with dolls on the shaved green lawns under the cedars of her childhood home, occasionally hearing the slow clop, clop of a passing horse beyond the confining hedges. Later she would have been taught to ride, and, inevitably, to ride to hounds, for her home in Ashwell was at the heart of the finest fox hunting country in England and her parents were both keen fox hunters. Perhaps, later still, she would have joined the eager throngs of debutantes, primped for her first ball, and eventually married some suitable neighboring landowner. Though by any flight of fancy it is difficult to imagine Beryl being content to spend her days in a silk-lined drawing room dispensing tea and gossip.

But in 1903 her father decided to emigrate to the burgeoning Protectorate of British East Africa, now Kenya. Beryl was only three years old when she was taken out to join him on an isolated pioneer homestead where the emphasis in education was on survival. Within eighteen months her parents had separated and her mother returned to England taking the eldest child, Richard, with her. Beryl remained on the farm at Njoro with her father and thus began a unique upbringing almost devoid of convention or restriction, which she called "a world without walls."

Beryl's father was fully occupied with the business of establishing his farm, so the child was left in the daily care of African workers. As naturally as breathing she learned the customs and languages of the numerous tribespeople who squatted on the farm: Nandi, Kipsigis, Luo, Kikuyu, even the occasional Masai herdsman. With these friends as mentors she ran barefoot, and often half naked, through primeval forests. She learned to hunt and track with native cunning, and to kill wild animals armed only with a spear. She became part of Africa and Africa became part of her.

Sometimes Beryl joined her father on his rounds of the farm, riding her pony, an Arab stallion named Wee MacGregor. As time went by she graduated to exercising the imported English thoroughbred racehorses that her father trained as a sideline to his farming interests. Before she was in her teens she was riding and handling horses that were too "difficult" for the African syces [grooms]. Her riding ability and knowledge of horses had become a legend in Kenya even before she trained the winner of the St. Leger.

It was a hard life and the presence of a thousand African migrant workers did not provide a leisurely existence for Beryl and her father. The days were long and arduous and the foes

of the pioneer settler were many. Marauding lions and leopards killed the stock—the stock that had survived tick fever
or other numerous endemic ailments. Other wild animals
trampled or grazed upon crops. The vagaries of climate—too
much sun and no rain, and then suddenly too much rain—had
to be contended with while the farm was literally hacked out
of the Mau forest.

Sometimes in the long dark evenings after the rows of thoroughbred horses had been bedded down, Beryl would sit before the blazing cedarwood fire and her father would read
aloud from the Greek classics by the light of a hurricane lamp.
Once she had learned to read, she read voraciously from any
book that came her way, and later her father appointed governesses—a chain of them—all heartily disliked. Two male
tutors were tolerated until the First World War called both
into service, when the rebellious Beryl was sent away to
school in Nairobi.

She was always a difficult pupil because she resented disci-
pline, and after three years she was expelled for inciting fellow
pupils to revolt. She returned happily to Njoro and became
"head lad" in her father's racing stable. Two weeks before her
seventeenth birthday, a tall, patrician, and extremely beautiful
young woman, Beryl was married to a neighboring farmer
who was twice her age. Shortly after her marriage, her father
went bankrupt and left the country, so at the age of eighteen
she obtained a trainer's license, took over the training of a
handful of horses and immediately produced winners. When
her marriage disintegrated she moved into a grass-thatched
hut, continued training, and was only twenty-three years old
when she trained the winner of the Kenya St. Leger. More success followed, as did a second brief marriage to a wealthy aristocrat. But the marriage failed when she became emotionally

entangled with an English prince, and she threw her career over without a backward glance when she became interested in the new sport of flying.

Beryl did not see flying as a sport, however. She saw it as a new and exciting way to earn a living. She obtained her pilot's license and quickly built up her flying hours, including a solo six-thousand-mile flight to England when she had only just over a hundred hours in her logbook. Then she went on to gain her commercial pilot's license—the first awarded to any woman in East Africa. In her flimsy, fabric-covered biplane she hired herself out as a big-game spotter to safari parties. Using cleared areas of scrub as temporary landing strips, she joined the hunters and flew each day looking for herds of elephant, especially the big "tuskers" sought by the trophy hunters. When the safari season ended, she ferried passengers to isolated "up-country" farms, carried the air mails to gold miners in Tanganyika, turned her two-seater into a flying ambulance, and occasionally worked as a relief pilot for a newly established airline. The solo flying she did across the bush was highly dangerous, given the technical restrictions of aircraft at that time and the wilderness over which she flew. She had no radio, and a forced landing—even assuming she survived it without injury—could have meant slow death from starvation or thirst, not to mention attack by wild animals. Her only concession to the dangers was to carry a phial of morphine in the pocket of her immaculate white flying suit, and a revolver.

In 1936 Beryl was the first woman to fly the Atlantic from east to west—the first person of either sex to fly from England to North America—and she became an international celebrity. There was a handful of famous aviators at the time represented in the United States by Charles Lindbergh, Amelia Earhart, and Wiley Post, and in England by Amy Johnson, Jim

Mollison, and Jean Batten; all had written their stories (or, in some cases, had them ghostwritten). It was therefore inevitable that Beryl should be asked to write about her achievement, but the book that resulted, *West with the Night*, was a revelation. Far from being a stereotyped version of how she learned to fly, followed by the Atlantic crossing, her memoir drew upon her childhood and equine experiences, as well as her aeronautical exploits, and was written in a style that earned praise from literary critics. But after a brief period of success during which the book reached number one on the *New York Times* bestseller list, it faded into obscurity, a forgotten victim of the Second World War.

When, forty years later, her beautifully phrased book was rediscovered and republished, doubt was thrown upon Beryl's ability to have written it. Friends of Beryl's third husband, the writer Raoul Schumacher, claimed it was he who had written Beryl's work. "She was nearly illiterate!" said some of her detractors, while others asked why—since she was so able— were there no other works? This collection of Beryl's short stories, discovered during research for her authorized biography, provide some answers.

After researching Beryl's fascinating career, meeting her, and discovering her range of talent, I find it incredible that anyone who knew her well could doubt her ability to write. Who else could have told the story of her childhood and other experiences with such depth and perception? No ghostwriter could have extracted the level of detail and produced it so sensitively.

The supposition that Beryl was illiterate is pure nonsense. She had an education all right, though it was not always formal in its structure. It was sufficiently good to enable her to pass her commercial pilot's examinations, including the difficult Navigation Theory paper. Her pilot's logbook reveals a firm, educated hand, and her surviving letters convey a light sense of humor and a neat phraseology. Her learning process was an uncoordinated mixture of the practical and the aesthetic, helped along on occasions by her well-educated father, and later still by the scholarly Denys Finch Hatton, who encouraged Beryl to educate herself.

Beryl herself always maintained that she was the sole author of her book. Equally, she claimed that it was her old friend, the French writer/aviator Antoine de Saint-Exupéry, who helped her to start writing her memoir (perhaps accounting for its poetic nature), and she never denied that Raoul helped her with editorial advice and support. There are some surviving pages of manuscript that bear Raoul Schumacher's handwritten edits, and Beryl herself acknowledged his "help and encouragement" in a foreword. But she wrote the major part of her memoir in the Bahamas and Raoul never visited her there.

Beryl herself seemed totally unconcerned about the theory that she had not written the book. When I discussed the subject with her she dismissed it, "Oh that old thing again!" Asked how she answered her detractors, she shrugged and said, "I don't bother. . . ."

Writing was only incidental to Beryl, to be cast off when she moved on to the next phase of her life. After her marriage to Raoul Schumacher foundered in 1948 she returned to Africa and embarked upon a second brilliant career training racehorses. Her long life was filled with adventure and achievement. Her other great successes—the horse training and the flying—were public, often in the glare of media coverage. But writing cannot be done in public. It is essentially a lonely profession and therefore it was easy for Beryl's detractors to cast doubt on her authorship.

My opinion is that Beryl—like many who have confined their writing to autobiography—found writing a chore. Though she called herself a writer during her American period and often made a show of retiring to her room "to work," she had difficulty in producing finished pieces of fiction. Nonetheless, during her American period Beryl published the stories contained in this anthology, some of which share the vivid classical quality that singles out _West with the Night_ as a great piece of writing. The others are of less interest as literature than for their historical background, because there is much in them that enhances what is known about Beryl's life.

Beryl cooperated with me in the writing of her biography, but she died before I could tell her that I was compiling this anthology, which was to be a surprise for her eighty-fourth birthday. I can therefore only imagine what her reaction would have been. "Really? How funny! Sit down and have a drink. Now . . . what shall we talk about?" To the end she remained essentially modest about her achievements. When she spoke of them at all it was matter-of-factly and when asked to elaborate, a dismissive wave of her long slim hands was inevitably accompanied with a scornful, "But it's all so long ago, no one will be interested in that."

Beryl's literary works are few, and that is our loss. But now that her autobiography promises to rank among the classics of our time she surely deserves the full, unequivocal credit for her remarkable writing ability, in addition to the acclaim that she has already received for her other achievements.

MARY S. LOVELL
Salisbury, England
March 1987

PART ONE

Something I Remember

This story and the two that follow are almost autobiographical and form a welcome addition, in Beryl's own words, to her memoir. I use the word almost because in each case the facts have been slightly exaggerated to provide a dramatic climax to real events. It may well be that originally she had written about these episodes for her memoir. It is known that her husband Raoul advised her to cut that work down and revise the chronology, and perhaps the resultant discards provided the basis for these individual short stories, which were finished at a later date.

At the time Beryl wrote this story, she was living on an isolated New Mexico ranch where she "raised turkey poults and did a lot of riding." She told me that Raoul was sometimes away due to war service and she was often bored and lonely. Recalling and writing about her childhood helped to pass the long evenings.

Wee MacGregor was Beryl's first horse. Her father bought him when Beryl was about six years old, and it is typical of Beryl that her first horse was an Arab stallion, a type not normally known for docility. But Beryl's remarkable riding ability was obvious even as a tiny child—she describes Wee MacGregor as an obedient pony.

It is not known whether the fight between Wee MacGregor and Chaldean actually happened. Certainly there was a filly in Beryl's stable called

[First published in *Collier's, The National Weekly*, January 1944.]

Reve d'Or in 1922; it was her father's parting gift when he left Kenya for Peru. The incident described here is more likely to be the reflection of several fights between stallions, witnessed by Beryl at Green Hills—the Njoro farm where she grew up.

_____

When I think about it, it seems to me that in twenty-odd years of breeding and training racehorses, I ought to have encountered at least one with human qualities. I have read about such horses but I have never known one and I can't help feeling a little cheated. Whenever I have heard someone say, "Now there's a horse so intelligent he's almost human," I have had to admit to myself a little sadly that no horse I can bring to memory ever deserved that laudatory phrase. Of course, it may be that such a comparison is, to a horse, of doubtful virtue. That was certainly the case with Wee MacGregor.

Wee MacGregor maintained throughout his life a gentle contempt for both men and the works of men, and I am convinced that his willing response to their demands was born wholly of tolerance. He rarely ignored a word or resisted a hand; and it was not until he began his blood feud with Chaldean that anyone realized the intensity of the fire that burned in his heart.

Wee MacGregor was an Arab. His coat was chestnut, and his mane and tail were black, and he wore a white star on his forehead—jauntily and a little to one side, more or less as an impudent street urchin might wear his cap. He was an urchin, too, by the standards prevailing in our stables. He was perfectly built but very small, and though he was a stallion, he was not bought to breed, certainly not to race, but only to work at carrying myself or my father—and even, if need be, to draw a pony cart. I still remember the day he came.

Horses were always coming and going on our farm in Kenya. Some arrived for training, and others left for the races at Nairobi, Eldoret, Nakuru, or even Durban, more than two thousand miles away. Until the advent of Wee MacGregor, they were all thoroughbreds of course and, to the uninitiated, they must have looked alike, except for color. They were tall, tense horses of supreme arrogance and insolent beauty. They were pampered, they were groomed, they were cherished like the heirs to so many thrones.

They were, I am afraid, a snobbish clique, for when Wee MacGregor was led for the first time to his stall (in the lesser stable) he was greeted with silence. Not even a stallion raised his voice, and the brood mares in their spacious boxes scarcely stirred. There may have been other reasons for it, but the controlled dismay with which our thoroughbreds looked upon Wee MacGregor was, in effect, similar to the way a gathering of the socially illustrious might view the arrival in their midst of a laborer with calloused hands.

Nevertheless, in the days that followed, the little Arab worked hard and kept his peace; he toiled with patience and gave everyone to understand that he bore no grudge and that his was a placid soul. He was intelligent, he handled beautifully, he refused no effort asked of him, and it may have been that if Chaldean had not come to the farm, we would never have been disillusioned about Wee MacGregor's pacific nature. But Chaldean did come—and on a bad day, too.

We were clearing the trees from our farm—or rather we were fighting the great Mau forest, which, in its centuries of unhampered growth, had raised a rampart of trees so tall I used to think their branches brushed the sky. The trees were cedar, olive, yew, and bamboo, and often the cedars rose to heights of two hundred feet, blocking the sun.

Men said the forest could not be beaten, and this was true, but at least my father made it retreat. Under his command, a corps of Dutchmen with hundreds of oxen and an axe to every man assaulted the bulwark, day after day, and in time its outer walls began to fall.

On one such day, my father said to me, "Get Wee Mac-Gregor and take this note to Mostert. The rains are due, and I don't want the teams bogged in the forest."

Christiaan Mostert was our foreman and when, an hour later, he took my father's message from my hand and read it, he looked upward involuntarily, but he could not see the sky.

"Ja," he said, "I see nothing, but I think the baas is right. I smell rain, and the monkeys have lost their tongues."

He spat on his hands and shouted an order, but it was too late. Thunder swallowed his voice, and rain swallowed the forest. It was a typical equatorial storm—instantaneous, violent, and all-encompassing. It made the world black, then split the blackness with knives of light. It made the great trees creak and the bamboos moan. Forest hogs ran for cover, terrified parrots darted in green and scarlet arcs through the lightning, and the oxen plunged and strained in their traces.

It was not a new thing for Christiaan Mostert, or for any of his men, or for me. It was new for Wee MacGregor, and yet the little Arab took the whole monstrous nightmare in his stride. He neither reared nor even trembled, and as I rode him from ox team to ox team through the roaring forest aisles, his manner was one of dutiful resignation.

Even when a massive cedar, ripped by lightning, fell across a span of oxen and broke the backs of two, he did not wince; and when Christiaan Mostert put rifle bullets into the suffering beasts, Wee MacGregor only tilted his ears in mild curiosity, as if the insanity of his masters had begun to bore him.

For an hour he worked, disdainful even of the storm, lending his strength to a bogged wagon more than once, carrying me back and forth with Mostert's orders to his men; and when the storm ended as abruptly as it had begun, Wee MacGregor met Chaldean for the first time.

Chaldean had arrived that day from England. He stood, bristling arrogance, blanketed and angry-eyed in the broad space between our stables. My father was there, standing proudly beside him, and a dozen syces and farm boys, marveling at his beauty.

It was more than beauty. It was pride in heritage and consciousness of ability, for Chaldean's breeding and his record were clean as fire. He was a descendant of St. Simon, and a champion, and his colts were champions and he knew it.

He was black and smooth as a rifle barrel and as hard. The cast of his head was classic. He was deep-chested and clean-legged and the promise of a magnificent stride lay in his height and in the power of his quarters. He was to Wee MacGregor as a Doric column to a beam of wood, and he clothed his beauty in insolence.

Wee MacGregor felt it. Straight from his labors in the forest, still wet with the rain that mingled with his sweat, he raised his head and looked upon this pampered paragon— and trembled. He let a low sound escape his throat, and Chaldean heard it.

For a moment, the two horses—one a drudge and one a prince—regarded each other, and then Chaldean whirled on his tether and reared from the ground and screamed the shrill scream of an angered stallion. He rose higher, against my father's strength, and beat the air with his forelegs and screamed again. My father swore and jerked him down, and the syces ran forward to hold him.

Wee MacGregor plunged, but I held him back. He fought the bridle, but I turned him. It did not last long, but it was not finished. I knew then, as I rode to the stable, that the giant thoroughbred and the little Arab had made their quarrel and what remained was only the settling of it.

Still under the pressure of regular work, you forget such things. If you have a stable of fifty horses, you have not time to concern yourself with the grudges and foibles of one or two. You remember certain rules and you follow them. The rule that two warring stallions must never meet is axiomatic—so self-evident that you take it for granted that they never will.

My days passed, and when on occasion I had to use Wee MacGregor again on some routine duty or other, it did not seem to me that anything about him had changed. He brooded a lot, the way some horses do, or appear to do, and often I would find him in his stall standing in the farthest corner, out of the light, staring at the wall and seeing nothing.

It is true that once or twice I noticed that the wooden latch on his door had been partly slipped back, but there again I thought nothing of it because many horses will, out of boredom, fondle a latch with their teeth or toy with a halter rope. I always shot the latch home and forgot about it.

When Reve d'Or came to the farm, Chaldean's ego began to assert itself to such an extent that at times he was almost beyond control. Reve d'Or was a whaler filly (that is to say, an Australian thoroughbred filly), a dark bay and beautiful in the eyes of horsemen, but I never knew why her daily passage down the areaway between Chaldean's stable and Wee Mac-Gregor's should have brought their vendetta to the white heat that it did; there were dozens of other mares and fillies on the place.

It may have been that, in fact, she was wholly forgotten

by both of them once they had established a new reason for their enmity, but however that was, her groom never led her past the stables without drawing from the little Arab and the haughty thoroughbred screams of mutual rage and hatred. It ought to have been obvious to everybody that one day this burning bitterness must bring a climax, but no one thought about it.

It was not so long a time that Reve d'Or had a lovely foal, and Chaldean (since he was of St. Simon strain) was, of course, its sire. Horse breeders are not given to romanticism in their work but rather to considerations of profit and loss, and a colt by Chaldean out of Reve d'Or gave great expectations to my father and to those horse-wise friends who frequented our house.

It is a strange but a true thing that the appearance of a new foal in a stable will always excite the stallions and even the geldings to the most exorbitant antics. They will neigh and scream and beat against their boxes in a kind of wild gaiety. If they are in pasture, they will gallop its length time and again, kicking their heels, drumming out the good word with swift and sparkling hooves like tireless performers at a week-long jubilee. No birthdays go unheralded. And yet, in the case of Reve d'Or's foal, Wee MacGregor was a silent bystander.

This, I suppose, was due to his breeding. Arabs are not so excitable as thoroughbreds, and Wee MacGregor was valued all the more for his steady (if increasingly dour) character. He had even got to the point where he no longer returned Chaldean's insults, but only stood and glared at his enemy from the darkest depths of his stall. He worked hard while Chaldean basked in the sun; he arrived home clotted with sweat while Chaldean fretted under the ministrations of some diligent syce; his feet were left unshod for labor while Chaldean's were deftly plated for glory on the track. We forgot, but Wee MacGregor remembered these things. He hoarded the memories until his heart was full of them and would hold no more.

It is a hideous thing to watch two stallions fight. If you are on the back of one, it is terrifying.

For many months, not a morning had passed on which Wee MacGregor had not seen me mount Chaldean and ride him away to his exercise. For many months, I had forgotten the half-open latch on Wee MacGregor's door, I had forgotten that patience and practice make for perfection. Nowadays I can only believe that Wee MacGregor knew it from the first.

He caught us not far from the house. The path we always took wandered through a wattle grove that had a clearing in it. It was a big clearing surrounded by trees and shaded by their lacelike leaves and yellow blossoms. The earth underneath was red clay and hard. It was so hard that it gave a kind of ring to Wee MacGregor's hooves—a bold and forthright ring, for he used no cunning in his attack; he did not come from behind.

He came straight for his enemy, not cantering or rushing headlong, but lifting his firm little legs high and proudly, making taut the bow of his neck, flaunting his black tail like a battle plume. Nor were his ears laid back in anger. They were alert, anticipant, and eager—as if this, at last, were the joyful moment he had dreamed of all his quiet life.

I remember that the little scraps of sunlight fallen through the leaves lay on his chestnut coat and burnished it like armor; I remember that his eyes were bright. I remember, too, that Chaldean swung round with graceful majesty to face this puny David and his shining courage. I could feel Chaldean's muscles harden; I could feel his veins swell to rigid ropes beneath his skin. I could hear the first notes of his battle cry, deep and low in his throat, and I looked around me.

Through the trees I could see our house, but it was far. No one was near—not my father, not a syce, not a farmhand. I might have dismounted, but you do not abandon a valuable horse to his fury; you do not throw away the rules. You hang on—and tremble. I hung on. I trembled. The two stallions were alone in their anger and I was alone in my fear.

When Wee MacGregor charged, when Chaldean screamed his challenge, when blood spurted on my clothes and on my bare arms, and the cyclones of dust hid all but trenchant teeth and hooves like iron cudgels, my fear was frozen still—and I was a forgotten watcher.

I watched the little Arab's first lunge. He came in, head outstretched, swift as a sword, using only his teeth—flashing his teeth—hoping to cripple Chaldean's foreleg. He was fearless. He was quick, and in this quickness he was deadly.

Chaldean went to his knees, parrying the thrust and screaming his war cry with what seemed the volume of a thousand trembling trumpets. The vibrations of that cry ran through my body.

Chaldean went down. He struck his shoulder on a root, gashing the flesh, adding crimson to our vortex of whirling color, but he rose again with inspired fury. He reared high, while I clung to him, and he caught the Arab on the flank, striking both blood and pain as a smith strikes fire from steel.

I suppose I cried out. I suppose I flailed my whip and let the reins cut my tugging hands. I was alone and not yet fifteen, and it may even have been that I wept, but these are things I don't remember. I only remember the sudden realization of the terrible power, the destructive strength that can pour from the sinews of this most docile of animals, this nodding slave of men.

Wee MacGregor fought with so cold a determination that he made almost no sound. It was clear at once that he wanted not just to win but to kill. It was clear, too, that he felt that his anger compensated for his lack of size.

Chaldean towered above him. He had advantages and he used them. He reared until the Arab was beneath him, then plunged and sank his teeth into Wee MacGregor's neck and held fast and reared again and hurled his enemy from him into the dust and blood; and there was a moment of silence.

There was a moment of silence as the little Arab found his legs and stood sucking breath into his lungs. The wound on his neck was deep and it was scarlet, but it might have been no wound at all. He gave no sign of pain.

For a frantic instant, I tried to turn Chaldean, to drive him home, but he would not budge. He knew what was coming, and it came.

If Wee MacGregor had fought viciously before, he fought insanely now. He came in with eyes like burning coals, and I tried to beat him off, but for him, I was not there. For him, nothing existed save his anger and his enemy. Abandoning caution, he closed, and the impact almost threw me from the saddle.

Again Chaldean caught him by the neck and hurled him bleeding to the ground, and again he rose, staggering a little now, but not hesitating. His courage was like a shield that beat away the thought of fear. Three times he came on and three times he fell before Chaldean's strength and fury. But on the fourth try, he found his moment.

I do not know how it happened, but somehow in the maelstrom of screams and dust and thudding hooves, the little

Arab caught in his teeth a strip of the pressure bandage bound around Chaldean's foreleg. The bandage had come undone. It was like a net, and the Arab meant to make it one. He held it firmly in his teeth and pulled, and Chaldean was helpless. He pawed and plunged and tottered and swayed, fighting to free himself. There was panic in him—and I prepared to leap from his back at last. It seemed madness to hang on for, if he fell, I should fall with him—perhaps under him.

I beat Wee MacGregor with my whip, sparing no strength, lashing his head and his neck and his withers, but he was aware of nothing save the promise of triumph. His teeth clamped tight on the bandage, he threw the whole power of his body into the effort of downing his enemy.

Chaldean faltered. He was trapped, and the Arab knew it. I knew it. I put my hands on the pommel and made ready to throw myself clear, I could hear voices coming up the road, but now there was not time. It was too late.

I was raising myself from the saddle when the bandage broke in Wee MacGregor's teeth. The ripping of the cloth and Chaldean's lunge were simultaneous. So, almost, was my own cry and Wee MacGregor's single shriek of pain when Chaldean's teeth closed on the little Arab's foreleg, twisting it, breaking the bone as if it were a stalk of corn. Chaldean reared high and, for the last time, threw his challenger to earth.

The Arab lay almost still, but he was not dead, and Chaldean would not have it so. Not I, but his rage was master. Wee MacGregor tried once more to rise, but the bone of his leg was broken through. David was down, and Goliath moved forward to kill him, but he did not.

My father had come, and with him, his men. They had bound grass to sticks and made torches of them and now they beat Chaldean back with fire. They thrust the fire in his face and beat him back, step by step, and shouted at him, and I gathered the reins tight in my hands, which were bleeding now, and urged him home at last, down the dusty road, not bothering to hold my tears.

Most times you destroy a crippled horse, but Wee Mac-Gregor was made to live, though he never worked again. He was brought home on a rope stretcher and for weeks he stood in his stall supported by a sling until, in time, he walked once more, with halting steps.

Of course, he was never any trouble after that; he could not have been. He was pensioned, as faithful horses often are, and he never again slipped the latch of his stall—or at least not more than once.

One day, or rather at the end of one day, when the sun was almost gone and I rode Reve d'Or through the clearing in the wattle grove, we came upon the little Arab standing still as marble in what had been the arena of his great defeat. He was older then, and the fire had gone from his eye, and his chestnut coat was dull in the horizontal light. But there he stood, looking not at Reve d'Or and not at me, but at the earth, and we passed him by. He did not whinny or make any sound or lift his head. He only stood there like a man with a dream.

But of course that was only the way it seemed to me. Horses are not like humans—at least no horse that I have ever known—and I suspect that he had come there only to catch the last warmth of the sun. I don't know, and so I can't be sure. It is all just something I remember.

The Captain and His Horse

"The Captain and His Horse" was the first short story written by Beryl while she was living in New York in 1943. It is based on a true incident—the group of men and horses did visit the Njoro farm during the First World War. When I interviewed Beryl in 1986 I had not seen this story, but she had a page of draft manuscript for it and we discussed that. She recalled the horse rather than the men, though she did remember playing cricket and learning how to fire a revolver.

The name she gave to the horse in the story was poetic license. Beryl thought the horse's name was "something funny like Jimmy . . . I can't remember exactly," she said. But there was a horse called the Baron in Beryl's life. He was one of her first racehorses when she started training and was part-owned by her great friend and lover, Tom Campbell Black.

The incident in this story probably happened in early 1915, for later that year Beryl was sent away to school in Nairobi. In 1917 when she was expelled for trying to incite a rebellion, she returned to Njoro to become "head lad" at her father's racing stable, and then she was clearly older than the girl portrayed here.

After the story was first published, Beryl's editor at Houghton Mifflin wrote to the South African writer Stuart Cloete, a mutual friend, asking

[First published in *Ladies' Home Journal*, August 1943.]

him if he had seen Beryl's "magnificent horse story" in a weekly magazine.
Cloete's reply reveals his exasperated amusement:

> *Yes I have read Beryl's magnificent horse story, and you will find my*
> *equally magnificent horse story in a forthcoming Collier's [*"Crusader," *first*
> *published in* Collier's, The National Weekly, 1943]. *I wrote mine*
> *some time before Beryl wrote hers and read it to her when she was in New*
> *York.*

Honi soit qui mal y pense . . .

The world is full of perfectly well-meaning people who are sentimental about the horse. They believe that God in His wisdom charged the horse tribe with two duties; the first being to serve man generally, and the second being to eat lump sugar from the palms of kindly strangers. For centuries the horse has fulfilled these obligations with little complaint, and as a result his reputation has become static, like that of a benevolent mountain, or of an ancient book whose sterling qualities most people accept without either reservation or investigation. The horse is "kind," the horse is "noble." His virtues are so emphasized that his character is lost.

The personalities of many horses have remained in my mind from early East African days. Horses peopled my life then and, in a measure, they still people my memory. Names like these—Cambrian, the Baron, Wee MacGregor—are to me bright threads in a tapestry of remembrance hardly tarnished after all these years.

Now there is war, and it is hard to say a thing or think a thing into which that small but most tyrannical of words does not insert itself. I suppose it is because of this that the name of the Baron comes most often to me—because of this and, of course, because, among other things, the Baron was himself a warrior. There was a war, too, when I was a girl of thirteen living on what was euphemistically called a Kenya farm, but which was in fact a handful of cedar huts crouching on alien earth and embraced by wilderness. That was the old war, the nearly forgotten war, but it had the elements of all wars: it bred sorrow and darkness, it bred hope, and it threw strong lights on the souls of men, so that you could see, sometimes, courage that you never knew was there.

Like all wars—like this one—it produced strange things. It brought people together who had never before had a common cause or a common word. One day it brought to my father's farm at Njoro a small company of sick and tired men—mounted on horses that were tired, too—who had the scars of bullets in their flesh.

It goes without saying that the men were cast of heroic stuff. I remember them. A man who has fought for six months in blinding desert heat and stinging desert cold and lives only to fight again has no respect for the word "heroic." It is a dead word, a verbal medal too nebulous to conceal even the smallest wound. Still, you can utter it—you can write it for what it is worth.

But these men came on horses. Each man rode a horse, each was carried to the restful safety of our farm not by an animal, but by his companion, by his battle friend.

"Who are they?" I asked my father.

He is a tall man, my father, a lean man, and he husbands his words. It is a kind of frugality, a hatred of waste, I think. Through all his garnered store of years, he has regarded wasted emotion as if it were strength lavished on futile things. "Save strength for work," he used to say, "and tears for sorrow, and space it all with laughter."

We stood that morning on the little porch of our mud-and-daub house, and I asked my father who these men were with torn clothes and bearded faces and harsh guns in such a gentle land. It is true that leopards came at night and that there were lions to be met with on the plains and in the valleys not far away. But we had learned to live with these and other beasts—or at least they had learned to live with us—and it seems to me now that it was a land gentle beyond all others.

"They are soldiers of the British army," my father said, "and they are called Wilson's Scouts. It is very simple. They have never seen you before, but they have been fighting for your right to grow up, and now they have come here to rest. Be kind to them—and above all, see to it that their horses want nothing. In their way, they are soldiers, too."

"I see," I said. But I was a child and I saw very little. In the days that followed, the tired men grew strong again and most of their wounds healed, and they would talk in the evening as they sat around our broad table. The men would sit under hurricane lamps whose flames danced when a joke was made, or grew steady again when there was silence. Sometimes the flames would falter, and I could stand in the room for long minutes nursing a failing lamp and hearing what there was to hear.

I heard of a German, General von Lettow-Vorbeck, who, with his Prussian-officered troops based in German East Africa, was striking north to take our country. It seemed that these troops were well-enough trained, that they responded to orders without question, like marionettes responding to strings. But they were lost men; they were fighting British settlers, they were trying to throw Englishmen out of their homes—an undertaking in which I sensed, even then, the elements of flamboyant ambition, and not a small measure of indiscretion.

They were well-enough trained, these Germans, but, among

other things, they had Wilson's Scouts to consider; hard-riding volunteer colonials whose minds were unhampered with military knowledge, but whose hearts were bitter and strong—and free. No, it seemed to me, as I listened to them, that the enemy they fought was close to his grave. And as things developed, he was, when I met the Baron, already anticipating its depth.

There was a captain in our small group of cavalrymen, and he would sometimes talk about the Baron—short snatches of talk of the kind that indicated that everybody everywhere must, of course, have heard of him. The captain would say things like this. He would say, "It looked difficult to me. There was a *donga* six feet across and deep with wait-a-bit thorns, and three of the enemy on the other side, but the Baron wasn't worried and so I couldn't be. We cleaned them out after a little skirmish—though the Baron caught one in the shoulder. He holds it still." And the other men would shake their heads and drink their drinks, which I knew was just a quiet way of paying tribute to the Baron.

He was the pride of the regiment, of course, but when I first saw him in the stable my father had given him near our thoroughbreds, I was disappointed. I couldn't have helped that; I was used to sensitive, symmetrical, highly strung horses, clean-bred and jealous of their breeding.

But the Baron was not like this. He was crude to look at. Surrounded by the aristocrats of his species, the Baron seemed a common animal, plebeian. It was almost as if he had been named derisively. At our first meeting he stood motionless and thoughtful—a dark brown gelding with a boxlike head. There was thick hair around his pasterns and fetlock joints, and he wore his rough coat indifferently, the way a man without vanity, used to war, will wear his tattered tunic.

It is a strange thing to say of a horse, but when I went into the Baron's stable I felt at once both at ease and a little inferior. I think it was his eyes more than anything—they were dark, larger than the eyes of most horses, and they showed no white. It wasn't a matter of their being kind eyes—they were eyes that had seen many things, understanding most of them and fearing none. They held no fire, but they were alive with a glow of wisdom, neither quiet nor fiercely burning. You could see in his eyes that his soul had struck a balance.

He turned to me, not wanting to smell my hair or to beg for food, but only to present himself. His breathing was smooth and unhurried, his manner that of an old friend, and I stroked his thick hard neck that was like a stallion's, because I could think of nothing else to do. And then I left quietly, though there was no need for silence, and walked through one of our pastures and beyond the farm into the edge of the Mau forest, where, if you were a child, it was easier to think.

I thought for a long time, concluding nothing, answering nothing, because there was nothing I could answer.

The war, the wounded men, the big thoughts, the broad purposes—all were still questions to me, beyond my answering. Yet I could not help but think that the dark brown gelding standing there in his stable was superior, at least to me, because he made it evident that he had no questions and needed no answers. He was, in his way, as my father had said, a soldier, too.

It is easy enough to say such a thing, but as one day nudged another through that particular little corridor of time the Baron proved himself a soldier—and it seems to me now, something more.

I don't think I ever learned the full name of the young captain who owned him, but that was not my fault. There was little formality about Wilson's Scouts. The men at our farm were part of a regiment, but more than that they were a brotherhood. They called their captain "Captain Dennis" or just Dennis. Wilson himself, the settler of Machakos who had first brought them together was simply "F.O.B." because those were his initials.

Captain Dennis took the Baron out of his stable one morning, and two of the other men got their horses, and when they were all saddled and bridled—while I leaned against the stable door watching the Baron with what must have been wistful eyes—Captain Dennis led the big gelding over to me and handed me the reins. The captain was a lanky man with fierce grey eyes and a warm smile that laughed at their fierceness—and I think at me as well.

He said, "You've been watching the Baron like that for weeks and I can't stand it. We're going to shoot kongonis with revolvers from horseback, and you're coming along."

I had a currycomb in my hand and I turned without saying anything and hung the comb on its peg in the stable. When I came out again my father was standing next to the captain with a revolver in his hand. It was a big revolver, and when my father gave it to me he said:

"It's a little heavy, Beryl, but then you never had much fun with toys. What the captain can't teach you, the Baron will. It doesn't matter if you don't hit a kongoni, but don't come back without having learned something—even if it's the knowledge that you can't shoot from horseback."

The captain smiled, and so did my father. Then he kissed me and I mounted the Baron and we rode away from the farm—the captain, two cavalry men, and myself—through some low hills and down into the Rongai Valley, where the kongonis were.

To say that it was a clear day is to say almost nothing of that country. Most of its days were clear as the voices of the birds that unfailingly coaxed each dawn away from the night. The days were clear and many-colored. You could sit in your saddle and look at the huge mountains and at the river valleys, green, and aimless as fallen threads on a counterpane—and you could not count the colors or know them, because some were nameless. Some colors you never saw again, because each day the light was different, and often the colors you saw yesterday never came back.

But none of this meant much to me that morning. The revolver slung at my waist in a rawhide holster, the broad, straight backs of the cavalrymen riding ahead, the confident pace of the Baron—all these made me feel very proud, but conscious of my youth, smaller, even, than I was.

We hit the bowl of the valley, and in a little while the captain raised his hand, and we looked east into the sun and saw a herd of game about a mile away, feeding in the yellow grass. I had hunted enough on foot to know the tricks: move upwind toward your quarry; keep the light behind you if you can; fan out; be quiet; if there is cover, use it. The captain nodded to me and I waved a hand to show that I would be all right by myself, and then we began to circle, each drifting away from the others, but still joined in the flanking maneuver.

The grass in the Rongai Valley is waist-high and it does not take much of a rise in the plain to hide a man and his horse. In a moment the Baron and I were hidden, and so were the men hidden from us, but the herd of game was just there toward the sun, gathered in a broad clearing—perhaps five thousand head of kongonis, zebras, wildebeests, and oryxes grazing together.

I rode loose-reined, giving the brown gelding his head,

watching his small alert ears, his great bowed neck, feeling the strength of his forthright stride—and I felt that he was hunting with me. He moved with stealth, in easy silence, and I dropped my hand to the revolver, self-consciously, and realized that it was really I who was hunting with him.

He was not an excitable horse, yet he seemed to become even more calm as the distance between the game and ourselves narrowed, while I grew more tense. I sat more rigidly upon the back of the Baron than anyone should ever sit upon the back of any horse, but I had the vanity of youth; I was not to be outdone—not even by soldiers.

By the time the identity of the game had become clear— the horns of oryxes reflecting sunlight like drawn rapiers, the ungainly bulk of wildebeests, zebras flaunting their elaborate camouflage, eland and kongonis in the hundreds—by the time the outlines of their bodies had become distinct to my eyes, I was so on fire with anticipation that I had forgotten my companions.

The Baron and I took advantage of what cover there was and crept up on the outer fringe of the herd until we could smell the dust they stirred to motion with their hooves. Then the Baron stopped and I leaned forward in the saddle. I was breathing unevenly, but the Baron scarcely breathed at all.

Not a hundred yards away, a kongoni stood in long grass, half buried in it. The sun was on him, playing over his sleek fawn coat, and he looked like a beast carved from teakwood and polished by age. He was motionless, he was still, he was alert. High in the shoulders, the line that ran sloping to his hips was scarcely curved, and it forewarned us of his strength and his speed.

It didn't occur to me that I might have been wiser in choosing a smaller animal. One half as big would have been faster than most horses, with perhaps more endurance, but this one was a challenge. I could not resist. In a quick instant of apprehension I peered in all directions, but there was no one near. There were only the Baron, the kongoni, and myself, none of us moving, none of us breathing. Not even the grass moved, and if there were birds they were motionless too.

Leaning low over the Baron's crest, I begin to whisper, smothering my excitement in broken phrases. I ease the reins forward, giving him full head, pressing my hands upon his neck, talking to him, telling him things he already knows: "He's big! He's the biggest of all. He's out of the herd; he's alone, he's ours! Careful, careful!"

The Baron is careful. He sees what I see, he knows more than I know. He tilts his ears, his nostrils distend ever so slightly, the muscles of his shoulders tighten under his skin like leather straps. The tension is so great that it communicates itself to the kongoni. His head comes up and he trembles, he smells the air, he is about to plunge.

"Now!"

The word bursts from my lips because I can no longer contain it; it shatters the stillness. Frightened birds dart into the air, the kongoni leaps high and whirls, but we are off—we are onto him, we are in full gallop, and as the tawny rump of our prey fades into the tawny dust that springs from his heels, I am no longer a girl riding a horse; I am part of the dust, part of the wind in my face, part of the roar of the Baron's hooves, part of his courage, and part of the fear in the kongoni's heart. I am part of everything and it seems that nothing in the world can ever change it.

We run, we race. The kongoni streaks for the open plain. Somewhere to the left there is the drumming of a thousand hooves and the voices of men—angry men with a right to be angry. I have committed the unpardonable; I have bolted their game, but I can't help it.

We're on our own now—the Baron and I—and no sense of guilt can stop us.

We gain, we lose, we hold it even. I grope for the revolver at my thigh and pull it from its sheath. I have used one before, but not like this. Always before it has been heavy in my hand, but now it is weightless; now it fits my hand. Now, I think, I cannot miss.

Rocks, anthills, leleshwa bush, thorn trees—all rush past my eyes, but I do not see them; they are swift streaks of color, unreal and evanescent. And time does not move. Time is a marble moment. Only the Baron moves, his long muscles responding to his will, surging in steady, driving rhythm.

Closer, closer. Without guidance the Baron veers to the left, avoiding the dust that envelops the racing kongoni, exposing him to my aim—and I do aim. I raise the gun to shoulder height, my arm sways, I lower it. No. Too far, I can't get a bead. Faster! It's no good just shooting. I've got to hit his heart. Faster! I do not speak the word; I only frame it on my lips, because the Baron knows. His head drops ever so slightly and he stretches his neck a bit more. Faster? There, you have it—this is faster!

And it is. I raise my arm again and fire twice and the kongoni stumbles. I think he stumbles. He seems to sway, but I am not sure. Perhaps it is imagination, perhaps it is hope. At least he swerves. He swerves to the right, but the Baron outgenerals him; the Baron is on his right flank before I can shift my weight in the saddle.

Then something happens. I want to shoot again, but I can't—there's nothing to shoot at. He's gone—our kongoni's gone. He's disappeared as if his particular god had that moment given him wings. The Baron slows, my hand drops to my side and I mumble my frustration, staring ahead.

It's a *donga*, of course—a pit in the plain, deeper than most, crowded with high grass, its sides steep as walls. Our prize has plunged into it, been swallowed in it, and there is nothing to do except to follow.

That's my impulse, but not the Baron's. He looks from side to side, sudden suspicion in his manner, tension in his body. He slows his pace to scarcely more than a canter and will not be urged. At the rim of the *donga* he almost stops. It is steep, but in the high grass that clothes it I can see the wake of the kongoni, and I am impatient.

"There! Get onto him!"

For the first time I slap the Baron with the flat of my hand, coaxing him forward. He hesitates, and there is so little time to waste. Why is he failing me? Why stop now? I am disappointed, angry. I can't return empty-handed. I won't.

"Now then!"

My heels rap sharply against his ribs, my hand is firmer on the reins, my revolver is ready—and the Baron is a soldier. He no longer questions me; surefooted and strong, half walking, half sliding, he plunges over the rim of the *donga* at such an angle that I brace myself in my stirrups and shut my eyes against the plumes of dust we raise. When it is gone, we are on level ground again, deep in grass still studded with morning dew— and the path of the kongoni is clear before us, easy to see, easy to follow.

We have lost time, but this is no place for speed. Our prey is hiding, must be hiding. Now, once more, we stalk; now we hunt. Careful. Quiet. Look sharply, watch every moving thing; gun ready, hands ready.

I'm ready, but not the Baron. His manner has changed. He is not with me. I can feel it. He responds, but he does not anticipate my will. Something concerns him, and I'm getting nervous too—I'm catching it from him. It won't do. It's silly.

I look around. On three sides we are surrounded by steep banks easier to get down than up—and just ahead there's nothing but bush and high grass that you can't see into. Even so there's a way out—straight ahead through the bush. That's where the kongoni went—it's where we'll go.

"Come on!"

I jab the Baron's ribs once more and he takes a step forward—a single step—and freezes. He does not tremble. With his ears and his eyes and by the sheer power of his will, he forces me into silence, into rigidity, into consciousness of danger.

I feel and see it at the same moment. Wreathed in leaves of shining grass, framed in the soft green garland of the foliage, there is an immense black head into which are sunk two slowly burning eyes. Upon the head, extending from it like lances fixed for battle, are the two horns of a buffalo. I am young, but I am still a child of Africa—and I know that these, without any question, are Africa's most dreaded weapon.

Nor is our challenger alone. I see that not one but a dozen buffalo heads are emerging from the bush, across our path like links in an indestructible chain—and behind us the walls of the *donga* are remote and steep and friendless. Instinctively I raise my revolver, but as I raise it I realize that it won't help. I know that even a rifle wouldn't help. I feel my meagre store of courage dwindle, my youthful bravado becomes a whisper less audible than my pounding heart. I do not move, I cannot. Still grasping the reins, but unaware of them, the fingers of my left hand grope for the Baron's mane and cling there. I do not utter them, but the words are in my heart: I am afraid. I can do nothing. I depend on you!

Now, as I remember that moment and write it down, I am three times older than I was that day in the *donga*, and I can humor my ego, upon occasion, by saying to myself that I am three times wiser. But even then I knew what African buffaloes were. I knew that it was less dangerous to come upon a family of lions in the open plain than to come upon a herd of buffaloes, or to come upon a single buffalo; everyone knew it— everyone except amateur hunters who liked to roll the word "lion" on their lips. Few lions will attack men unless they are goaded into it; most buffaloes will. A lion's charge is swift and often fatal, but if it is not, he bears no grudge. He will not stalk you, but a buffalo will. A buffalo is capable of mean cunning that will match the mean cunning of the men who hunt him, and every time he kills a man he atones for the death at men's hands of many of his species. He will gore you, and when you are down, he will kneel upon you and grind you into the earth.

I remember that as I sat on the Baron's back the things I had heard about buffaloes swept swiftly into my mind. I remember fingering the big revolver, suddenly becoming heavy in my hand, while the buffaloes moved closer in strategic order.

They stood in an almost mathematical semicircle across the only avenue of escape from the *donga*. They did not gather together for the charge, they did not hurry. They did not have to. They saw to it that every loophole was blocked with their horns, and it seemed that even the spaces between their bodies were barred to us by the spears of light that bristled from their bright, black hides. Their eyes were round and small and they burned with a carnelian fire. They moved upon us with slow leisurely steps, and the intensity of their fury was hypnotic. I could not move.

I would not think, because to think was to realize that behind us there was only a wall of earth impossible to climb in time.

As the nearest bull raised his head, preliminary to the final charge, I raised my revolver and with strange detachment, watched my own hand tremble. It wasn't any good. Thinking of my father, fear changed to guilt and then back to fear again, and then to resignation. All right—come on, then. Let's get it over. It's happened to lots of others and now it's going to happen to me. But I had forgotten my companion. All this time the Baron had not moved. Yet neither had he trembled, nor made a sound.

You can find many easy explanations for the things that animals do. You can say that they act out of fear, out of panic, that they cannot think or reason. But I know that this is wrong; I know now that the Baron reasoned, though what he did at the precise instant of our greatest danger seemed born more of terror than of sense.

He whirled, striking a flame of dust from his heels; he reared high into the air until all his weight lay upon his great haunches, until his muscles were tightened like springs. Then he sprang toward the farthest, steepest wall—while behind us came the drumming, swelling thunder of the herd.

For perhaps a hundred yards the *donga* was broad and flat, and then it ended. I remember that the wall of earth loomed so closely in front of my eyes that they were blinded by it. I saw nothing, but just behind us I could hear the low, the almost soothing undertones of destruction. There was a confident, an all-but-casual quality in the sound; not hurried, hardly in crescendo, not even terrifying, just steady—and inescapable.

Another minute, I thought—a whole minute at least. It's a lot of time; it's sixty seconds. You can do a lot of living in sixty seconds.

And then the Baron turned. I do not know how he turned—I do not know how, running at such speed, he could have turned so swiftly and so cleanly—and I do not know how it was that I stayed in the saddle. I do know that when, at a distance of less than a hundred feet, we faced the onrushing buffaloes once more, they had been beaten, outgeneralled, frustrated; they had lost their battle. An instant ago they had presented an impassable barrier, but now their ranks were spread; now their line was staggered and there were spaces between their beautiful, embracing horns that not one but two horses might have galloped through.

The Baron chose the widest breach and sprinted. He moved toward the open end of the *donga* in great exultant leaps, springing like a reedbuck, laughing in his heart. And when the *donga* was far behind us and the sun was hot on our backs and sweat stood on the Baron's flanks, we came slowly up the wagon track that led to the farm.

I remember that my father and Captain Dennis were talking near the doorway of our house when I rode by, and it may have been that they were smiling; I am not sure. But at least I said nothing and they said nothing, and in a few days all the soldiers left, and it was not until five years had passed that I heard the Baron's name again.

My father spoke it first. We sat at our table one night, and with us sat the colonel of the East African Mounted Rifles. He was not an imposing man; he was red-faced and he looked a little like the colonels in the cartoons you used to see, though of course he was out of uniform.

The war was over and the men had returned to their farms—or some men had. Only a handful of Wilson's Scouts survived, and the colonel and my father talked about that, and then my father asked about Captain Dennis, and the colonel's face got redder. At least he made a grimace with his lips that could only have meant displeasure.

"Dennis," he said, "ah, yes. We had a lot of confidence in him, but he proved a fool. Went dotty over some horse."

My father and I looked at each other. "The Baron," my father said.

The colonel nodded. "That was it. The Baron—big brute with a head like a cartridge case. I remember him."

"What happened?" said my father.

The colonel coughed. He flipped a large hand over on the table and shrugged. "One of those things. CO sent Dennis through von Lettow's lines one night to pick up a spot of news. It was south of Kilimanjaro. Not nice country, but he got through on that clumsy half-breed of his—or almost got through, that is."

"They got him, did they?" said my father.

"Got him in the face with grenade shrapnel," said the colonel. "Not fatal though. With a little sense he would have made it. He clung to that horse and the horse brought him almost all the way back. Then Dennis went off his chump. Disobeyed orders. Had to be rescued. Blasted fool."

My father nodded but said nothing.

"Blasted fool," repeated the colonel. "He was within a mile of our lines with all the information we wanted—then he quit."

"It seems hard to believe," I said.

"Not at all," said the colonel, looking at me with stern eyes. "It was that horse. The brute suddenly went under. Dennis found he'd been shot in the lung. The Baron went down and Dennis wouldn't leave him—sat there the whole night with his face half shot away, trying first aid, holding the brute's head in his lap." The colonel looked at my father with sudden anger. "He'd disobeyed orders. You see that, don't you?"

My father let a smile, half gay, half sad, twist his lips. "Oh clearly! Orders are orders. No room for sentiment in war. You had Captain Dennis court-martialed, of course?"

A hurricane lamp makes almost no sound, but for a long time after my father's question there was no sound but the sound of our hurricane lamp. It gave a voice to silence—the colonel's silence. He looked at both of us. He looked at the table. Then he stared at the wrinkled palms of his clumsy hands until we thought he would never utter another word, but he did.

He stood up. "It took a little time," he said, "but finally Dennis recovered—the Baron died with his head toward our guns. In the end I had them both decorated for bravery beyond the call of duty—the captain and his horse. You see," the colonel added angrily, "I'm afraid I'm a blasted fool myself."

The Splendid Outcast

"The Splendid Outcast" is a fascinating insight into the world of horse-sales and is based on a real event. The horse whom Beryl calls Rigel in her story (after Rigel Beta Orionis, a star particularly visible in the night skies of Kenya) was actually Messenger Boy.

During 1928, shortly after Beryl married the wealthy young aristocrat Mansfield Markham, the couple were in England on honeymoon. Beryl was already a successful trainer, having the winners of the classic Kenya St. Leger and several feature-races as well as numerous minor winners to her credit. She was anxious to improve the bloodline of the horses in her stable and when Messenger Boy was entered for auction at Newmarket, she went with Mansfield to bid for him.

Messenger Boy's breeding was even more impressive than that of Rigel. His sire was Hurry On, winner of the St. Leger in 1916. Never beaten on the turf, Hurry On sired three Derby winners and his trainer, the great Fred Darling, always regarded him as the best horse he had ever trained. To add to this, Messenger Boy's dam was Fifinella, the last filly to win the English Derby and she also won the Oaks in that same year (1916). It would be difficult to envisage a more perfect pedigree and under normal circumstances a foal from this union should have fetched a huge sum at auction, probably even beyond Mansfield's resources.

[First published in *Saturday Evening Post*, September 1944.]

The chestnut colt foaled in 1924 and though showing great promise was a difficult horse to ride and manage. Vicious and unpredictable, in 1927 he killed his groom and attacked Fred Darling, injuring the latter so badly that he was in hospital for weeks. Darling later said that Messenger Boy was one of the few truly insane horses he ever came across during his career.

Mansfield had severe misgivings but Beryl was delighted when she acquired the horse for the remarkably low price of "several hundred pounds." Mansfield told his nephew, Sir Charles Markham, that within weeks of the horse's arrival in Kenya Beryl was using him as a daily hack. Beryl told her friend Doreen Bathurst Norman that she had "simply turned the horse out into a field for a week or so and then got on and rode it," but later she confessed, "Well, he was a bit of a handful at first."

Messenger Boy went on to become one of the leading sires in Kenya racing.

The stallion was named after a star, and when he fell from his particular heaven, it was easy enough for people to say that he had been named too well. People like to see stars fall, but in the case of Rigel, it was of greater importance to me. To me and to one other—to a little man with shabby cuffs and a wilted cap that rested over eyes made mild by something more than time.

It was at Newmarket, in England, where, since Charles I instituted the first cup race, a kind of court has been held for the royalty of the turf. Men of all classes come to Newmarket for the races and for the December sales. They come from everywhere—some to bet, some to buy or sell, and some merely to offer homage to the resplendent peers of the Stud Book, for the sport of kings may, after all, be the pleasure of every man.

December can be bitterly cold in England, and this December was. There was frozen sleet on buildings and on trees, and I remember that the huge Newmarket track lay on the downs below the village like a noose of diamonds on a tarnished mat. There was a festive spirit everywhere, but it was somehow lost on me. I had come to buy new blood for my stable in Kenya, and since my stable was my living, I came as serious buyers do, with figures in my mind and caution in my heart. Horses are hard to judge at best, and the thought of putting your hoarded pounds behind that judgement makes it harder still.

I sat close on the edge of the auction ring and held my breath from time to time as the bidding soared. I held it because the casual mention of ten thousand guineas in payment for a horse or for anything else seemed to me wildly beyond the realm of probable things. For myself, I had five hundred pounds to spend and, as I waited for Rigel to be shown, I remember that I felt uncommonly maternal about each pound. I waited for Rigel because I had come six thousand miles to buy him, nor was I apprehensive lest anyone should take him from me; he was an outcast.

Rigel had a pedigree that looked backward and beyond the pedigrees of many Englishmen—and Rigel had a brilliant record. By all odds, he should have brought ten thousand guineas at the sale, but I knew he wouldn't, for he had killed a man.

He had killed a man—not fallen upon him, nor thrown him in a playful moment from the saddle, but killed him dead with his hooves and with his teeth in a stable. And that was not all, though it was the greatest thing. Rigel had crippled other men and, so the story went, would cripple or kill still more, so long as he lived. He was savage, people said, and while he could not be hanged for his crimes, like a man, he could be shunned as criminals are. He could be offered for sale. And yet, under the implacable rules of racing, he had been warned off the turf for life—so who would buy?

Well, I for one—and I had supposed there would not be

two. I would buy if the price were low enough, because I had youth then, and a corresponding contempt for failure. It seemed probable that in time and with luck and with skill, the stallion might be made manageable again, if only for breeding—especially for breeding. He could be gentled, I thought. But I found it hard to believe what I saw that day. I had not known that the mere touch of a hand, could in an instant, extinguish the long-burning anger of an angry heart.

I first noticed the little man when the sale was already well on its way, and he caught my attention at once, because he was incongruous there. He sat a few benches from me and held his lean, interwoven fingers upon his knees. He stared down upon the arena as each horse was led into it, and he listened to the dignified encomiums of the auctioneer with the humble attention of a parishioner at mass. He never moved. He was surrounded by men and women who, by their impeccable clothes and by their somewhat bored familiarity with pounds and guineas, made him conspicuous. He was like a stone of granite in a jeweler's window, motionless and grey against the glitter.

You could see in his face that he loved horses—just as you could see, in some of the faces of those around him, that they loved the idea of horses. They were the cultists, he the votary, and there were, in fact, about his grey eyes and his slender lips, the deep, tense lines so often etched in the faces of zealots and of lonely men. It was the cast of his shoulders, I think, the devotion of his manner that told me he had once been a jockey.

A yearling came into the ring and was bought, and then another, while the pages of catalogues were quietly turned. The auctioneer's voice, clear but scarcely lifted, intoned the virtues of his magnificent merchandise as other voices, responding to this magic, spoke reservedly of figures: "A thousand guineas ... two thousand ... three ... four! ..."

The scene at the auction comes to me clearly now, as if once again it were happening before my eyes.

"Five, perhaps?" The auctioneer scans the audience expectantly as a groom parades a dancing colt around the arena. There is a moment of near silence, a burly voice calls, "Five!" and the colt is sold while a murmur of polite approval swells and dies.

And so they go, one after another, until the list is small; the audience thins and my finger traces the name, Rigel, on the last page of the catalogue. I straighten on my bench and hold my breath a little, forgetting the crowd, the little man, and a part of myself. I know this horse. I know he is by Hurry On out of Bounty—the sire unbeaten, the dam a great steeplechaser—and there is no better blood than that. Killer or not, Rigel has won races, and won them clean. If God and Barclays Bank stay with me, he will return to Africa when I do.

And there, at last, he stands. In the broad entrance to the ring, two powerful men appear with the stallion between them. The men are not grooms of ordinary size; they have been picked for strength, and in the clenched fist of each is the end of a chain. Between the chain and the bit there is on the near side a short rod of steel, close to the stallion's mouth—a rod of steel, easy to grasp, easy to use. Clenched around the great girth of the horse, and fitted with metal rings, there is a strap of thick leather that brings to mind the restraining harness of a madman.

Together, the two men edge the stallion forward. Tall as they are, they move like midgets beside his massive shoulders. He is the biggest thoroughbred I have ever seen. He is the most beautiful. His coat is chestnut, flecked with white, and his mane and tail are close to gold. There is a blaze on his face—wide and straight and forthright, as if by this marking he proclaims that he is none other than Rigel, for all his sins, for all the hush that falls over the crowd.

He is Rigel and he looks upon the men who hold his chains as a captured king may look upon his captors. He is not tamed. Nothing about him promises that he will be tamed. Stiffly, on reluctant hooves, he enters the ring and flares his crimson nostrils at the crowd, and the crowd is still. The crowd whose pleasure is the docile beast of pretty paddocks, the gainly horse of cherished prints that hang upon the finest walls, the willing winner of the race—upon the rebel this crowd stares, and the rebel stares back.

His eyes are lit with anger or with hate. His head is held disdainfully and high, his neck an arc of arrogance. He prances now—impatience in the thudding of his hooves upon the tanbark, defiance in his manner—and the chains jerk tight. The long stallion reins are tightly held—apprehensively held—and the men who hold them glance at the auctioneer, an urgent question in their eyes.

The auctioneer raises his arm for silence, but there is silence. No one speaks. The story of Rigel is known—his breeding, his brilliant victories, and finally his insurgence and his crimes. Who will buy the outcast? The auctioneer shakes his head as if to say that this is a trick beyond his magic. But he will try. He is an imposing man, an experienced man, and now he clears his throat and confronts the crowd, a kind of pleading in his face.

"This splendid animal—" he begins—and does not finish. He cannot finish.

Rigel has scanned the silent audience and smelled the unmoving air, and he—a creature of the wind—knows the indignity of this skyless temple. He seems aware at last of the chains that hold him, of the men who cling forlornly to the heavy reins. He rears from the tanbark, higher and higher still, until his golden mane is lifted like a flag unfurled and defiant. He beats the air. He trembles in his rising anger, and the crowd leans forward.

A groom clings like a monkey to the tightened chain. He is swept from his feet while his partner, a less tenacious man, sprawls ignobly below, and men—a dozen men—rush to the ring, some shouting, some waving their arms. They run and swear in lowered voices; they grasp reins, chains, rings, and swarm upon their towering Gulliver. And he subsides.

With something like contempt for this hysteria, Rigel touches his forehooves to the tanbark once more. He has killed no one, hurt no one, but they are jabbing at his mouth now, they are surrounding him, adding fuel to his fiery reputation, and the auctioneer is a wilted man.

He sighs, and you can almost hear it. He raises both arms and forgoes his speech. "What," he asks with weariness, "am I offered?" And there is a ripple of laughter from the crowd. Smug in its wisdom, it offers nothing.

But I do, and my voice is like an echo in a cave. Still there is triumph in it. I will have what I have come so far to get—I will have Rigel.

"A hundred guineas!" I stand as I call my price, and the auctioneer is plainly shocked—not by the meagerness of the offer, but by the offer itself. He stares upward from the ring, incredulity in his eyes.

He lifts a hand and slowly repeats the price. "I am offered," he says, "one hundred guineas."

There is a hush, and I feel the eyes of the crowd and watch

the hand of the auctioneer. When it goes down, the stallion will be mine.

But it does not go down. It is still poised in midair, white, expectant, compelling, when the soft voice, the gently challenging voice is lifted. "Two hundred!" the voice says, and I do not have to turn to know that the little jockey has bid against me. But I do turn.

He has not risen from the bench, and he does not look at me. In his hand he holds a sheaf of bank notes. I can tell by their color that they are of small denomination, by their rumpled condition that they have been hoarded long. People near him are staring—horrified, I think—at the vulgar spectacle of cash at a Newmarket auction.

I am not horrified, nor sympathetic. Suddenly I am aware that I have a competitor, and I am cautious. I am here for a purpose that has little to do with sentiment, and I will not be beaten. I think of my stable in Kenya, of the feed bills to come, of the syces to be paid, of the races that are yet to be won if I am to survive in this unpredictable business. No, I cannot now yield an inch. I have little money, but so has he. No more, I think, but perhaps as much.

I hesitate a moment and glance at the little man, and he returns my glance. We are like two gamblers bidding each against the other's unseen cards. Our eyes meet for a sharp instant—a cold instant.

I straighten and my catalogue is crumpled in my hand. I moisten my lips and call, "Three hundred!" I call it firmly, steadily, hoping to undo my opponent at a stroke. It is a wishful thought.

He looks directly at me now, but does not smile. He looks at me as a man might look at one who bears false witness against him, then soundlessly he counts his money and bids again, "Three fifty!"

The interest of the crowd is suddenly aroused. All these people are at once conscious of being witnesses, not only before an auction, but before a contest, a rivalry of wills. They shift in their seats and stare as they might stare at a pair of duelists, rapiers in hand.

But money is the weapon, Rigel the prize. And prize enough, I think, as does my adversary.

I ponder and think hard, then decide to bid a hundred more. Not twenty, not fifty, but a hundred. Perhaps by that I can take him in my stride. He need not know there is little more to follow. He may assume that I am one of the casual ones, impatient of small figures. He may hesitate, he may withdraw. He may be cowed.

Still standing, I utter, as indifferently as I can, the words, "Four fifty!" and the auctioneer, at ease in his element of contention, brightens visibly.

I am aware that the gathered people are now fascinated by this battle of pounds and shillings over a stallion that not one of them would care to own. I only hope that in the heat of it some third person does not begin to bid. But I need not worry; Rigel takes care of that.

The little jockey has listened to my last offer, and I can see that he is already beaten—or almost, at least. He has counted his money a dozen times, but now he counts it again, swiftly, with agile fingers, as if hoping his previous counts had been wrong.

I feel a momentary surge of sympathy, then smother it. Horse training is not my hobby. It is my living. I wait for what I am sure will be his last bid, and it comes. For the first time, he rises from his bench. He is small and alone in spirit, for the glances of the well-dressed people about him lend him nothing. He does not care. His eyes are on the stallion and I can see that there is a kind of passion in them. I have seen that expression before—in the eyes of sailors appraising a comely ship, in the eyes of pilots sweeping the clean, sweet contours of a plane. There is reverence in it, desire—and even hope.

The little man turns slightly to face the expectant auctioneer, then clears his throat and makes his bid. "Four eighty!" he calls, and the slight note of desperation in his voice is unmistakable, but I force myself to ignore it. Now, at last, I tell myself, the prize is mine.

The auctioneer receives the bid and looks at me, as do a hundred people. Some of them, no doubt, think I am quite mad or wholly inexperienced, but they watch while the words "Five hundred" form upon my lips. They are never uttered.

Throughout the bidding for Rigel, Rigel has been ignored. He has stood quietly enough after his first brief effort at freedom; he has scarcely moved. But now, at the climax of the sale, his impatience overflows, his spirit flares like fire, his anger bursts through the circle of men who guard him. Suddenly, there are cries, shouts of warning, the ringing of chains and the cracking of leather, and the crowd leaps to its feet. Rigel is loose. Rigel has hurled his captors from him and he stands alone.

It is a beautiful thing to see, but there is terror in it. A thoroughbred stallion with anger in his eye is not a sight to entrance anyone but a novice. If you are aware of the power and the speed and the intelligence in that towering symmetrical body, you will hold your breath as you watch it. You will know that the teeth of a horse can crush a bone, that hooves can crush a man. And Rigel's hooves have crushed a man.

He stands alone, his neck curved, his golden tail a battle plume, and he turns, slowly, deliberately, and faces the men he has flung away. They are not without courage, but they are without resource. Horses are not tamed by whips or by blows.

The strength of ten men is not so strong as a single stroke of a hoof; the experience of ten men is not enough, for this is the unexpected, the unpredictable. No one is prepared. No one is ready.

The words "Five hundred" die upon my lips as I watch, as I listen. For the stallion is not voiceless now. His challenging scream is shrill as the cry of winter wind. It is bleak and heartless. His forehooves stir the tanbark. The auction is forgotten.

A man stands before him—a man braver than most. He holds nothing in his hands save an exercise bat; it looks a feeble thing, and is. It is a thin stick bound with leather—enough only to enrage Rigel, for he has seen such things in men's hands before. He knows their meaning. Such a thing as this bat, slight as it is, enrages him because it is a symbol that stands for other things. It stands, perhaps, for the confining walls of a darkened stable, for the bit of steel, foreign, but almost everpresent in his mouth, for the tightened girth, the command to gallop, to walk, to stop, to parade before the swelling crowd of gathered people, to accept the measured food gleaned from forbidden fields. It stands for life no closer to the earth than the sterile smell of satin on a jockey's back or the dead wreath hung upon a winner. It stands for servitude. And Rigel has broken with his overlords.

He lunges quickly, and the man with a bat is not so quick. He lifts the pathetic stick and waves it in desperation. He cries out, and the voice of the crowd drowns his cry. Rigel's neck is outstretched and straight as a sabre. There is dust and the shouting of men and the screaming of women, for the stallion's teeth have closed on the shoulder of his forlorn enemy.

The man struggles and drops his bat, and his eyes are sharp with terror, perhaps with pain. Blood leaves the flesh of his face, and it is a face grey and pleading, as must be the faces of those to whom retribution is unexpected and swift. He beats against the golden head while the excitement of the crowd mounts against the fury of Rigel. Then reason vanishes. Clubs, whips, and chains appear like magic in the ring, and a regiment of men advance upon the stallion. They are angry men, brave in their anger, righteous and justified in it. They advance, and the stallion drops the man he has attacked, and the man runs for cover, clutching his shoulder.

I am standing, as is everyone. It is a strange and unreal thing to see this trapped and frustrated creature, magnificent and alone, away from his kind, remote from the things he understands, face the punishment of his minuscule masters. He is, of course, terrified, and the terror is a mounting madness. If he could run, he would leave this place, abandoning his fear and his hatred to do it. But he cannot run. The walls of the arena are high. The doors are shut, and the trap makes him blind with anger. He will fight, and the blows will fall with heaviness upon his spirit, for his body is a rock before these petty weapons.

The men edge closer, ropes and chains and whips in determined hands. The whips are lifted, the chains are ready; the battle line is formed, and Rigel does not retreat. He comes forward, the whites of his eyes exposed and rimmed with carnelian fire, his nostrils crimson.

There is a breathless silence, and the little jockey slips like a ghost into the ring. His eyes are fixed on the embattled stallion. He begins to run across the tanbark and breaks through the circle of advancing men and does not stop. Someone clutches at his coat, but he breaks loose without turning, then slows to an almost casual walk and approaches Rigel alone. The men do not follow him. He waves them back. He goes forward, steadily, easily and happily, without caution, without fear, and Rigel whirls angrily to face him.

Rigel stands close to the wall of the arena. He cannot retreat. He does not propose to. Now he can focus his fury on this insignificant David who has come to meet him, and he does. He lunges at once as only a stallion can—swiftly, invincibly, as if escape and freedom can be found only in the destruction of all that is human, all that smells human, and all that humans have made.

He lunges and the jockey stops. He does not turn or lift a hand or otherwise move. He stops, he stands, and there is silence everywhere. No one speaks; no one seems to breathe. Only Rigel is motion. No special hypnotic power emanates from the jockey's eyes; he has no magic. The stallion's teeth are bared and close, his hooves are a swelling sound when the jockey turns. Like a matador of nerveless skill and studied insolence, the jockey turns his back on Rigel and does not walk away, and the stallion pauses.

Rigel rears high at the back of the little man, screaming his defiant scream, but he does not strike. His hooves are close to the jockey's head, but do not touch him. His teeth are sheathed. He hesitates, trembles, roars wind from his massive lungs. He shakes his head, his golden mane, and beats the ground. It is frustration—but of a new kind. It is a thing he does not know—a man who neither cringes in fear nor threatens with whips or chains. It is a thing beyond his memory perhaps—as far beyond it as the understanding of the mare that bore him.

Rigel is suddenly motionless, rigid, suspicious. He waits, and the grey-eyed jockey turns to face him. The little man is calm and smiling. We hear him speak, but cannot understand his words. They are low and they are lost to us—an incantation. But the stallion seems to understand at least the spirit if not the sense of them. He snorts, but does not move. And now the jockey's hand goes forward to the golden mane—neither hurriedly nor with hesitance, but unconcernedly, as if it had rested there a thousand times. And there it stays.

There is a murmur from the crowd, then silence. People look at one another and stir in their seats—a strange self-consciousness in their stirring, for people are uneasy before the proved worth of their inferiors, unbelieving of the virtue of simplicity. They watch with open mouths as the giant Rigel, the killer Rigel, with no harness save a head collar, follows his Lilliputian master, his new friend, across the ring.

All has happened in so little time—in moments. The audience begins to stand, to leave. But they pause at the lift of the auctioneer's hand. He waves it and they pause. It is all very well, his gestures say, but business is, after all, business, and Rigel has not been sold. He looks up at me, knowing that I have a bid to make—the last bid. And I look down into the ring at the stallion I have come so far to buy. His head is low and close to the shoulder of the man who would take him from me. He is not prancing now, not moving. For this hour, at least, he is changed.

I straighten, and then shake my head. I need only say, "Five hundred," but the words won't come. I can't get them out. I am angry with myself—a sentimental fool—and I am disappointed. But I cannot bid. It is too easy—twenty pounds too little, and yet too great an advantage.

No. I shake my head again, the auctioneer shrugs and turns to seal his bargain with the jockey.

On the way out, an old friend jostles me. "You didn't really want him then," he says.

"Want him? No. No, I didn't really want him."

"It was wise," he says. "What good is a horse that's warned off every course in the Empire? You wouldn't want a horse like that."

"That's right. I wouldn't want a horse like that."

We move to the exit, and when we are out in the bright cold air of Newmarket, I turn to my friend and mention the little jockey. "But he wanted Rigel," I say.

And my old friend laughs. "He would," he says. "That man has himself been barred from racing for fifteen years. Why, I can't remember. But it's two of a kind, you see—Rigel and Sparrow. Outlaws, both. He loves and knows horses as no man does, but that's what we call him around the tracks—the Fallen Sparrow."

PART TWO

Brothers Are the Same

This story was written during the final months of World War II. Beryl had moved from New Mexico and was living on a ranch in Elsinore in Southern California. Raoul had just been released from active service and placed on general reserve; it was a period of great personal happiness. This is the first of Beryl's stories that was not written in the first person and the style of writing shows some departures from her earlier work. One can only conjecture how much of it is total fiction and how much based upon a childhood experience. Perhaps it was based upon some gossip Beryl had heard whispered around the firesides of her African friends.

Although the story "Brothers Are the Same" seems on first consideration to have been written out of her deep knowledge of African culture, Raoul told his friend, John Potter, that he had been obliged to comb a reference library for information on Masai tribal customs which Beryl was not able to provide. It appears the story's plot may have been his, while Beryl provided the background that Raoul wove into the story. This was the first story published under her name for which Beryl was not solely responsible, and it appears to have been very much a joint effort.

Although this story may have been a product of Raoul's fertile imagination it is a compelling character study and there is enough of Beryl's writing style in it to convince me that it was not merely ghostwritten.

And the reader can be sure that Beryl knew firsthand the horror of a

[First published in Collier's, The Weekly Magazine, February 1945.]

lion's attack, the brute strength, the overwhelming sounds and smell, for as a small child she was attacked by the supposedly tame lion belonging to a friend: "What I remember most clearly of the moment that followed," she wrote, "are three things—a scream that was barely a whisper, a blow that struck me to the ground, and, as I buried my face in my arms [I] felt Paddy's teeth close on the flesh of my leg. I remained conscious, but I closed my eyes and tried not to be. It was not so much the pain as it was the sound. The sound of Paddy's roar in my ears will only be duplicated, I think, when the doors of hell slip their wobbly hinges, one day, and give voice and authenticity to the whole panorama of Dante's poetic nightmare" [reprinted by kind permission of the Beryl Markham Estate, from West with the Night *by Beryl Markham].*

———————

They are tall men, cleanly built and straight as the shafts of the spears they carry, and no one knows their tribal history, but there is some of Egypt in their eyes and the look of ancient Greece about their bodies. They are the Masai.

They are the color of worn copper and, with their graceful women, they live on the Serengeti Plain, which makes a carpet at the feet of high Kilimanjaro. In all of Africa there are today no better husbandmen of cattle.

But once they were warriors and they have not forgotten that, nor have they let tradition die. They go armed, and to keep well-tempered the mettle of their men, each youth among them must, when his hour comes, prove his right to manhood. He must meet in combat the only worthy enemy his people recognize—the destroyer of their cattle, the marauding master of the plains—the lion.

Thus, just before the dawning of a day in what these Masai call the Month of the Little Rains, such a youth with such a test before him lay in a cleft of rock and watched the shadowed outlines of a deep ravine. For at least eight of his sixteen

years, this youth, this young Temas, had waited for his moment. He had dreamed of it and lived it in a dozen ways—all
of them glorious.

In all of the dreams he had confronted the lion with casual
courage, he had presented his spear on the charging enemy
with steadiness born of brave contempt—and always he had
won the swift duel with half a smile on his lips. Always—in
the dreams.

Now it was different. Now as he watched the place where
the real lion lay, he had no smile.

He did not fear the beast. He was sure that in his bones and
in his blood and in his heart he was not afraid. He was Masai,
and legend said that no Masai had ever feared.

Yet in his mind Temas now trembled. Fear of battle was a
nonexistent thing—but fear of failure could be real, and was.
It was real and living—and kept alive by the nearness of an enemy more formidable than any lion—an enemy with the
hated name Medoto.

He thought of Medoto—of that Medoto who lay not far
away in the deep grass watching the same ravine. Of that Medoto who, out of hate and jealousy over a mere girl, now
hoped in his heart that Temas would flinch at the moment of
his trial. That was it. That was the thing that kept the spectre
of failure dancing in his mind, until already it looked like
truth.

There were ten youths hidden about the ravine, and they
would stage and witness the coming fight. They had tracked
the lion to this, his lair, and when the moment came, they
would drive him, angered, upon Temas and then would judge
his courage and his skill. Good or bad, that judgement would,
like a brand mark, cling to him all his life.

But it was Medoto who would watch the closest for a sign,

a gesture, a breath of fear in Temas. It was Medoto who would spread the word—Medoto who surely would cry "Coward!" if he could.

Temas squirmed under the heavy, unwholesome thought, then lifted his head and pierced the dim light with his eyes. To the east, the escarpment stood like a wall against the rising sun. But to the north and to the west and to the south there were no horizons; the grey sky and the grey plain were part and counterpart, and he was himself a shadow in his cleft of rock.

He was a long shadow, a lean shadow. The *shuka* that he wore was now bound about his waist, giving freedom to his legs and arms. His necklace and bracelets were of shining copper, drawn fine and finely spiraled, and around each of his slender ankles there was a copper chain.

His long hair, bound by beaded threads, was a chaste black column that lay between his shoulders, and his ears were pierced and hung with gleaming pendants. His nose was straight, with nostrils delicately flanged. The bones of his cheeks were high, the ridges of his jaw were hard, and his eyes were long and dark and a little brooding. He used them now to glance at his weapons, which lay beside him—a spear, a rawhide shield. These, and a short sword at his belt, were his armament.

He lowered his glance to the place he watched. The ravine was overgrown with a thicket of thorns and the light had not burst through it yet. When it did the lion within it would wake, and the moment would come.

A feeling almost of hopelessness surged through him. It did not seem that he, Temas, could in this great test prove equal to his comrades. All had passed it; all had earned the warrior's title—and none had faltered. Even Medoto—especially Me-

doto—had proven brave and more than ready for his cloak of
manhood. Songs were sung about Medoto. In the evenings in
the *manyatta* when the cattle drowsed and the old men drank
their honey wine, the girls would gather, and the young men,
too, and they would chant to the heroes of their hearts.

But none chanted to Temas. Not yet. Perhaps they never
would—not one of them. Not even . . .

He shook his head in anger. He had not meant to think of
her—of Kileghen of the soft, deep-smiling eyes and the reedbuck's grace. Even she, so rightly named after the star Venus,
had only last night sung to Medoto, and he to her, laughing
the while, as Temas, the yet unproven, had clung to the saving
shadows, letting his fury burn. Could she not make up her
mind between them? Must it always be first one and then the
other?

He saw it all with the eye of his memory—all too clearly.
He saw even the sneer of Medoto on the day the elder warrior,
the chief of them all, had tendered Temas his spear with the
wise words: "Now at last this weapon is your own, but it is only
wood and steel and means nothing until it changes to honor,
or to shame, within your grasp. Soon we shall know!"

And soon they should! But Medoto had laughed then. Medoto had said, "It seems a heavy spear, my comrade, for one so
slight—a big weight for any but a man!" And Temas had made
no answer. How could he with Kileghen leaning there against
the *boma* as though she heard nothing, yet denying her inno-
cence with that quiet, ever-questing smile? At whom had she
smiled? At Medoto for his needless malice—or at Temas for
his acceptance of it?

He did not know. He knew only that he had walked away
carrying the unstained spear a little awkwardly. And that the
joy of having it was quickly dead.

Now he spat on the earth where he rested. He raised a curse against Medoto—a harsh, a bitter curse. But in the midst of it he stiffened and grew tense. Suddenly he lay as still as sleep and watched only the ravine and listened, as to the tone of some familiar silence.

It was the silence of a waking lion, for morning light had breached the thicket, and within his lair the lion was roused.

Within his lair the lion sought wakefulness as suspicion came to him on the cool, unmoving air. Under the bars of sunlight that latticed his flanks and belly, his coat was short and shining. His mane was black and evenly grown. The muscles of his forelegs were not corded, but flat, and the muscles of his shoulders were laminated like sheaths of metal.

Now he smelled men. Now as the sunlight fell in streams upon his sorrel coat and warmed his flanks, his suspicion and then his anger came alive. He had no fear. Whatever lived he judged by strength—or lack of it—and men were puny. And yet the scent of them kindled fire in his brooding eyes and made him contemplate his massive paws.

He arose slowly, without sound—almost without motion—and peered outward through the wall of thorns. The earth was mute, expectant, and he did not break the spell. He only breathed.

The lion breathed and swung his tail in easy, rhythmic arcs and watched the slender figure of a human near him in a cleft of rock.

Temas had risen, too. On one knee now, he waited for the signal of the lifted spears.

Of his ten comrades he could see but two or three—a tuft of warrior's feathers; here and there a gleaming arm. Presently all would leap from the places where they hid, and the Masai battle cry would slash through the silence. And then the lion would act.

But the silence held. The interminable instant hung like a drop that would not fall, and Temas remembered many of the rules, the laws that governed combat with a lion—but not enough, for stubbornly, wastefully, foolishly, his mind nagged at fear of disgrace—fear of failure. Fear of Medoto's ringing laughter in the *manyatta*—of Kileghen's ever-questing smile.

"I shall fail," he thought. "I shall fail before Medoto and, through his eyes, she will see my failure. I must fail," he said, "because now I see that I am trembling."

And he was. His hand was loose upon the long steel spear—too loose, the arm that held the rawhide shield was hot and too unsteady. If he had ever learned to weep he would have wept—had there been time.

But the instant vanished—and with it, silence. From the deep grass, from the shade of anthills, from clustered rocks, warriors sprang like flames, and as they sprang they hurled upon the waiting lion their shrill arrogant challenge, their scream of battle.

Suddenly the world was small and inescapable. It was an arena whose walls were tall young men that shone like worn gold in the sun, and in this shrunken world there were Temas and the lion.

He did not know when or how he had left the rock. It was as if the battle cry had lifted him from it and placed him where he stood—a dozen paces from the thicket. He did not know when the lion had come forward to the challenge, but the lion was there.

The lion waited. The ring of warriors waited. Temas did not move.

His long Egyptian eyes swept around the circle. All was perfect—too perfect. At every point a warrior stood blocking the lion from improbable retreat—and of these Medoto was one. Medoto stood near—a little behind Temas and to the right. His shield bore proud colors of the proven warrior. He was lean and proud, and upon his level stare he weighed each movement Temas made, though these were hesitant and few.

For the lion did not seek escape, nor want it. His shifting yellow eyes burned with even fire. They held neither fear nor fury—only the hard and regal wrath of the challenged tyrant. The strength of either of his forearms was alone greater than the entire strength of any of these men; his speed in the attack was blinding speed, shattering speed. And with such knowledge, with such sureness of himself, the lion stood in the tawny grass, and stared his scorn while the sun rose higher and warmed the scarcely breathing men.

The lion would charge. He would choose one of the many and charge that one. Yet the choice must not be his to make, for through the generations—centuries, perhaps—the code of the Masai decreed that the challenger must draw the lion upon him. By gesture and by voice it can be done. By movement, by courage.

Temas knew the time for this had come. He straightened where he stood and gripped his heavy spear. He held his shield before him, tight on his arm, and he advanced, step by slow step.

The gaze of the lion did not at once swing to him. But every eye was on him, and the strength of one pair—Medoto's—burned in his back like an unhealed scar.

A kind of anger began to run in Temas's blood. It seemed unjust to him that in this crucial moment, at this first great trial of his courage, his enemy and harshest judge must be a wit-

ness. Surely Medoto could see the points of sweat that now
rose on his forehead and about his lips as he moved upon the
embattled lion. Surely Medoto could see—or sense—the
hesitance of his advance—almost hear, perhaps, the pounding of his heart!

He gripped the shaft of his spear until pain stung the muscles of his hand. The lion had crouched and Temas stood suddenly within the radius of his leap. The circle of warriors had
drawn closer, tighter, and there was no sound save the sound
of their uneven breathing.

The lion crouched against the reddish earth, head forward.
The muscles of his massive quarters were taut, his body was a
drawn bow. And, as a swordsman unsheaths his blade, so he
unsheathed his fangs and chose his man.

It was not Temas.

As if in contempt for this confused and untried youth who
paused within his reach, the lion's eyes passed him by and fas-
tened hard upon the stronger figure of another, upon the figure of Casaro, a warrior of many combats and countless victories.

All saw it. Temas saw it, and for an instant—for a shameless
breath of time—he felt an overwhelming ease of heart, relief,
deliverance, not from danger, but from trial. He swept his
glance around the ring. None watched him now. All action, all
thought was frozen by the duel of wills between Casaro and
the beast.

Slowly the veteran Casaro sank upon one knee and raised
his shield. Slowly the lion gathered the power of his body for
the leap. And then it happened.

From behind Temas, flung by Medoto's hand, a stone no
larger than a grain of maize shot through the air and struck the
lion.

No more was needed. The bolt was loosed.

But not upon Casaro, for if from choice, the regal prowler of the wilderness had first preferred an opponent worthy of *his* worth, he now, under the sting of a hurled pebble, preferred to kill that human whose hand was guilty.

He charged at once, and as he charged, the young Temas was, in a breath, transformed from doubting boy to man. All fear was gone—all fear of fear—and as he took the charge, a light almost of ecstasy burned in his eyes, and the spirit of his people came to him.

Over the rim of his shield he saw fury take form. Light was blotted from his eyes as the dark shape descended upon him—for the lion's last leap carried him above the shield, the spear, the youth, so that, looking upward from his crouch, Temas, for a sliver of time, was intimate with death.

He did not yield. He did not think or feel or consciously react. All was simple. All now happened as in the dreams, and his mind was an observer of his acts.

He saw his own spear rise in a swift arc, his own shield leap on his bended arm, his own eyes seek the vital spot—and miss it.

But he struck. He struck hard, not wildly or too soon, but exactly at the precise, the ripened moment, and saw his point drive full into the shoulder of the beast. It was not enough. In that moment his spear was torn from his grasp, his shield vanished, claws furrowed the flesh of his chest, ripping deep. The weight and the power of the charge overwhelmed him.

He was down. Dust and blood and grass and the pungent lion smell were mingled, blended, and in his ears an enraged, triumphant roar overlaid the shrill, high human cry of his comrades.

His friends were about to make the kill that must be his. Yet his hands were empty, he was caught, he was being dragged. He had scarcely felt the long crescentic teeth close on his thigh, it had been so swift. Time itself could not have moved so fast.

A lion can drag a fallen man, even a fighting man, into thicket or deep grass with incredible ease and with such speed as to outdistance even a hurled spear. But sometimes this urge to plunder first and destroy later is a saving thing. It saved Temas. That and his Masai sword, which now was suddenly in his hand.

Perhaps pain dulled his reason, but reason is a sluggard ally to any on the edge of death. Temas made a cylinder of his slender body and, holding the sword flat against his leg, he whirled, and whirling, felt the fangs tear loose the flesh of his thigh, freeing it, freeing him. And, as he felt it, he lunged.

It was quick. It was impossible, it was mad, but it was Masai madness, and it was done. Dust clothed the tangled bodies of the lion and the youth so that those who clamored close to strike the saving blows saw nothing but this cloud and could not aim into its formless shape. Nor had they need to. Suddenly, as if *En-Gai* himself—God and protector of these men of wilderness—had stilled the scene with a lifted hand, all movement stopped, all sound was dead.

The dust was gone like a vanquished shadow, and the great, rust body of the lion lay quiet on the rust-red earth. Over it, upon it, his sword still tight in his hand, the youth lay breathing; bleeding. And, beyond that, he also smiled.

He could smile because the chant of victory burst now like drumbeats from his comrades' throats—the paeans of praise fell on him where he lay, the sun struck bright through shattered clouds; the dream was true. In a dozen places he was hurt, but these would heal.

And so he smiled. He raised himself and, swaying slightly like any warrior weak in sinew but strong in spirit from his wounds, he stood with pride and took his accolade.

And then his smile left him. It was outdone by the broader, harder smile of another—for Medoto was tall and straight before him, and with his eyes and with his lips Medoto seemed to say: "It is well—this cheering and this honor. But it will pass—and we two have a secret, have we not? We know who threw the stone that brought the lion upon you when you stood hoping in your heart that it would charge another. You stood in fear then, you stood in cowardice. We two know this, and no one else. But there is one who might, if she were told, look not to you but to the earth in shame when you pass by. Is this not so?"

Yes, it was so, and Temas, so lately happy, shrank within himself and swayed again. He saw the young Kileghen's eyes and did not wish to see them. But for Medoto's stone, the spear of Temas would yet be virgin, clean, unproved—a thing of futile vanity.

He straightened. His comrades—the true warriors, of which even now he was not one—had in honor to a fierce and vanquished enemy laid the dead lion on a shield and lifted him. In triumph and with songs of praise (mistaken praise!) for Temas, they were already beginning their march toward the waiting *manyatta*.

Temas turned from his field of momentary triumph, but Medoto lingered at his side.

And now it will come, Temas thought. Now what he has said with his eyes, he will say with his mouth, and I am forced to listen. He looked into Medoto's face—a calm, unmoving face—and thought: It is true that this, my enemy, saw the shame of my first fear. He will tell it to everyone—and to her.

So, since I am lost, it is just as well to strike a blow against him. I am not so hurt that I cannot fight at least once more.

His sword still hung at his side. He grasped it now and said, "We are alone and we are enemies. What you are about to charge me with is true—but, if I was a coward before the lion, I am not a coward before you, and I will not listen to sneering words!"

For a long moment, Medoto's eyes peered into the eyes of Temas. The two youths stood together on the now deserted plain and neither moved. Overhead the sun hung low and red and poured its burning light upon the drying grass, upon the thorn trees that stood in lonely clusters, upon the steepled shrines of drudging ants. There was no sound of birds, no rasping of cicada wings, no whispering of wind.

And into this dearth, into this poverty of sound, Medoto cast his laugh. His lips parted, and the low music of his throat was laughter without mirth; there was sadness in it, a note of incredulity, but not more, not mockery, not challenge.

He stared into the proud unhappy face of Temas. He plunged the shaft of his spear into the earth and slipped the shield from his arm. At last he spoke.

He said, "My comrade, we who are Masai know the saying: 'A man asks not the motives of a friend, but demands reason from his enemy.' It is a just demand. If, until now, I have seemed your enemy, it was because I feared you would be braver than I, for when I fought my lion my knees trembled and my heart was white—until that charge was made. No one knew that, and I am called Medoto, the unflinching, but I flinched. I trembled."

He stepped closer to Temas. He smiled. "It is no good to lie," he said. "I wanted you to fail, but when I saw you hesitate I could not bear it because I remembered my own hour of fear.

It was then I threw the stone—not to shame you, but to save you from shame—for I saw that your fear was not fear of death, but fear of failure—and this I understood. You are a greater warrior than I—than any—for who but the bravest would do what you have done?" Medoto paused and watched a light of wonderment kindle in Temas's eye. The hand of Temas slipped from his sword, his muscles relaxed. Yet, for a moment, he did not speak, and as he looked at Medoto, it was clear to both that the identical thought, the identical vision, had come to each of them. It was the vision that must and always will come to young men everywhere, the vision of a girl.

Now this vision stood between them, and nothing else. But it stood like a barrier, the last barrier.

And Medoto destroyed it. Deliberately, casually, he reached under the folds of his flowing *shuka* and brought from it a slender belt of leather crusted with beads. It was the work and the possession of a girl, and both knew which girl. Kileghen's handiwork was rare enough, but recognized in many places.

"This," said Medoto, "this, I was told to bring, and I was told in these words: 'If in his battle the young Temas proves himself a warrior and a man, make this belt my gift to him so that I may see him wear it when he returns. But if he proves a coward, Medoto, the belt is for you to keep.'"

Medoto looked at the bright gift in his hands. "It is yours, Temas!" He held it out. "I meant to keep it. I planned ways to cheat you of it, but I do not think a man can cheat the truth. I have seen you fight better than I have ever fought, and now this gift belongs to you. It is her wish and between us you are at last her choice." He laid the belt on the palm of Temas's open hand and reached once more for his shield and spear. "We will return now," Medoto said, "for the people are waiting. She is waiting. I will help you walk."

But Temas did not move. Through the sharp sting of his wounds, above his joy in the promise that now lay in his hands, he felt another thing, a curious, swelling pride in this new friendship. He looked into the face of Medoto and smiled, timidly, then broadly. And then he laughed and drew his sword and cut the beaded belt in half.

"No," he said. "If she has chosen, then she must choose again, for we are brothers now and brothers are the same!"

He entwined one half of the severed belt in the arm band of Medoto, and the other half he hung, as plainly, on himself.

"We begin again," he said, "for we are equal to each other, and this is a truth that she must know. She must make her choice on other things but skill in battle, since only men may judge a warrior for his worth!"

It was not far to the _manyatta_ and they walked it arm in arm. They were tall together, and strong and young, and somehow full of song. Temas walked brokenly for he was hurt, and yet he sang:

> _Oi-Konyek of the splendid shield_
> _Has heard the lowing of the kine . . ._

And when they entered the gates of the _manyatta_, there were many of every age to welcome Temas, for his lion had been brought and his story told. They cheered and cried his name and led him past the open doors to the peaceful earthen houses to the _singara_, which is the place reserved for warriors.

Medoto did not leave him, nor he Medoto, and it was strange to some to see the enemies transformed and strong in friendship, when yesterday their only bond was hate.

It was strange to one who stood against the _boma_ wall, a slender girl of fragile beauty and level, seeking eyes. She was as young as morning, as anticipant. But this anticipation quickly dimmed as she saw the token she had made, one half borne hopefully by Medoto, the other as hopefully carried by Temas!

Both sought her in the gathered crowd, both caught her glance and gave the question with their eyes. Both, in the smug, self-satisfied way of men, swaggered a little.

So the girl paused for an instant and frowned a woman's frown. But then, with musing, lidded eyes, she smiled a woman's smile—and stranger yet, the smile had more of triumph in it, and less of wonder, than it might have had.

PART THREE

The final four stories are based on fictional, mainly romantic, situations of a type in great demand during the war—and immediate postwar—years by a public that dictated a requirement for escapist entertainment. These stories lean heavily on Beryl's African, equine, and aviation background. Though originally published under Beryl's name, the three stories in Part Three were probably certainly ghostwritten by Raoul Schumacher, for the style is clearly identical to that of the handful of short stories published by him. Nevertheless, they will be interesting to admirers of Beryl Markham; her experiences add dimension to the thin plots.

Appointment in Khartoum

The threads of Beryl's own life can be seen in the experiences of the young aviatrix flying what she takes to be a chauvinistic, male passenger across the Sudd. Beryl flew this route many times, and her description of flying through a violent storm and the forced landing may well be grounded in personal experience, for her logbook records such an occurrence during her solo flight to England in 1932.

The heroine of "Appointment in Khartoum" is an American girl, and there is contemporary Allied patriotism as well as romance in the ending of the story, which was written in early 1944 when the war was still at its height. But the slight plot forces one to wonder why Kensing—apparently such a brilliant pilot—could not, himself, have flown to Khartoum.

The *babu* desk clerk was apologetic. He wore a red fez upon his narrow head, and he emphasized his regret by shaking the fez from side to side rhythmically, like a band leaders' baton. No, the plane for Khartoum had not arrived. It would not arrive. The weather was bad. He was immensely, abjectly, miserably sorry, but there was no other available plane in Jerba,

[First published in *Collier's, The National Weekly*, April 1944.]

and would Mr. Kensing be kind enough to sit down and drink some tea?

Mr. Kensing would not. He was tall, and when he leaned over the desk, the *babu* seemed to shrink visibly—fez and all.

"Thank you very much—and blast your tea! I want a plane. I wired for a plane. My business can't wait. Telegraph Nairobi and don't stand there shaking that silly cap!"

The girl in the rawhide chair looked up from her year-old copy of a sports magazine and concluded that the stranger had a foul temper. He was obviously English, plainly in a hurry, and probably connected with the Foreign Office. War had dumped some peculiar people into the heart of Africa— urgent people with a common loathing for delay. They wore their tempers on their sleeves and went around tearing up red tape as if it were confetti.

She looked through the fly-specked window of what was euphemistically, perhaps even sarcastically, called the Hotel Jerba. Had it been called the Jerba Opera House, it would have made as much sense. It was a ten-room corrugated-iron shack with medieval plumbing, and with the Anglo-Egyptian Sudan for a garden. It had an airport with two gently sagging hangars, which now, before the slow stalking wind, were beginning to tremble as if anticipating the impending storm. The plane that had brought the Englishman had gone. No other plane would arrive from Nairobi that day—perhaps not for many days.

She put her magazine aside, wondering somewhat skeptically just how important the young man's business might be. Then she shrugged. It didn't matter.

Or did it? As if she had been made alert by some pinprick of an idea, she sat erect in the chair, then leaned forward, an expression of sudden interest in her face. Perhaps, she thought, just perhaps . . .

She watched the restless stranger pace the floor with enormous strides—enormous, but uneven. His slight limp was apparent enough to her, but he himself ignored it with magnificent disdain. He stared at the little desk clerk who was furiously clicking his telegraph key—and waited.

When the answer came, the *babu* punched it out on a typewriter and handed the sheet to the Englishman, who read it out loud in staccato syllables: ALL PLANES GROUNDED. SUGGEST MR. KENSING GET MEREDITH IF POSSIBLE AND AT OWN RISK. SELFRIDGE.

Mr. Kensing crumpled the sheet and swore beautifully, but with British restraint. He lowered his head and crept toward the *babu* as if he were going to pounce. "Meredith, eh? So there is a pilot here! Why the devil didn't you tell me that? Where is this fellow, Meredith? This is wartime. Move!"

The *babu* moved. He moved a little like someone quite lately struck over the head with a sandbag—uncertainly, warily. He came around the desk that was made of crude planking and aimed a brown, unstable finger at the girl in the rawhide chair.

With notable lack of gallantry he said, "That, sir, I am very sorry, please forgive, is this fellow Miss Meredith—a woman, you will observe."

"A woman?" Mr. Kensing uttered the word with plain incredulity, almost with distaste. He took three steps toward Diana Meredith and stared at her, around her, and through her. He wiped his forehead with a very smart blue handkerchief. "I beg your pardon—but are you . . ."

"A woman?" Diana smiled and looked at her trousers. "Don't let the slacks fool you. Skirts would be silly out here."

"I'm sorry. I didn't mean that. I'm looking for a pilot and a plane."

Diana stood up and shook her chestnut hair into place. Her

eyes were about on a level with Grey Kensing's shoulders, and she had to tilt her head upward to speak to him.

"I know," she said. "I couldn't help hearing. I'm a pilot and I have a plane. The war has grounded me, and I've been hoping for a chance." Her voice was confident, but eager. "I thought if I could prove my usefulness . . ." She hesitated, then let the sentence die on her lips.

Grey Kensing was shaking his head a little wearily but with unmistakable firmness. "Terribly sorry, Miss—Meredith is it?—my pilot would have to be a man, of course. Can't trust girls or amateurs, you know, on business matters—war matters. You have the plane. Now if you could suggest some pilot . . . some professional . . ."

Grey Kensing stopped talking abruptly because he had no one to talk to. Diana was halfway to the door before she turned. There was a blaze of anger in her smoke blue eyes, but she kept her voice cool.

"This is Africa," she said. "The facilities are somewhat limited. So is the supply of pilots. I would suggest you cable London—they might send you one."

She didn't slam the door; she closed it quietly and went across the runway, biting her lip and fighting the rising wind.

Professional pilot! For three years, she had flown her one-plane taxi service into almost every corner of central, east, and north Africa under commercial license—until the war had grounded her. Now, thousands of miles from Texas—and home—she was not only useless but had to be reminded of it by an impatient Englishman.

She swung open the door of the small hangar with a good deal more strength than required. Midmorning light poured over the yellow wings and fuselage of her tiny Avian. It was a biplane with an open cockpit, few instruments, and a galaxy of patches that, to Diana, were no indication of weakness, but only so many symbols of character and integrity.

"My dear young lady!"

She swung round with less surprise than annoyance. My dear young lady indeed! She muttered the phrase in her mind. Grey Kensing looked scarcely four years older than she, yet there he stood in the hangar doorway, talking like a character out of a third-rate play—looking like one, too—handsome, and better dressed than made sense in this windy wilderness.

She didn't answer. She waited.

He indicated the Avian with a resigned but disappointed gesture of his hand. "So that's what you call your plane. That's what you expect to get me to Khartoum in—bad weather and all!" He looked angry, even desperate.

Diana nodded. "That," she admitted, "is what I call my plane. I've flown over half of Africa in it and I expect to fly over the other half in the same machine. As for getting to Khartoum in it, I'm sorry I made the suggestion. I could get you there—storm or no storm—but you don't trust women pilots, and that's that. You'll have to excuse me now. I'm closing the hangar." She moved toward the door with quick, determined steps.

Grey Kensing sighed. He moved toward the plane. He said, "Miss Meredith, please don't be coy. I didn't come out here in order to sell whisk brooms. I have a job to do for my government—your government, too, incidentally. It's a small job perhaps, but it's important, and I have got to be in Khartoum by morning. You offered to fly me. I'm accepting the offer. I can't do anything else."

Quite as casually as if he were himself the owner of the Avian—albeit not a proud owner—Grey Kensing tossed a briefcase and a small overnight bag into the locker, then turned again to Diana, whose face bore an expression of mingled bewilderment and fury.

She had concluded that she could either slam the hangar door in his face or swallow her pride for the sake of the chance to get off the ground again. Once she had got him across ths Sudd and safely to Khartoum, he might be generous enough to admit that she could fly. Everything helped. A lot could depend on this one flight. She decided against slamming the hangar door. Instead, she opened it wider, and together, in brittle silence, they pushed the plane out onto the runway.

As she got into her seat behind the instrument board, Diana thought she saw just the glimmer of a smile on Grey Kensing's lips. She wasn't sure, but it seemed to her a challenging smile . . .

If you are a pilot with a morose turn of mind and wish to escape the world, you need only fly north from Jerba. When the great green Sudd begins to crawl under your wings, you have at least escaped the world that men know and walk upon and quarrel over. The Sudd is the dregs of Africa, the backwash of the Nile, a flat never-ending swamp garrisoned by crocodiles. It spreads between Jerba and Malakal. It seems to wait for planes to fall—a vast receptacle, hopeful of misfortune.

To Diana, the Sudd, in any weather, was a nightmare. In a storm it was delirium come true, but any way you looked at it, you were a fool to fly over it if you didn't have to.

She was flying over it and she supposed that she didn't really have to. She sat at the controls of the Avian and told herself that normally, under the promise of such foul weather, she wouldn't have budged from the runway. Still, when you wanted a chance at something, you did strange, even foolhardy things. That was one reason. The other—well, it was hardly clear in her mind, nor was she sure she wanted it to be. She was not going to admit that Grey Kensing's outspoken disbelief of her ability had influenced her for a moment.

She looked to the east and saw the storm clouds rolling toward her like smoke from a burning forest. The familiar stench of the Sudd began to invade the cockpit, and she eased back on the stick and climbed . . .

She was cruising at a hundred miles an hour when the storm hit. At first, there was no rain; it was all wind and darkness. Diana experienced the eerie sensation of seeing the wings of her plane and all else that was visible swallowed in the gloom until she and Grey Kensing seemed borne wholly by magic and the roar of her engine. It was not a new sensation. She and the Avian were intimate with storm, but somehow today it was disquieting.

When the rain came, lightning came with it, ripping the black fabric of the sky, framing the Avian in momentary halos of brilliance and, as abruptly, leaving it to darkness.

Diana was suddenly alone. It was the aloneness of concentration—of swiftly moving hands, of concerned eyes darting from instrument to instrument, of feet, sensitive, steady, alert on the rudder bar—the aloneness of caution, of determination, of competence. She was alone as she had been a thousand times before, and when the bland voice of Grey Kensing came to her through her earphones it was as startling as a hand suddenly placed upon her shoulders.

"How far to Malakal?"

She snorted. Ten minutes of storm and he was already anxious for a runway.

"An hour, I think—maybe more." She had to scream it into the mouthpiece, outshouting both the engine and the thunder, but there was a sharpness in her voice not common to her. She wanted to add, "Maybe two hours—four—six! If you're afraid, we'll turn."

But he wasn't afraid. She knew he wasn't afraid, and even that knowledge vaguely annoyed her; he was simply cold and critical and obsessed with getting to Khartoum.

The storm had risen to its full malevolence, and she felt, as she had often done, the real enmity of the elements—their hatred of men's intrusion into the sky. Wind struck at the little airplane with hammer blows, lightning blinded its eyes, darkness made it blunder on its way. And below it all lay the Sudd.

She worked in silence, neither complaining to herself nor aloud. What disturbed her most was that, after all her countless hours in the air, she was being compelled to prove herself once more—and to a brusque and even arrogant young man she had never seen before and never wanted to see again.

She put her head out of the cockpit and stared down, but the air was opaque as an angry sea. The guiding ribbon of the Nile had not yet appeared.

A muffled metallic cough—louder to her than thunder had ever been—came to her ears. Of all sounds in the world, this one sound is, to a pilot, the most significant, the most hated, the most feared. Diana couldn't believe it, but there it was. She wouldn't believe it, but it was true. Now at last it had happened. Now, in the full temper of the storm, the Avian was failing her. It was dying on her.

The splutter increased—sharp staccato barkings of the exhaust, the roar of the engine fighting to live, the cough again, the hesitance, the silence amidst sound, the hush of the powerless prop.

She bit her lip, remembering the worn petrolflex that she had not been able to replace. Air in the fuel tube. Airlock. Her fingers closed on the throttle. It was no good. She eased forward on the stick. She had to. They were falling, losing altitude, circling toward the Sudd. She steadied the plane and thrust it into the wind, working for time, but there was no time.

She lifted the speaking tube and said into it, "You had better hang on. We're going down." Her voice was even, but heavy with bitterness—filled with bitterness. There was no fear in it, only admission of defeat and failure.

Under a flash of lightning she saw Grey Kensing leaning forward as if intent upon something in his hands. Then the lightning was gone, and his infuriatingly calm British voice came to her through the earphones: "Swamp underneath, I believe. Bad show, isn't it?"

"Bad show!" Diana blurted it out loud. Did he always respond to everything with moth-eaten English clichés? She thrust her head out of the cockpit as she caught the altimeter reading with the tail of her eye. Two thousand feet and losing altitude fast. She couldn't see anything below. She didn't particularly want to. She knew what was there.

At five hundred feet, she saw what was there—a motionless mat of green scum, steamy with the falling rain, flat as an airport, inviting, beckoning. She circled, keeping the plane aloft almost with the strength of her will, catching the wind, letting it lift her so long as it would.

It was not long. The dead engine was dragging the Avian inexorably earthward, swampward. At a hundred feet, she saw the ridge of shining clay jutting away from the morass and she was suddenly calm. Calm—and angry, and bitter. She had a choice to make; crash on the ridge, or be sucked into the swamp. It didn't matter which, but the first seemed the least ignominious. She said into the speaking tube, "I'm sorry, but this is it!" and began to sideslip. She made a bird of the Avian, spilling air from one wing, then from the other—teetering, sliding on the wind like a falling hawk, dropping.

She had no time to look at Grey Kensing but she was somehow conscious of his poised rigidity as they fell. He was silent, unmoving, vindicated in his distrust of women pilots for whatever satisfaction there was in it. There couldn't be much, she was thinking. And then they struck.

They didn't land, they struck; the little plane hit the clay ridge squarely with both wheels and then skidded, leaped into the air, and struck again. The jolt was more sickening than painful. It hurled Diana forward in her safety belt until she thought the canvas would break. Not once—twice—three times—four. She thought the jolting would never stop, and then, abruptly, it did.

It stopped and, except for the driving rain, there was silence. No other sound. Not even thunder. A terrible silence. A silence of defeat and despair and emptiness.

She looked at Grey Kensing. He didn't turn: he didn't say a word. He wouldn't, she thought. He was unbuckling his safety belt—slowly, methodically, as if they had come down not in the world's most miserable swamp, but on a paved airport lined with lights. He was imperturbable, superior, hateful.

He clambered out of the plane and reached to help Diana, saying nothing.

Manners, she thought, those inbred, meaningless, English manners!

She took his hand and got out and looked at him. His dark hair was ruffled, there was a little trickle of blood on his cheek. Not much, but a little. He pulled a handkerchief out of his pocket and patted the trickle neatly. Then he looked at his watch, at Diana, at the Avian.

"Airlock, I think," he said. "Have you a spanner?" He didn't say, "Are you all right" or "Are you hurt?" Just, "Airlock, I think. Have you a spanner?" It was exactly as if he had said, "Could I bother you for a match?"

Diana opened her mouth, then closed it again. "Spanner?" Well that was English for wrench. He wanted a wrench. This obviously nonmechanical, perfectly groomed young Englishman wanted a wrench.

She wanted to laugh, but before she knew it, she had got the box open and was handing him the wrench.

She wanted to swear, too, but she wasn't very good at it, so she didn't. She walked around the plane peering at every strut and joint and wheel. It was intact. Rugged and tough and ready, the little Avian stood there—one wheel on soft clay, the other on fairly hard ground. Not a scratch on her. There was a devilish, minxlike quality in her tip-tilted attitude. Diana shook her head. Why, of all times, should this have been the time for failure! Why couldn't she have been alone when it happened?

She looked around her. The storm was waning, but the rain had stirred the Sudd until its stench was thick as mist. They were on an island of rain-sleek clay—an island perhaps twelve yards wide and four hundred yards long. Normally the Avian required about six hundred yards for a takeoff—in dry weather. Two hundred yards less meant a lot, especially on a wet surface. Still, there were the doughnut tires. They helped—or were said to, anyway.

She went round to the cowling and saw that it was open and that Grey Kensing's head was under it. He was making a noble effort but probably didn't know a carburetor from a wing flap. Manlike, he thought he had to do something.

She rolled up her sleeves. She had humored his ego long

enough. They were lucky to be alive whether he knew it or not—Khartoum or no Khartoum. If they got out of here, he could spend the rest of his life cursing women pilots and the crates they flew in. It didn't matter anymore. She was dejected and impatient—and worried.

She said, "Better let me handle it. I know the engine."

He said, "Get some tape."

She hesitated, making no effort to stem her annoyance. "Mr. Kensing," she said.

He didn't lift his head, but he lifted his voice. He roared "Tape, dammit!"

A moment later she stood beside him, tight-lipped, furious, groping for effective words and not finding them—but the tape was in her hand. When he said, "Wire," she got it. When he said, "Pliers," she got them. When, finally, after what seemed ages, but was only ten minutes, he turned his grease-stained face toward her and pointed to the cockpit, she got behind the controls without a word. If she had had a word, she couldn't have uttered it. It wouldn't have come.

She had a vision of his explaining his lateness in Khartoum, explaining it in clipped English terms: "Girl pilot—American, I think—best I could do. Put me smack down in the Sudd with a frayed petrolflex—had to fix it myself. Man's job, flying. Shouldn't permit—"

Smothering her resentment, Diana watched him return from his inspection of what had to be the runway. She had looked it over herself, of course, but that had not been enough—not for Grey Kensing. He walked round the cowling and put his hands on the propeller with such confident ease that she did not stop him.

"Contact?" he said.

"Contact!" she snapped.

The engine roared and he got into his seat. He had taken over. He had simply taken over, and there she sat, in her own plane, waiting for a signal to take off.

The astonishing thing was that he confidently expected her to perform the miraculous. He ignored the soft going, the shortness of the run, the direction of the wind. He just lifted his hand, as if flying were child's play, and Diana (like an obedient child) took off.

It was as simple as that; and, as the Avian shook the Sudd from her heels—quite as nonchalantly as Grey Kensing might have done—she told herself that never in her twenty-one years had she disliked anyone so much, unless it was herself at that moment for having left her single chance to prove her mettle behind her on that scum-surrounded ledge.

Malakal for fuel, then Omdurman, and then Khartoum just across the White Nile. No more storm, and the evening sky was blue as heavy glass. The adobe huts of Omdurman stood in the valley like nursery blocks on a green rug. Diana sighed, as she always did when she saw the airport—flat and yellow and capacious as a Texas plain.

She sighed, but with more relief than she had ever done. It was not only the flight that was ended. So too was this enforced companionship with the maddening, arrogant—and yet strangely casual—Grey Kensing.

He had made Khartoum—and with half an hour to spare. Yet, so long as he remembered that flight, he would inevitably recall it as the flight on which a girl pilot—or would-be pilot—had put him down.

When they had landed and he had once more helped her out of the cockpit in that precise and dutiful manner of his, he bowed a little hesitantly, mumbled his thanks, and asked if she needed a lift into town. His hair was tousled, the bruise on his cheek had turned slightly blue, and his shirt had grease on it. Diana decided that, for the first time, he looked eminently human, but she did not dwell upon the discovery.

She shook her head. No. No, thanks. It was nice of him to offer the lift, but she couldn't. Had to get a mechanic on the machine right away. Things to see to . . .

She smiled and he smiled—somewhat painfully it seemed—and then he was gone, walking away from her, tall, erect, overcoming his limp by the sheer pride of his carriage.

Diana watched him for a moment, then leaned against the wing of her plane, pulled off her helmet and let the wind blow idly through her hair. That was that, she thought. Grey Kensing—embodiment of a fine, self-centered man. She wondered why he had bothered to thank her at all. Habit, no doubt. He'd probably thanked bus drivers and doormen in exactly the same way. Mustn't be rude to the working classes, you know!

She thought of the entry she would make in her pilot's logbook: "Jerba to Khartoum—Pilot, Self. Passenger, Grey Kensing." Under "remarks" she would, of course, write: "Forced landing—Sudd," and she would write it with bitterness. Any chance she might have had to fly regularly again, to revive her air service and put it to wartime needs, instead of carrying lion and elephant hunters from place to place, would be gone now.

She sighed and turned to the Avian. She would get a mechanic to repair the petrolflex, and she would return to Jerba in the morning. She was unaccountably depressed, but she couldn't shake it off. She began to check over the plane as was her habit, but she went about it mechanically, almost without interest. When she got to the front cockpit, she glanced at the seat Grey Kensing had occupied, then turned back again.

Something had caught her eye. It was a scrap of white paper, a used envelope crumpled into a ball. It lay on the floor beside the seat.

Diana looked at it, hesitated, then reached into the cockpit. She got the little ball of paper and compressed it in her hand as if to toss it to the ground but she didn't. Something kept her from it. She unfolded the envelope with a childish feeling of guilt and saw there was writing on its back.

It was scrawled, uneven writing, scarcely legible. As she read, she recalled the brief moment when Grey Kensing had sat, head forward, silhouetted by the blazing sky, intent on something in his hands. This then was what it had been.

She made her lips move slowly, though she read in silence, bewildered silence, almost unbelieving silence:

"I wish to make it clear that, should this plane be found wrecked, it will in no way be the fault of the pilot, Miss Meredith. She made the flight altogether at my insistence and has acted with skill and courage. Grey Kensing."

That was all—or Diana thought it was. She stared at the crumpled envelope with blurred eyes. She turned it over and over again in her fingers, but it was not until she had stood there like that for a long time that she noticed the typewritten words on the front of the envelope—the words that had been used by someone to address Grey Kensing—and it was what followed his name that caught her eye. "Grey Kensing," the clean-cut letters spelled, "Grey Kensing, DFC."

Distinguished Flying Cross! She didn't know whether anger, embarrassment, or shame was the uppermost of her emotions. Perhaps it was a combination of the three. Grey Kensing, DFC. A war ace—and she, Diana, had undertaken to show him how to cross the Sudd in a storm! It was worth a laugh, but there was no laughter in her heart. She wanted to crawl into a hotel room and lock the door and just stay there until her Avian was ready to fly back to Jerba once more.

As she stood there, with the gallant and generous note in her hand, a lump came into her throat and would have been followed by tears if she hadn't held them back. It was obvious enough that in the midst of the storm over the Sudd—at the moment when the forced landing had become inevitable— Grey Kensing had thought not so much of his own safety as he had thought of Diana's honor and reputation as a pilot. If, by chance, he had been killed, and she had lived, that little note, scratched out up there in the wild, resentful sky, would have absolved her of his death. All danger over, he had of course thrown the note from the plane but, as nearly always happened, the wind had hurled it back again, back to her.

Grey Kensing, DFC. She repeated the name and, repeating it, found answers to some of the questions in her mind. She knew now that he had been decorated for bravery. She could guess the rest. His limp must be the result of battle injury. He had been retired out of the service and put into civilian work. The gruff manner, the impatience, the seeming rudeness—all these were to cover the disappointment, the bitterness that must come to a fighting man no longer bearing arms, to a pilot no longer able to fly.

She shook herself out of her reverie. An airport attendant had come up, and she went through the routine of presenting her papers and arranging for the care of the plane, then she walked slowly toward one of the shining cars that served the airport as taxis.

She said, "Grand Hotel," to the Egyptian driver—and said it listlessly.

In a few minutes, the driver stopped before a deep veranda

that looked down upon the dreaming Nile, but Diana, who loved the river, did not look at it now. She gave the driver a note and waived the change.

In a few minutes, a Sudanese boy was leading her along the dark, fan-cooled corridor toward her room. She was still in her flying clothes, and a few curious people had stared at her as curious people do, but she was unaware of them.

The Sudanese boy stopped and opened a door, and she was thanking him and fumbling in her pocket for change when another door opened and Grey Kensing stepped into the corridor. He was in fresh clothes and immaculate once more. He came toward her, trying, as always, to hide his modest limp, and Diana thought that his smile had lost its challenge, its gently mocking quality.

He said, "You ought to have come with me. I asked you." Diana nodded and found herself stupidly groping for words. A little impatiently, she handed the waiting boy a few coins, and when he had left and they were alone, she saw that her unsteady fingers had dropped the crumpled envelope that she had found in the plane and that Grey Kensing had stooped to pick it up.

For a moment, she could say nothing. He had recognized it, of course, and was doubtless wondering why she had clung to it all the way from the airport. Nor could she have explained it to him. But she tried. She said, "I—it must have blown back. I'm afraid I read it. It was good of you."

He moved closer to her and looked questioningly into her eyes.

"About the forced landing," she said. "I wanted to make a better showing. I . . ."

His hands were on her shoulders before she could finish— large hands, strong but strangely gentle. He looked down upon her, smiling. The abrupt, cold manner, the icy reserve were suddenly gone, and his eyes were warm. He shook his head.

"No," he said, "I don't see. I didn't write that note out of kindness, but out of simple respect for a fellow flier and a master of the craft. I'd made a mistake in judging you and I had to make it right. That was just the beginning."

He took her arm in his and began to march her solemnly down the corridor and toward the broad veranda busy with white-clad Sudanese boys, tinkling glasses, and uniforms of a dozen nations.

When they were comfortable in the wicker chairs and he had ordered champagne cocktails, he reached across the table and took Diana's hand in his own.

"You see," he explained, "a mistake like mine takes a lot of undoing—weeks, months, years perhaps! It's a big job—even for an Englishman. So big, in fact, I'm going to need an ally."

Diana laughed. "Your traditional ally?" He nodded. "America," he said and lifted his glass to hers.

"Contact?"

"Contact!"

The Nile was silent, and yet as Diana peered through the trees that stood in dutiful attendance upon its banks, the river seemed to glow with a wise and age-old smile—placid, knowing and, beyond all things, content.

Your Heart Will Tell You

Juanita, the surprisingly pliant heroine of "Your Heart Will Tell You," flew her airplane into the desert to search for her childhood friend. Beryl could provide the background to this story with complete confidence for she had done the same thing many times in her Avro Avian, searching for fellow aviators whose airplanes had failed to report to their intended destination. However, it is difficult to believe that Beryl would have put herself in the same situation as Juanita, who continued her search even when she knew it meant using up the fuel required to fly to safety.

Perhaps Beryl was repeating the words of her own flying instructor, Tom Campbell Black, in Peter's response to Juanita's suggestion to fly to the rescue, "[It's] a fool's errand so long as there's a rescue party on the way. A good flier never risks the same accident twice. If you want to be good, remember that. You can't fly on your emotions. . . . It's the harebrained pilots that make people mistrust flying, the hero boys full of daredevil nonsense from the last war, all anxious to have their necks broken in another one." It sounds like Tom, careful and precise; but Tom was responsible for many such rescues himself, including that of the famous Ernst Udet (one of the pilots in Richtofen's crack Red Baron fighter squadron in the First World War).

[First published in *Ladies' Home Journal*, January 1944.]

Peter Shaw had got out of the cockpit and was leaning against the fuselage of his Avro, tugging at the chin strap of his helmet, when Juanita ran up. Several shades of East African dust were caked on his face, and his eyes were bloodshot. He was obviously dead tired, and there was justification for his impatience, which he presently displayed by breaking the strap and throwing the helmet on the ground. The act released his black hair, so that its smothered curls began to come alive in the wind. Dust or no dust, Peter was handsome by any standard, and Juanita had never been more aware of it; his features were too clean-cut to take harm from a bit of dirt, and his eyes too bold to suffer much from weariness or wind. His nose was straight as a blade and his lips were full. Beyond that, he had flat cheeks, which, at the moment, he was diligently scrubbing with the back of his hand.

Juanita came to him gently, and he grinned. It was a good grin, and he took her lightly in his arms and kissed her on the forehead, then held her a little away from him, appraising, with mock solemnity, her wide apart blue eyes, her shining, sun yellow hair.

"Hello, monkey," he said. "I'm glad I made it."

"Made what?" Juanita disengaged herself and looked at the Avro. She thought that it sagged a bit on the port side, but on the whole it looked pretty sound. She began to smile—and then the smile didn't come. Nothing came but a strange uneasiness, then a sharp awareness. She looked at the Avro again. Of course it sagged—a longeron was snapped like a piece of kindling struck with an axe—and the front seat, Michael's seat, was empty. She did not question Peter. She moved closer to him and put a hand on his arm and waited.

He glanced at his plane and swore softly. "My first forced landing," he explained. "The rains are on and I couldn't find

Marsabit. That was yesterday. It was getting dark and I had to come down in that darned lava desert about eighty miles north of the post." He handed her his flying map, marked clearly with a pencil dot. "Right there," he said. "Snapped a longeron getting down—and I'll never know how I managed to get off."

"And Michael?"

"He's all right. We don't have to worry." He spoke quickly but with weariness in his voice. "In the morning I saw I couldn't get the plane off with both of us in it—too much weight. We talked it over and Michael had to stay. It was the only way out. I left him what water there was and flew to Marsabit. They're sending a camel caravan out to get him." He managed a tired smile. "And that's the story. Now how about some tea?"

They had left the runway behind them and, walking arm in arm, had reached the little jungle of bougainvillea that guarded the veranda of her father's house.

Juanita was thoughtful. "That would be the Koroli Desert," she said, looking at the map again. "It's supposed to be one of the worst."

He nodded. "I can confirm it. It's terrible."

For a moment she was silent. She paused with her hand on the latch of the heavy *lamu* door that, like a portcullis, confronted the surrounding wilderness. She swept the wayward locks of blond hair away from her forehead as if meaning him to see the whole of her face as she turned it to him.

"Peter," she said hesitantly, almost with an air of apology, "I know you're worn out—and perhaps this is silly for me to say. I'm not used to this kind of thing yet—but shouldn't something more be done? Shouldn't you go back for Michael? If he's eighty miles north of Marsabit, camels won't reach him for days." She swept her hand toward the runway. "There's my plane; if you took the seats out to lighten it—or—" She paused again a little awkwardly, as if feeling that without the right to do it she was questioning his judgement. "It won't be dark for hours," she said. "I thought that perhaps—" Groping for words, she saw that Peter was looking down at her with surprise in his eyes, and she gave it up.

"Darling," he said firmly, "you never went in for heroics or hysterics before; you oughtn't to start now. Michael wouldn't expect me to chance my plane, or yours, on a fool's errand so long as there's a rescue party on the way. A good flier never risks the same accident twice. If you want to be good, remember that. You can't fly on your emotions." His voice was almost paternal. He was the teacher again, as she had known him in the cockpit—calm, sensible, sound. It was the quality that had given her such confidence in him. "It's the harebrained pilots that make people mistrust flying," he had often told her, "the hero boys full of daredevil nonsense from the last war, all anxious to have their necks broken in another one."

No, she conceded to herself, you couldn't fly on your emotions. Peter had confronted her with her own philosophy of sanity and realism, and she could not criticize him for it. If one man were lost in a desert, nothing could be gained by losing two. This must be—this was—truth. But still—

For a moment, she glanced back through her childhood memory, seeing herself and the redheaded Michael running forever, barefoot and happy, through the forest paths. She looked up at Peter and contrived a smile. "I'm sorry," she said. "He's such an old, old friend—and I can't help thinking."

"You needn't," said Peter. "The camels will find him."

She knew that he was right. But she had to tell herself that he was, had to check herself on the verge of stupidly insisting that he take her plane and go back after Michael. She had to close the doors of her mind against the sudden thought that in Peter's place, Michael would have gone back, would have insisted on going back.

A long time afterward, when it was midafternoon, she was still trying to shut that obstinately persisting thought out of her mind, the way the drawn curtains of her father's house were shutting out the equatorial sun, unchallenged master of this land even here in the foothills of Mount Kenya, whose crest was eternally studded with ice. Here in the long living room it was almost dark, and almost cool, and within the cedar walls there was an atmosphere—almost—of peace.

In a broad leather chair that leaned its back against a tier of bookshelves, she sat staring at the opposite wall without seeing it. What she saw was Peter's crippled plane as he maneuvered it, so cleverly and so carefully, from the runway and started for Nairobi. It had been gone for an hour, but the drone of it seemed scarcely dead in her ears.

She was being stupid, she told herself. Stupid and vain. Like the vain, stupid women who demanded that their men be heroes, because the men they read about and saw in films and perhaps dreamed about were always heroes. The kind of heroes who got themselves cut to ribbons or blown to bits for no better reason than to let some woman salve her silly ego with the thought, "He did it for me!"

She ought to be rejoicing that Peter wasn't that kind of hero. That he'd done the sensible, the right things, the things that were as wise and safe for Michael as for Peter himself. The surest way of getting Michael out of that desert alive had been to leave him there, with water, to make for Marsabit and send those camels out to bring him back. The camels were certain to do it. In a little time, perhaps in only a few hours, the word would come that all was well, and she would be glad that she'd been sensible, too, as sensible as Peter, and left a man's problem for men to cope with.

But she stirred in her chair, and pushed her hair back from her forehead with a quick, almost fretful gesture, as if her hand could brush away the question that was in her mind. She did not want to think. Beyond everything she did not want to think. But she did not know why this was so.

She closed her eyes and held them closed while Ismail, the Somali houseboy, entered the room on noiseless feet and performed his special rite. Every afternoon at just this hour he lit the incense. It was incense brought from Aden, near the Red Sea, and, as a Somali, he had a reverence for it. It was nostalgia made sweet, and its fragrance, blended of myrrh and frankincense, was as much a part of the Martin house as Ismail himself.

Perhaps it was the act itself, performed in silence except for the hypnotic rustle of Ismail's *khansa*, that made Juanita sleep. Certainly she had not intended to. She sat still in the deep chair and nodded like a drowsy child, a troubled child, and when she awoke—not with a start, but gently—her eyes were on the little iron brazier where the incense burned. As she watched the blue smoke, dreamily at first, it seemed to her that it rose erratically. Then, in the half-light of the curtained room, it seemed to make a kind of pattern, dimly remembered but familiar.

North from Marsabit toward the Kenya-Ethiopia border, the Koroli Desert spreads with the aimlessness of all deserts, admitting no boundary save the sky. But to the practiced eye, to the desert-born, the Koroli Desert is clearly marked with the symbols of its special character. It is no sea of yellow sand lapping at the shores of an occasional oasis; it is a crowded desert, dry as bleaching bones, but furnished, as few deserts are, with countless monstrous black lava shapes, sculptured and bequeathed by some cataclysm-minded god, aeons ago. The dismal monuments rise at every hand, and a man among them is to himself, and to them, without existence; he is better than lost. His being is without significance. If he has water, he can delude himself while it lasts. If he has hope, he can sing; if he has courage, he can work—it hurries time.

Michael was hurrying time. He both worked and sang. Fairly tall, his body had a wiry, whiplike quality; the distinguishing feature of his face was its simplicity. A lean face, starred with freckles, surmounted by a mop of reddish hair and lighted with blue eyes, it obviously had never concealed a secret and masked few, if any, doubts. It was open and unperturbed.

He wore the uniform of an officer of the King's Africa Rifles: khaki shorts, a tunic of the same stuff, bearing mathematically spaced pockets, a military helmet. A metal water bottle dangled from a strap hung over his shoulder and now and then swung in wide arcs as he strained and sweated against a black rock and dragged it from the clearing he had planned. He was making a runway for an airplane, and the job was plainly impossible. He sang gaily—but with no tone and no respect for melody—the chorus of Schubert's melancholy "Serenade," and the impassioned words wandered without goal or audience through the labyrinth of rock.

He had cleared a space perhaps twenty feet wide and fifty feet long—scarcely enough room, he thought, in which to toss a cat, much less swing it. But it didn't matter. There would probably be no plane anyway, but the job kept him occupied while he waited for the camels.

"Under my window, deep in the shadows"—he sang loudly, apparently unaware that, since there were no shadows anywhere within the scope of his sight, the words were mildly ironic—"sings the nightingale."

He paused there, unsure of the verse, indifferent to the fact that the only bird within view was a vulture, mute, intent, ploughing the sky back and forth on hopeful wings. Having paused in his singing, he reproached himself for having sung at all. It made his throat dry. He reached down for the water bottle at his hip, held it to his ear and shook it. This morning it had gurgled; now it only tinkled. He wanted to drink, but rejected the impulse, thinking of tomorrow.

According to his watch, it was an hour past noon. He had a handful of dates wrapped in a handkerchief. He ate four of them and put the little bundle that remained into the pocket of his shirt. He was hungry and his mouth seemed dry as the sand he waded in, but he felt that he was getting used to the heat. It was everywhere, coming up from the earth, radiating from the lava boulders, pouring even from his body so that, to himself, he seemed no longer alien to the desert, but a part of it.

He remembered that, in theory, a man without sufficient water was supposed to die after forty-eight hours of such exposure, but he counted this as nonsense. The brief spasms of dizziness that were beginning to plague him as he worked were, he decided, due to fatigue; he had moved a lot of rock; all that he needed was to rest.

He closed his eyes and crouched against a shaft of rock that jutted from the sand. He was breathing with some effort, but that would soon pass. He groped in a pocket and brought out a square of shining paper. It was a print of a careless snapshot taken some years ago as Juanita Martin and he had stood hand in hand over the body of a marauding leopard they had trapped together. It had been their first great adventure. He did not dwell upon it, but when he returned it to his pocket, the urge to sing had left him. Still, he did not allow himself a maudlin sigh; it was pointless to wish.

For a long time now he had discounted himself as a romantic figure, and it seemed to him that all the girls he had ever known had upheld him in this judgement. He was irrevocably the constant friend, the old dependable—the good sound wine that never sparkled.

He shook his water bottle again, ruled temptation down, and began to labor over a rock. It was heavy, but he pried it from its hollow and lifted it with both arms, holding it against his body. He struggled toward the edge of his tiny clearing, sinking to his ankles in the sand, shaking his head against the salt sweat that blinded his eyes.

He could not have seen the almost buried blade of lava that ran across his path, for he stumbled over it with the rock in his arms, and went down swearing mildly at his clumsiness. He was not hurt. Not even his fingers were hurt; the fall was gentle, and it was not until he stood up again and began automatically to dust his clothes that he saw that his water bottle had burst open under the impact of the rock and had poured its contents on the sand. He did not reach for it, nor make any move. He stood swaying a little with the heat of the desert crowding him, watching the dark spot the cupful of water had made at his feet. Finally he took one of the two cigarettes that were left to him and lit it and drew the smoke in deeply.

Under my window, deep in the shadows—aimlessly the words wandered through his mind, but did not reach his lips. The smoke from his cigarette rose from his hand straight to the sky like a rope at a magician's bidding. He observed it idly, feeling the dizziness again, and closed his eyes until it had passed.

Well, he thought, here it was—the classic desert tragedy, a stranded man without water. It was so hackneyed, so melodramatic a situation as to be almost shameful. At the thought of it he tried to smile, but he knew that the effort was false. He knew that it was the sun and not fatigue that was draining the strength from his legs and his arms and making his vision more blurred, moment by moment. He had known it for hours.

Now it came again—the weakness that ran through his body like a fever and, like a fever, left him trembling and yearning to let himself fall upon the sand and stay there, forgetting everything. But once more he waited until it had gone, steadying himself, staring at his burning cigarette as if sanity—and even hope—were to be found only in the contemplation of the little rod of grey smoke that tapered toward the sun.

Smoke. Closing his eyes, he remembered a game they used to play—Juanita and he—a game with smoke. It had been simple. You built a fire somewhere on the veld, not too far from the farm, and you kept yourself hidden. Then with your hat, or with a sheaf of grass, you broke the smoke into puffs and made signals like the natives. Three short puffs and a long one, for instance, always meant "Come quickly, the fort is falling." It had been fun to make the signal and see how long it took for your most special friend to find you and arrive, breathless, with a handful of stone or a *Wandorobo* bow and arrow for your support against the enemy.

Three short puffs and a long one. Almost dreamily, with half a smile on his lips, Michael Cole knelt in the sand and lighted a scrap of paper from his pocket. Crawling on his knees, he collected bits of desert grass and threw them on the feeble flame. He found the stems of dry thorns and added them to it one by one like a miser paying pennies. He would have searched farther had he found the strength to move another step, but, like the water in the broken bottle, the strength had run out of him.

When the flame had grown to the size of a small bush, he pulled his battered hat from his head, and time after time, until he began to fall into what he supposed was sleep, he sent the smoke upward in three short puffs and then a long one, while there was willingness in his arms, the childish message.

Desert grass and thorns are not long-burning. For perhaps five minutes the little fire smoldered, and when it went out he was unconscious of it. He lay with his red hair in the sand, breathing slowly while his sole companion, the vulture overhead, swung nearer on rigid wings.

Juanita got to her feet and stood for a moment, trembling. She walked over to the brazier and watched it closely. The smoke from the incense rose in an unbroken band of blue.

"It was a dream," she said. "It couldn't have been a signal. Not for me."

She went to the window and opened the curtains on the empty sky. She thought of her meagre sixty hours of flying time, her uncertain skill with compass and calculator, her constant concern with the vastness of the land. She thought of Peter's face, looking the way it would look at her if he knew about the futile, senseless thing she wanted to do, the utterly unreasonable reason why she wanted to do it.

"He's right," she said. "I couldn't—"

But she took the map that Peter had left with her and held it tightly in her hand. She looked at her watch. She took her flying goggles from a drawer in the table. Peter's face was still watching her. She answered what it was saying.

"I know," she said. "I'll never find him."

Sleep had gone from her eyes and they were shining

strangely. She ran through the house and out along the path to the runway that had been, when she and Michael were children, a field of grass to others, but to them a hundred things: a sea, a jungle, a city with gleaming streets, an undiscovered world—a desert.

"The fort is falling," she murmured as she ran, "the fort is falling!"

From the air the Koroli Desert seems especially designed to conceal a stranded man. In the midst of a hundred thousand lava rocks, some tall as a man, some prone like resting human figures, some kneeling like men at prayer or men digging for water—where is the man himself? He is everywhere and so does not exist at all.

After hours at the controls of her Gypsy Moth, Juanita Martin knew, if she had not known it before, how complete despair could be. Cautiously, she had clung to her course, anxiously she had pored over Peter's map in the painful knowledge that figures, the cold needle of the compass, the comfortless chart across her knees were, in her hands, the fallible links between herself and Michael. Yet nowhere, she assured herself, had she gone wrong.

There, to the west, neither like silver nor like blue nor even shining, but dull as rust and sullen in the sun, sprawled Lake Rudolf. Before her, under the belly of the plane, beyond her, behind her and to the east there was the desert. Had it not spread in all directions past the limit of sight, it might have been the ruins of an ancient city burned to earth, the fallen columns of its buildings in a charred jumble, its symmetry vanished with age. Disconsolately she realized that a single man lost here might be lost forever, and in the realization she admitted that if Peter's reason had seemed to her without sympathy, it had still been reason. Here, at the prompting of a childhood memory—a wisp of smoke—she flew under the guidance of little else but impulse on an impossible errand.

She could still turn back. The hot swift wind that invaded the open cockpit scorched her cheeks. For better vision she had pushed her goggles from her eyes, and they wept from the sting and the glare. But these were physical discomforts, far less important than the dawning knowledge that she was afraid.

She was caught between two fears. With little more than an hour of daylight left, she might turn back to Marsabit before dark, and the fear that lack of courage might force her to do it was no less than the fear that nightfall might find her still above the hostile land—and without fuel.

Again and again she circled over what, according to her calculations, would be the dot that Peter had indicated on his map. Nowhere was there any sign of life. Inscrutable and silent, the desert waited beneath her wings, and in the end she turned.

She could not fly forever staring with blinded eyes on an unvarying scene that yielded her nothing. For what, to her, was time without end, she had hung like this—on hope and on those feeble wings—and there was nothing. Sick in her heart, she pressed the rudder bar and mapped her course to Marsabit, and counted herself a fool. She had proven nothing save that Peter had, after all, been right.

Unreasonably she let frustration turn to anger, and anger to imprudence. She pushed the throttle, accelerating the little plane almost beyond its limit of speed, and roared toward Marsabit. Minutes and miles disappeared behind her, hand in hand, and the voice of the Gypsy Moth jeered of failure, and the tears in her eyes were not from wind alone.

When she saw the camel caravan stirring the dust in lazy

wisps from the desert, she was halfway to Marsabit and the sun lay low and red upon the farthest dunes. Inexperienced though she was, it did not take her more than a moment to compute that the caravan was off its course, not by much, but by enough to miss its goal by several miles.

She did not hesitate. If she had thought, she would not have turned back again, but she did not allow herself to think. She banked the plane in a wide, clear arc and flew once more toward the desert in what was left of the day's last light. She flew low in a kind of urgent despair, swinging the little craft back and forth not five hundred feet above the ground, ignoring her dwindling supply of fuel, handling the controls with careless intimacy born not of skill, but of bitterness and desperation.

Now she began to wonder if she had not been committed to this search, not just from the moment Peter had flown to Nairobi, but long before, years before, perhaps. Vague questions that had never confronted her began to rise in discomforting shapes to cloud her vision. She began to speculate on her love for Peter, on its whirlwind beginning at the dance at the Muthaiga Club in Nairobi, a beginning that had been without question, perhaps even without understanding. She could not be sure—but now, each time she envisioned Peter's appealing, masculine figure, his carefree manner, his dark eyes so often lighted with gaiety, the slight unprepossessing presence of Michael Cole was in the vision, too, until both men were confused and mingled in her memory.

Impatiently, she banished thought and tried to concentrate on the task at hand. She had not enough fuel with which to return to Marsabit, and dusk was not far off. Shadows of rock had begun to spread themselves on the desert like an army of men preparing for sleep, but there was no man among them. Nor would there be, she decided. She had failed miserably in a wild, quixotic quest. More—as a pilot she was guilty of the ultimate sin: she had allowed herself no safety, no retreat.

The drone of the plane and the coming of night and the hopelessness made her want to sleep, as if sleep could drug discouragement and make fear numb. At a thousand feet she leveled the craft and held it level, flying north. Below her the desert was cooling; the tone and feel of the wind in the wires and on the wings were changed. The light was failing. And it seemed to come not from the sky in which she flew, but from the earth, making the sand translucent and the black rocks gleam. Once more she swung the plane east and then south.

She was almost incapable of thought or action when she saw below her the grooves that the wheels of a plane had left, deep and evenly spaced in the shifting sand. By morning, perhaps within another hour, the night wind would have erased the sign.

Without thought she began to spiral earthward, without even wondering whether she was capable of side-slipping deftly enough to make the almost impossible landing. Cautiously, boldly, as if she had done it a thousand times, she pushed the stick to the left and put pressure on the right rudder bar and then reversed the action, tipping the plane from side to side, spilling the air from its wings until it began to fall like a wounded hawk, until the earth came up like darkness and struck the craft and the sound of tearing wires and fabric and snapping wood burst in her ears and she felt her body plunge against the belt that held her in the cockpit, and consciousness left her.

When she recovered consciousness the sun had gone and massive shadows stalked the desert. She was dazed and her legs were numb but there was no pain, no blood. She was not hurt, but she saw that her plane had lost a wing against a jutting rock. It would not fly from this place. She unfastened the safety belt and climbed down and stared about her. There was neither movement nor breath of life.

She shouted, but there was no answer. She groped in the plane and got a water bottle, then a flashlight, and swung its hard, white beam from rock to dune and from dune to rock, and there was nothing.

She moved away from the plane into the forest of shapeless masses, stumbling as she walked, calling Michael's name and receiving, in turn, an echo. Despair began to fill her heart and would have filled it, but the light fell upon a smudge of ash at her feet, black ash, pitifully small, and dead, but hoarded like a wealth of gold dust in a hand-scooped hollow. A small dead fire. With a scorched, battered hat beside it. She followed the tracks Michael had made with his dragging feet until she found him, not fifty feet beyond, his red hair seemingly no longer red, but dimmed by the color of the sand he lay in, the skin of his face scorched and peeling, his eyes closed.

She dropped her light and lifted his head from the sand and brought the water to his clenched lips and poured it on them and forced it into his mouth. After a long, long time he stirred and his eyes looked up into hers. Still uncertain, he lifted a hand, touched her cheek.

"How did you know?" His voice was a child's voice, trailing across the edge of sleep.

She seemed to hear, but very far away, Peter's patient, sensible voice reminding her that you couldn't fly on your emotions. Or live by them. She didn't attempt to answer Michael except by the pressure of her heart against his cradled head. She had always known, she thought now, that her heart would find its way to Michael.

The Transformation

The tall, rough-handed, blunt John Craig in this story could well be based on Beryl's first husband, Jock Purves. Beryl was sixteen when she married Jock, a former Scottish International Rugby Football player, twice her age. He was a neighbor of Beryl's father, and the scene where the storyteller meets John has a ring of reality about it. "I used to ride through a corner of his pastures, and I found him there one morning stretching wire on fence posts. . . ." Beryl's marriage to Jock lasted less than two years and it is tempting to think that John's clumsy yet confident ability on his farm, and his inability to relate emotionally to the needs of the sensitive Anne, might cast some light on Beryl's own situation.

Jock eventually returned to London where he became a sports journalist for The Times. Perhaps this struck Beryl as just as unlikely an occurrence as the profession provided for John Craig at the end of this story.

———————

I first saw him at a gunsmith's shop in Nairobi. He was a huge man, young—twenty-six, perhaps—and he knew nothing of guns, nor did he want to. He was new to Kenya, but not to farming, and he had bought a tract of uncleared land up near the Mau forest, where leopards had of course begun to prey

[First published in *Ladies' Home Journal*, January 1946.]

upon his livestock. He needed a rifle, he explained to the clerk; and as he examined three or four, I saw that he handled them without respect or appreciation. His hands were strong and insensitive, and he would jerk open the breech of a finely made weapon as if it were a rusted piece of machinery. In the end he chose a light Springfield of excellent design and walked away holding it as if it were an axe.

The clerk shook his head and looked at me. "He'll prop windows open with it," he said, "and let the barrel rust."

"I suppose so," I said. I didn't care whether or not he split wood with it, but I remembered the way he used his hands.

It proved to be the way he used everything. As we learned more of him we saw that his mind was as harsh as his touch. He was not cruel, but there was no sentiment in him that one could see, nor much curiosity except about material things that he could turn to his needs. What he did not understand he shrugged away. But he worked wonders with what he knew.

In very little time he cleared a hundred acres of his farm, blasting the stumps of massive trees, dragging boulders with teams of oxen, and finally gouging the soil in precise and parallel furrows—for he did not seem to plough the land, but to harass it with a kind of anxious fury until it bore. He had no talent for the earth and pretended none, but he knew it chemically and made it yield.

His house was built in a matter of weeks. It stood high and alone on the rim of the Rongai Valley—a dark intrusion on the gentle skyline. It was clean and square and bleak. Nothing could get into it that he did not want to get in, and among those things was cheer as other people knew it. Still, as a house, it was beyond criticism. It was solid, tight—a flawless shelter—and when the last nail had been sunk into its cedar planking, John Craig decided to marry.

It was not an extraordinary decision except that it was so deliberately made and that, to the surprise of everyone, he set his mind on the one girl who was almost beyond his reach and certainly beyond his understanding. She was Anne Barton, whom Craig had met not more than twice, and who was in any case in love with another man, Larry Abbot, an independent pilot, the possessor of countless friends, but with not a shilling to his name.

Everyone knew about Anne and Larry; they seemed almost of a single identity, though for all of that it was a strange relationship. For three years their eventual marriage had been taken for granted, but it remained "eventual"; it had never happened, simply because Larry remained too improvident to make it happen. Yet Larry and Anne were inseparable, and his adoration of her must have been as plain to John Craig as it was to everyone; still it had no effect on him. He was ready to marry and Anne Barton was the girl he wanted.

He went to Anne and made his fantastic proposal with such bluntness as can come only from a man of massive ego, and he was turned away with more grace, but with equal bluntness.

Anne Barton was essentially feminine, essentially gentle, and she had more wisdom at twenty-two, I think, than is commonly combined with beauty. She was a slender girl with chestnut hair that shone above deep eyes with a curious light in them. Perhaps they were sad eyes—they were at least musing—but she had a wealth of laughter nonetheless, laughter hoarded, as it were, against the moment and the friend. She lived alone in Nairobi, working as a secretary in order to live, but for the love of the world she worked at being a sculptress; and while she had never had formal training in this, her hands could and did communicate to clay the strange intensity that was always in her eyes.

Of course she turned John Craig away, but not with anger or out of any affectation of outraged pride. She told him that he ought to see more of women—of other women.

"It's not enough just to be a man," she said, "even a strong and competent man. Women are not beggars, John. They don't have to take what's offered them. They choose, and the qualities they want are not what you think them to be. It's strange you haven't learned that. But one day you will."

He went away then, a giant of a man, stung deeply, yet proud and unbelieving because he could not believe in anything except himself—and I cannot say that he ever changed in that. And yet because of what happened a little later, during his inevitable quarrel with Larry Abbot, I am not sure, nor will I ever be.

I was myself a free-lance pilot in those days, and since Larry had taught me much of what I knew about flying, we saw each other almost daily at the Nairobi airport. His passion for the work was so intense that he had no room in his head or heart for the business of it. He made a living with his two planes, but it was a bare living when in East Africa at that time he might have made a small fortune. He was a slender man—about twenty-four then—with nothing arresting about him except searching grey eyes, fine hands, and a smile that he seemed to reserve for small tragedy. Everything held a meaning for him, and he would spend hours in his plane alone and often by night because, as he once said, he was fascinated by "the furnishings of darkness."

All in all, he was as different from John Craig as a plane is different from a plough; and it was this difference, among other things, that made it seem inevitable that he and Anne must one day marry. And yet, though he was deeply in love with her, he was equally in love with solitude and Anne was afraid of that. Very often he would slide into the cockpit of his plane, wave a hand, and take off, to be gone for days on a profitless flight. He would fly into Tanganyika, or Abyssinia, or perhaps into the Belgian Congo, and when he came back, strangely refreshed, he would go to Anne, finding her in her tiny studio of half-born figures of clay, and they would talk for hours and laugh together—and make dreams that never came true. He offered her everything of the spirit, and she returned in kind and seemed happy. Yet, being a woman, she could want fulfillment of a kind he did not understand, and his repeated plea for marriage was turned back again and again because she believed that he thought of it too lightly—not as the profound and deep responsibility she wanted it to be. This was the constant hurt to him, so it was natural that, when word of Craig's heavy-handed proposal to Anne reached Larry's ears, he was shocked and angered—shocked by what seemed to him the boorishness of it, and angered because it had never occurred to him that, marriage or not, Anne was not wholly his own.

"Craig may not know any better," Larry said to me, "but it's no excuse! How can you go to a woman you scarcely know and say, 'Look, I've got a farm and a new house and some cows, and now I want you for a wife'? What kind of man will do that?"

We were standing by the hangar at the airport, waiting for the low clouds to rise from the runway. Larry's rusty hair was tangled by the antics of a feeble morning breeze, his flying clothes—shirt, slacks, and sneakers—were crumpled, but somehow neat. He swung his goggles from his forefinger in a little nervous arc.

"What kind of man?" he demanded again.

I didn't answer at once. I knew what kind of man, but I also knew about Larry—about his gentle irresponsibility, the ease with which he could detach himself from practical matters. It seemed to me that he was half a man, the sensitive, generous, and forever-undecided half, while John Craig was the other half—muscle, mind, and ego. Neither man was complete. Each, I thought, lacked the virtues of the other, and because of that their mutual contempt in the end must congeal into hard constructive hatred, though at that time they barely knew each other by sight.

"John Craig is not a subtle man," I said. "But he meant no insult to Anne. He just doesn't understand gentleness or tact."

"Or much else," said Larry, "except his farm and his boorish vanity. What he can't bend, he wants to break. But there are ways of curing that."

He shrugged then and went into the hangar, and I went toward my own plane, which was already on the runway.

My father's farm and John Craig's were neighboring, and I would fly up from Nairobi on weekends or when the business of transporting mail and hunters into the hinterland slacked off a bit. On those occasions I would sometimes see John working in his fields or with his cattle. He was unchanging, outwardly content in his loneliness—tall, rough-handed, blunt. Somehow he gave the impression of a man cut off from the society of other men by the mere fact that he did not know their language of casual talk and quick laughter, and could not learn it.

I used to ride through a corner of his pastures, and I found him there one morning stretching wire on fence posts. His tools were a small bar with a claw in it and a hammer. He could catch the wire in the claw, then draw it taut against the post, and staple it. Twice while I watched he broke the heavy strands as if they were clotheslines, because when his strength began to pour through his massive arms, he seemed unable to check it. Of course, when he was finished his fence was tighter than anyone else's.

When the work was done, and not until then, he looked up and nodded. In the bright Kenya sun his large tanned face was at once striking and a little pathetic. He wiped sweat from his jaws and his neck and stood waiting for my opinion of his place. I could see the question in his eyes. They were the eyes of an arrogant child demanding praise. But at the same time they were guarded and sharp with challenge.

We were on a rise of ground, and from my saddle I could look over his farm. It was finished. It was so complete, so precisely arranged that it might have been a painting by a commercial draftsman. It was too orderly, and I felt that even the cattle had taken their places in the various fields out of deference to the whole design.

"What do you think of it?" he said.

"You've made a fine thing of it. It's like a blueprint—exactly like a blueprint."

The comparison pleased him. He looked proudly at what he had built. Then at once he turned on me in frowning petulance.

"Good," he said, "good! Then tell me this. You've lived here all your life, and you know Anne Barton. If my farm is what you say it is—is there any reason why she shouldn't want to live on it?"

Perhaps a Breton peasant might have asked that question— some man to whom a woman was no more than a practical complement to his cow barns, his henhouse, and his kitchen. But Craig was no peasant.

"There's nothing wrong with your farm," I said. "But women don't marry farms. Not Anne, at least, and it's time you knew it."

He only shrugged. "She can't live on dreams," he said, "or on air—especially with a man who spends most of his time in the middle of one or the other." It was an obvious reference to Larry, and it was all the sharper for the truth that was in it. But more than that there was disdain in it, and contempt.

"It's true that Larry is no farmer," I said. "He'd be no good at it. But then, you're no flier—and probably if you tried you would be no good at that."

He straightened immediately and cocked his head a little to one side, as if he couldn't believe what I had said, and I knew that I had blundered. He was no man to admit inferiority in anything, and now he felt challenged, though indirectly, by a man he instinctively and jealously hated.

"A plane is a machine, isn't it?" he said.

I nodded. "A plane is a machine." It would have been futile, I thought, to point out that such planes as we then flew were something more than just machines—and something less. They were fledgling things of wood and wire and cloth. More often than not they were equipped with engines too powerful for their fragile frames, or—as in Larry's Klemm—with engines so feeble as almost to require of the pilot the sensitive touch of a pianist to keep them in harmony with the weather and the wind.

And yet John Craig was saying, "I know machines. I can handle machines, though I never thought it much of a way to test a man. Still, it seems the idea appeals to women—men in ships, men in planes, men with their feet off the ground. Well, if that's what's wanted, it's easy enough. I'll fly."

It seemed at the moment no more than a boast born out of simple masculine pride. It was as if he had said, "I know women. I can handle women!"

I reined my horse toward my father's farm. Glancing back, I

saw that Craig had undertaken to split a log of cedar for his fence. He did not do it patiently by the use of a wedge and hammer, but by wrathful, even wild, blows of his enormous axe; and somehow that picture came into my mind at once, when two days later, to the astonishment of both Larry and myself, Craig strode across the Nairobi airport and demanded that Larry teach him to fly.

It was a strange and disquieting moment. Nurtured by silence, the enmity of each toward the other had grown and taken the formless and unreasonable shape of all things that thrive without light. There was no understanding, not even enough for anger.

They looked at each other for a moment: Larry, slender, motionless, outwardly at ease, smiling his bittersweet smile; and Craig, big, but bigger still with arrogance, framed in the hangar door. Craig held a scrap of newspaper in his hand. It was the small advertisement Larry had run for months, not really to increase his income but to please some insistent friend who sold such ads. There it was, in John Craig's hand, and he was saying:

"You're Abbot, aren't you? Well, as you know, I'm John Craig, and I want to fly. You can show me the tricks."

All the condescension in the world was in his voice—all the patronizing inflection of the sturdy realist addressing the dreamer. And the dreamer might easily have laughed him away. It was what I hoped for, expected, I think. But there were more subtle shades to Larry's nature. I looked at his face and saw that he was still smiling his dry, mirthless smile. His grey eyes, aglow with irony, were very steady and very thoughtful. He knew the challenge for what it was. He shifted his glance from Craig's face to Craig's massive hands that were like great, insensitive clamps. Then he looked with meaning at the fragile little plane already shivering on the runway under the morning wind. The plane was sky blue, and on its fuselage was neatly painted the name: *ANNE*. He turned to me and nodded toward the scrap of newsprint in John Craig's hand.

"The power of the printed word," he said, smiling his sardonic smile, "it brings all things to all men. All right, Craig, we fly."

They took off at once: Larry at the controls, with more than a hint of disdain in his manner; Craig in the rear cockpit, his shoulders squared in arrogance. And when at last the little craft was airborne, droning its reproach against the sky, I could not help thinking that no smaller world could be contrived for two men so hateful of each other. But in an instant they were gone, and with time and distance closed behind them I went about my own work, servicing my plane for a routine flight to Mombasa.

What happened after that is difficult to tell, because part of the story is lost.

I returned just before dark, landing my Avian on the rough plot we called an airport, and I saw then that Larry Abbot and John Craig had not come back. There was no word, nor any sign of them, but I was not immediately worried. I saw to it that flares were lighted on the edges of the runway, and then I went into Nairobi, telling myself that they would come in by night.

But they did not come in that night, nor the next night, nor the night after that, and there was no message. There was nothing.

On the second day I went to Anne and told her what had happened, and I saw at once that she was afraid for Larry—for both of them. She did not hate John Craig, but she feared the fury of his jealousy and strength. And she knew Larry; she knew his tenacity, his determination to humiliate the big man. It was like a knife against a bludgeon.

"It's not just a legend," she said, "that this country does strange things to men. They get drunk on the bigness of it. They throw restraint away, and reason goes with it. They should not be together in that plane!"

She was not given to hysteria, but she was deeply concerned. I watched her pace her tiny, cluttered workshop, a slender, vital, yet very feminine girl. Almost a child, I thought, and it came to me that she was out of place among her pedestals and lumps of clay. It was make-believe, and I suddenly knew why, because I remembered that once she had stood with a clay figure that she had made, and had looked at it heavy in her hand, and then had said, "I wish it were a child— my child." It was a thing that Larry could never understand because it would have meant the sacrifice of his constant flirtation with unreality. It would have meant responsibility, regularity, worry—the coarser threads that go into the weaving of happiness. Nor could John Craig have understood it.

I stood up and moved toward the door. "I'll take off in the morning," I said, "toward Marsabit. They went north."

We had no radios then; nor any shortwave station in East Africa, for that matter. When a plane vanished, you did the simple thing: you looked for it, hoping that if it had force-landed, it had found some better place than the vast Mau forest, the slopes of Kilimanjaro, or the steaming elephant country to the south. I knew all the hopes. I had searched before for lost planes—and found a few.

But I did not find this one. No one ever did, though there were countless parties organized. And then, after eleven interminable days and nights, we learned by messenger that two men had crawled one morning from the rim of the Koroli Desert to the shelter of an Indian trader's camp. They were John Craig and Larry Abbot, of course—and they were nearly dead.

Men have been lost and found before—many in Africa, some in the Koroli Desert, a place of monstrous rocks burning in a sea of sand—and most times such men have a story to tell, and they tell it. These men did not. A few natives and settlers remembered seeing the plane in broad daylight and clear weather. Some said its course was erratic, its control unstable. Others said it flew straight for the desert, willfully guided there. Perhaps it does not matter, and perhaps the story of John Craig's and Larry Abbot's eleven days and nights in that prison of rock and sand does not matter either, since neither man would ever speak of it.

And yet, one wonders. I, at least, am haunted now and then by the patchwork story of the Indian trader who nursed them, in his way, for many hours, and who seemed, when I spoke to him long afterward, an incurious man, but one of precise memory. He was a Sikh, and I remember his great turban of dirty cloth that seemed so white against his earthy skin, so fresh above his tired eyes.

"I saw them at dawn, memsahib," he said, "not men to the eye, but mounds of flesh for jackals. Yet they breathed, and the jackal does not touch what breathes, memsahib. I brought them here."

His trader's shack—his *duka*—was four walls of mud and daub, his merchandise the cherished luxuries and tinsel of a dozen native tribes. The men had crawled, he said, part way, and he had helped and guided them. They needed water and he had given that, and bathed their lips and burning eyes until they slept.

"Then they were not hurt," I asked, "except by the sun?"

He looked at the sun, as if to question it, and then he looked at me. "The sun, memsahib, may sometimes choke a man, but it leaves no mark upon his throat."

I hesitated, but he would not be hurried. "Which man?" I finally asked.

The old Sikh shrugged. He was explicit. "The mark of the big one was on the throat of the other. A strong mark, memsahib—a death mark—but the fingers of the big one's hand were broken." He smiled musingly. "A little man can break a little bone," he said.

"I see," I told him and nodded.

So it had come to that. I wondered what had given impetus to that silent, lonely struggle in the sand. Two men—both strong, but one immense—shuffling, swaying, groping, each for the other's life. A knife against a bludgeon—the quick, sharp cleverness of Larry, the knotted muscles of Craig.

"And after that?" I turned again to the Sikh.

"There was blood on both," he said. "And this, memsahib, was a strange thing to my eye—that when I found them, the wounds of each were wrapped, with care, in the clothing of the other!"

I got no more from him, and never will; it was all he knew. But when I left, he handed me a crumpled note in Larry's writing—a note the Sikh had picked up from the floor where Craig had lain.

"I cannot read, memsahib. Does this have meaning?"

To me it had. It was the kind of note that was exchanged between the cockpits when the roar of the engine was too loud for speech. I read it slowly.

"Better admit you can't fly, Craig—just yet, and maybe

never. You're over the Koroli, and in trouble. I can take over, and I will—when you ask it. Give your pride a breather. Live and learn."

That was it—Larry, smiling still, and still sardonic, watched the little plane under Craig's thick-handed guidance plunge and tremble over the hot, swift currents of the desert. And there was Craig, out of control, trampling the rudder bar, clutching the stick as if it were his heavy axe—and swearing to God that he would see them crash on the Koroli sand before he asked for help. And they had crashed because each must test the mettle of the other like sabres crossed in battle. Steel against steel. Pride against pride. Male against male.

And yet, in the end, as the old Sikh said: "The wounds of each were wrapped, with care, in the clothing of the other!"

Enemies—comrades for a while—but they did not become friends. It would be easier to say that whatever they had endured had bound them together and made them friends, but it wasn't so. They never spoke again—and yet they were not the same again. It was as if two disparate elements had been somehow ground in a crucible until each took essence from the other.

A little later Anne and Larry were married, and after that Anne had the child she wanted, and a certain crispness crept slowly into Larry's manner and into his life—an alertness, a sense of direction. He planned air routes and turned his dreams into money. He bought equipment and was as hard as iron in the bargaining. He gained stature; and friends who knew him for his bittersweet smile and his careless ways admired him later for what they called his "drive." Success came to him, and a woman's happiness to Anne.

Craig saw her once to say good-bye. His arrogance had strangely crumbled, and with it his farm. It became in time no

longer the draftsman's drawing, but a warm and happily dis-
ordered place of foraging livestock and uneven fields. At last
he sold it and wandered out of Africa—disconsolately, I suppose—but I had word of him.

Years later a friend from England said to me, "Do you remember Craig?" and again I saw the big man as he had once
stood with his great angry axe, splitting a tree as if he were
Vulcan forging armor for the gods.

"I remember Craig," I said.

"He's a doctor now," my friend said, "a surgeon in a children's clinic of the London slums."

I looked at him closely, and then I said the only thing that I
could say—the only thing that would come to my mind: "A
doctor? A surgeon? With those enormous hands?"

My friend nodded, smiling a little. "Yes," he said, "with
those enormous hands."

PART FOUR

The Quitter

"The Quitter" was the last story Beryl wrote. It was written at the Santa Barbara cottage set high in a wooded canyon that had once been the romantic hideaway of her friends Leopold Stokowski and Greta Garbo.

It was an unhappy time for Beryl and for Raoul. He had begun to drink heavily and put on weight. The little writing Raoul produced would not sell, and the couple had severe financial difficulties. The problems were not one-sided. Beryl was scornful of failure and treated Raoul badly. Her frequent extramarital relationships further contributed to the breakdown of the union, and their rows became frequent and violent.

Beryl evidently wrote this story herself—probably out of financial desperation—but when she presented it to Raoul for editing (prior to its submission to a publisher), he was still sulking after a violent disagreement. He refused to help and Beryl was deeply upset. She submitted the unedited manuscript, but it was rejected. Consequently she turned to an old friend—the writer Stuart Cloete—for help. Cloete edited the story, which was later accepted for publication. It is perhaps the change in editor that accounts for the distinctive style of this story.

All the story's ingredients are those of Beryl's own life: the problems of a trainer, the thrill and apprehension of racing; the despair of a woman facing financial ruin; the greatness of a horse. Beryl was always at her best

[First published in Cosmopolitan, June 1946.]

when writing about horses. She understood horses in a very special way and, more than any man, not even excluding her beloved father, they were the real love of her life.

"The Quitter" may have been the last thing that Beryl ever wrote, though some years ago there was a manuscript of an unfinished novel— believed to be the novel that she was working on jointly with Raoul, when she visited Kenya and Somalia in 1947, a year after this story was writ- ten—among the papers at Beryl's cottage in Nairobi. That manuscript disappeared some time after 1983.

Mat Dixon's lips were unmoving. He looked at the girl through grey, reluctant eyes that gave no answer. His hands were folded on the desk, where he kept them in a single hard- ened fist as if they held the word she wanted. English sunlight lay in the room in golden ribbons, giving glow to things not meant to glow, but it lent no warmth to the girl's precisely sculptured face.

Sunlight on marble, Mat Dixon thought. He watched her move in her chair, not petulantly, but with a kind of regal im- patience, as she always moved when she asked for the impos- sible and intended to get it. Perhaps beauty alone did that to some women, Dixon thought. It gave them arrogance the way great strength gives arrogance to certain men.

"Sheila Berkeley?" people said. "Ah, yes—the beautiful one!" Too true, perhaps, for she wore her beauty with a shrug as if it were an ermine wrap of which she could say, "I suppose it is lovely, but then I've had it so long!"

Dixon opened his hands and looked at his empty palms. It was no good temporizing. "Sheila, I can promise nothing," he said.

For a moment the girl in the blue tweed suit, expertly cut and altogether immaculate, made no reply. Finally she said, "I own the greatest racehorses in England—or so I am told. I employ, in yourself, the best of all possible trainers—or at least the most expensive. I am fortunate, I know, in having the paragon of jockeys, not to say that most attractive of men, your son Kent, to ride for me. And yet . . ."

"And yet," said Dixon, "I cannot promise to win a race—or predict the outcome. I cannot encourage you to bet the whole of what you have left on the chance that Templar, great as he is, will win the Classic. Nor can I swear that he will lose it. A horse is no machine, no jockey can bring a miracle to pass—and any trainer who says otherwise is nothing but a lying fraud!"

He left the desk and strode across the tiny room, a lean man aged like a leather whip. He turned on her. "Why do you race?" he asked. "Why—of all people—do you race?"

"For money, Mat." She smiled saying it. "I race for money. My father didn't, and when he died he was already lost, or nearly lost through sweet but ruinous sentiment. He loved the noble horse. I prefer pounds sterling. Does that shock you? I can't help it. I'm in no position to help it. Templar cost my father ten thousand pounds. One way or another I must get it back."

"He's earned it ten times over."

She shrugged. "Not for me—and tomorrow we run in the Classic. It may be rumor, but I've heard that some people make money on racing—those who know the tricks."

Mat did not yield. "Templar may not win," he said. "He and Kent will fight to win. They may lose, but they will fight to win. I can't say more. You can't ask more."

"I do ask more!" She got to her feet and stood before him. She was not tall, but she was slender, and she was as cleanly made as any thoroughbred.

Conformation, Dixon thought, but not much else. Breeding, but too small a heart. You saw it everywhere—in men, in horses, and in women.

"I must ask more," she said. Calm had gone out of her voice, and in its place there was an edge of panic, of urgency. "Mat, they're closing in. I'm going to lose it all—the house, the grounds, everything father left—to creditors. Call it my fault. Say I threw the money away, gambled it away. It's true, but I don't know how to live without spending. I've got to win on this race, can't you see? It doesn't matter if Templar loses so long as I know how to bet. Fix it for me, Mat, fix it! I don't care how!"

He was coldly quiet. "I care," he said, "and Kent cares. He's not my son and the most respected rider in England for nothing. He will not fix the race, nor will I. Templar will be ridden to win. He will not be held back in order to insure your bet, Sheila. That's what you are hinting, and I tell you it can't be. If you lose—well, then you lose, but you don't quit. Some do, but not, I hope, the daughter of Jeff Berkeley. It wouldn't be . . ."

"Sporting?" she asked. "Is that the word? Shall we be trite, Mat?" She stepped closer to him and met his eyes in open contest. "Look," she said, "you've known me all my life, and you know that I will not submit to living on a pauper's income under the sorrowful eyes of my friends. I will not submit to public disgrace for my debts. If I could sell Templar I would. I would sell him together with all the trumped-up tales and fiction and nonsense about his great heart, his magnificent spirit, and all the rest. But my father's will prevented me from doing that. So I am trapped. And yet not quite!" He watched her upturned, flawless face, and saw that the arrow was coming. "If you cannot promise what I ask," she said, "I'm still not beaten. Kent loves me. He always has—and you and I both know it!"

Long ago he had seen Sheila use her charms as a musician uses notes and strings. She could create many moods in men, and not the least of these was desire. Kent was a man like other men—and young—as young as she. As children, the two had played together, and the boy's loyalty to that friendship, his admiration of her beauty, had grown with the years. Now he was great—or close to greatness—in his craft, his art. Not yet a Fred Archer, but close and coming closer.

Mat Dixon felt a thickness in his throat—a fear—but he straightened a little, accepting her challenge.

"We promise a clean race—Kent and I—and nothing more."

She smiled once, with easy certainty. And then abruptly she was gone. Mat heard her Bentley start and swing away. He did not have to look through the window to know that she would find Kent—probably near Templar's stall. Kent was as honest as spring rain—had always been. But Sheila was as lovely as spring itself and harder to deny. And yet—to throw a race, a career and all one's honor away for a girl—for one like that . . .

"Not my son," Mat Dixon said.

He spat the thought away and went out into the cleansing air. But he saw the girl's blue Bentley near Templar's stall and knew there was cause for doubt.

Kent Dixon stood by the stable gate on whose arch was stenciled the words: "On the Turf, and Under It, All Men Are Equal." It was hardly profound, and maybe it wasn't true, but he and his father had always liked to think it was.

He took his thoughts from the legend and looked into the

blue compelling eyes of Sheila Berkeley. He was plainly torn between conflicting things. His face—an inquiring, forthright face, masking no secrets, was somber now. Unlike most riders, he was tall—as tall as the great Fred Archer had been. He was lean, of course, almost as lean as the rails he loved to ride against. And he was hard. In most things he was hard, with the thonglike hardness of those who can, with feeling hands and constant will, direct the unleashed power of a thoroughbred. But was he hard in this?

He swung his glance from the girl to the old and intimate horizon, then back again to the lavish fortune of her hair.

"Kent, I'm lost," she said, "unless you help." And he listened.

He listened to each word and watched her tears. He held her close—and this he had not done since childhood days, vanished days. Not since the incident—the incident they never spoke of now. Had it not been for that, he thought, he might have struck her for what she was begging him to do.

But he remembered the long ago day when Sheila had been trapped in a loose-box by an angry stallion. It was a stallion the tawny-haired girl had loved with courageous passion—but not with understanding.

She had loved his smooth and massive beauty, but all the while there was fear in her, and this she fought because of him, but she did not know how to keep evenly burning the flame of his spirit. In those days she thought that love and admiration were enough, and she offered both. She went boldly one morning into the stallion's loose-box and closed the door behind her.

It was not a new thing; she had done it before—timidly, at first, and then with greater ease. But on this morning the stallion was at his feed, and she entered too quietly. Startled, he turned on her and let his fright blaze into fury. He whirled and tried to reach her with his teeth and with his hooves.

For long and terrifying minutes, she cringed under the feed-box, beating him off with her tiny riding hat, weeping—for fear, and for his faithlessness.

It was Kent who found her, Kent who got her out, and in his boyish arms she had sought comfort for her terror and her childish sorrow.

An incident, he thought, of no importance. And yet it seemed to shut her heart against so many things. It was as if forever afterward she had been afraid to open it lest more hurt enter it. She hated horses now, and from that simple hate worse things had grown—cynicism, hardness. One day something might happen to change all that—one day.

Now she needed him—and more than anything else, he wanted her to need him. It was his chance, and yet he knew that what she asked of him—the whole of his honor, of Templar's honor too, in a way—was a heartbreaking gift to make.

He held her at arm's length and looked at her and shook his head. "You don't know, Sheila, what it means to cheat in a race. Sometimes you read about it. More often you hear rumors, usually untrue. You get to thinking that all riders cheat to win—or to lose. You think it's natural, but it isn't. Not for me."

Tears made stars of her eyes, "I know it, Kent." She was pleading now. "But I appeal to you because I must. I've done wrong things—spent money out of boredom, out of loneliness maybe. I've borrowed it falsely on false promises. I admit that. Now I'm confronted with disgrace, and I can't bear it. I have four days to produce four thousand pounds. And if I fail, I'm leaving England, Kent."

He did not flinch, nor speak, nor make any gesture. But

longing and indecision were suddenly in his eyes. She kissed him full upon the mouth. "I'm betting against Templar," she said. "Don't let me down!" And then she vanished.

Night left its post, and race day came. Mat Dixon's stables, immaculate and gleaming, like the barracks of some proud regiment, were hushed but active. Each of the many stables around the great grandstand was a guarded camp in which some hoped-for Achilles of the turf abided moodily, or some too-eager Hector fidgeted on polished hooves while a thousand husbandmen and handlers counted hours and, throughout the land, ten million Englishmen plotted bets.

Some horses tremble before a race, some ease the tensions of their nerves by spurts of anger, and there are some who brood. But all are conscious of the day—sensible of the approaching trial—wanting it, living toward it. For the thoroughbred who races because he must is not often seen on any track; he cannot win, not even against a poorer horse with a love of running in his heart. Sinew and bone and blood make a horse, but spirit makes a horse race.

Templar was quiet, statue-still. His the great name, his the obligation to be calm. He watched and waited.

A big horse, he dwarfed the grooms. A gleaming horse, his chestnut coat accepted light like amber. Wise in his way, his eyes were large and deeply knowing, and his ears—scarcely longer than the finger of a man—were tilted as if to catch each tick of passing time.

Kent Dixon looked at him and shook his head. "Templar," he said, "this ought to be your race. You want it, and you've got it in you. I have wanted it for years, but now . . ." He did not finish.

With sadness in his hands, he stroked the shoulder of the

stallion. "You can't always win," he said, and, saying it, he turned to see his father in the doorway.

Mat Dixon smiled to see a horse that he had trained within an inch or two of that improbable goal, perfection, to see his son, motherless from birth, conform so closely to what he wanted in a son. These things brought fulfillment near to him. He thought it would be nearer, if now—today—he might see this son, a product of his heart, ride Templar, a product of his skill, to victory in that race all horsemen longed to one day win. But his smile passed swiftly, for the eye of his memory saw another smile challenging his own.

"You're worried, Kent," he said. "It's Sheila."

Kent nodded. His eyes, grey like his father's, were somber now and inward looking. But they held a knowledge.

"It's partly Sheila," he said. "But you mustn't hate her. She can't help having been born to what she was. I love horses; I was born to it. She loves luxury, wastefulness. She was born to that, but one day she will change."

"She was born to selfishness," Mat Dixon said. "She was born with a hollow heart! Forget the girl—until tomorrow. Today we race. Today—"

Kent stopped him. He took his hand from Templar's shoulder. "We may not win," he said. "We may not even place. I have to tell you that." He watched his father's lips tighten now, the muscles of his jaw set hard. He went on, "There's a fault in Templar. You can't see it, but it's there. At times I feel it in my hands during workouts, during races. I've told you that, I tell you now, again."

Mat Dixon fought his rising doubt, his rising anger. Was he being told, being warned in these blunt terms that the girl had won against him—that Templar would be held from probable victory on this trumped-up theory of a hidden fault? Had he trained thoroughbreds for forty years for this? He ran expert eyes over Templar's magnificent body. This horse was perfect, as perfect as a horse could be.

Mat spat into the straw bedding. True, Kent had twice before hinted at some hidden fault in the great stallion—some inherent weakness he seemed to sense but constantly disproved by winning race after race on Templar. Mat Dixon let his anger go in a soundless sigh. There was no better rider in England than his son, but perhaps no more uneven a judge of horses—and of women.

Mat looked at his watch. In a few hours they would be at the post. On fire with this futile love, this futile faith in Sheila, Kent clearly planned to throw the race. Well, a single splinter of time would tell. There would be an instant, Mat knew, an instant of decision when Kent would have to cheat, or not cheat. At the point of that sharp moment, he would have to check Templar—or ride Templar. All plans, all other things aside, it was a question as to whether his son, at the final point, the crucial point, could discard his honor for a lovely face.

He thought not. Surprisingly he smiled. "I trust you, Kent, to do your best. I trust Templar to give his best. He always has; he always will. He's not a quitter—you will not make him one."

He left the stall and went into the sunlight like a man unburdened. His son made a hopeless gesture with his hands and stared at the brooding horse.

By midafternoon the Newmarket grandstand overflowed with people until, from a distance, it was like the mouth of some huge horn of human plenty. The people were tense, the thrill of the impending contest already burning in their blood.

For not time, but struggle, is the essence of a horse race—not stopwatch figures, but rivalry. Who cares how brief the

time, how shaved by tenths of seconds, so long as in that time
a man's heart may add its tiny drumbeat to the massive music
of pounding hooves? Deplore the bets, bewail the gambling,
but all of this is not what it seems, for there are people who
will bet on a horse for love of him. And, if he loses, they will
bet on him again, not caring much, so long as they can see him
run. Saint Simon—Seabiscuit—Gallant Fox. What clings to
these remembered names is not the smell of gathered money.
It is a certain aura that the valiant and the deep of heart leave
always in their passing.

Templar was building such a name. His character was such
that men too shrewd to do it would bet on him against all
comers, at all times, since not to do it seemed a faithless thing.

The crowd was for Templar. And the crowd had voice, a single voice that could swell like the sound of surf, or subside like
a waning tide. It could indicate many things—hope, anger,
pleasure, sometimes contempt. It could ride the moment. And
the moment came.

The paddock opening was cleared, and through this clearing, lined with men whose labor and whose skill was fiber to
the sport, the horses filed.

All were great—or so it seemed—all magnificent, or so
they looked. No eyes save expert ones could find a fault. But
there were such eyes.

The eyes of trainers were sharp, and they were quick. They
penetrated style and manner and gleaming coats to see, beneath, a lurking weakness or hidden strength. The trainers bit
their pipes, or rubbed their jaws; they watched the horses and
pondered on their chances.

But not Mat Dixon. He stood apart, alone among the many,
and saw a thing he did not want to see. Templar was last to
leave the paddock for the track, and as he left with Kent, re-

splendent in his gold and purple silks, a glistening head—the head of Sheila—shone as she moved in the swaying crowd.

In a moment she was at the stallion's side, and Mat Dixon saw his son's firm hands draw gently on the reins. He saw Templar pause—nervous now, for the time was near—and he saw, but did not hear, the exchange of words between Kent and the girl. It was short, as casual as a greeting. But it was more. Much more. It was a question and an answer. It was decision.

With it, the girl turned and went, unhesitating, toward the betting booths. Graceful, vivid among the hundreds, she was like a self-assured child walking in a wood.

Kent watched her go, then straightened in the saddle, but he did not seek his father's face. He leaned forward, and he spoke softly to Templar.

The stallion dipped his shapely head and flicked his hooves as if to say that, lacking wings, he could still fly. And then they cantered up the track and took the cheering of the crowd. It swelled and thinned and swelled again, and when it tapered to its final hush, Mat Dixon found his box, his binoculars in hands more tense than they had ever been at any race in forty racing years.

He did not turn toward Sheila's box, and she did not look toward him. Expressionless, unspeaking, they waited for the start.

A struggle, a shout, a soothing voice, horses fighting to be free. The starter's hand poised high; the barriers, inanimate but tense. Such is the prelude to a race.

There is a stillness, a nervous murmur from the crowd, and then again a stillness. The starting gate has every eye; the moment is unbreathing. It dangles like a drop that will not fall. But then it does; a drop of time falling—fallen.

Mat Dixon saw the barrier rise and heard the swift, familiar thunder of the crowd. He saw the human sea surge toward the rail. He heard the cry "They're off!" But he did not add to the cry.

The start was clean with no horse left behind and no horse far enough ahead to be alone. The field of twelve was like a cloud, close-bunched and dark and building speed. It passed the stands where people now were motionless, making no sound, hearing nothing save the velvet drumming on the turf.

Templar was last, restrained by Kent—a band of weightless color bending low. Both horse and rider knew such things as must be known. Both horse and rider knew such things as others knew—or more. They did not press, or fight the field, or flaunt the power that they had. Not yet. Not now.

They did not seek the rail. In one quick move they might, Mat Dixon thought, but now they played the cautious game, and played it well.

The turn was made, the pace increased, and the back stretch spread before the swiftly gliding little storm of crouching men and faster drumming hooves.

A horse called Ariel had the lead—a driving bay with piston stride—hard, rhythmic, and determined. Behind him—just behind—was Chanticleer, running heavily, but fast. This was the one to fear, Mat Dixon knew, the one to watch. He was well ridden, and he never tired. Time and again he had plunged to victory against smoother, fleeter horses through sheer weight of muscle and strength of sinew—through that and heart. Chanticleer had heart. So had Templar—and the two had never met, till now.

Mat Dixon raised his glasses to his eyes and let a smile bend his lips—tentative but full of hope. He swore in silence for his doubt of Kent. The boy was riding.

The boy was riding hard, and now the crowd gave out a stirring growl that rose to thunder, broke to cheers then steadied on the single cry: "Templar!"

For Kent was doing what he did so well. The field—the moving cloud—had thinned as if a wind had scattered it. Twelve horses reached the final turn, but only three were fighting for the lead—black Chanticleer, the bay Ariel, and Templar like rusty gold. The rail, the inside track, was needed now—and Kent was taking it. He had no room: they gave him none, but he was taking it.

Deftly, with unerring hands, he edged Templar so close to the rigid bars that it seemed both horse and rider must crash against them. But they did not crash. They fought their way.

The voice of the crowd rose clear and vibrant. Mat Dixon laughed aloud for pride and threw his laughter toward the cool blonde head of Sheila Berkeley, who did not hear and did not move.

Like a blade, the boy cut Ariel from the race. The turn was made, and the homestretch was a battleground for two— Templar and Chanticleer.

Silence again. The crowd is still. The swallows flying low, swing lower. A throat is cleared, a hat is crushed in nerveless hands. The grandstand creaks.

Desperately, blindly almost, surely with pain in lungs and heart, the two Titans, each with outstretched neck, each with burning, ebbing strength, beat back the time, shame the distance and loom closer length by length.

There is no dust on this green turf, this English turf, the air is clean. The end of a race is clearly seen by any eager eye— at times, too clearly—at such a time as this.

Mat Dixon saw it. Thousands saw it. The cool, unruffled Sheila saw it. Perhaps Chanticleer himself saw Templar sud-

denly give ground when there was at last no hand's breadth to
be spared.

It was a little ground, not much. So little that at first nobody
believed it. Could Templar quit? He never had. Could Templar lose? That came to every horse, but this was strange. He
seemed at once, to slow his stride—to fight, yet not to fight.
He seemed at once to lose his heart, to lose his will—to yield,
breath by breath, to Chanticleer, a massive shadow now, blot-
ting the glow of courage that, until this moment, had clung to
Templar's name.

Mat Dixon rose and let his glasses dangle on their strap.
They had no purpose now. He did not need them to see the
end—to see Templar fall back, held surely by a subtle hand—
Kent's hand, held so cleverly that the mimicry of courage was
almost real as the two great gleaming thoroughbreds bore
down fighting (so it seemed) for victory.

Templar was close—a neck behind—and the burden that
he carried then was more than man and leather. For the crowd
had jeered. The crowd's hosannas had turned to scorn, as wine
can turn to vinegar.

And before these jeers, he lost. Before the throng's contempt, he failed—a blood-gold champion, shamed, discred-
ited, not because he did not win, but because in the eyes of
those who watched, in the eyes of those who believed in him,
he quit.

Night came, inevitable and kind. The grandstand stood de-
serted, as empty as the half-born moon that shone upon it.
The Classic was over; the Classic was won, and the name
Chanticleer rolled on the tongue of racing England.

Mat Dixon sat alone. It seemed to him that here in the bar
of the Boar's Head Inn, among the scattered voices of unwor-

ried men, he could be more alone than if he sat before the portraits on his cottage walls—the champion thoroughbreds, the
silver trophies, the pictures of his son.

He seldom drank, but now he tried and found it bitter in his
throat. It answered nothing, changed nothing. For the tenth
time, he pushed the half-full glass away.

He could not believe what he had seen, but he had seen it.
Behind closed eyes, he still could see it, the greatest horse in
England quitting when a race was nearly won. Being forced to
quit—there was no escape from that, he thought—because
his own son had sold his name, his whole integrity, for a woman's smile and a thatch of shining hair.

Well, her inheritance was safe, her purse was full, her shame
avoided. Certainly she had bet against her own Templar, sure
in the knowledge he would be robbed of his victory. How bra-
zen it now seemed—Kent's effort to convince him of a hidden
weakness in the stallion, when, today, Mat Dixon had watched
his favorite, and the people's favorite, beat the best that England offered—pass them as lightly as a shadow—until the
end.

Until the end. He cupped his hands against his eyes and
tried not to think. He looked at his glass but did not touch it.
He couldn't sit here forever. He would have to face the boy.

He put his hands on the edge of the table and began to rise,
then paused. Kent stood before him, confronted him, blocked
his exit. There was no fear in the boy's face, no repentance.
His eyes were as hard as his father's, and as bitter. They caught
the accusing stare and threw it back.

"Say it," his father said. "Say what you came to say."

Kent stepped back then. He was breathing deeply, and
when he spoke, the movement of his lips was imperceptible.

"The race killed Templar," he said. "He died three hours ago."

Somewhere in the room a stranger was laughing. Somewhere a glass tinkled against another glass. Somewhere a clock marked time. But all of these sounds were silence to Mat Dixon. He rose in silence, hearing nothing, and faced his son with unbelieving eyes.

"I know what's on your mind," Kent said. "I know why you're here. Maybe you had a right to wonder, even to doubt, but you were wrong. We worked to win. I never rode harder. Templar never fought harder. But it's more than that—too much more."

He paused and motioned his father to a chair. Mat Dixon sat in it, waiting.

"Down the homestretch we were winning," Kent said. "You saw it, everybody saw it. We were coming home—and then it happened. The thing I tried to tell you about happened. Templar broke. He went on fighting, but his strength was gone. I felt it leave his body. I felt it running out under my hands and knees. I could do nothing. I couldn't even have slowed him if I had tried. He went on to the end—and lost."

"And died," Mat Dixon said.

Kent stared at the knuckles of his hands. "And died," he said, "two hours later. We brought him back; he tried to eat, but couldn't—and you weren't there.

"I sent for Kimberly and the other vet. It wasn't any good. He was dead when they got there."

Mat Dixon reached for his glass but did not lift it. "You found out why?" Mat Dixon asked. "Thoroughbreds don't die like that. They die, but not like that."

Kent stared at the paneled wall, through it, beyond it. "I did what had to be done," he said. "I had an autopsy. I had to know—and now I know. Listen, Dad." He swung his eyes to the eyes of the older man. "Listen," he said, "for the whole of his life—and for the whole of every race he ran and won, and for those he tried to win—Templar had one lung. Not two like every other horse, but one. He was born that way. We know that now, but he never knew it. He was a racehorse and he had to run, begged to run. That's how he died, that's why he died and why he lost today—breathing hard because he could breathe no other way—fighting, wondering perhaps why each race seemed longer, why every horse seemed stronger than he. But fighting—fighting always, all the way—until he broke, with ten thousand heartless fools calling him a quitter!"

He swung around as if to hide the blur that dimmed his eyes. In an instant he had pushed through the carefree, laughing men and was gone.

For a long time Mat Dixon sat unmoving. Once in the history of English racing a horse had died like that. It was on the records. And now Templar. One lung. Not two like every other horse but one. And still to race, still to fight with every breath too small, each stride a memory of pain. Was there courage in such a horse? Was there heart?

He left the inn and plodded blindly toward his stables in the night. One thing was in his thoughts—one lurking thing. Since Templar lost, then Sheila must have won. It wasn't easy to think of a horse dying for that. It burned in him, and he went to Templar's stall and stood outside it, hoping to forget.

It was empty now. The deep-eyed stallion was gone—the honest one. He turned, then stopped.

The weeping in the empty stall was deep and unashamed—woman's weeping. He took a step, then stopped again; he could not leave. He heard the voice and knew it. He heard the other voice, and it was Kent's. He could not keep himself from glancing through the door.

Moonlight lay like hoarded treasure on the straw. The golden girl crouched in it, kneeling, crying. And Kent was there, as soft-spoken as a man should be when a woman cries.

"He tried to win," he said. "I told you to bet on him—and he tried to win."

"I know it, Kent." She lifted her face and the moonlight caught it. Sorrow had softened it. Tears had gentled it.

"I bet it all," she said, "all on Templar and on you. I couldn't have borne it otherwise. I know that now. I lost everything, and so I am free. I'm free to work—at something, anything. Don't let me be a quitter, Kent."

He smiled and stroked her hair as if she were a child he remembered—a sobbing child frightened by a horse she loved.

"You saw him run," he said, "you saw him break. Templar was half a horse inside—and still he ran. Can we be quitters now?"

Illustrations by Gaye C. Chapman

LEOPARD

Contents

THIS BOOK offers you exciting ideas for fifteen different theme parties, with many variations. For each party, we suggest the suitable age group, venue and number of guests; give ideas for invitations, decorations, games and prizes; suggest a menu and a party cake, and provide tempting recipes. Following the theme parties are more recipes for favourite party fare, basic cakes and frostings, as well as an excellent section on all sorts of games — traditional, quiet, active — suitable for group or individual play.

COOKERY RATING

Easy: simple to make
Medium: a little more skill needed
Advanced: for confident cooks

Party Planning

D O YOU HAVE A CHILD'S PARTY coming up? A little forward planning will help to turn the day into a memorable occasion. Parties can be small-scale fun or grand-scale productions. The best parties are often the most simple, and a little creative effort will go a long way to ensuring a successful, hassle-free event.

A particular theme can add lots of fun to a party for any age group. A theme can be the springboard for more ideas on decorations and food — as well as invitations, cake, games, prizes and guests' clothing. A party theme is a good starting point for planning, and adds interest all round.

Vampire Blood (see page 47)

Fairy Bread (see page 94)

Moon Buggy Wheels (see page 55)

WHEN, WHERE AND WHO

The first step in planning any party is deciding where it is to be held. There are so many options: the home, garden, park, zoo, amusement park, bowling centre, restaurant, theatre, cinema, pop concert, beach, swimming pool or boat. Your area may offer a special venue, in or out of doors. Ask your local council for information if you are new to the neighbourhood. A particular hobby could suggest a venue; a picnic and riding party could be held at a local riding school, for example.

The venue, day and length of the party will determine the number of guests you can accommodate, afford and deal with. It makes things easier if some of the invited children know one another. Your child, as the host, should draw up the guest list. Even very young children have firm ideas on whom they want to invite. If you can't cope with a large number, say so at the beginning, and give your child a number to work with — for example, 6 or 10. A small group of happy children can form the basis of a terrific party. A large party, consisting of different age groups, not familiar with each other, can separate into small fragments and will be harder to organise for games.

FOOD, THEMES AND FUN

Having chosen the venue, step two is the all-important choice of the type of food to be served. The venue can dictate the menu. At home, or in your garden, it is easy to have traditional party fare with all the trimmings. It helps to keep the food away from the play area, in another room or a different corner of the garden. Try (not always easy) to serve the food as an event on its own.

For parties at outdoor venues, such as the park, beach, or riding school, the food should be simpler and easy to transport. Parties held in restaurants offer the easiest food option, but can be expensive.

Zoos, amusement parks and bowling centres often cater for parties and will give you special rates. If you are taking the children to the theatre, cinema or a pop concert, remember to plan for a time to provide party food and the cake. If transport is a problem, plan for the closest venue — the nearest park, or restaurant. Alternatively, have a mock dinner party at home.

Whether you take the children out to eat, or have the party at home, remember the magic ingredient itself — the cake. A party's not a party without one. Always supply plenty to

drink. Child's play is thirsty work, and children consume large quantities at parties. In fact, they often drink more than they eat.

Some children react badly to artificial food colourings and sweeteners. In a party of very young children, check with other parents that there are no food allergies.

To ensure that you relax, enjoy yourself and pass on a happy feeling, a couple of good helpers (or more if the guests are very young) will be a valuable asset on the day.

Party games are usually voted the best part of the entertainment and children love them. Step three of your plan is to draw up a list of games. Think about when to start them, about what time you plan to serve the food and cut the cake. The programme for games should be varied — 10 minutes is usually long

enough for most games. Find all the equipment you need for each game well before the guests arrive — thimbles, scarves for blindfolds and so on. Your written list will help you keep an eye on the time and your programme and keep things moving. It helps to be flexible. If a particular game is a roaring success, let it run on for a while, in place of the next one on the list.

Pages 102 to 110 contain lots of ideas for a variety of games, from the traditional to the new, to suit all ages.

If you have chosen a theme for the party, try not to get too carried away with fancy dress ideas. Choose themes with which parents are going to be able to cope. Many parents are very busy and can't sit up for two nights at the sewing machine making a costume. Try not to make dressing up too competitive — some parents will

head for the nearest hire service, while others won't be able to afford it and their children will feel their outfits aren't good enough.

Consider what might be easy. If most guests or their parents are keen horse-riders or hikers, an equestrian or camping party will present no problems. Beach clothes can make cheap and colourful outfits. Children who go to martial art classes will immediately have a costume for a judo or Japanese party. You'll find a selection of themes later on in this book, all of which can offer you a whole party plan, or can be adapted to suit your own particular group.

INVITATIONS

Written invitations are fun for all age groups. Children love to receive them. They give essential information to parents, and provide definite arrival and departure times. Parents transporting young children will appreciate having your telephone number close to hand.

Make or buy the party invitations, and send them about two weeks in advance. The best invitations are often handmade. Design yours so that they reflect the type of party it will be — a clown shape for a clown party, for example. Coloured card is inexpensive and easily found.

Stationery stores sell attractive invitations with blank spaces for filling in the time, place, and date. There is usually a large selection of invitations; you're almost certain to find the one that fits your kind of party.

Remember to include start and finish times, your street address — add a small map on the back of the card if your street is hard to find — and add your telephone number. Include any special information such as what to wear, or alternative

Exciting decoration sets the mood for a Disco Party (page 86)

arrangements in case of rain. It's useful to ask guests or their parents to R.S.V.P., so that you have a clear idea of the numbers of guests to expect.

THEMES, TRIMMINGS AND PARTY IDEAS

All of the suggested themes in this book can be adapted to suit your own special requirements and imagination. If your time is limited, don't try to make everything for the party — all the food, the cake, invitations, outfits, decorations, as well as organising the games. Do what you are best at, like making the cake and food, then buy the decorations and invitations. Get the children involved and ask a friend or two to help on the day.

SWEETS

Once children start to visit other people's homes or go to pre-school, they soon discover the delights of sweets, ice-creams and salty things in packets. Most children love sweet things and expect them at parties.

If there is a health reason for sweets not being allowed, or if you prefer not to offer them, there are other delicious and healthy alternatives. Small boxes of sultanas, raisins, dried apples or apricots are popular with most children, so are dried banana chips and unsalted peanuts.

Sweets tied up in bags are a favourite take-home party favour and chocolate bars are acceptable inexpensive prizes. On pages 98 to 101 you will find tempting and attractive suggestions for sweets and candies.

BALLOONS

Balloons are a must for any party, whatever the age. Tie a few to the gate or doorknocker to make your house easy to find. Colourful and cheap, balloons give a boost to all decorations regardless of the theme, and children love taking them home afterwards. Try to have plenty of spares on hand to replace the ones which burst just as the children are about to leave.

Don't think you can forget the balloons just because the party is outdoors. In a large field or park, a bunch of balloons tied to the nearest tree makes your group easy to spot. Get the children to blow them up before the party or have a balloon-blowing contest. If you want to use hundreds for a big event, use a lilo or air bed pump.

Helium balloons are fun and can be obtained from speciality shops. Party shops sell a range of shapes and colours of balloons, as well as the skinny-sausage variety which can be twisted and shaped into animals or initials for that extra touch.

Very small children may be startled by balloons bursting, and will need comforting. Remember, too, that children — even older ones — should not put pieces of burst balloon in their mouths as they can easily choke.

FANCY DRESS

Crêpe paper is a wonderful stand-by for decorating or making a fancy dress. It's cheap and can be tied, stitched, stapled, or pinned. It can be used in almost any theme; it will make a dramatic cape for a vampire, a cloth and a deep frill to encircle a table, or a flower-petal hat.

Felt is another fantastic fabric for making a quick fancy dress, or for decorating existing clothes with cut-out stars, letters or stripes. It needs only to be tacked on, for easy removal after the party. It can also be glued to

Card, glitter and balloons add a festive touch to the Space Party (page 50)

cardboard or other surfaces. Available in a multitude of colours from most haberdashery departments, it has the added advantage of being cheap. Do remember, though, to remove felt additions from ordinary clothes afterwards, before putting the clothes in the wash. Felt colours, like those of crêpe paper, do run.

Paper streamers, available from most supermarkets, add a festive touch, as do party hats, masks and tooters. Party hats or masks can also be made to enhance a theme. Most stationers have a range of light card or coloured paper. Add glue, staples, hat elastic and a sprinkling of glitter, and you can create a cast of thousands.

First Party

IT IS HARD to resist having a party for your baby's first birthday, even if the child is not aware of the occasion. It provides a pleasant opportunity to spend the day with other new mothers. Grandparents often want to attend. Keep it simple. Pick a shady spot in the park and spread out the picnic blankets.

Age group: one
Venue: park or botanical garden
Number of guests: minimal

Invitations
Invite guests by telephone, or a card with a large 'one', a single candle or any other card you can find suggesting 'one'.

Decorations
Bright and colourful plastic picnic ware is best, as paper plates and cups get knocked over too easily and can be chewed. Tie a bunch of balloons to a tree to mark your picnic spot, but keep the balloons out of reach of babies, and be prepared to comfort those who are frightened by a bursting balloon.

Food
Check with other mothers which foods they have introduced. Most babies of this age will eat biscuits, yoghurt, jelly and cup cakes. For the mums and older children, have French bread, a few good cheeses, suitable dips and pieces of fruit. Drumsticks are easy to carry and are a savoury welcome to most adults at a child's party, but remember to remove the splinter bone and cartilage before giving one to a baby to gnaw.

Cake: a Gingham Dog cake is simple to make.

Games
Bring along soft rubber or fabric balls or rattles for each baby. A packet of colourful plastic bangles will amuse them. Have plenty of safe toys on hand. When babies tire, prams or strollers will provide a soothing change and give you the opportunity for a walk in the park.

Party Favours
The soft balls and plastic bangles you brought along.

GINGHAM DOG CAKE

Preparation time: 50 minutes
Cooking time: 40 minutes
Easy

1 x 350 g packet cake mix or one
 quantity of butter cake batter
 (see page 96)
2 quantities butter icing (see page 96)
green food colouring
Smarties for decoration

1. Preheat oven to 180°C. Grease and line an 18 x 28 cm shallow tin. Make the cake according to directions on the packet or recipe. Pour mixture

into prepared tin and bake for 35–40 minutes or until cooked. Cool.

2. Cut cake into sections as shown in diagram. Discard shaded pieces and assemble pieces as shown, joining the pieces with a little butter icing.

3. Divide remaining icing in half and use one half to cover the top and sides of the cake. Leave to set. Using a ruler and a fine skewer, prick lines on the dog's body, dividing it into squares (see photograph).

4. Tint remaining icing green or another colour. Fill an icing bag fitted with a writing tube or use a paper bag with the tip cut off. Pipe lines on the cake, following the marks, then decorate with more lines and dots as shown. Arrange Smarties to make the dog's collar, nose and eye, securing them with dabs of icing.

Gingham Dog Cake

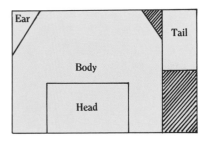

Gingham Dog Cake

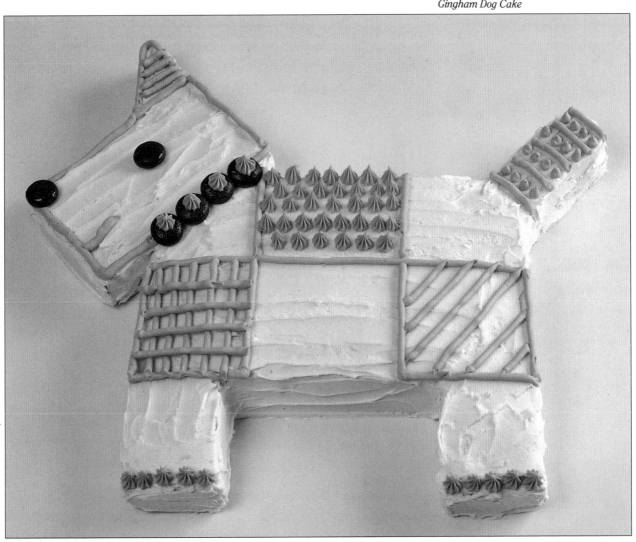

Clown Party

THE SECOND and third birthdays are an excellent opportunity for a small-scale party. Invite other children from the neighbourhood or local playgroup. Two or three parents would be helpful, as toddlers need assistance and attention. Holding the party in the garden means that no-one has to worry about spilt drinks and allows parents to relax too. Keep the party short. Toddlers tire quickly and will probably need a nap after an hour or two of activity and social interaction in a group.

Age group: two or three years
Venue: the garden
Number of guests: 4–6

Invitations
Cut out a clown-face card. Include the time, date, your address and telephone number.

Decorations
Before the party, check that the area is childproof. Put away sharp gardening tools and other hazardous items. Garden furniture will be fine for adults: children will enjoy using a plastic plate and cup on the lawn. Tie balloons to a tree, and put up a garden umbrella if the day is hot. Have a basin of water and a few facecloths nearby.

Clockwise from left: Cherry Crunch, Clown Faces, Baskets of Tricks, Peach Dream, Fairy Biscuits, Harlequin Dip and Number Sandwiches.

Basket of Tricks

segments with grapefruit knife and reserve. Scoop out membrane, leaving orange shells intact.
3. To serve, cut jellies into cubes. Combine with orange segments, assorted fruits and marshmallows. Spoon into orange shells. Add a pretty flower to garnish. Chill before serving.

Fairy Biscuits

FAIRY BISCUITS

Preparation time: 15 minutes
Cooking time: nil
Makes about 12
Easy

1 x 250 g packet plain biscuits
125 g cream cheese, softened
1 cup hundreds and thousands

1. Lay biscuits out on a board or tray, with the flat side facing upwards.
2. Spread each biscuit with a little cream cheese and sprinkle with hundreds and thousands.

NUMBER SANDWICHES

Preparation time: 45 minutes
Cooking time: nil
Serves 10
Easy

1 loaf sliced bread
butter for spreading
fillings

1. Spread slices of bread thinly with butter. Spread 10 slices or half the loaf with filling and top with slices of buttered bread.
2. Cut sandwiches into number

Food
Some toddlers may have special food or drink preferences: check with their parents. Suggested menu: Fairy Biscuits, Number Sandwiches, Basket of Tricks, Clown Faces, Cherry Crunch, Peach Dream, Harlequin Dip.

Cake: a Clown's Head cake is fun and easy to make.

Games
Children aged two and three enjoy water and sand play. A baby bath filled with water, and with a good assortment of containers from the pot cupboard or plastics shelf, will be popular. If you haven't a sandpit, make a sand tray on the same lines: a large, shallow plastic or metal container filled with clean sand, some plastic cups, and a beach bucket, is a veritable honey-pot for small children. Group games could include *Ring-a-ring-a-rosy*; *Hide-and-seek*; *The Farmer in the dell*; *Follow-the-leader*; *On the bank, in the river*. Bubble

blowing is fun for three-year-old children. *Wobbling bunnies* is, too.

Party Favours
Sweets or bags of dried fruit, and one or two balloons.

BASKET OF TRICKS

Preparation time: 30 minutes plus chilling time
Cooking time: nil
Serves 6
Easy

½ x 85 g packet red jelly
½ x 85 g packet green jelly
3 oranges
assorted fresh or unsweetened canned fruits, cut up e.g. strawberries, bananas, canned peaches
6 marshmallows, cut into quarters

1. Prepare jellies, using a little less water than packet directs. Pour into small, shallow tins and refrigerate until jellies are firm.
2. Cut oranges in half, cut out fruit

shapes. Skewer each sandwich with a small flag with the individual child's name written on it.

3. Cover with plastic wrap or damp greaseproof paper to prevent sandwiches from drying out.

FILLINGS
Egg Mayonnaise
Mash together 7 hardboiled eggs, 3 tablespoons mayonnaise and pepper to taste. Divide mixture between 10 slices bread. Top with finely shredded lettuce.

Carrot and Cheese
Combine 5 finely grated carrots, 125 g finely grated cheese, 2 mashed hardboiled eggs, 1 stalk finely chopped celery and 1 tablespoon plain yoghurt or sour cream. Divide between 10 slices of bread.

Tropical Delight
Drain 1 x 425 g can crushed pineapple. Stand 10–15 minutes to allow all excess moisture to drain away. Combine with 1 x 100 g packet roughly chopped marshmallows, 1 cup sultanas, 1 cup shredded coconut and 4 tablespoons sour cream. Mix thoroughly and spread over 10 slices bread.

Number Sandwiches

Cherry Crunch

CHERRY CRUNCH

Preparation time: 15 minutes
Cooking time: 10 minutes
Makes 30
Easy

30 g butter
2 tablespoons honey
2 tablespoons brown sugar
2 cups cornflakes
½ cup chopped glacé cherries

1. Preheat oven to 180°C. Line 30 deep muffin tins with paper cake cases.
2. Place butter, honey and sugar in a small pan. Heat gently until frothy. Combine cornflakes and cherries in a large mixing bowl. Stir in butter mixture and mix well.
3. Spoon into paper cake cases. Bake for 5–10 minutes. Remove from oven and cool on a wire rack.

Clown Faces

Peach Dream

CLOWN FACES

Preparation time: 20 minutes
Cooking time: nil
Serves 10
Easy

1 litre vanilla ice-cream
10 ice-cream cones
½ cup shredded coconut
20 Smarties for eyes
10 glacé red cherries
1 licorice strap
5 small red snakes

1. Scoop ice-cream into balls on a large flat tray. Arrange cones on top of ice-cream and place in freezer until firm.
2. Decorate ice-cream with coconut for hair, Smarties for eyes and a cherry for each clown's nose. Cut licorice into fine strips 1 cm long and place vertically on top of and below each Smartie. Finish each face with half a red snake for the mouth. Serve at once.

PEACH DREAM

Preparation time: 10 minutes
Cooking time: nil
Serves 8
Easy

1 x 425 g can peach slices
500 g litre vanilla ice-cream
¼ cup orange juice
few drops vanilla essence
2 cups milk, chilled
orange slices for garnish

1. Drain peach slices and chill well. Put into a blender bowl with ice-cream, orange juice, vanilla essence and milk. Blend until smooth.
2. Pour into tumblers and serve at once, garnished with orange slices.

HARLEQUIN DIP

Preparation time: 30 minutes
Cooking time: nil
Serves 10
Easy

6 hardboiled eggs
2 tablespoons mayonnaise
2 tablespoons sour cream
2 tablespoons finely chopped fresh parsley
1 tablespoon poppy seeds
2 tablespoons finely chopped red capsicum
rice crackers for serving

Harlequin Dip

1. Mash hardboiled eggs with mayonnaise and sour cream. Lightly brush a small bowl with oil. Spoon egg mixture into bowl and pack firmly. Chill in the refrigerator for 1 hour.

2. Invert egg mould onto a flat serving plate. Cover a third of the top and sides of the egg mixture with finely chopped parsley, one third with poppy seeds and remaining third with capsicum. Press on lightly. Surround egg mixture with rice crackers to serve.

CLOWN'S HEAD CAKE

Preparation time: 1½ hours
Cooking time: 45 minutes
Easy

2 x 350 g packets cake mix or
    2 quantities butter cake (see page 96)
1 quantity butter icing (see page 96)
red food colouring
blue food colouring
Smarties
1 licorice strap
1 chocolate finger biscuit
red crêpe paper
shirring elastic

1. Preheat oven to 180°C and grease two 20 cm round cake tins. Make the cakes according to directions on the packet or following recipe. Turn into prepared tins and bake for 40–45 minutes or until cooked. Cool.

2. Cut a hat and a pompom from one cake (see diagram). Use the second cake for the face.

3. Divide butter icing in half. Set aside one half to decorate the face. Divide the remaining half into thirds. Place one-third in one bowl and colour it deep red for the pompom. Place the remaining two-thirds in another bowl and colour it deep blue for the hat.

4. Ice the pompom and hat cakes red and blue respectively, covering tops and sides. Ice the face cake separately, spreading the reserved plain icing over top and sides of face.

5. To assemble: carefully place the hat in position, so the curve at the base of the hat fits into the top of the face. Place pompom on top of hat.

Clown's Head Cake

Cover the join between hat and face with Smarties, and use Smarties on the face for eyes and mouth. Use small strips of licorice for eyelashes and a long strip for the mouth. Cut the chocolate finger in half for the nose. Make a ruffle, using the red crêpe paper and shirring elastic, to finish the neck trim.

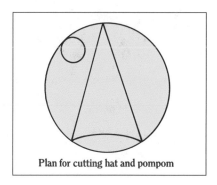

Plan for cutting hat and pompom

ZooParty

A ZOO PARTY works well for younger children. If you have a zoo in your town, you might like to arrange a visit to the zoo first, and follow it with a party at home. Another option is to check with the zoo to see if they have facilities for small functions, and take a picnic party along. Alternatively, you could have your own special Zoo Party in the garden, as outlined here.

Invite guests to come dressed as their favourite animal. A costume doesn't have to be elaborate. A paper face mask or snout, a pinned-on tail, and ears made of cardboard and hat elastic will do the trick very well.

Age group: four to seven
Venue: zoo, or your garden
Number of guests: up to 10

Invitations
Make cards shaped like elephants or your child's favourite animal. Invite guests to dress as an animal and to bring their favourite stuffed animal toys to the party too.

Clockwise from left: Birds' Nests with Sweet and Sour Sauce, Moo Juice Shakes, Elephant Ears, Growling Gorilla Tamers, Animal Shapes, Cats' Faces and Three Blind Mice.

Cat Faces

Decorations
Collect as many stuffed animal toys as you can from friends and neighbours to add to your own child's collection. Place these in appropriate groups around the garden — all the bears together, the wombats together, and so on. Make zoo signs for each collection — Elephant Enclosure, Reptile House or Platypus Pool — and hang these up. Make enclosures for the groups out of twisted chains of coloured crêpe paper, tied on sticks. Decorate a table of nibbles with a crêpe paper frill, and hang a ZOO KIOSK sign over it. Use paper plates or cups decorated with jungle greenery or animals, or use brightly coloured plastic tableware.

Food
The menu offers Growling Gorilla Tamers, Moo Juice Shakes, Birds' Nests with Sweet and Sour Sauce, Three Blind Mice, Animal Shapes, Elephant Ears, and Cat Faces.

Cake: serve a Piggy Cake.

Games
Play *The farmer in the dell*, *What's the time, Mr Wolf?*, *Bat the balloon*, and *Wobbling bunnies*. Have a *Blow the balloon* race. Play *Balloon dress-ups*, and have a sack race.

Play *Paddy's black pig* for a good laugh.

Or play *Animalia*. Blindfold six children. Let the others watch. Line up the blindfolded children in a row, not using their names, so that they do not know who their neighbours are. Taking each in turn, and identifying her by touch only, give her an animal; snake, lion and so on. Let each child practise the sound of their animal; hissing, grunting or roaring. Then get them to move out of line and turn around a few times, until the line is thoroughly muddled.

They then have to remake the row in its original order, by listening to the sounds made by each other and placing themselves in the right relative position. Remaining children watch to see if the order is correctly achieved. Observers and players then swap places and the game continues.

Another game is *No paws allowed*. Put a whole apple onto a paper saucer, one for each guest. Place the saucers on the floor. When all the children are kneeling at a saucer, with hands clasped behind their backs, give a starting signal. They have to eat the apples without using their hands at all. The first to finish is the winner.

Prizes and Party Favours
Animal biscuits wrapped in cellophane, animal-shaped rubbers, plastic zoo animals (buy a bag and split it, wrapping each individually).

CAT FACES

Preparation time: 40 minutes
Cooking time: 15 minutes
Makes 24
Medium

½ cup golden syrup
⅓ cup brown sugar
60 g butter
2¼ cups plain flour
2 teaspoons mixed spice
beaten egg, to glaze
1 quantity buttercream frosting (see page 96)
Smarties and licorice for decoration

1. Preheat oven to 180°C and lightly grease oven trays. Combine golden syrup, brown sugar and butter in a pan. Stir over low heat until melted and smooth. Cool to room temperature.
2. Sift flour and spice together into a large bowl. Add cooled syrup mixture and stir well to combine.
3. Roll out half the dough on a lightly floured surface to 2 mm thickness. Cut into 5 cm rounds and place on prepared trays. Roll out remaining dough and cut into long triangles for cats' 'ears'. Brush a little beaten egg onto ears and attach to top of pastry rounds. Bake for 10 minutes until browned. Cool 2–3 minutes on trays before lifting onto wire racks to cool.
4. Spread face of biscuits with frosting and leave ears plain. Decorate with Smarties for eyes and mouth. Cut licorice into 6 thin strips and arrange 3 strips either side of mouth for whiskers.

ANIMAL SHAPES

Preparation time: 25 minutes
Cooking time: 20 minutes
Makes 18
Easy

4 sheets ready-rolled shortcrust pastry
125 g tasty cheese, grated
125 g cream cheese, softened
¼ cup sour cream
2 tablespoons chopped fresh parsley
1 egg yolk
sesame seeds

1. Preheat oven to 190°C and lightly grease a flat oven tray. Place two sheets of pastry on a lightly floured surface. In a bowl combine cheeses, cream, parsley and egg white.
2. Divide cheese mixture between pastry sheets and spread over each sheet. Top with remaining pastry. Roll out pastry lightly so that the layers join together. Using animal shaped cutters, cut pastry into a variety of shapes. Brush surface with beaten egg yolk and sprinkle with sesame seeds.
3. Bake in oven for 15–20 minutes until pastries are lightly puffed and golden. These are best served warm, though they are still tasty at room temperature.

Animal Shapes

BIRDS' NESTS WITH SWEET AND SOUR SAUCE

Preparation time: 40 minutes
Cooking time: 25 minutes
Serves 10
Easy

10 chicken wings
1 egg white
¼ cup cornflour
1 teaspoon soy sauce
90 g rice vermicelli noodles
oil for deep-frying

SAUCE
¼ cup white vinegar
¼ cup white sugar
¼ cup tomato sauce
¼ cup water
1 tablespoon cornflour

1. Remove wing tip and discard. Cut wing through the joint into two sections. Push chicken flesh to one end of the bone, using a sharp knife to cut through tendons and pry the flesh away from the bone.
2. Place chicken in a large bowl, with egg white, cornflour and soy sauce. Mix with hands, turning and coating chicken until no flour lumps remain.
3. Heat oil until very hot. Add a few strands of noodles to test oil temperature. Noodles should puff almost immediately (if they don't, discard them and heat oil further). Cook noodles, half at a time. As soon as noodles puff, lift out with a wire strainer and drain on absorbent paper. Lift chicken wings out of mixture one at a time, and drop into hot oil. Fry about six at a time for 3–5 minutes until chicken is golden and cooked through.
4. To prepare sauce: blend together all ingredients in a small pan until smooth. Bring to the boil, stirring over medium heat and boil for 1 minute.
5. To serve: arrange chicken wings on top of noodles on a large serving plate and drizzle a little sauce over the chicken. Serve remaining sauce separately.

Birds' Nests with Sweet and Sour Sauce

Growling Gorilla Tamers

2. Remove stones from prunes and replace with almonds. Pipe frosting into cavity with almonds. Cut licorice strap into fine short strips and attach with a little frosting to represent whiskers. Attach a larger piece for the tail and pieces of cherry or muskstick for eyes.

3. Chop jelly into cubes and spoon onto a flat white plate. Arrange 'mice' on top of jelly and chill until ready to serve.

MOO JUICE SHAKES

Preparation time: 5 minutes
Cooking time: nil
Serves 6
Easy

400 g fruit-flavoured yoghurt
2 tablespoons honey
1 teaspoon vanilla essence
2 ripe bananas or ¼ peeled seeded
  rockmelon
2 cups chilled milk
4 scoops vanilla ice-cream
grated nutmeg

1. Place all ingredients except nutmeg in a blender bowl. Cover and blend at high speed for 3 minutes.
2. Pour into six glasses and sprinkle with a little grated nutmeg. Serve immediately.

Moo Juice Shakes

GROWLING GORILLA TAMERS

Preparation time: 15 minutes
Cooking time: 15 minutes
Serves 10
Easy

10 bananas
200 g chocolate chips
foil for wrapping

1. Preheat oven to 180°C. Peel bananas leaving skin and banana joined at base. Stud banana liberally all over with chocolate chips. Bring up skin to surround banana and wrap tightly in foil.
2. Bake bananas for 10–15 minutes. Remove foil and serve warm. Banana will be lightly cooked and chocolate will be melted throughout.

THREE BLIND MICE

Preparation time: 30 minutes plus
  chilling time
Cooking time: nil
Serves 20
Easy

1 x 85 g packet yellow jelly
20 prunes
20 almonds
½ quantity vanilla flavoured buttercream frosting (see recipe page 96)
1 licorice strap
red cherries or musksticks

1. Make jelly according to instructions on packet using only 1½ cups water. Chill until jelly is set firmly.

Three Blind Mice

ELEPHANT EARS

Preparation time: 15 minutes
Cooking time: 10 minutes
Makes 15
Easy

oil for deep-frying
1 x 125g packet poppadums
poppy seeds

1. Heat oil until surface appears to be moving and oil is hot. Drop in one poppadum to test it. Poppadum should expand and puff almost immediately. If it does not, allow oil to get hotter.
2. Cook poppadums in hot oil a few at a time, lift out of oil and whilst still hot sprinkle with poppy seeds. Drain on absorbent paper.

Piggy Cake

PIGGY CAKE

Preparation time: 1 hour
Cooking time: 50 minutes
Easy

2 x 350 g packets cake mix or
    2 quantities butter cake batter
    (see page 96)
1 quantity butter icing
    (see page 96)
few drops pink food colouring
1 licorice strap
Smarties
2 cups coconut
green food colouring

1. Preheat oven to 180°C. Grease and line both a 20 cm round and a 20 cm square cake tin. Make the cakes according to directions on the packet or following recipe. Divide mixture evenly between prepared tins and bake for 40–50 minutes or until cooked. Leave cake to cool in tin before turning out. Trim the cakes so they are both the same height.
2. From the square cake, cut a 10 cm round for the snout and two ears (see diagram 1). Colour butter icing pale pink. Use two-thirds to cover the round cake and the ears. Colour remaining one-third of the icing a darker shade of pink and use this to cover the snout.
3. Place the cake on a covered cake board, positioning snout and ears appropriately (see diagram 2). Use Smarties for eyes and nostrils. Cut the licorice strap to form whiskers, ears and eyelashes. Colour the coconut green, sprinkle around the head and decorate with Smarties and any remaining licorice strips.

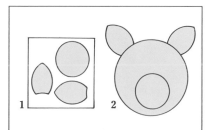

1. Placement diagram for cutting snout and ears.
2. Assemble the iced cake pieces on a board.

19

Wild West Party

THIS CAN BE held indoors or out. Before the party, ask your local grocer for some very large cardboard boxes; with windows cut in the sides, these make excellent forts and hiding places.

Make headbands from tape or ribbon for each brave. Add cardboard feathers to the back, and add face paint for extra fun. Borrow a collection of wide-brimmed felt hats for cowhands from friends. Brown paper, cut into fringed strips, makes good chaps when pinned to the sides of jeans. Large handkerchiefs or square scarfs make good neckerchiefs. Alternatively, invite guests to create their own Wild West costumes.

Age group: four to ten
Venue: house or garden
Number of guests: up to 10

Invitations
Cut out wigwam shapes from folded cardboard. Paint patterns on the outside and invite Cowhands and Braves to join you out on the prairie for a hoedown and a wardance.

Decorations
Paint the outside of big cardboard boxes with poster paints, to create forts and homesteads. Make one or two wigwams from blankets draped over broomsticks. Pin crêpe paper or felt, cut into Indian patterns, on the blankets to decorate wigwam walls. Draw a few prickly cactus plants on big sheets of card or paper, paint and cut out the shapes and pin these up as wall or fence decor.

Food
Wild West Beans, Desert Coolers, Shaggy Dog Faces, Cheese Wheels, Side Saddle Grits, Prairie Wings and Cactus Juice.

Cake: welcome the pardners to a Wagon or Fort cake.

Games
Divide the children into teams of Cowhands and Indians for a game of tag, with each team trying to round up all the other team's members. Play *Hot potato*, *Musical saddles* (or cushions), *Pin the tail on the donkey* (or horse). Have a *Knee balloon race*.

An excellent indoor game is *Captives*. Children are divided into two teams, the Sheriffs and the Braves. Sheriffs cover their eyes and count to 100 while Braves scatter throughout the house and hide. The Sheriffs then seek out all those in hiding. When a Sheriff finds a Brave, the Brave is taken captive and taken back to a previously-decided jail-house. The first Brave taken there has to hold on to the jail-house bars — the leg of a table or side of a chair — with one hand. The next captive taken has to hold hands with the first. Each succeeding captive links hands with the last, so that the captives form a chain.

Meanwhile, those Braves who are still in hiding have to sneak back to the prison, and free the captives as quietly as possible. A Brave may free only one captive at a time, and must free the captive who is last in the chain. Once free, a Brave goes off to hide again. The object of the game — for the Sheriffs to capture all the Braves — may take a while to achieve!

Prizes and Party Favours

Small plastic Wild West toy figures (buy a bag from a department store and split it up); silver nuggets (pieces of fudge or cookies wrapped in silver foil) and water pistols.

Clockwise from left: Desert Coolers, Wild West Beans, Side Saddle Grits, Cactus Juice, Prairie Wings, Shaggy Dog Faces, and Cheese Wheels (centre)

SIDE SADDLE GRITS

Preparation time: 10 minutes
Cooking time: 10 minutes
Serves 10
Easy

5 cobs corn
1 tablespoon sugar
125 g butter
thick toothpicks (older children only)

1. Peel away green covering from cobs of corn and remove 'silk'. Break cobs in half. Place corn into a large pan of cold water, add sugar and a few outer leaves of the corn. Bring to boil and cook 8–10 minutes until corn is tender.
2. Drain corn and toss in butter. Insert a toothpick in each end of the corn to serve.

Shaggy Dog Faces

Wild West Beans

SHAGGY DOG FACES

Preparation time: 20 minutes
Cooking time: 2 minutes
Makes 18
Easy

4 cups Rice Crispies
1½ cups icing sugar, sifted
1 cup desiccated coconut
3 tablespoons cocoa
250 g vegetable fat
a little frosting or icing
shredded coconut
jelly beans
red glacé cherries
white or pink marshmallows

1. In a bowl combine Rice Crispies with icing sugar, coconut and cocoa. Melt vegetable fat over gentle heat, cool slightly and pour over dry ingredients. Stir to mix thoroughly.
2. Divide evenly between paper cake cases. Chill in the refrigerator to set.
3. Attach decorations with a little icing — coconut for hair, pieces of jelly beans for eyes, a glacé cherry for mouth and a marshmallow for a hat.

WILD WEST BEANS

Preparation time: 15 minutes
Cooking time: 15 minutes
Serves 10
Easy

200 g corn chips
1 x 440 g can baked beans
150 g ham, cut into 1 cm pieces
200 g grated processed cheddar cheese

Cactus Juice

1. Preheat oven to 180°C. Spread a layer of corn chips on a large flat platter. Spoon over a quarter of the baked beans, sprinkle with a quarter of the ham and cheese. Top with corn chips and repeat layers until all ingredients are used. Finish with a light sprinkling of cheese.
2. Heat through in the oven for 10–15 minutes until cheese melts. Serve hot with a few extra corn chips if desired.

CACTUS JUICE

Preparation time: 10 minutes plus
   chilling time
Cooking time: nil
Serves 10
Easy

2 litres apple juice
2 tablespoons honey
½ cucumber, seeded and finely sliced
1 x 750 ml bottle lemonade, chilled
1 x 750 ml bottle soda water, chilled
ice-cubes
fresh mint leaves for garnish

1. Mix together apple juice, honey and cucumber. Pour into a large serving jug or bowl and chill thoroughly.
2. To serve: add lemonade, soda, and ice-cubes. Float a few mint leaves as a garnish.

DESERT COOLERS

Preparation time: 30 minutes plus
  freezing time
Cooking time: nil
Makes 12
Easy

1 fresh pineapple
500 ml plain yoghurt
1 x 85 g packet lemon flavoured
  jelly
2 cups shredded coconut

1. Peel pineapple and remove any
brown spots and eyes. Cut pineapple
in half, and remove core. Cut each
half in three wedges, and cut wedges
in half horizontally. This will give 12
small wedges in all. Insert a lollipop
stick into each wedge. Place in freezer
until partially frozen.
2. Mix together yoghurt and jelly
crystals and stir briskly over a bowl of
warm water until yoghurt has thinned
and crystals are beginning to dissolve.
3. Dip each wedge of pineapple into
yoghurt mixture then dip into
coconut. Stand sticks in a piece of
polystyrene or chunks of vegetables,
and return to freezer until frozen.

Desert Coolers

Cheese Wheels

CHEESE WHEELS

Preparation time: 20 minutes
Cooking time: nil
Serves 8
Easy

250 g processed or mild cheddar, sliced
  into 1cm slices
chunks of cabana, gherkins and dried
  apricots
toothpicks

1. Using a round scone cutter, cut
cheese slices into discs.
2. Thread 2 cheese discs onto each
toothpick, alternating with a cabana,
gherkins and apricots. For younger
children, omit toothpicks and pile
onto biscuits.

HINT
Cabana is a continental salami style
sausage similar to cabanossi. It is
available at large supermarkets and
delicatessens. Whole cherry tomatoes
can be used instead of apricots.

Wagon Cake

WAGON CAKE

Preparation time: 1¼ hours
Cooking time: 40 minutes
Easy

2 x 350 g packets cake mix or
    2 quantities butter cake batter
    (see page 96)
3–4 tablespoons cocoa
hot water
1 quantity basic butter icing
    (see page 96)
red food colouring
yellow food colouring
12 round chocolate biscuits
2 licorice strips
chocolate chips

1. Preheat oven to 180°C. Grease both a 14 x 8 cm cylindrical loaf tin and a 14 x 8 cm loaf tin. Make the cakes according to directions on the packet or following recipe. Divide mixture between prepared tins and bake for 35–40 minutes or until cooked. Cool. Cakes may need to be trimmed to equal length.
2. Dissolve cocoa in hot water. When cool beat into half the butter icing. Divide the remaining portion in half again, colouring one yellow and one red.
3. Make two piles of four round chocolate biscuits, joining the biscuits together with a little butter icing. Cover the rectangular cake with chocolate butter icing and smooth with a knife, to form the base of the wagon. Place the two piles of chocolate biscuits on a plate to act as a support for the cake and position the wagon base on these. To make the top of the wagon, cover the cylindrical cake in strips of red and yellow icing. Smooth with a knife. Place the top onto the wagon base

PRAIRIE WINGS

Preparation time: 50 minutes
Cooking time: 10 minutes
Makes 24
Medium

12 chicken wings
1 cup plain flour
½ teaspoon garlic powder
½ teaspoon cinnamon
½ teaspoon black pepper
½ teaspoon dried oregano
½ teaspoon dried parsley flakes
pinch paprika
oil for deep-frying

1. Cut chicken wings into three pieces, cutting through joints. Discard wing tips. Using a sharp knife cut flesh around the top of each joint through to the bone. Push flesh down, prying it away from the bone until it is all pushed to one end but still intact.
2. Mix together flour, herbs and

spices in a large plastic bag. Add chicken and shake bag to coat chicken with flour.
3. Remove chicken from flour and deep-fry in hot oil for 3–5 minutes until crisp, golden and cooked through. Drain on absorbent paper and serve hot.

Prairie Wings

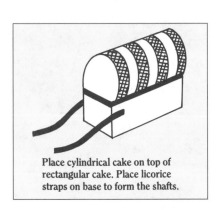

Place cylindrical cake on top of rectangular cake. Place licorice straps on base to form the shafts.

and join with icing.

4. Cut strips of licorice to cover the join of the two cakes. Cut two more strips to form the shafts. Attach these to the sides (see diagram). Pipe the child's name along the side of the wagon in white butter icing, using a piping bag. Pipe spokes on the remaining four chocolate biscuits to form wheels. Attach these to each corner of the wagon, using icing. Sprinkle chocolate chips over the plate to represent the ground.

FORT CAKE

Preparation time: 1½ hours
Cooking time: 45 minutes
Easy

1 x 350 g packet cake mix or
   1 quantity butter cake batter
   (see page 96)

ICING
½ quantity butter icing (see page 96)
1½ tablespoons cocoa
1 tablespoon hot water
½ cup icing sugar
water
2 x 200 g packets chocolate finger
   biscuits
Wild West figures

1. Preheat oven to 180°C. Grease and line a 20 cm square cake tin. Make the cake according to directions on the packet or following recipe. Turn into prepared tin and bake for 40–45 minutes or until cooked. Cool before turning out.
2. To prepare icing: dissolve cocoa in hot water to form a thick paste. Add to butter icing, and beat well to blend. Coat cake with icing and place on a cake board.
3. Prepare plain icing by mixing icing sugar and a little water to a piping consistency. Pipe 'Happy Birthday' and the birthday child's name onto the cake.
4. Cut about 1 cm off the ends of eight biscuits and place these at intervals around the cake, cut ends down (see diagram 1). Use the remaining biscuits to surround cake completely to give a fort effect (see diagram 2). Place Wild West figures at appropriate places on cake and on the board outside the fort.

Fort Cake

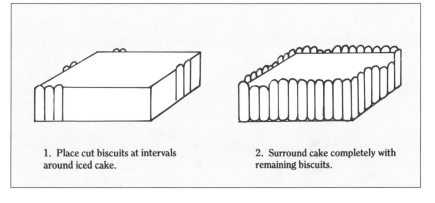

1. Place cut biscuits at intervals around iced cake.

2. Surround cake completely with remaining biscuits.

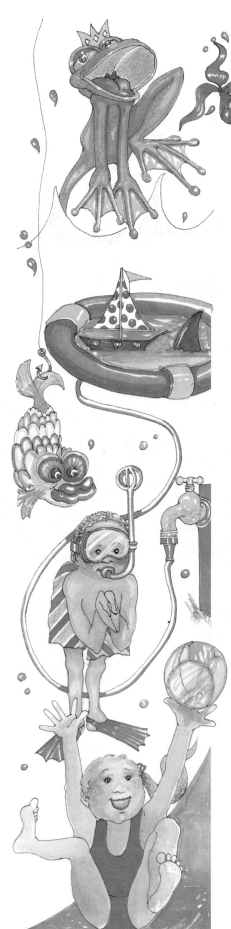

Water Party

THIS IS TERRIFIC for younger children, and sometimes tempts the older mavericks too. Best held in summer, it can also be very successful in a mild autumn or hot spring season. While the children enjoy splashing, your garden benefits as well.

It's wise to check with the local council in very hot weather, to see if water restrictions are currently in force.

You don't need a pool for a water party — the basic equipment is a hose, a sprinkler, and one or two sheets of plastic (inexpensive sheets are obtainable from most hardware stores or gardening outlets). It helps to have neighbours who won't mind a bit of noise for a couple of hours.

Dress requirements are simple: guests wear swimming costumes and bring a towel. It is a good idea to ask them to bring a change of clothes, so that if they get too chilly, they can change and warm up.

Age group: four to eight
Venue: the garden
Number of guests: 10–12

Invitations
Cut out a fish shape from folded card. Borrow your child's wax crayons and draw scales and features in white or yellow wax, then paint over the wax with blue watercolour — you'll get a glistening wet fish effect. As well as giving the details of the party, add a note about the theme, for example, 'This is a water party. B.Y.O. towels, wear a swimming costume, and let's make a splash!'

Decorations
Cut out paper fish and boat shapes from coloured card and hang them from trees and shrubs. Cut blue and green crêpe paper into wavy narrow strips, and hang the streamers from the washline or eaves to make fronds of seaweed. Pinch or pull the edges of the crêpe for a wavy effect. Paper plates, cups and napkins featuring fish are available from most stores.

Food
Fish 'n Chips, Pizza Subs, Rainbow Pond, Tropical Fish on sticks, Frankfurter Sailboats, Shark-infested Waters, Life Savers.

Cake: Tiny the Tugboat will add a nautical touch.

Games
Spread a sheet of plastic on the lawn and turn the hose on lightly, so that a steady trickle of water runs across the sheet. This makes an invitingly slippery surface and becomes a water slide, whether on the level or on a slight slope.

Alternatively, hand out three big

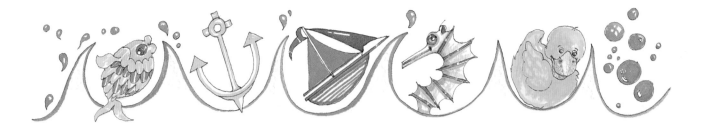

balloons. Have the children stand in a circle around the sprinkler, with the sprinkler turned up high. Children must throw the balloons across the water fountain, to the child opposite. With three balloons being thrown simultaneously, and often being deflected by the sprinkler, this game leads to a giggling tumble of children scrambling to catch errant balloons.

Play *Jump the broom*, substituting the sprinkler for the broom.

Bring out a bowl of soapy water and have a bubble-blowing competition. Bubbles can be blown through plastic pipes, twists of plastic-coated wire, or through the 'O' formed by a forefinger tip touching the thumb.

Play *Sardines*, *On the bank*, *In the river*, or *Froggy, froggy, may we cross your shining river?* Have a *Fishing competition* or a *Water race*.

Prizes and Party Favours
Marshmallow fish or frogs from the local sweet store; small plastic water toys such as boats or ducks, or ping-pong balls. Water pistols.

Clockwise from left: Pizza Subs, Shark Infested Waters, Rainbow Pond, Frankfurter Sailboats. Tropical Fish on Sticks, Fish 'n Chips, Lifesavers, The Big Wheel.

Rainbow Pond

FISH 'N CHIPS

Preparation time: 45 minutes
Cooking time: 30 minutes
Serves 10
Medium

750 g white fish fillets
1 egg, lightly beaten
¼ cup milk
1 cup plain flour
2 cups dried breadcrumbs
8 potatoes
oil for deep-frying
lemon wedges or vinegar for serving

1. Cut fish into 3cm pieces, removing any bones. Beat together egg and milk. Coat fish in flour, dip in egg mixture, then into breadcrumbs. Press crumbs on firmly. Chill until ready to cook.
2. Peel potatoes. Cut potato lengthways into 1cm wide finger lengths. Rinse under cold water and pat dry in a tea-towel or kitchen paper. Heat oil in a deep fryer, lower half the chips into the oil and cook for 5 minutes. Lift out and drain on absorbent paper. Reheat oil and repeat process with remaining chips.
3. When ready to serve: reheat oil and cook chips until crisp and golden. Drain on absorbent paper and keep warm in the oven. Cook fish, a few pieces at a time, for 1–2 minutes until golden and cooked through. Drain on absorbent paper and keep warm. Serve hot with a little vinegar or lemon wedges.

*If fish pieces take longer to cook than 2 minutes, the oil isn't hot enough — increase the temperature to ensure fish cooks on the inside without burning on the outside.

Fish 'n Chips

RAINBOW POND

Preparation time: 35 minutes plus
chilling time
Cooking time: 2 minutes
Serves 10
Easy

4½ cups apple juice
1 x 85 g packet orange-flavoured
jelly
1 x 85 g packet lime-flavoured
jelly
1 x 85 g packet strawberry-flavoured
jelly
1 x 425 g can apricot halves, well
drained
½ ripe honeydew melon, with the flesh
shaped into balls by a melon baller
1 x 250 g punnet strawberries, hulled
and halved
yoghurt, cream or ice cream for serving

1. Make up different jelly flavours separately using apple juice instead of water. Allow to cool until mixture thickens slightly.
2. To assemble: into a clear glass 2 litre serving bowl pour thickened orange jelly mixture and apricot halves. Refrigerate until set.
3. Gently spoon lime jelly and melon balls on top of apricot layer. Refrigerate until set.
4. Spoon on strawberry jelly and strawberry halves as a final layer. Chill for several hours until firmly set.
5. When jelly is set, serve accompanied by ice-cream, freshly whipped cream or plain yoghurt.

LIFE SAVERS

Preparation time: 25 minutes
Cooking time: 1 hour
Makes 10
Medium

2 egg whites
½ cup caster sugar
300 ml thickened cream
raspberry jam for spreading
fine red ribbon

1. Preheat oven to 150°C. Grease an oven tray and sprinkle liberally with cornflour, or line tray with baking paper. Mark 5 cm circles on it.
2. Beat egg whites into stiff peaks. Add sugar, a tablespoon at a time, beating well between each addition.
3. Fill a piping bag and pipe around edge of circles on tray. Bake for 20–30 minutes or until meringue is dry. Turn oven off, letting meringues dry in cooling oven.
4. Near serving time, join meringues together in pairs with jam and cream. Thread ribbon through centre and around rings, lifebuoy-style. (If filled too far in advance, meringues become moist and soft.)

Life Savers

Shark-infested Waters

SHARK-INFESTED WATERS

Preparation time: 5 minutes
Cooking time: nil
Serves 8
Easy

1 x 850 ml can pineapple juice
1 cup orange juice
½ cup lime juice cordial
3 passionfruit
1 x 285 ml bottle dry ginger ale
2 x 285 ml bottles lemonade, chilled
1 orange, cut into segments
2 slices pineapple, cut into 1cm chunks
ice-cubes

1. In a large jug or bowl, mix together juices, cordial and passionfruit. Chill thoroughly.
2. Stir in ginger ale and lemonade. Add orange and pineapple together with a few ice-cubes.

Frankfurter Sailboats

The Big Wheel

FRANKFURTER SAILBOATS

Preparation time: 15 minutes
Cooking time: 5 minutes
Makes 8
Easy

8 frankfurters
8 long bread rolls
soft butter
8 short bamboo skewers
4 single cheese slices, halved diagonally
8 cherry tomatoes
tomato sauce, mustard and gherkin relish, as desired
celery, carrot and zucchini sticks for serving

1. Place frankfurters in a pan, cover with cold water and slowly heat until boiling. Drain.
2. Split rolls and spread lightly with butter, if desired. Place a frankfurter in each roll.
3. Insert a skewer into each cheese slice, then through a tomato. Stand skewers upright through one end of each frankfurter with cheese at the top to make sails. Serve with condiments and vegetable sticks.

TROPICAL FISH ON STICKS

Preparation time: 15 minutes plus chilling and freezing time
Cooking time: 2 minutes
Serves 10
Easy

3 oranges
1 x 85 g packet orange-flavoured jelly
½ cup orange juice

1. Peel oranges leaving outer white pith intact. Break oranges into segments, arrange them on a flat tray and place in the freezer until frozen.
2. Make jelly with orange juice instead of water. Cool in the refrigerator until jelly begins to thicken.
3. Skewer orange segments with toothpicks. Dip each segment into jelly, allowing drips to fall back into bowl. Stand each toothpick in a piece of polystyrene or a potato and place in the freezer to set. For younger children, remove toothpicks before serving. Serve frozen.

THE BIG WHEEL

Preparation time: 30 minutes
Cooking time: 20 minutes
Makes 1 cake with 12 sections
Medium

2 cups self-raising flour
30 g butter cut into small pieces
⅓ cup caster sugar
¼ cup sultanas
1 egg, beaten
150 ml milk
½ cup strawberry jam or other jam, warmed
6 musksticks or thick licorice twists

1. Preheat oven to 220°C and grease a 20 cm ring tin with melted butter. Sift flour into a large bowl. Rub in butter lightly, using fingertips.
2. Mix in sugar and sultanas. Combine egg and milk. Make a well in the centre of the flour. Pour in liquid all at once, reserving about a teaspoon for glazing. Mix quickly into a soft dough.
3. Turn onto a floured board (use self-raising flour). Knead lightly. Roll out to form a rectangle about 1.5 cm thick. Spread jam over dough. Roll up as a swiss roll and cut into 2 cm lengths. Place in prepared tin cut side up. Glaze with milk. Bake for 15–20 minutes or until golden brown. Mixture should be just leaving the sides of the tin. Cool on wire rack. Insert musksticks or licorice, as spokes on the wheel. Serve sliced and spread with butter.

Pizza Subs

1. Preheat oven to 180°C and grease two 18 x 28 cm shallow tins. Make cakes according to directions on the packet or following recipe. Pour into prepared tins and bake for 35 minutes or until cooked. Cool.
2. Cut base of boat out of first cake (see diagram 1). Cut second cake into 3 pieces for top decks (see diagram 2).
3. Tint one-third of prepared buttercream frosting bright blue and cover first tier. Cover the remaining three pieces with untinted frosting, then assemble as shown in the photograph.
4. Make portholes from round candies. Cut snakes lengthways into strips and use them to make deck trim. Press marshmallows and candle in place, and finish with a small anchor.

PIZZA SUBS

Preparation time: 20 minutes
Cooking time: 15 minutes
Makes 12
Easy

6 long bread rolls
250 g butter, melted
1 cup tomato purée
1 tablespoon tomato paste
1 teaspoon dried oregano
pinch dried basil
pinch sugar
500 g mozzarella cheese, finely grated
1 green capsicum, halved, seeded and finely sliced
1 red capsicum, halved, seeded and finely sliced
250 g ham, cut into 1 cm pieces
1 x 225 g can pineapple pieces, drained

1. Preheat oven to 200°C. Split rolls in half lengthways. Brush cut surface and outside crust with melted butter.
2. Combine tomato purée, tomato paste, herbs and sugar. Spread over cut surface of bread. Top with grated cheese and arrange capsicum, ham and pineapple over surface.
3. Bake for 10–15 minutes or until cheese melts and browns. Serve hot.

TINY THE TUGBOAT

Preparation time: 50 minutes
Cooking time: 35 minutes
Easy

2 x 350 g packets cake mix or 2 quantities butter cake batter (see page 96)
2 quantities buttercream frosting (see page 96)
blue food colouring
red and white round candies
red snake jujubes
white marshmallows
candle
a small toy anchor

Tiny the Tugboat

31

Pirate Party

T HIS THEME is enormously popular with children aged from five to nine. Providing a costume at the door as each guest arrives takes very little preparation beforehand, and gets the party going quickly. Make each guest an eyepatch from a triangle of black cardboard and a piece of hat elastic. Make gold earrings from brass curtain rings with a loop of cotton attached, to loop over the ears. If you have an old curtain or table cloth that's due for the ragbag, tear it into triangles or strips, and have each child tie the strips around their heads to add to the piratical look. You could make more elaborate additions: cardboard swords for each guest, and cummerbunds.

Age group: five to nine
Venue: house or garden
Number of guests: up to 12

Invitations
Folded card, cut to the shape of a treasure chest and suitably illustrated by the host, could be opened to invite fellow brigands aboard the *Good Ship Tamsin Martin* (use your child's name). If you are providing eye patches and scarves, ask guests to wear jeans. Alternatively, ask them to dress as pirates.

Decorations
Paint parrots, treasure chests, and palm trees on large sheets of card or butcher's paper. Cut these out and pin them up. As a highlight, draw a sailing ship with a Jolly Roger flying from the topmost mast. Hang other flags from the ceiling or from trees. Add cardboard cut-out sharks and a mermaid or two. A washing basket filled with balloons makes a good treasure chest; even the most blood-thirsty pirate enjoys balloons.

If the party is held in the evening, pirates' lamps add to the atmosphere and are easy to make. For each, you need a paper packet, sand, water, a glass jar and a candle. Half-fill the packet with sand. In the sand, stand

a glass jar which is one-quarter full of water. Stand the candle in the water. When the candle is lit, the paper packet will glow with a soft light. (Should the lamp be knocked over accidentally, the sand and water will dowse the flame quickly.)

Food
Calculated to make the hungriest pirate's mouth water — Wooden Legs, Pirate Ships, Banana Planks, Cannon Balls, Deadly Decks and Poison Potion.

Cake: Long John Silver's Treasure Chest.

Games
Have a hat-making session early in the party, so that each child makes a

triangular pirate's hat for her- or himself. Make these from sheets of newspaper, or from butcher's paper cut to the same size as newspaper.

Use tapes of traditional sea shanties for musical accompaniment to play *Musical hats*, *Musical sets*, or *Jump the shark* (otherwise known as *Jump the broom*). Play *Pass the oranges*; have a *Balloon fight*, or a *Knee balloon race*. Arrange a treasure hunt and a three-legged race. Have a *Back-to-back race*.

Make steps out of chairs, and have the steps lead up to a tabletop covered with brown paper. Place a pile of soft cushions, or a mattress, on the floor at the far side of the table. As a forfeit, or for children who go out during other games, let them walk the plank by climbing onto the table and jumping off into the cushions.

Play *The Captain's coming*. Nominate one side of the room to be port, and another to be starboard. Also nominate places or pieces of furniture to be a rowboat, the anchor, the main mast, the cannon etc. All children group in the centre of the

Clockwise from left: Wooden Legs, Banana Planks, Deadly Decks, Poison Potion, Cannon Balls and Pirate Ships.

Wooden Legs

30 minutes or until chicken is cooked through, turning and basting chicken every 10 minutes. Chicken is cooked when juices run clear if pierced through the thickest section of the leg.

3. Tie 2 pretzels to the base of each leg with a long chive, to represent Long John Silver's crutch. Serve hot or cold.

POISON POTION

Preparation time: 30 minutes plus overnight standing time
Cooking time: 5 minutes
Makes 10 cups
Easy

6¼ cups boiling water
5 cups sugar
2 lemons, juiced and rind finely grated
2 large oranges, juiced and rind finely grated
30 g citric acid
15 g tartaric acid
15 g Epsom salts

1. Pour boiling water over sugar in a pan, then stir over gentle heat until sugar dissolves. Stir in grated rind and strained juice.
2. Stir in remaining ingredients. Cover with a cloth and leave overnight. Pour into sterilised bottles and store in the refrigerator. When ready to serve, dilute with iced water.

Poison Potion

room. Call out the key phrase and add a command, for example 'The Captain's coming — run to starboard!' or, 'The Captain's coming — scrub the decks!' The last person to reach starboard or to start scrubbing the decks is out. Other commands could be to salute, to run to the rowboat, to lift the anchor and so on.

Play *Shipwrecked*, a type of tag. Scatter cushions on the floor. Only the catcher (or Shark) may touch the floor. The other children must flee the Shark, moving only from cushion to cushion. Anyone landing in the sea (i.e. on the floor) is shipwrecked, and may be caught by the Shark.

Prizes and Party Favours
Pieces of eight (chocolate coins covered in gold foil). Popcorn necklaces. Stickers featuring parrots, rainbows or boats. Bars of silver (muesli or chocolate bars wrapped in silver foil).

WOODEN LEGS

Preparation time: 10 minutes
Cooking time: 40 minutes
Serves 10
Easy

10 chicken drumsticks

BASTE
4 tablespoons dark soy sauce
1 tablespoon honey
1 clove garlic, crushed
1 tablespoon tomato sauce
20 pretzels
10 long chives, soaked for 5 minutes in hot water

1. Preheat oven to 200°C. Place drumsticks on a wire rack in a baking dish containing a little water. Roast in the oven for 10 minutes.
2. To prepare baste: combine all remaining ingredients except pretzels and chives and brush the baste over chicken drumsticks. Roast a further

34

CANNON BALLS

Preparation time: 25 minutes
Cooking time: 5 minutes
Serves 8
Easy

500g sausage meat
½ cup crushed, plain savoury biscuits
¼ cup grated tasty cheese
1 egg, lightly beaten
¼ cup evaporated milk
1 tablespoon fruit chutney
pinch pepper
oil for shallow frying

1. In a bowl combine all ingredients except oil. Take small portions and form into 2cm balls. Shallow-fry in oil until browned and cooked through. Serve hot on wooden toothpicks.

NOTE
These can be made one or two days ahead and reheated.

DEADLY DECKS

Preparation time: 20 minutes
Cooking time: 25 minutes
Makes 18
Medium

500 g sausage meat
2 tablespoons plain flour
2 tablespoons tomato sauce
1 small onion, grated
1 tablespoon chopped fresh parsley
1 x 350 g packet prepared puff pastry
beaten egg
tomato sauce for serving

1. Preheat oven to 200°C. In a pan combine sausage meat, flour, sauce, onion and parsley. Stir over low heat for 2–3 minutes, then simmer for another 10 minutes. Turn out onto a plate to cool.
2. Roll out pastry thinly. Cut into strips 8–10 cm wide. Spoon meat mixture down the centre of each strip, leaving a margin on pastry edges to fold over. Brush edges with milk or water and fold over to seal.
3. Glaze pastry with a little beaten egg. Cut into 10 cm lengths. Arrange, seam side down, on prepared trays and bake for 15 minutes, or until pastry is brown and crisp. Serve hot with tomato sauce.

Cannon Balls

Deadly Decks

Pirate Ships

PIRATE SHIPS

Preparation time: 30 minutes
Cooking time: 15 minutes
Makes 24
Medium

1¾ cups plain flour
90 g butter
1 tablespoon iced water
2 egg yolks
¼ cup barbecue sauce
1 stick cabanossi or other sausage, cut into 1 cm slices
60 g mozzarella cheese, grated
1 onion, finely chopped
4 gherkins, thinly sliced

1. Preheat oven to 200°C.
2. Sift flour into a bowl. Rub in butter until mixture resembles coarse breadcrumbs. Mix together iced water and egg yolks. Add to mixture and work through with a flat-bladed knife.
3. Mould into a ball and knead lightly. Roll out two-thirds of pastry thinly on a floured board. Cut out pastry shapes to fit boat-shaped or tartlet tins, line each hollow or tin with pastry and prick pastry with a fork. Bake for 10 minutes or until pastry is golden.

Banana Planks

BANANA PLANKS

Preparation time: 10 minutes
Cooking time: nil
Serves 10
Easy

5 ripe bananas, peeled and quartered lengthways
5 passionfruit, pulped
5 kiwi fruit, peeled and chopped
¼ small pineapple, peeled, cored and roughly chopped
1 litre vanilla ice-cream
1 cup chocolate flavoured syrup
10 ice-cream wafers

1. Arrange two banana quarters in each individual sundae dish. Spoon over passionfruit pulp, kiwi fruit and pineapple chunks.
2. Arrange 2 small scoops of ice-cream over fruit in each dish. Drizzle over a little chocolate sauce and garnish with an ice-cream wafer.

4. Roll out remaining pastry thinly and cut into triangles to form sail shapes. Thread a toothpick through centre of each pastry sail. Lay them flat on a lightly greased oven tray and bake for 5–7 minutes or until golden.

5. Spoon barbecue sauce into the base of each pastry case. Top with gherkin, onion and grated cheese. Place a slice of cabanossi in the centre of each boat and return to the oven for 5 minutes or until cheese melts and browns lightly. Remove from oven and while still hot, insert pastry sail. Serve immediately.

LONG JOHN SILVER'S TREASURE CHEST

Preparation time: 1 hour
Cooking time: 45 minutes
Medium

2 x 350 g packets cake mix or
   2 quantities butter cake batter
   (see page 96)
1 quantity butter icing (see page 96)
2 tablespoons coffee essence
chocolate sprinkles
5 toothpicks
200 g marzipan
extra coffee essence
licorice
chocolate gold coins
costume jewellery

1. Preheat oven to 180°C and grease two 20 x 8 cm loaf tins. Make the cakes according to directions on packet or following recipe. Turn mixture into prepared tins and bake for 40–45 minutes. Cool.

2. Add coffee essence to the butter icing and ice the top and sides of one of the cakes to form the chest, and the top and sides of the other cake to form the lid. Reserve enough icing for final decoration.

3. Place one cake on a cake board, and sprinkle the top with chocolate sprinkles. This forms the base of the chest. Secure five toothpicks along the back edge of the bottom cake, against which to rest the lid (see diagram 1).

4. Knead the marzipan until pliable. Add enough coffee essence to make marzipan a dark brown and continue

Long John Silver's Treasure Chest

to knead to distribute the colour evenly. Roll out and cut two 20 x 3 cm strips. Lay these over the two ends of the lid to look like straps. Using the remaining marzipan, form a handle and a keyhole for the chest. Cut licorice into a keyhole shape and place on the marzipan before securing to the cake.

5. To the remaining butter icing, add extra coffee essence to make the icing a darker brown. Fill a piping bag, and using a plain nozzle pipe around the edges and bottom of the chest, and pipe initials on the lid.

6. Fill the chest with chocolate gold coins and costume jewellery. Secure handle to chest. Place the lid on the cake, resting it against the toothpicks at the rear edge (see diagram 2).

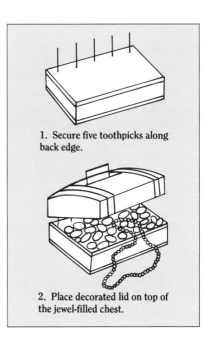

1. Secure five toothpicks along back edge.

2. Place decorated lid on top of the jewel-filled chest.

Kite Party

This one is great for high flyers. It's a party that can be enjoyed by most ages. If it is held for younger children, parents will probably get involved too.

Plan to hold the kite-flying time of the party in the nearest open space — the park or a football field. Have the business part of it (eating and kite-making) at home.

Before the party, check that kites will be clear of power lines in the kite-flying area, and check the safest route for walking to it. On the way there and back, younger children could make a chain by holding onto a length of rope in pairs. All children should be seen safely across busy roads or intersections.

Age group: five to eleven
Venue: home and an open space, such as the park
Number of guests: up to 10

Invitations

Make cardboard kites small enough to fit into envelopes for posting. Write party details on the kite face. Add a tail made from thread and twists of coloured tissue paper. If the weather is likely to be cool, remind guests to bring jackets to wear outside.

Clockwise from top left: Swirls and Twists, Kite Cake, Smooth Landings, Clouds, Kite Tails, High Flying Kites, Reels of String, and Air Pockets.

Decorations

Before the party, make a selection of kites in different colours, shapes and sizes, with lots of help from the host and possibly the host's friends too. Paper kites are inexpensive and quick to make. If you enjoy sewing, try making fabric kites from brightly coloured polyester, using wire and bamboo for framing. Use these to decorate the party area. You can give these away at the end of the party as prizes, or keep some aside for Christmas or birthday gifts.

From kite to kite, fly coloured paper streamers, and hang bunches of balloons where the breeze will catch them so that they bob and rustle. A small electric fan, placed safely on a shelf, will keep streamers and balloons moving too. A rainbow, painted on butcher's paper, makes an effective backdrop.

Straw baskets containing the makings for kites — scissors, glue, rolls of tissue and coloured paper, strips of light bamboo cut to size, adhesive tape and string — will be needed later in the party and will help set the scene from the start.

Food

The menu offers High Flying Kites, Kite Tails, Swirls and Twists, Reels of String, Smooth Landings, Clouds and Air Pockets.

Cake: make a Kite cake.

Games

Arrange a *String hunt* for guests as they arrive. Collect all the string afterwards and re-use it for flying kites later.

Clear a good floor area, and have a kite-making session as soon as all the guests have assembled. Younger children may need a little help; for this age group, it is easiest to have the kite-paper cut to size, and twists of tail tissue prepared beforehand. Older children will be much more adventurous. The kites you made for party decorations will be a source of inspiration. Some children might want to make two or three different kites.

If the children are old enough, have a competition to see who can invent the most novel kite, or whose kite is the most decorative.

While the glue is drying, have a game of *Balloon dress-ups*, or play *Find the bell-ringer*.

Before going out kite-flying, serve the party food, keeping the cake aside for your return.

Take some of the kites you made as decorations to the park too, in case a couple of the kites made by guests prove to be aerodynamically disastrous.

At the park, have kite-flying competitions; whose kite can fly highest, or longest? Have a kite race. Try sending messages up the kite strings.

On your return home, serve the cake and nibbles.

Prizes and Party Favours

The kites you made, balloons, small wind-chimes, whistles, blow-out streamers.

Reels of String

REELS OF STRING

Preparation time: 30 minutes
Cooking time: 15 minutes
Makes about 40
Easy

750 g cocktail frankfurters
1 sheet frozen puff pastry, thawed
milk
tomato sauce for serving

1. Preheat oven to 180°C. Cut between frankfurters to separate and set aside. Brush pastry with a little milk. Cut into strips about 5 mm x 10 cm.
2. Wrap pastry around each frankfurter and secure with a toothpick at each end.
3. Place on an ungreased baking tray. Bake for 10–15 minutes or until pastry is golden. Serve with tomato sauce.

HINT
These can be prepared in advance, and frozen in their uncooked state.

Just before the party, remove them from the freezer and bake them.

It is best to remove toothpicks first if serving them to very young children.

SWIRLS AND TWISTS

Preparation time: 20 minutes
Cooking time: 15 minutes
Makes 32
Easy

2 sheets frozen puff pastry, thawed
¼ cup tomato sauce
1 cup shredded tasty cheese
milk

1. Preheat oven to 200°C. Brush one sheet of pastry with tomato sauce. Sprinkle with cheese. Place remaining sheet of pastry on top. Roll lightly with a rolling pin to seal sheets together. Brush with milk.
2. Cut pastry into 16 strips. Cut each strip in half. Twist each piece several times. Place on an ungreased baking tray and bake for 10–15 minutes or until golden brown.

Swirls and Twists

Clouds

CLOUDS

Preparation time: 20 minutes
Cooking time: 2 minutes
Makes about 24
Easy

250 g vegetable fat
3 cups Rice Crispies
1 cup icing sugar, sifted
1 cup desiccated coconut
1 cup dried milk powder
assorted sweets for decoration

1. Soften vegetable fat over low heat until just melted. Combine remaining ingredients and pour over vegetable fat. Mix well together.
2. Spoon into small paper cake cases. Decorate as desired, or leave plain. Chill until set. Keep refrigerated until required.

HINT
For a delicious variation, add chopped dried fruit or glacé cherries, sultanas or raisins to the Clouds before chilling.

41

Smooth Landings

High Flying Kites

HIGH FLYING KITES

Preparation time: 1 hour plus 20
   minutes chilling time
Cooking time: 10 minutes per batch
Makes about 30
Easy

125 g butter
½ cup sugar
1 egg
½ teaspoon cinnamon
1½ cups plain flour
2 tablespoons cornflour
100 g marshmallows
100 g chocolate
2 x 10 cm lengths licorice
1 cup glacé icing to decorate
food colouring

1. Preheat oven to 220°C and grease
an oven tray. Cream butter and sugar
together until pale, light and fluffy.
Beat in egg until mixture is smooth
and creamy. Sift together cinnamon,
plain flour and cornflour. Add to
butter mixture, and mix well with a

flat-bladed knife. Form mixture into a
ball. Chill covered in the refrigerator
for 20 minutes.
2. Roll out dough on a lightly floured
board to 5 mm thick. Cut dough into
diamond shapes of equal size.
Arrange on prepared tray and bake
for 8–10 minutes or until biscuits are
a pale golden brown. Remove from
oven and cool on tray.
3. Place marshmallows and chocolate
in a heatproof bowl. Place over
simmering water and stir over a low
heat until melted.
Cut licorice into 10 cm lengths.
Spread the underside of half the
biscuits with a little chocolate mixture
and place a piece of licorice on a
pointed edge of the biscuit to
represent the tail of the kite.
4. Decorate the top of the remaining
biscuits with glacé icing tinted several
colours. Place in the oven (180°C) for
5 minutes to set. Remove from oven
and cool slightly prior to joining
biscuit halves.

SMOOTH LANDINGS

Preparation time: 5 minutes
Cooking time: nil
Serves 8
Easy

4 small ripe bananas
2 cups milk
2½ cups crushed ice
½ cup passionfruit pulp

1. Slice banana and place in a
blender bowl. Add milk and ice, and
blend for 1 minute.
2. Add passionfruit pulp and blend
for 15 seconds. Pour into tumblers
and serve immediately.

Kite Tails

42

AIR POCKETS

Preparation time: 5 minutes
Cooking time: 5 minutes
Makes 8 cups
Easy

⅓ cup oil
½ cup uncooked popcorn
1 clove garlic, crushed
2 tablespoons grated romano or
  parmesan cheese
½ teaspoon onion salt
¼ teaspoon dried oregano
¼ teaspoon dried basil

1. Heat oil in a large pan. Add all the popcorn. Cover and cook, shaking pan, until popcorn stops popping.
2. Combine all remaining ingredients. Toss popcorn in the mixture. Serve freshly made in individual bags or cups.

Air Pockets

KITE TAILS

Preparation time: 20 minutes
Cooking time: 15 minutes
Makes 50
Easy

1 x 375 g packet prunes
125g mozzarella, cut into 1 cm pieces
13 rashers rindless bacon, cut into
  5 cm lengths
toothpicks (omit for younger children)

1. Remove stones from prunes. Insert a piece of cheese in the centre of each prune. Wrap in a piece of bacon. Secure with toothpicks.
2. Refrigerate until required. Bake at 180°C for 10–15 minutes or until bacon is crisp and cheese melts.

Kite Cake

KITE CAKE

Preparation time: 45 minutes
Cooking time: 40 minutes
Easy

1 x 350 g packet cake mix or
  1 quantity butter cake batter
  (see page 96)
2 quantities buttercream frosting
  (see page 96)
food colouring
licorice straps
ribbon

1. Preheat oven to 180°C and grease and line an 18 x 28 cm shallow tin. Make the cake according to directions on the packet or following recipe. Pour mixture into prepared tin and spread evenly. Bake for 30–40 minutes or until cooked. Stand 5 minutes before removing from tin. Cool.
2. Divide frosting into four equal portions. Colour each portion differently.
3. Cut cake to form a diamond-shaped kite as shown in diagram. Slit cake horizontally in half. Spread the bottom half of the cake with a quarter of the frosting using alternating colours. Top with second half of cake. Cut 2 x 20 cm x 1 cm strips of licorice. Push into frosting in the centre of cake, inserting it at pointed edge of the diamond.
4. Place on a large board. Cover sides and top of cake with frosting, alternating colours. Place a strip of licorice lengthways down the centre of the cake and another strip widthways across the centre. Trim licorice so it extends 1 cm beyond edge of cake.
5. Tie bows from ribbons and attach to the kite tail and corners of the kite cake.

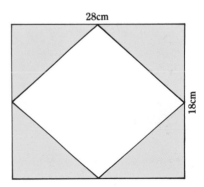

43

Spooky Party

THIS IS a very easy and popular party idea and costumes are no problem. Even the shyest child will enjoy dressing up for this occasion. Inexpensive all-black costumes can be created for magicians, witches, black cats, bats, spiders, or skeletons with the bones painted in white. Easy all-white outfits made with sheets might be for ghosts and mummies. More elaborate costumes could be created for vampires, Frankensteins and devils. Hideous masks and other delightful accessories can be bought from newsagents and party speciality shops, or made by guests.

This theme can be adapted: have a Monster Party, Mask Party or Halloween Party instead, on the same lines. For Halloween, make grinning lamps out of hollowed-out pumpkins with candles inside them.

Age group: six to ten
Venue: house, garden or garage
Number of guests: up to 12

Invitations
Draw a skeleton on black card, or cut out a haunted house, owl or ghost shape. Include a reminder to wear something spooky.

Decorations
Drape the table in dark grey. Provide grey, silver or black paper plates and cups. Use spray-on cobwebbing where it won't affect the food. Encourage a spooky atmosphere with green or dim lighting. Candles and sparklers add a good effect, but remember to put them safely out of harm's way. Suspend cut-outs of spiders, owls, witches and lanterns from the ceiling. Use black balloons. Make a few ghosts from white sheets draped on coathangers: add black felt eyes, and hang them in dark corners.

If you want to use dry ice to create smoky effects, remember that dry ice **must** be kept safely out of reach at all times, as it causes very severe burning and skin damage. Under no circumstances should dry ice be touched with bare hands.

Food
Bleeding Fingers; Broomsticks; Bites that go Crunch in the Night; Mouse Traps; Skeleton Ribs; Squelch and Crunch; Frozen Black and Goo; Ghostmallows; Vampire Blood.

Cake: a Halloween cake. Use 'magic' candles that die out for a few seconds then re-light themselves again.

Games
Play *Murder in the dark*, *Wrap the mummy*, *Blind man's bluff*, *Sardines*, *Musical torch*, *Hangman*, *Guess in the dark*, and *Taste and guess*.

Prizes and Party Favours
Inexpensive tricks from magic shops such as fake blood and dracula teeth. Rats and snakes (the jujube variety, sold in most sweet shops at a low cost).

44

MOUSE TRAPS

Preparation time: 15 minutes
Cooking time: 5 minutes
Serves 10
Easy

10 slices bread
butter for spreading
Vegemite or Marmite
250 g cheese, finely grated
5 tablespoons tomato sauce

1. Preheat grill on high. Toast bread on both sides. Spread thinly with

butter and Vegemite or Marmite. Sprinkle with grated cheese. Spoon 2 teaspoons of tomato sauce on top of cheese.

2. Place under hot grill and cook until cheese melts and tomato sauce spreads. Serve immediately.

Clockwise from left: Frozen Black and Goo, Broomsticks, Skeleton Ribs, Vampire Blood, Mouse Traps, Bleeding Fingers, Squelch and Crunch. Centre: Bites that go Crunch in the Night and Ghostmallows.

Ghostmallows

Broomsticks

GHOSTMALLOWS

Preparation time: 25 minutes
Cooking time: 10 minutes
Makes about 25
Easy

2 cups white sugar
6 teaspoons liquid glucose
6 teaspoons gelatine
1½ cups water
10 cups cornflour (only used for moulding, so the cornflour can be re-used)
peppermint essence, optional
licorice shapes for decoration

1. Place sugar, glucose, gelatine and water in a pan and bring to the boil. Boil 2 minutes, remove from the heat and cool.
2. Place cornflour in a deep baking dish and pack in very firmly. Make indentations in the cornflour using a single egg (a hard-boiled one is easier to use since there is less chance of breaking). Alternatively, use a small bowl to form indentations.

3. Add essence to sugar syrup. Beat with an electric mixer for 10 minutes or until mixture is thick, white and frothy. Spoon mixture into recesses in cornflour. Allow to set. Lift out of cornflour and attach small pieces of licorice to represent eyes. This is best done with a little icing if you have any left over, otherwise a dab of jam or unset marshmallow mixture will do the trick.

BROOMSTICKS

Preparation time: 20 minutes
Cooking time: 5 minutes
Makes 24
Easy

6 frankfurters
24 pretzels
1 cup grated cheese
¼ cup tomato sauce

1. Place frankfurters in a pan of cold water. Bring just to boiling point and drain immediately. Cut each frankfurter into four pieces. Insert a pretzel into each frankfurter and set aside.
2. Combine cheese and tomato sauce in a pan. Melt over very low heat.
3. To serve: dip frankfurter 'brooms' into melted cheese mixture.

BITES THAT GO CRUNCH IN THE NIGHT

Preparation time: 50 minutes
Cooking time: 20 minutes
Serves 10
Medium

250 g pumpkin, peeled and seeds removed
1 sweet potato, peeled
2 carrots, peeled
2 potatoes, peeled
oil for frying
garlic powder

1. Using a potato peeler or a sharp paring knife, peel off paper-thin slices of vegetables. Place vegetables on a large clean tea-towel or absorbent paper and pat gently to dry.
2. Heat oil in a deep-fryer until oil sizzles when tested with a piece of vegetable. Drop in a few pieces of vegetable at a time and fry until crisp and golden. Lift out of oil and drain on absorbent paper. Repeat with remaining vegetable slices. While still

hot, sprinkle liberally with garlic powder. Serve warm or store in an airtight container until required.

VARIATIONS
These are scrumptious when sprinkled with cinnamon sugar or dusted with a light sprinkling of icing sugar, instead of garlic powder.

SKELETON RIBS

Preparation time: 15 minutes plus overnight marinating time
Cooking time: 1 hour
Serves 6
Easy

2 racks beef ribs

MARINADE
⅔ cup soy sauce
juice of 2 lemons
2 teaspoons freshly grated ginger
¼ cup grainy mustard
½ cup brown sugar
6 shallots, chopped
1 cup tomato purée
pinch pepper

1. Mix together all ingredients for marinade and pour over ribs. Cover and marinate overnight in the refrigerator.
2. To cook ribs: place on a rack in a roasting pan. Brush or spoon marinade over ribs. Barbecue or bake at 200°C for 45 minutes–1 hour, basting frequently. Serve hot.

Skeleton Ribs

Bleeding Fingers

BLEEDING FINGERS

Preparation time: 20 minutes
Cooking time: 1 hour
Makes 20
Medium

2 egg whites
½ cup white sugar
1 cup desiccated coconut
½ cup raspberry or strawberry jam

1. Preheat oven to 150°C. Line a baking tray with baking paper or grease and dust liberally with cornflour.
2. Beat egg whites until stiff peaks form. Beat in sugar, one tablespoon at a time, and continue beating until mixture is thick and glossy. Fold through coconut. Fit a piping bag with a plain 2 cm tube and fill it with the meringue mixture. Pipe 8 cm lengths onto prepared tray.
3. Bake in oven for 5 minutes, reduce heat to 130°C and cook for a further 45–50 minutes until fingers are dry and crispy. Turn off oven and leave meringues to cool.
4. In a pan heat jam over low heat

until thin and runny. Remove meringues from tray in oven and dip into jam, allowing excess to drip away. Place on a rack to cool.

VAMPIRE BLOOD

Preparation time: 10 minutes
Cooking time: 10 minutes
Makes 2 litres
Easy

1.25 litres water
1.5 kg sugar
30 g citric acid
2 teaspoons raspberry essence
few drops red food colouring (optional)

1. Heat water and sugar in a pan, to boiling point, stirring until sugar is dissolved. Boil for 5 minutes.
2. Pour into a large jug, add citric acid and stir until dissolved. Set aside until cold. Stir in raspberry essence and a little food colouring if you wish. Pour into sterilised bottles. Serve 1 tablespoon of cordial diluted with iced water to taste.

Frozen Black and Goo

SQUELCH AND CRUNCH

Preparation time: 30 minutes
Cooking time: 40 minutes
Makes 18–20
Medium

BISCUIT BASE
1 cup brown sugar, firmly packed
1 egg
2 cups self-raising flour
2 tablespoons cocoa
125 g butter
2 tablespoons milk

MARSHMALLOW TOPPING
½ cup sugar
2 teaspoons gelatine
½ cup water
1 teaspoon vanilla essence
green food colouring (optional)
silver cachous

1. Preheat oven to 180°C. Lightly
grease a flat oven tray. Mix together
sugar, egg and half the flour and
cocoa, sifted together. Melt butter
over gentle heat. Stir in milk and pour
into the dry ingredients.
2. Beat well for 2–3 minutes. Add the
rest of the sifted dry ingredients and
mix well. Take small portions, roll
into balls and arrange on prepared
trays. Press down with a fork and
bake for about 15 minutes or until
lightly browned. Cool.
3. To prepare topping: combine
sugar, gelatine and water in a small
pan. Stir over low heat until boiling.
Simmer, without stirring, for 3–4
minutes, then cool.

Squelch and Crunch

FROZEN BLACK AND GOO

Preparation time: 30 minutes plus
    freezing time
Cooking time: nil
Serves 10
Easy

1 litre vanilla ice-cream
50 g chocolate chips or pieces
3 tablespoons chocolate-flavoured
    syrup
1 x 250 g punnet strawberries, hulled
    and chopped
3 tablespoons strawberry-flavoured
    syrup
100 g pink and white marshmallows
8 small wooden ice-cream sticks

1. Soften ice-cream at room
temperature until soft but still firm.
Divide ice-cream into thirds. Into the
first third mix chocolate chips and
chocolate syrup. Spoon evenly into
eight waxed paper cups. Place in
freezer.
2. Into the second third add
strawberries and strawberry syrup.
Spoon evenly on top of the chocolate
mixture. Return cups to freezer.
3. Into the remaining ice-cream mix
the marshmallows. Spoon on top of
the strawberry and chocolate mixture
in cups. Insert an ice-cream stick and
freeze for a minimum of three hours
to set firm. Peel waxed cups away
from ice-cream and replace in freezer
to harden.

HINT
It is important to use a good quality
ice-cream for this recipe, since the
lesser quality ice-creams tend to
become runny very quickly after
softening.

4. Stir in vanilla essence and colouring. Beat with an electric beater until thick and fluffy. Spoon on top of biscuits and decorate with silver cachous.

NOTE
Do not top the biscuits with marshmallow until the day they are to be eaten, because they will soften.

HALLOWEEN CAKE

Preparation time: 1½ hours
Cooking time: 45 minutes
Medium

2 x 350 g packets cake mix or
    2 quantities butter cake batter
    (see page 96)
jam
1 quantity butter icing (see page 96)
¼ teaspoon grated orange rind
orange food colouring
almond paste
yellow food colouring
licorice

1. Preheat oven to 180°C. Grease 2 metal jelly moulds. These must be 3-cup capacity and should be vertically ribbed. Make the cake according to directions on the packet or following recipe. Turn into prepared moulds and bake for 40–45 minutes or until cooked. Cool.
2. Level the top of each cake and spread the cut surface with jam. Sandwich the two cakes together. Place on a cake rack.
3. To prepare topping: add orange rind and orange food colouring to butter icing. Cover the cake completely (see diagram 1). Knead the almond paste until soft, and work in a little yellow food colouring. Mould a top and stem for the pumpkin. Place these on the cake. Cut licorice shapes for a face and fasten them to the cake, using some of the icing (see diagrams).

NOTE
If no vertically ribbed jelly moulds are available, bake two cakes in plain 3-cup capacity pudding basins, and cut vertical serrations in them to provide a pumpkin effect.

Halloween Cake

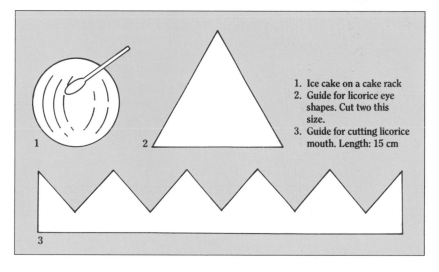

1. Ice cake on a cake rack
2. Guide for licorice eye shapes. Cut two this size.
3. Guide for cutting licorice mouth. Length: 15 cm

Space Party

THIS IS ALWAYS a very popular party theme for young children. Many children have remnants from past presents or events to create a costume. Costumes can also be made from boxes, paper, silver foil or packing oddments like polystyrene chips. Children could dress as space creatures, Martians, astronauts or spacecraft. Florist's wire makes good antennae and a small box, covered in foil, makes a convincing hand-held transmitter.

Age group: six to ten
Venue: garage or basement
Number of guests: up to 12

Invitations
A flying saucer made from two paper plates, joined by a single staple at the side. Invite your guests to board the Intergalactic Starship for a trip to the Outer Nebulae.

Decorations
Cover the party table with butcher's paper, then place a layer of dark blue cellophane over that. The effect is a deep translucent blue. Scatter silver foil stars or comet's tail streamers across the table top. Float silver or black balloons from the ceiling. Make paper stars, suns, and planets, paint or colour them and add sprinklings of glitter; hang these from light fittings, curtain tracks and the tops of doors. Cover the windows with blue or green cellophane to filter the daylight, or put cellophane covers over the light fittings for unearthly light effects. (Remember to keep the cellophane a safe distance from the bulb itself.) Cut comets and asteroids from silver foil, to pin up on the walls.

Food
Star Dust, Outer Space Shapes, Galactic Discs, Moon Rocks, Meteors, Space Wheels, Foaming Craters, Space Spuds, Moon Moguls, Moon Buggy Wheels.

Cake: the Outer Space Cake will fill inner spaces.

Games
Make a cassette of space music before the party, and use this for music games. Play *Guess in the dark*, *Magpies*, the *Flour game*, *Hedgehogs*, *Mystery matchboxes*. Or play a variation of *What's the Time, Mr Wolf?* with a change of title — *What's the time, Darth Vader?*

I Went to Mars is a popular and challenging game. The first child announces: 'I went to Mars, and I took a . . .' and names any object — 'I went to Mars, and I took a pencil.' The next one has to repeat the object and add another. 'I went to Mars and I took a pencil and an apple.' The third will add a new object, always keeping the list in order: 'I went to Mars, and I took a pencil, an apple and my dog.' Turns continue around the circle for as long as possible.

Prizes and Party Favours
Small magic tricks, packets of glittery stars (available from most stationers), bubble pipes, novelty straws, and star dust (sherbet).

FOAMING CRATERS

Preparation time: 10 minutes
Cooking time: nil
Serves 8
Easy

1 x 250 g punnet strawberries, washed
   and hulled
8 large scoops vanilla ice-cream
2 x 750 ml bottles lemonade

Foaming Craters

1. Purée strawberries until smooth.
Divide purée evenly between eight tall
tumblers.
2. Place a scoop of ice-cream in each
glass and top with lemonade, being
careful mixture does not overflow.
Serve immediately.

*Clockwise from top left: Space Wheels,
Moon Buggy Wheels, Foaming Craters,
Moon Moguls, Star Dust, Galactic Discs,
Meteors, Space Spuds, Outer Space Shapes
and Moon Rocks.*

a further 20 minutes or until 'wheels' are golden and crispy to touch. Remove from oven and cool on a wire rack.

5. Whip cream with sugar and vanilla until thick. Crumble Flake bar and chop Violet Crumble or honeycomb bars into spiky-shaped chunks.

6. To assemble: halve wheels horizontally. Scrape out any moist mixture in the centre. Spoon or pipe whipped cream into the cavity, and top with spikes of chocolate and honeycomb bars.

MOON ROCKS

Preparation time: 15 minutes
Cooking time: 30 minutes
Makes 24
Medium

2 cups white crystal sugar
300 ml water
4 tablespoons malt vinegar
½ teaspoon bicarbonate of soda

1. Line 2 deep muffin trays with 24 paper cake cases. Place sugar, water and vinegar in a large pan, bring slowly to the boil and stir until sugar dissolves. Wash any sugar crystals down the sides of the pan with a wet brush before mixture boils.

2. Boil rapidly without stirring until

Space Wheels

SPACE WHEELS

Preparation time: 45 minutes
Cooking time: 40 minutes
Makes 24
Medium

1 cup water
125 g butter, cut into small pieces
1 cup plain flour, sifted
3 eggs, beaten
300 ml thickened cream
1 tablespoon sugar
1 teaspoon vanilla essence
1 x 30 g bar Flake or chocolate bar
2 x 45 g bars Violet Crumble or
    chocolate-coated honeycomb

1. Preheat oven to 190°C. Lightly grease a baking tray and mark 10 cm circles on the tray.

2. Place water and butter in a pan and bring to the boil. Add flour all at once and immediately beat until smooth with no lumps remaining. Return to heat and cook over low heat for 2–3 minutes or until mixture leaves the sides of the pan. Remove from heat and cool slightly.

3. Beat in egg a little at a time, beating well between additions. When all the egg has been added, the mixture should be glossy and thick enough to have a wooden spoon stand up in it.

4. Fit a piping bag with a plain 2 cm tube and fill it with mixture. Pipe around edge of marked rounds to give doughnut shapes. Bake for 20 minutes or until 'wheels' puff. Reduce heat to 160°C and continue cooking

Moon Rocks

mixture starts to change colour and turns golden. Remove from heat immediately and stand 2 minutes.

3. Add bicarbonate of soda and stir through toffee mixture. The mixture will froth up immediately so it is important to use a pan large enough to allow for the expansion. Pour frothing mixture into prepared trays and stand at room temperature until set and crisp.

METEORS

Preparation time: 40 minutes
Cooking time: 10 minutes
Makes about 40
Medium

1 cup water
125 g butter, cut into small pieces
1 cup plain flour, sifted
3 eggs, lightly beaten
2 tablespoons sugar
½ teaspoon cinnamon
oil for deep-frying

COATING MIXTURE
1 cup caster sugar
1 teaspoon cinnamon
1 teaspoon nutmeg

1. Place water and butter in a pan and bring to the boil. Add the flour all at once and beat immediately until smooth with no lumps remaining. Return to heat and stir over low heat for 2–3 minutes or until the mixture leaves the sides of the pan. Cool slightly.

2. Beat in egg, a little at a time, until mixture becomes smooth and glossy. Combine sugar and ½ teaspoon cinnamon, and stir this evenly through the mixture.

3. Heat oil in a deep-fryer. The oil will be hot enough when a 2 cm cube of bread becomes golden brown in 20 seconds when dropped into it. Spoon teaspoonfuls of the mixture into hot oil. Fry for 1–2 minutes or until golden brown, puffed and cooked through. Drain well on absorbent paper.

4. Prepare coating mixture by combining ingredients in a bowl. Toss hot puffs in coating and serve immediately while still warm.

Outer Space Shapes

OUTER SPACE SHAPES

Preparation time: 1 hour plus 20
  minutes chilling time
Cooking time: 10 minutes per batch
Makes about 30
Easy

125 g butter
½ cup sugar
1 egg
½ teaspoon cinnamon
1½ cups plain flour
2 tablespoons cornflour
100 g marshmallows
100 g chocolate
2 x 10 cm lengths licorice
1 cup glacé icing to decorate
food colouring

1. Preheat oven to 220°C and grease an oven tray. Cream butter and sugar together until pale, light and fluffy. Beat in egg until mixture is smooth and creamy. Sift together cinnamon,

plain flour and cornflour. Add to butter mixture, and mix well with a flat-bladed knife. Form mixture into a ball. Chill covered in the refrigerator for 20 minutes.

2. Roll out dough on a lightly floured board to 5 mm thick. Cut dough into star and moon shapes of similar size. Arrange on prepared tray and bake for 8–10 minutes or until biscuits are a pale golden brown. Remove from oven and cool on tray.

3. Place marshmallows and chocolate in a heatproof bowl. Place over simmering water and stir over a low heat until melted. Spread the underside of half the biscuits with a little chocolate mixture.

4. Decorate the top of the remaining biscuits with glacé icing, tinted several colours. Place in oven at 180°C for 5 minutes to set. Remove from oven and cool slightly prior to joining identical biscuit halves.

Star Dust

cook 1 minute. Remove from heat. Gradually blend in milk a little at a time, beating until smooth. Stir over medium heat until boiling; boil for 3 minutes. Remove from heat.
3. Stir in mayonnaise, half the cheese, then corn and ham. Spoon mixture into vol-au-vent cases and sprinkle with remaining cheese. Heat in oven for 10 minutes until cheese is melted and the filling is hot.

GALACTIC DISCS

Preparation time: 10 minutes
Cooking time: 8 minutes
Makes 12
Easy

12 gingernut biscuits
12 white marshmallows
24 licorice straws
12 Smarties

1. Preheat oven to 150°C. Line a muffin tray with 12 paper cake cases, and place a gingernut biscuit in each case. Top with a marshmallow. Heat in the oven for 5 minutes, or until biscuit softens and takes on the shape of the container and marshmallow softens slightly.
2. Remove from the oven and immediately insert 2 licorice sticks into each marshmallow as antennae; place a Smartie in the centre.

NOTE
If marshmallow sets prior to inserting licorice, either return it to the oven for a minute more or attach the licorice with a little icing or frosting.

Galactic Discs

STAR DUST

Preparation time: 15 minutes
Cooking time: nil
Serves 10
Easy

3 cups icing sugar
1 teaspoon food colouring
2 x 25 g packet Fruit Tingles or acid drops
¼ teaspoon bicarbonate of soda
½ teaspoon cream of tartar
1 teaspoon citric acid
10 licorice straws

1. Place sugar into a large bag, add a few drops of food colouring and shake bag vigorously until sugar is evenly coloured. Transfer to a large bowl.
2. Place Fruit Tingles or acid drops into a food processor or blender and process until finely chopped. Add to icing sugar with bicarbonate of soda, cream of tartar and citric acid. Mix well until ingredients are evenly distributed.

3. Spoon into individual bags and add a licorice straw through which to suck sherbet mixture.

MOON MOGULS

Preparation time: 25 minutes
Cooking time: 15 minutes
Serves 10
Easy

10 x 8 cm precooked vol-au-vent cases
40 g butter
2 tablespoons plain flour
1 cup milk
1 tablespoon mayonnaise
125 g cheese, grated
1 cup corn niblets, cooked
125 g ham, finely chopped

1. Preheat oven to 180°C. Place vol-au-vent cases onto a flat ungreased oven tray.
2. Melt butter in pan, lift off heat and stir in flour. Return to low heat and

54

MOON BUGGY WHEELS

Preparation time: 15 minutes
Cooking time: nil
Serves 10
Easy

10 bagels
butter
10 round slices ham
20 cherry tomatoes, halved
20 green cocktail onions, halved
toothpicks (omit for younger children)

1. Slit bagels horizontally in half.
Spread lightly with butter. Place a
slice of ham on one half of each
bagel, top with second half of the
bagel.
2. Insert a toothpick into a tomato
half and top with a green cocktail
onion. Arrange 4 tomato and onion
'bolts' around the edge of each bagel.
Serve.

SPACE SPUDS

Preparation time: 40 minutes
Cooking time: 1 hour 10 minutes
Serves 10
Easy

5 large potatoes
heavy duty foil
2 tablespoons sour cream
20 g butter
1 egg
1 tablespoon mayonnaise
1 tablespoon chopped chives
3 seafood sticks, finely sliced
125 g tasty cheese

1. Preheat oven to 190°C. Wash
potatoes until skin is clean and free of
dirt, then wrap them tightly in heavy
duty foil. Bake for 1 hour or until
tender when pierced with a skewer.
Remove from oven and allow to stand
until cool enough to handle.
2. Cut potatoes in half, leaving foil
intact. Scoop out flesh with a metal
spoon and mash until smooth. Beat in
cream, butter, egg, mayonnaise and
chives. Stir the seafood stick slice
through the potato mixture.
3. Spoon mixture back into potato
halves, top with cheese and heat in
oven for 10 minutes until cheese is
melted and lightly browned.

Outer Space Cake

OUTER SPACE CAKE

Preparation time: 40 minutes
Cooking time: 50 minutes
Easy

1 x 350 g packet cake mix or 1 quantity
  butter cake batter (see page 96)
500 g cream cheese, softened
¼ cup sifted icing sugar
1 teaspoon vanilla
a little milk if necessary
redcurrant jelly or raspberry jam
aluminium foil
toothpicks
red sweets
pipe cleaners
2 small space figures

1. Preheat oven to 180°C. Grease,
line and grease again a 20 cm round
cake tin. Make the cake according to
directions on the packet or following
recipe. Pour mixture into prepared tin
and bake for 50 minutes or until
cooked. Cool. Place cake on board.
2. Beat cheese until very soft and
creamy. Beat in icing sugar and
vanilla. If necessary, beat in a little
milk to give a spreading consistency.
3. Swirl mixture over cake, building
up peaks and craters as pictured.
Make a 'river' with jelly or jam.
4. Use two balls of crumpled foil for
the spaceship body. Fold strips of foil
concertina fashion for the steps.
Cover 3 toothpicks with foil for
antennae, and stick a red sweet on the
end of each. Cover pipe cleaners with
foil, and bend into position to make
the legs of the spaceship. Place space
figures in position.

Character Party

THIS PARTY IS built around the theme of a favourite nursery rhyme, book or movie. The chosen title will provide a variety of ideas for fancy dress, and can be adapted to suit most age groups. Characters to dress as could include traditional or current favourites — Robin Hood, Snow White, Sherlock Holmes, Mowgli or any recent movie hero.

Age group: six to ten
Venue: house or garage
Number of guests: up to 12

Invitations

Make a mask card, or buy a packet of paper masks and write the invitation on the back of each one. Ask your guests to come dressed as their favourite character. As a passport to the party, ask guests to bring a self-portrait of their character.

Decorations

A few weeks before the party, start collecting old magazines and coloured newspaper supplements featuring pop or movie stars. Pin these up around the party area. Make a banner on a sheet of butcher's paper, announcing the Hall of Fame, and hang that over the door or on the gate. As the guests arrive, hang their passport portraits around the walls.

Pin up a large piece of blank butcher's paper on one wall, and have a bowl of mixed poster paint nearby. Have arriving guests 'sign in' to the Hall of Fame by dipping their hands in the paint, making a hand print on the paper, and then signing their characters' names beneath. (If the bowl of paint is placed on newspaper, and you have a wet facecloth and a bowl of clean water nearby, hands can be quickly cleaned afterwards.)

Paper plates, cups, and matching paper tablecloths featuring current movie heroes or Disney characters are available from speciality party shops.

Food

Batwing Biscuits, Superman Sausages, Mickey Munchies, Snow White Surprise, Melon Jaws, Bluebeard's Bundles, and Mad Hatter Punch.

Cake: a Rupert Bear cake.

Games

Use music from a popular movie to play games such as *Pass the parcel, Jump the broom, Musical statues* and *Musical chairs.* Play the *Chocolate game* or have a *Guessing competition.*

Play *Partners.* Before the party, draw up a list of famous partners — Miss Piggy and Kermit, Robin Hood and Maid Marion, Peter Pan and Wendy, and so on. Write each name on a piece of paper. At the start of the game, pin a name on the back of each child, not allowing them to see their own names. Then each child must establish who he or she is, by asking questions of the other players. ('Am I an animal? What colour am I?') Answers should be given in the form of clues — 'You're green' — without giving away the name, until players arrive at the right identity. Once each child has correctly guessed who they are, they then search for their partners, whose names, of course, they can see.

Prizes and Party Favours

Badges, party whistles, small puzzle games.

SNOW WHITE SURPRISE

Preparation time: 30 minutes plus
   30 minutes freezing time
Cooking time: nil
Serves 10
Easy

2 litres vanilla ice-cream
10 white marshmallows
10 thin strips of licorice
20 Smarties
4 glacé cherries, cut into quarters

1. Using a large ice-cream scoop, place 10 scoops of ice-cream on a flat tray. Make 10 more scoops using a

small scoop. Place these on top of large scoops. Freeze for 30 minutes to become firm.

2. Remove from freezer and top each one with a marshmallow for a hat. Tie licorice around 'neck' to form a scarf. Place Smarties on small scoops of ice-cream for eyes and add one-quarter of a glacé cherry for the mouth. Return to freezer until ready to serve.

Clockwise from left: Mickey Munchies, Superman Sausages, Melon Jaws, Mad Hatter's Punch, Snow White Surprise, Bluebeard's Bundles, and Bat Wing Biscuits.

Bluebeard's Bundles

BLUEBEARD'S BUNDLES

Preparation time: 1 hour
Cooking time: 25 minutes
Makes 40
Medium

125 g uncooked prawns, shelled,
   deveined and finely chopped
250 g chicken mince
1 small carrot, finely chopped
4 cups finely chopped spring onions or
   shallots
1 tablespoon soy sauce
2 tablespoons fish sauce
pinch pepper
about 40 fresh (or frozen and thawed)
   won ton wrappers
vegetable or peanut oil for deep-frying
extra soy sauce for serving

1. In a bowl combine chopped
prawns, chicken mince, carrot, spring
onions, sauces, and pepper to taste.
Mix lightly but thoroughly.
2. Place 1 teaspoonful of the mixture
in the centre of each wonton wrapper.
Moisten edges lightly with water.
Gather up 4 corners of wrapper
together and seal.
3. Heat about 2 cups oil in a wok or

Melon Jaws

MELON JAWS

Preparation time: 20 minutes
Cooking time: nil
Serves: depends on size of melon
Easy

1 long oval shaped melon, chilled
2 glacé cherries, black olives or
   2 cherry tomatoes

1. Place melon on a large tray. If
melon is not sitting firmly on tray, cut
off a thin slice underneath to give a
flat base.
2. Mark melon with the tip of a sharp
knife to give a cutting guide. Cut out a
jagged edge to represent a mouth.
Cut a 'V' from the other end to
represent the shark's tail.
The 'V' shape that has been removed
will form the fin. Secure it to the top
of the shark's body with toothpicks or
a fine skewer.
3. Attach 2 glacé cherries for the
shark's eyes with toothpicks. Cut into
thin slices to serve.

heavy-based pan until hot. Fry 5–6 at a time, over 3–4 minutes, turning once. Drain on paper towels. Serve hot with soy sauce for dipping.

MAD HATTER'S PUNCH

Preparation time: 15 minutes plus
    chilling time
Cooking time: 4 minutes
Serves 10
Easy

150 ml water
1 cup sugar
1 x 850 ml can pineapple juice
1 cup orange juice
juice 2 large lemons
2 passionfruit
5 cups black tea, chilled
2 x 285 ml bottles dry ginger ale,
    chilled
fresh mint sprigs
1 cup pineapple chunks
1 ripe firm banana, sliced

1. Heat water and sugar in a pan, stirring over gentle heat until sugar dissolves. Boil for 3 minutes. Set aside to cool.
2. When cold, mix in fruit juices and passionfruit. Chill thoroughly. When needed, combine with tea and ginger ale in a bowl over crushed ice. Add mint sprigs, pineapple and banana slices to serve.

Bat Wing Biscuits

Mad Hatter's Punch

BAT WING BISCUITS

Preparation time: 35 minutes plus
    1 hour chilling time
Cooking time: 10 minutes
Makes 12
Easy

90 g butter, softened
2 tablespoons golden syrup
1 tablespoon cream
¼ teaspoon almond essence
1¾ cups plain flour
strips of licorice
2 tablespoons cocoa
3 tablespoons icing sugar

1. Preheat oven to 190°C and lightly grease a flat oven tray. Using a wooden spoon, beat together softened butter, golden syrup, cream and almond essence, and blend well. Gradually stir in flour to make a firm dough (in hot weather you may need to add a little extra flour).
2. Knead the dough lightly until smooth. Wrap and chill in the refrigerator for 1 hour or until firm enough to handle.
3. Roll out biscuit dough on a lightly floured board to 5 cm thickness. Cut biscuits into the shape of 'bat wings'. Press strips of licorice into biscuits to form bat 'veins'. Bake in oven for 7–10 minutes until firm and golden. Cool on tray.
4. To serve: combine cocoa and icing sugar and sprinkle liberally through a fine strainer over the biscuits.

Superman Sausages

paper piping bags with mixtures. Place frankfurter on roll and pipe a blue 'S' along its length. Pipe a yellow 'S' next to the blue 'S'. Serve at once.

MICKEY MUNCHIES

Preparation time: 5 minutes
Cooking time: nil
Serves 10
Easy

1 cup plain rice crackers
1 cup banana crisps
1 cup shredded coconut
1 cup unsalted peanuts
1 cup raisins
2 cups toasted muesli
4 cups fresh popcorn
1 cup sunflower kernels or pumpkin
   seeds

1. Combine all ingredients in a large bowl and mix well. Spoon into individual bags or containers for serving.

Mickey Munchies

SUPERMAN SAUSAGES

Preparation time: 25 minutes
Cooking time: 10 minutes
Serves 10
Medium

10 continental frankfurters
5 long bread rolls
butter for spreading
tomato sauce
1 x 200 g tub cream cheese
2 tablespoons mayonnaise
1 teaspoon mild mustard
yellow and blue food colouring

1. Place frankfurters on griller tray and cook under a hot griller for 10 minutes, turning once. The skin should have a blistered appearance and frankfurters be warmed through.
2. Slit rolls horizontally and place on a serving platter cut side up. Spread thinly with butter and liberally with tomato sauce.
3. Combine cream cheese, mayonnaise and mustard, and mix well. Tint half the mixture bright yellow and the other half blue. Fill two

RUPERT BEAR

Preparation time: 1¼ hours
Cooking time: 40 minutes
Easy

2 x 350 g packets cake mix or
  2 quantities butter cake batter
  (see page 96)
½ cup coconut
3–4 tablespoons seedless jam
1½ quantities butter icing (see page 96)
yellow food colouring
red food colouring
3 licorice straps
1 chocolate button
50 g cooking chocolate

Rupert Bear Cake

1. Preheat oven to 180°C. Grease and line two 22 x 32 cm Swiss roll tins. Make the cakes together according to directions on the packet or following recipe. Stir in coconut. Pour mixture into prepared tins and bake for 30–40 minutes. Cool before trimming the tops off to give a flat surface. Sandwich cakes together with jam.

2. Cut a paper pattern of Rupert, using diagram 4 as a guide. Using the pattern, cut a Rupert shape from the cake. Then cut the paper pattern into two pieces, separating the face from the shoulders and scarf. Remove the face pattern, leaving the shoulder and scarf pattern on the cake.

3. Ice the Rupert face (see diagram 1) with butter icing. Divide the remaining butter icing in half. Colour one part yellow and the other part red, with food colouring. Cut the scarf from the shoulder pattern, giving three pieces. Leave the two shoulder patterns on the cake, so the scarf

shape is free for icing (see diagram 2).

4. Fill an icing bag with yellow icing. Pipe around the edges of the scarf. Fill in scarf with the remaining yellow icing.

5. Use narrow strips of licorice to make the plaid pattern on the scarf and outline it with long licorice strips.

6 Put half the red icing into a piping bag, and pipe around the edge of the

scarf (see diagram 3). Spread the remaining red icing over the shoulders to give Rupert his red jersey. Use narrow strips of licorice as a nose and outline his mouth (see diagram 4). Halve the chocolate button to make two half circles for eyes. Melt the cooking chocolate and use a pastry brush to paint Rupert's chocolate mouth.

1. Cut away face from paper pattern, and ice the face.

2. Cut scarf from pattern and ice.

3. Pipe on Rupert's scarf.

4. Place licorice in position for ears, nose and mouth.

Picnic Party

THE PARK OR local nature reserve is a great place to hold a Picnic party. Everyone can run their legs off and work up an appetite. It also solves the problem of accommodating large numbers of children if your child wants the whole class to attend. The park provides plenty of scope for outdoor team games, too. Games of tag or hide-and-seek are good. Be well prepared and have a list of chosen activities made out before you get there. If you have a very large group, you may need extra adults or teenagers to help you. It is essential to remember everything before you leave home — use the checklist.

Age group: six to twelve
Venue: park or local reserve
Number of guests: up to 20

Invitations
Make a card in the shape of a soccer or cricket ball, or a sausage. Give good, clear instructions of when and where to meet. Be precise about pick-up time as many large parks close their gates at sunset. Provide an alternative should the heavens open, and ask children to bring raincoats and sunhats to cover all eventualities.

Clockwise from left: Maggot Mounds, Bugs in Rugs, Ant Floater, The Sausage Sizzle, Porcupines, Butterfly Cakes and Insy Winsy Spiders.

Decorations

Bunches of balloons tied to trees and parked cars make your group easy to find. Make a banner from an old sheet, or a poster, announcing the event: 'Susan's Party', and tie it between two bushes. Take picnic rugs and multi-coloured plastic picnic ware.

Food

Pack individual picnics with all the party trappings. If barbecues are provided, have a sausage sizzle or serve satays. Suggested menu: Insy Winsy Spiders; Porcupines; Bugs in Rugs; Ant Floaters; Maggot Mounds, and Butterfly cakes.

Cake: a Snake cake will be popular.

Games

Cricket, soccer, or volley-ball; a treasure hunt, a *Tug of war*; play *Grandmother's footsteps*; *Pass the parcel*; *Overpass, underpass*; or have a *Water race*. Have a *Hot Potato Relay* and play *Sardines*.

Prizes and Party Favours

Inexpensive skipping ropes — hand them out early if necessary. Clickers, whistles, colourful balls and badges.

Park Checklist

For the picnic: a fold-up table and chairs, or rugs and ground sheets.
For the meal: plastic plates and cups, napkins, cutlery, sharp knife, salad bowls, tablecloth.
Barbecue: large serving plates and barbecue tools. Check beforehand whether you need to take along fuel, hot plate or grill. A scraper to clean the barbecue before cooking.
Food extras: as well as prepared party food, remember to take sauces, pepper, salt, and salad dressing. Take candles for the cake, and matches to light them.
It's very important to have enough to drink. Any extra can always be taken home, but children will consume a large amount of fruit juice, soft drinks or water, especially if the day is hot.

Equipment: your pre-planned games programme will remind you of the sporting equipment needed. It is a good idea to put all these items in a clothes basket so that they are together for easy finding. Remember to take a good thick rope for the tug of war. Take a loud whistle.
Take a big garbage bag for collecting waste at the end of the party. Collecting the rubbish could be organised as a team game, with the winning team being the one whose sector is tidied first.
First Aid Equipment: a good basic first aid kit is essential. Add to it spare toilet paper, tissues, insect repellent and sunscreen. A container of moist paper towels will be useful too.
Safety Notes: if the reserve is a large one where children could get lost, take 5 minutes at the start of the party to discuss safety with them. Arrange a signal that calls them back to you — three blasts on a whistle to indicate time for lunch or a team game.
Make sure children don't wander into the forest alone. A head count every now and then will alert you to strays.

Maggot Mounds

MAGGOT MOUNDS

Preparation time: 20 minutes
Cooking time: 12 minutes
Makes 40
Easy

2 x 250 g packets desiccated coconut
1 x 410 g can condensed milk
2 teaspoons vanilla essence
glacé cherries and coloured sprinkles
    for decoration (optional)

1. Preheat oven to 180°C and grease oven trays. In a bowl combine coconut, add the condensed milk and vanilla. Mix until thoroughly combined. Drop a teaspoonful at a time on to prepared trays, leaving 2.5 cm between each mound.
2. Decorate with glacé cherries or sprinkles. Bake for 10–12 minutes, or until lightly browned. Remove from trays immediately, and cool.

THE SAUSAGE SIZZLE

Preparation time: 50 minutes
Cooking time: 20 minutes
Serves 10
Easy

1.5 kg barbecue sausages
6 onions, finely sliced
2 teaspoons oil
60 g butter, melted

EXTRA INGREDIENTS
buttered long bread rolls
barbecue and tomato sauces
grated cheese
shredded lettuce
coleslaw
sliced tomato
shredded carrot
mayonnaise

1. Bring a large pan of water to the boil. Drop in sausages, reduce heat and cook for 5 minutes. Drain and cool. Pierce sausages with a fork or skewer.
2. Place onion slices on a large sheet of foil and drizzle a little oil and butter over them. Wrap securely. Place sausages and onions over hot coals and barbecue, turning frequently, for 10–15 minutes or until sausages are browned and onions are soft when you unwrap foil to test them.
3. To serve: place onions and sausages onto a large platter and allow guests to construct their own 'sausage roll' with the extra ingredients.

The Sausage Sizzle

Insy Winsy Spiders

INSY WINSY SPIDER

Preparation time: 40 minutes
Cooking time: 15 minutes
Makes 24
Medium

1 x 340 g chocolate cake mix
100 g chocolate
30 g butter
4 licorice straps
3 cups shredded coconut, tinted green
½ cup glacé icing (optional)
a little grated chocolate (optional)
24 red Smarties

1. Preheat oven to temperature recommended on the cake mix packet. Grease 24 shallow muffin pans. Make up cake mix according to the directions on the pack. Fill each muffin tin two-thirds full with cake mixture. Bake for 10–15 minutes or until cooked when tested. Cool on a wire rack, rounded side facing upwards. Place a clean oven tray underneath.
2. Melt chocolate and butter in a small heatproof bowl over simmering water. Remove from heat and beat well.
3. Spoon chocolate over cakes, ensuring that each cake is completely covered. The excess that drips onto the tray underneath may be re-melted and used to pour over cakes. Allow chocolate to set.
4. Cut licorice straps into thin lengths 3 cm long. Attach eight of these lengths to each cake as spiders' legs; insert them into the cake or attach with a little glacé icing.
5. Cut Smarties in half and place cut side down in chocolate icing at one end of cake to form eyes. Arrange spiders on coconut on a large platter. If you wish, decorate with a little glacé icing to highlight spiders' features and sprinkle cakes with chocolate to make furry bodies.

Butterfly Cakes

PORCUPINES

Preparation time: 30 minutes
Cooking time: 40 minutes
Serves 8
Medium

500 g minced chicken
½ cup soft white breadcrumbs
1 egg white
1 x 230 g can water chestnuts, finely
   chopped
1 clove garlic, finely chopped
6 shallots, finely chopped
1 tablespoon light soy sauce
½ teaspoon sesame oil
2 cups long grain white rice
lettuce or cabbage leaves for steaming

1. Combine chicken, breadcrumbs,
egg white, water chestnuts, garlic,
shallots, soy and sesame oil, mixing
well.
2. Using wet hands, mould mixture
into 3cm balls. Roll balls in uncooked
rice, pressing gently to make rice
stick.
3. Place rice balls in the top of a
steamer lined with lettuce leaves.
Steam over boiling water for 35–40
minutes until the rice is tender and
the meat balls are cooked through to
the centre. Serve hot or cold.

BUTTERFLY CAKES

Preparation time: 40 minutes
Cooking time: 15 minutes
Makes 24
Medium

1 quantity butter cake (see page 96)
1 x 300 ml carton cream, whipped
sifted icing sugar for sprinkling

1. Preheat oven to 180°C. Line 24
muffin tins with paper cake cases.
2. Prepare cake batter. Spoon
mixture into paper cases. Bake for 15
minutes or until cooked when tested.
3. Cool on a wire rack. Cut a slice
from the top of each cake. Cut in half
to form wings. Top cakes with cream
and wings to make butterflies. Dust
with a little icing sugar.

ANT FLOATER

Preparation time: 20 minutes
Cooking time: 15 minutes
Makes 6 cups concentrate
Easy

pulp of 12 large passionfruit
3 teaspoons tartaric acid
3 cups water
3 cups sugar

1. Put passionfruit pulp into a bowl,
stir in the tartaric acid. Heat water
and sugar together until boiling,
stirring until sugar dissolves. Then
boil for 10 minutes.
2. Add passionfruit pulp, cover and
leave until cold. Bottle and seal
securely. Serve diluted with iced water
or sparkling soda water.

Ant Floaters

Porcupines

Bugs in Rugs

BUGS IN RUGS

Preparation time: 20 minutes
Cooking time: 15 minutes
Makes 12
Easy

12 cocktail frankfurters
3 slices bread
½ cup tomato sauce
¼ cup melted butter
2 tablespoons poppy seeds
toothpicks

1. Preheat oven to 180°C. Lightly grease an oven tray. Pierce frankfurters all over with a fork.
2. Spread a little tomato sauce on bread slices. Cut each slice of bread into quarters. Place a cocktail frankfurter diagonally on each quarter of bread. Bring up edges and secure with a toothpick. Brush liberally with melted butter and sprinkle with poppy seeds.
3. Place on prepared oven tray, and bake for 10–15 minutes until bread is crisp and lightly brown. Remove from oven and serve hot or cold.

SAMMY SNAKE

Preparation time: 30 minutes
Cooking time: nil
Easy

1 quantity of buttercream frosting
  (see page 96)
green food colouring
1 packet of 6 jam rollettes
assorted decorations: licorice straps,
  licorice allsorts (cut in diamond
  shapes), Smarties and assorted
  sweets
shredded coconut, tinted green

1. Tint buttercream to desired shade of green with a little food colouring.
2. Place jam rollettes on a tray or flat platter, joining together with some buttercream frosting to form a curved snake. Spread remaining buttercream over snake.
3. Decorate using your favourite sweets. Sprinkle coconut around snake to represent grass. Chill until firm.

Sammy Snake

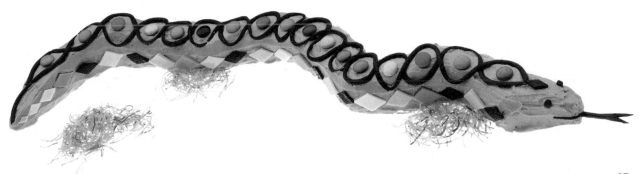

Dinner Party

T HIS PARTY makes a novel change from noisy Saturday afternoon bunfights. It is easy for working parents to arrange, as food can be prepared in advance and the table set the evening before. Parents or older siblings could enter into the spirit of things by serving the meal on silver trays, and acting the part of waiters to the sophisticated; draping a white cloth over one arm, and wearing white cotton gloves (available from most gardening shops, and not expensive). Invite guests to wear Formal Dress. They will enjoy dressing up in borrowed evening finery — long swishy skirts and flouncing feather boas, bow ties and jackets.

Age group: four to ten
Venue: home
Number of guests: up to 8

Invitations
Make invitations from black card, decorated with silver glitter on the front. Use a silver pen or white crayon to invite guests to a Soirée at Six Thirty. Ask them to wear Formal Dress and remind them to R.S.V.P.

Clockwise from left: Melon and Strawberry Cocktail, Number Cake, Tossed Salad, Chewy Chocolate Ice Cream Sundae, Spaghetti Bolognaise and Garlic Bread.

Decorations

Make the table setting as elegant as possible. Borrow a silver candelabra and use it as the centrepiece, with floral decorations around it and along the length of the table. Use tall plastic wine glasses with long stems to serve sparkling apple juice. Fold the table napkins into Lady Windermere Fans or other decorative shapes. Make small place cards for each guest. Write the menu out in flowing cursive writing, on a piece of card or mock parchment, and have it displayed on the table. Play soft background music and keep the lights low.

As each guest arrives, announce them formally. Serve them each a cocktail; fruit juice in long-stemmed plastic glasses, topped with a cherry, twisted slice of orange and tiny paper umbrella, with a novelty plastic swizzle stick. For extra impact, you could serve these in frosted glasses. To frost, dip the rim of each glass in egg white, then into caster sugar, and let the frosting harden in the fridge for ten or fifteen minutes before pouring the drinks.

As this is an evening party, guests will probably be ready for their meal soon after arriving. Plan to have the games after dinner, and have guests seated not later than half an hour after arriving.

Food

Entrée: Melon and Strawberry Cocktail.

Main course: Spaghetti Bolognaise, served with tossed salad and garlic bread.

Dessert: The Number Cake, or Chewy Chocolate Ice-cream Sundaes.

Melon and Strawberry Cocktail

Cake: The Number Cake, made from choux pastry, could be served as a party cake, or could be served as an elegant dessert at the end of the meal. For a change from birthday candles, use thin tapers or sparklers instead. These will have extra impact if the cake is served in a darkened room.

Games

After dinner, plan half an hour of quiet games such as *Hangman*, *Making words*, or *Hat making*. Have a *Memory test* or play *Mystery matchboxes*. More active games later could include *Bat the balloon*, *Wrap the mummy*, the *Chocolate game* or charades. Play *Hedgehogs*, *Find the bell ringer*, and *Balloon dress-ups*. A *Broomstick relay* is lots of fun, as is *Blindfold drawing*.

Prizes and Party Favours

Inexpensive toy jewellery , novelty party hats, and cocktail accessories — tiny umbrellas, fancy swizzle sticks and small decorations (buy a packet of these and divide the contents into groups of three or four items, wrapped in cellophane). Party blowout tooters and whistles.

Spaghetti Bolognaise

MELON AND STRAWBERRY COCKTAIL

Preparation time: 20 minutes plus 1 hour chilling time
Cooking time: nil
Serves 6
Easy

½ rockmelon
½ honeydew melon
1 x 250 g punnet strawberries
1 tablespoon lemon juice
1 teaspoon sugar
fresh mint for garnish

1. Scrape seeds out of the centre of melons. Scoop out flesh using a melon baller, or peel and cut into 2 cm chunks. Wash and hull the strawberries and slice into halves. Toss fruit in sugar and lemon juice and chill for 1 hour.
2. Spoon fruit into six glass bowls or tall parfait-style glasses. Garnish with sprigs of mint and serve.

SPAGHETTI BOLOGNAISE

Preparation time: 20 minutes
Cooking time: 1 hour
Serves 6
Easy

1 tablespoon vegetable oil
750 g minced beef
2 onions, finely chopped
1 clove garlic, crushed
1 x 425 g can of tomatoes
1 tablespoon lemon juice
2 tablespoons tomato paste
1 beef stock cube
½ teaspoon dried basil
½ teaspoon dried oregano
½ teaspoon sugar
3 tablespoons cold water
1 tablespoon plain flour
grated cheese for serving
385 g spaghetti
1 tablespoon oil (extra)

1. To make Bolognaise sauce: heat oil in a large pan. Add mince and cook in the oil until meat browns and separates into small pieces. Add garlic and onion, and fry a further 5 minutes.
2. Add tomatoes, tomato paste, lemon juice, stock cube, herbs and sugar. Stir to combine. Simmer for 40 minutes, stirring occasionally and breaking up tomato. Blend flour and water together to form a smooth paste. Add to meat mixture and return to boil, stirring constantly. Pour over cooked spaghetti and serve sprinkled with cheese.
3. To cook spaghetti: bring a large pan of water to the boil, add oil. Add spaghetti to rapidly boiling water, pushing spaghetti in gently until it is all submersed in the water. Stir once and boil rapidly for approximately 8 minutes or until firm but cooked through. Drain and serve immediately, topped with Bolognaise sauce.

Tossed Salad

TOSSED SALAD

Preparation time: 15 minutes
Cooking time: nil
Serves 6
Easy

SALAD
1 lettuce, washed
2 tomatoes, washed
¼ cucumber, thickly peeled
2 stalks celery, washed
1 carrot, peeled
6 mushrooms

DRESSING
1 tablespoon oil
1 tablespoon white vinegar
3 tablespoons mayonnaise
1 tablespoon finely chopped fresh
   parsley

1. Tear lettuce into bite-sized pieces and place in a large salad bowl. Remove core section from tomatoes and cut into quarters. Slice cucumber and celery. Cut carrot into thin sticks and quarter mushrooms. Arrange salad vegetables on top of lettuce and toss lightly.
2. To prepare dressing: combine all ingredients in a screwtop jar and shake well. Pour dressing over salad just before serving.

Chewy Chocolate Ice-cream Sundae

GARLIC BREAD

Preparation time: 15 minutes
Cooking time: 15 minutes
Serves 6
Easy

2 French bread sticks
200 g butter, softened
3 cloves garlic, crushed

1. Preheat oven to 180°C. Slice French sticks into 3 cm slices, cutting all the way through. Arrange bread on a large sheet of foil and re-form the shape of the loaf.
2. Cream together butter and garlic until light and very soft. Spread bread liberally on one side of each slice and place back on foil. Push slices together and wrap loaf tightly.
3. Bake bread in oven for 10–15 minutes. Partially open foil packets and serve.

CHEWY CHOCOLATE ICE-CREAM SUNDAE

Preparation time: 15 minutes
Cooking time: 5 minutes
Serves 6
Easy

1 litre vanilla ice-cream
3 Mars Bars
½ cup cream
2 Milky Ways
1 Flake, crumbled
1 Scorched Peanut Bar, broken into
    small pieces
6 ice-cream wafers

1. Roughly chop Mars Bars in small pieces and place in a heatproof bowl with cream. Heat over simmering water until melted. Cool slightly. Slice Milky Ways into 1 cm slices.
2. Place a small scoop of ice-cream into each of six parfait glasses. Divide half the Mars Bar mixture, Milky Way pieces and Scorched Peanut Bar between the glasses. Top each serving with another scoop of ice-cream then top with remaining Mars mixture, Milky Ways and Scorched Peanut Bars. Sprinkle with crumbled Flake and insert an ice-cream wafer on top of each glass. Serve immediately.

NOTE
Chocolate bars with flavoured creamy fillings and peanut brittle can be substituted for Mars Bars, Milky Ways and Scorched Peanut Bars.

Number Cake

NUMBER CAKE

Preparation time: 1 hour
Cooking time: 1 hour
Medium

CAKE
1 cup water
60 g butter, cut into small pieces
1 cup plain flour
1 teaspoon sugar
3 eggs

TOPPING
500 ml cream
1 tablespoon sugar
1 teaspoon vanilla essence
2 cups glacé icing (see page 96) or
    150 g melted chocolate
assorted sweets for decoration

1. Preheat oven to 210°C. Grease an oven tray and mark on it, as a large number, the child's age. Heat water and butter in a pan and bring to the boil. Sift flour and sugar together and add all at once to boiling butter and water mixture. Remove from heat and beat well until no lumps remain and mixture is thick. Return to low heat and stir until mixture leaves the sides of the pan. Remove from heat and cool.
2. Beat eggs lightly. Add a little at a time to flour mixture, beating well after each addition. When all the egg has been added, the mixture should be thick and glossy.
3. Spoon or pipe batter onto prepared tray in the shape of the number required. Bake for 20 minutes or until puffed. Reduce heat to 180°C and cook for a further 30–40 minutes or until golden, and crisp to touch. Remove from oven and cool on a wire rack.
4. To prepare topping: whip cream with sugar and vanilla until soft peaks form. Slit cake in half horizontally, fill with cream and replace top.
5. Place filled cake on a wire rack with a clean oven tray underneath. Warm icing or melt chocolate and pour immediately over the cake, allowing excess to drip off. If needed, the excess may be re-melted and poured over again. Before icing or chocolate cools, top with an assortment of sweets and add candles.

United Nations Party

T HE UNITED NATIONS party allows children a special opportunity to talk about the origins of their own families, and is fun for older children. Asking guests to come dressed in the national dress of a member of their family, or of their favourite country, will lead to a very colourful and interesting variety of dress. Many will be able to borrow items of national dress — Dutch clogs or lace caps, saris, kimonos, happy coats — and will be able to augment these with appropriate extras from their own wardrobes; black trousers with happy coats, for example.

Age group: seven to eleven
Venue: home
Number of guests: up to 12

Invitations

Make paper fans and write the invitations on those, or make small strings of flags, with the front coloured in, and the different parts of the invitation — time, place, address and so on — written on the back of each flag. Thread these together with cotton. Invite each guest to make their chosen country's national flag on a big sheet of paper, and to bring that to the party. Also ask each guest to make and bring their own 'passport', showing their country of origin, a self-portrait, and a description of themselves.

Decorations

Make flags and bunting from coloured paper or butcher's paper, and string these up about the party room. You may also be able to borrow bunting from your local supermarket or garage — supermarket bunting often shows world flags.

Display a globe or map of the world near the door. As each guest arrives, ask them to mark their chosen country with a yellow flag or sticker. Have a clothesline and pegs ready to hang each guest's national flag. Cut a

potato-print stamp, or find a pictorial rubber stamp, and stamp their 'passports'.

A local travel agency may lend you posters of exotic faraway places for displaying on the walls, or you could collect suitable pictures from coloured magazines and pin those up. Hang travel brochures on pieces of string from the ceiling.

Food

Serve a multi-national menu — Hawaiian Delights, Italian Fruit and Chocolate Cassata, Indonesian Satay with Peanut Sauce, Middle Eastern Hummus, Chinese Spring Rolls, mini Italian Pizzas and Island Coolers.

Cake: for an international flavour make an Australia cake.

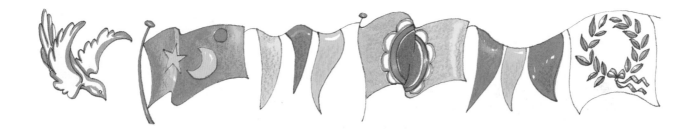

Games

As an ice-breaker, ask all the guests to sit in a circle. Taking turns, each child stands, shows his or her national dress, and talks about it and the country from which it comes. Encourage them by asking questions about what language is spoken there, what the capital city is, and why they have chosen it.

Play *Making words*, using the names of countries and cities as the starting point.

Play *Musical sets*, *Trains and stations*, *Taste and guess*, and *Chopsticks and marbles*. Have a doughnut eating race and play *Guess in the dark*. Play *Postman's holiday*, using countries and capital cities instead of town or street names.

Prizes and Party Favours

Incense sticks, paper fans, packets of origami paper, pencil sharpeners made like world globes, or extra-long pencils tipped with small flags.

Clockwise from left: Indonesian Satay with Peanut Sauce, Australia Cake, Island Coolers, Mini Italian Pizzas, Middle Eastern Hummus, Hawaiian Delights, Italian Fruit and Chocolate Cassata, Chinese Spring Rolls.

Chinese Spring Rolls

Indonesian Satay with Peanut Sauce

1. Slice bread into 10 thick slices. Spread with butter, and top with slices of ham.
2. Halve each slice of pineapple horizontally and place on top of ham. Top with cheese.
3. Place under a preheated griller until cheese melts and browns. Cut into fingers to serve.

HINT
As a variation, make these delicious snacks on small rounds of pita bread instead of crusty bread.

Hawaiian Delights

CHINESE SPRING ROLLS

Preparation time: 35 minutes
Cooking time: 30 minutes
Makes 12
Medium

250 g chicken breasts, skinned and
    finely chopped
1 tablespoon oil
6 shallots, finely sliced
200 g fresh bean sprouts
3 mushrooms, finely chopped
1 tablespoon chicken stock
1 tablespoon soy sauce
2 teaspoons cornflour mixed with
    1 tablespoon cold water
10–12 spring-roll wrappers (or use
    filo pastry sheets cut into
    20 cm squares)

1. Preheat oven to 200°C. Add chicken and oil to a preheated wok or pan. Stir-fry for 2–3 minutes. Add shallots, bean sprouts and mushrooms. Stir-fry for 2 minutes.
2. Mix together chicken stock, soy sauce and blended cornflour. Add to wok, stirring until sauce thickens. Allow mixture to cool. Drain off excess liquid.
3. Divide mixture into 12 portions. Place one portion in the centre of a spring-roll wrapper. Fold over sides. Roll up into a parcel and seal with a little water. Bake all parcels for 30 minutes until golden brown, or deep-fry in hot oil for 3–5 minutes and drain on absorbent paper. Serve hot.

HAWAIIAN DELIGHTS

Preparation time: 20 minutes
Cooking time: 5 minutes
Serves 10
Easy

1 loaf crusty bread
butter for spreading
10 slices sandwich ham
5 slices canned pineapple
10 slices processed or cheddar cheese

INDONESIAN SATAY WITH PEANUT SAUCE

Preparation time: 45 minutes plus
   overnight marinating time
Cooking time: 15 minutes
Makes 50
Easy

SATAY
1.5 kg lean pork or chicken
3 onions, chopped
1 cup soy sauce
3 cloves garlic
¾ cup white vinegar
juice 2 lemons
2 teaspoons turmeric
1 teaspoon cumin
ground black pepper
skewers

PEANUT SAUCE
2 tablespoons oil
2 onions, finely chopped
2 cloves garlic, crushed
1 cup coconut cream
juice 1 lemon
2 tablespoons soy sauce
2 tablespoons tomato sauce
2 teaspoons chilli sauce (optional)
½ cup crunchy peanut butter

1. Cut meat into bite-sized cubes.
Place in a large bowl. Place remaining
satay ingredients in a food processor
or blender and process to a purée.
Pour purée over meat and toss well to
coat cubes thoroughly. Cover and
refrigerate overnight to marinate.
2. Thread meat onto skewers. Grill or
barbecue for 5–10 minutes, turning
frequently.
3. To prepare peanut sauce: heat oil
in a large pan. Sauté onions and
garlic until onions are soft. Add all
remaining ingredients except peanut
butter. Bring to the boil, stirring
constantly. Reduce heat and simmer
for 3 minutes. Stir in peanut butter.
Spoon sauce over satays. Serve warm
or cool, with any remaining sauce in
a small bowl as an accompaniment.

HINT
If using wooden skewers, soak them
in cold water for at least 20 minutes
before threading the meat onto them.
This will prevent them from burning
when grilled.

Italian Fruit and Chocolate Cassata

ITALIAN FRUIT AND CHOCOLATE CASSATA

Preparation time: 20 minutes plus
   freezing time
Cooking time: nil
Serves 15

2 litres vanilla ice-cream (see note)
30 g white chocolate, roughly chopped
60 g dark chocolate, roughly chopped
1½ cups walnuts, roughly chopped
1½ cups slivered almonds
1½ cups raisins
1 cup red cherries, halved
1 x 100 g pkt marshmallows, halved
½ cup strawberry flavouring
extra strawberry flavouring

1. Lightly brush a 3 litre pudding
basin with oil. Invert on a rack to
drain away excess.

2. Soften ice-cream slightly and
transfer to a large chilled bowl. Add
white and dark chocolate, nuts,
raisins, cherries, marshmallows and
strawberry flavouring. Mix through
ice-cream until only just combined.
Spoon into prepared pudding basin
and return to freezer to become firm.
3. To serve: invert pudding basin
onto a serving plate, and cover with a
warm cloth for 1 minute. Gently shake
plate and bowl together until ice-
cream is released. Drizzle a little
strawberry flavouring over ice-cream.

NOTE
Use a good quality ice-cream for this
recipe. The lesser quality ice-creams
melt and lose volume very quickly on
softening.

Middle Eastern Hummus

Mini Italian Pizzas

MIDDLE EASTERN HUMMUS

Preparation time: 20 minutes plus
   overnight soaking time
Cooking time: 1 hour
Makes about 4 cups
Easy

1½ cups chick peas
1 cup lemon juice
⅓ cup water
2 tablespoons white vinegar
3 cloves garlic, chopped
1 cup tahini paste
2 tablespoons olive oil
extra olive oil to serve
mild paprika
10 pita breads

1. Place chick peas in a large pan,
cover with hot water and leave to soak
overnight.

2. Drain and return to saucepan.
Cover with hot water again. Bring to
the boil and cook for about 1 hour or
until soft.
3. Drain. Place chick peas in a food
processor or blender. Process to a
purée with lemon juice and water.
Add vinegar, garlic, tahini and olive
oil. Process again to a creamy paste.
Adjust seasoning. Add more lemon
juice, if required. Drizzle a little olive
oil over the top and sprinkle with
paprika. Serve accompanied with pita
bread cut into quarters.

HINT
Tahini paste is a thick paste made
from a base of crushed sesame seeds
with a little water, salt and lemon
juice. The consistency is similar to
peanut butter. It is readily available at
large supermarkets or delicatessens.

ISLAND COOLER

Preparation time: 5 minutes
Cooking time: nil
Serves 8
Easy

1 x 850 ml can pineapple juice
¼ cup lemon juice
½ cup coconut milk
1 x 1 litre bottle lemonade
Ice cubes
Pineapple slices for serving

1. Mix together juices and coconut
milk. Transfer to a large jug. Chill
thoroughly.
2. Just before serving add lemonade.
Garnish with a few ice-cubes and a
slice of pineapple.

Island Cooler

MINI ITALIAN PIZZAS

Preparation time: 35 minutes
Cooking time: 20 minutes
Makes 8
Easy

2 sheets frozen shortcrust pastry,
    thawed
¼ cup tomato sauce
2 slices ham, chopped
1 x 225 g tin sliced pineapple, drained
    and chopped
1 stick cabanossi or other sausage,
    sliced thinly
4 mushrooms, chopped
2 cups shredded cheese

1. Preheat oven to 180°C. Cut circles
of pastry using a large scone or biscuit
cutter. Alternatively, cut each sheet
of pastry into four circles, using a
sharp knife and a glass. Spread each
circle with tomato sauce. Top with
ham, pineapple, cabanossi slices and
mushrooms. Sprinkle with cheese.
2. Place on an ungreased baking
tray. Bake for 15–20 minutes or until
pastry is crisp and cheese has melted.
Serve hot from the oven.

HINT
Thinly sliced rings of onion can be
added for a tasty variation.

Australia Cake

AUSTRALIA CAKE

Preparation time: 45 minutes
Cooking time: 25 minutes
Easy

2 x 350 g packets cake mix or
    2 quantities butter cake batter
    (see page 96)
½ quantity buttercream frosting
    (see page 96)
500 g icing sugar
¼ cup cocoa
½ cup boiling water
1 teaspoon butter
250 g desiccated coconut
1 small Australian flag and candles for
    decoration

1. Preheat oven to 180°C. Grease
and line two 22 x 32 cm Swiss roll tins
with greaseproof paper and grease
again. Make cakes according to
directions on the packet or following

recipe. Divide mixture between
prepared tins and bake for 20–25
minutes or until cooked when tested.
Cool in tins for 5 minutes before
turning out onto a wire rack to cool
completely.
2. Spread one cake with frosting and
place other cake on top. Mark shape
of Australia on cake, using diagram as
a guide. Use a sharp knife to cut out
the shape.
3. Sift together icing sugar and
cocoa. Stir in boiling water and
butter. Blend until smooth, with the
consistency of cream. Add a little
extra water if necessary. Place cake
on a rack over a clean tray. Drizzle
chocolate mixture over cake and allow
it to flood over the sides, ensuring
cake is completely covered with
chocolate. Sprinkle liberally with
desiccated coconut. Stand 30 minutes
until icing sets.

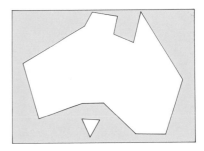

4. Lift cake onto a large board.
Decorate with an Australian flag and
candles.

HINT
To adapt the shape of this cake to
that of another country, simply trace
the required map outline from a large
atlas and use the tracing as a cutting
guide. Decorate with appropriate
flags.

SportsParty

WHAT TO WEAR poses no problem at all for this party theme, which is great fun for older children. Guests can dress in their own sports gear, or be invited to dress as their favourite sports heroes. They will have their own sports outfits to use, or could raid the wardrobes of friends and neighbours.

Before the party, set up a mini-golf course in your garden or garage. Pieces of cardboard make good slopes, loose bricks create low side walls, and tunnels can be constructed from cardboard boxes cut in half, or shoe boxes. Bottle sleeves made from paper, through which the ball must be putted, add a challenge. Have a golf club (borrowed from neighbours if necessary) for each player, and play with used golf balls.

Set up a ping-pong table in the carport. Invest in an inexpensive ping-pong set (table net, two or four bats and ping-pong balls) if you don't already have one. Ping-pong is a perennial favourite and the investment will be a popular one in the long term.

Age group: eight to eleven
Venue: home
Number of guests: up to 10

Invitations
Cut out cardboard cricket balls from folded red card, or cut single ping-pong bat shapes and write the invitations on those. Invite the team to join you for a sports tournament, and give kick-off time.

Decorations
Borrow all the sports equipment you can from friends. Use it to give a sporty flavour to the party room. Hang crossed hockey sticks, tennis racquets or cricket bats on the wall, and add cricket scarves, hats, football boots and ice-skates. Pin up a rugby jersey or two. If you can, borrow victors' shields and cups from the local sports club and display these as well, or paint mock shields on cardboard and hang those up. Big cheerleaders' pom-poms are easy to make, using strips of coloured crêpe paper taped onto lengths of bamboo.

Food
Serve Bats and Balls, Soccer Balls, Soft Pitch, Sportstar Stamina, Throw in the Bat, and Players' Meat Pies. Add a big bowl of orange wedges for refreshment at half-time.

Cake: score a point with the Racquet cake.

Games
Play ping-pong or mini-golf. Arrange a *Tug of war*, a *Blow the balloon* race and a game of balloon tennis, where balloons are batted from team to team instead of tennis balls. Play *Bat the balloon*; bob for apples, and have a *Doughnut eating race*.

Or play *Bean bag hockey*. The

equipment needed for this is simple — a small beanbag, two chairs, and two newspapers, each rolled up tightly and tied with string to form a stick.

Divide the children into two teams, and line them up on opposite sides of the room, facing each other. Give each member of one team a number, from left to right, and number the other team with the same numbers from right to left. The teams will then face each other like this:

$$1 \quad 2 \quad 3 \quad 4 \quad 5$$
$$5 \quad 4 \quad 3 \quad 2 \quad 1$$

In the centre of the floor, place the newspaper sticks and the beanbag. Place a chair against each far wall, in the middle. Each chair represents a goal for one team.

The referee must call out one of the team numbers. At the call, the two team members of that number have to run forward, pick up a newspaper stick, and try to hit the beanbag into goal between their team's chair legs; then sticks have to be replaced in the centre. The referee can keep the pace very fast. The team with the most

goals at the end of the allotted time, or when the whistle goes, wins.

Prizes and Party Favours
Tennis and ping-pong balls, inexpensive sun visors, small bottles of coloured zinc to protect noses from sunburn, aniseed balls.

Clockwise from left: Sportstar Stamina, Players' Meat Pie, Throw in the Bat, Bats and Balls, Soccer Balls and Soft Pitch

Bats and Balls

in a heatproof bowl over simmering water, and stir over a low heat until melted. Spread the underside of half the flat biscuits with a little chocolate marshmallow mixture.

4. Decorate the top of the remaining biscuits with glacé icing tinted several colours. Place in the oven (180°C) for 5 minutes to set. Remove from oven and cool slightly, prior to joining biscuit halves. Decorate balls with glacé icing and allow to set on a wire rack.

SPORTSTAR STAMINA

Preparation time: 25 minutes plus chilling time
Cooking time: 20 minutes
Makes 8 cups
Easy

4 large lemons
1½ cups sugar
2 cups water
1 cup lemon juice
1 litre extra cold water
lemon slices for serving

1. Peel rind from lemons as thinly as possible. Put in a pan with sugar and 2 cups water. Simmer for 20 minutes. Strain and set aside until cold.
2. Stir lemon juice and 1 litre water into the cold syrup and chill well. Serve in tall tumblers over crushed ice and top each with a lemon slice.

Sportstar Stamina

BATS AND BALLS

Preparation time: 1 hour plus 20 minutes chilling time
Cooking time: 10 minutes per batch
Makes about 50
Easy

125 g butter
½ cup sugar
1 egg
½ teaspoon cinnamon
1½ cups plain flour
2 tablespoons cornflour
100 g marshmallows
100 g chocolate
2 x 10 cm lengths licorice
1 cup glacé icing (see page 96)
food colouring

1. Preheat oven to 220°C and grease an oven tray and a shallow muffin tray. Cream butter and sugar together until pale, light and fluffy. Beat in egg until mixture is smooth and creamy. Sift together cinnamon, plain flour and cornflour. Add to butter mixture, and mix well with a flat-bladed knife. Form mixture into a ball. Chill covered in the refrigerator for 20 minutes.

2. On a lightly floured board roll out two-thirds of the dough to 5 mm thick. Cut dough into bat and racquet shapes of similar size. Arrange on prepared tray and bake for 8–10 minutes or until biscuits are a pale golden brown. Remove from oven and cool on tray. Shape remaining dough into footballs, soccer balls and cricket balls. Bake these for 5–10 minutes in shallow muffin containers to prevent them rolling everywhere. Remove from oven and cool on tray.

3. Place marshmallows and chocolate

SOFT PITCH

Preparation time: 5 minutes
Cooking time: nil
Makes 6
Easy

⅓ cup crunchy peanut butter
½ cup plain yoghurt
1 tablespoon chopped chives or shallots
1 tablespoon peanut or vegetable oil
1 teaspoon soy sauce or soy manis
fresh vegetables for serving

1. Beat together peanut butter and yoghurt. Add remaining ingredients except vegetables, and stir well.
2. Spoon into four small bowls or ramekins and place on serving plates. Surround with strips and slices of raw vegetables.

NOTE
Soy Manis is an Indonesian-style soy sauce which has a delicious, slightly sweet, soy flavour.

Soft Pitch

Soccer Balls

SOCCER BALLS

Preparation time: 30 minutes
Cooking time: nil
Makes 40
Easy

1 cup very finely chopped dried
    apricots
1 cup desiccated coconut
½ cup sweetened condensed milk
extra desiccated coconut

1. In a bowl combine apricots, coconut and condensed milk, mixing very thoroughly.
2. Take 2 teaspoons of mixture and form into a small ball. Repeat with remaining mixture. Toss balls in extra desiccated coconut. Place in the refrigerator and chill well.

NOTE
These can be made a week ahead and stored in an airtight container in the refrigerator.

HINT
Chopping dried fruit is easy if you use sharp scissors dipped in boiling water.

Throw in the Bat

Players' Meat Pie

THROW IN THE BAT

Preparation time: 20 minutes
Cooking time: 20 minutes
Makes 12
Easy

½ cup plain flour
1 egg
¼ cup milk
½ cup water
12 chipolata sausages or cocktail
    frankfurters
tomato sauce or baked beans to serve

1. Preheat oven to 210°C. Lightly oil
12 small muffin tins.
2. Sift flour into a bowl. Whisk
together egg, milk and water, and
gradually add to flour. Whisk until
batter is smooth.
3. Place a sausage in each prepared
muffin cup. Bake for 5 minutes.
Whisk batter again and quickly pour
around sausages in cups. Bake 10–15
minutes more until well risen and
browned. Serve hot with tomato sauce
or baked beans.

PLAYERS' MEAT PIE

Preparation time: 35 minutes
Cooking time: 1½ hours
Makes 1
Medium

PIE BASE
1 sheet frozen ready-rolled shortcrust
    pastry

PIE TOP
1 sheet frozen ready-rolled puff pastry

FILLING
1 tablespoon oil
30 g butter
750 g blade steak, trimmed and cubed
2 cups beef stock
pinch pepper
2 tablespoons cornflour
1 cup water
1 tablespoon worcestershire sauce

1. Preheat oven to 200°C. Line the
base of a 23 cm pie plate with pastry.
Trim edges. Rest in the refrigerator
until required.
2. To prepare filling: heat oil and
butter in a large frypan. Add meat in
batches and brown well. Drain off
excess fat. Return meat to pan with
stock and pepper to taste. Simmer,
covered, for 40 minutes or until meat
is tender.
3. Blend cornflour with a little water
to form a smooth paste. Blend in
remaining water and worcestershire
sauce. Add to meat and return to the
boil, stirring until thickened. Simmer
5 minutes, remove from heat and
cool.
4. Fill pie case with meat. Wet pastry
edges with a little water. Top with puff
pastry sheet. Trim edges and press
together to seal. Make a cut in the
centre of pastry top with a sharp
knife. Brush top with milk and bake
for 35–40 minutes or until puffed and
golden.

NOTE
This may be made into individual
party pies by lining muffin tins with
shortcrust pastry. Fill with meat and
top with rounds of puff pastry. Bake
for 10–15 minutes or until golden
brown.

BADMINTON RACQUET CAKE

Preparation time: 1¼ hours
Cooking time: 40 minutes
Medium

2 x 350 g packets cake mix or
    2 quantities butter cake batter
    (see page 96)
1 quantity butter icing (see page 96)
3 tablespoons cocoa
2 tablespoons hot water
Smarties

1. Preheat oven to 180°C. Grease and line both a 20 cm round cake tin and a 20 cm square cake tin. Make the cakes according to the directions on the packet or following recipe. Divide mixture between prepared tins and bake for 35–40 minutes or until cooked. Cool.

2. Dissolve cocoa in hot water and cool. Mix cocoa with half the butter icing, leaving remaining butter icing plain. Reserve ½ cup plain butter icing for decoration.

3. Trim the sides of the round cake to give an oval shape (see diagram 1). Cut the square cake vertically in three, to give two pieces each 8 cm wide and one narrower piece (see diagram). The remaining piece is not used so you could use it in another recipe.

4. Join the small ends of the two rectangular pieces of cake together with a little icing. Cover completely with plain butter icing. This forms the handle of the racquet.

5. Place the handle on a cake board, leaving enough room for the head of the racquet. Using the chocolate icing, ice the top of the oval cake smoothly, leaving an uniced 1.5 cm rim around the outside.

Using the plain icing, ice the sides of the cake and the 1.5 cm rim, covering the edges of chocolate icing slightly so that the two colours join together evenly.

6. Fill a piping bag with the reserved ½ cup of plain icing. Pipe lines over the chocolate icing to represent the strings on the racquet (see diagram 3). Place a row of Smarties around the outer edge of the cake where the chocolate icing and the plain butter icing meet (see diagram 4).

7. Transfer the head of the racquet to the cake board and join it to the handle with a little icing. Use Smarties around the base of the handle to represent a hand grip. Using a star nozzle, pipe a row of rosettes around the base of the cake.

HINT
Instead of using Smarties to decorate the cake, pipe rosettes in their place. For rosettes, make an extra ½ quantity of butter icing and colour it part red, part yellow.

Badminton Racquet Cake

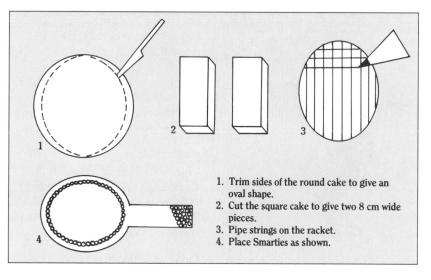

1. Trim sides of the round cake to give an oval shape.
2. Cut the square cake to give two 8 cm wide pieces.
3. Pipe strings on the racket.
4. Place Smarties as shown.

Disco Party

T HIS IS POPULAR with older children, who enjoy it all the more if it is held at night rather than in the afternoon. If you have a garage, basement or family room that can be cleared and used strictly for party purposes, so much the better. Furnishings in the party room are minimal, to allow space for dancing — heaps of scatter cushions are usually sufficient. Guests usually find no problem in assembling an appropriate wardrobe, often borrowed from older brothers or sisters. Neighbours might appreciate a word of warning before the event.

Age group: ten to twelve
Venue: home
Number of guests: up to 12

Invitations
Cut up popular teenage or motorbike magazines and make a collage of pictures on the front of each invitation. Alternatively, cut card into hamburger-shaped invitations and have the host illustrate the front of each card. Invite the gang over to a wild rage.

Decorations
Cover the table with a shiny black or red vinyl tablecloth and use red paper serviettes with glossy coloured paper plates and mugs. Tie bunches of brightly-coloured balloons to lengths of thin stick, wind red crêpe paper round the sticks, and prop these on the table and on window ledges. Invest in a few differently coloured light bulbs, and exchange these for the plain ones in your light fittings; or hang up a string of coloured lights.

Food
Serve Mini Burgers, Shoe String Fries, Chilli Con Carne, Guacamole and Corn Chips, American Hot Dogs, Pecan Chocolate Brownies, Apple Pie and Disco Delight Biscuits.

Cake: tune in with the Ghetto Blaster.

Games
Turn the room into a disco and have the host be responsible for equipment and sound. Dancing will be the main feature of the party, but you could suggest a few alternatives to keep things moving; dancing competitions, for example, or a variation of *Hop and pop*, during which guests must keep dancing whilst trying to pop each other's balloons.

For a complete change of pace, suggest a break for *Murder in the dark*, *Guess in the dark* or *Charades*.

Prizes and Party Favours
Fake fingernail sets, inexpensive earrings or other jewellery, sunglasses, badges and novelty straws.

SHOE STRING FRIES

Preparation time: 20 minutes
Cooking time: 30 minutes
Serves 10
Medium

2 kg large potatoes, thinly peeled
vegetable oil for deep-frying

1. Wash and thoroughly dry
potatoes. Cut lengthways into fine
shoestring lengths. Pat potatoes dry
with absorbent paper.
2. Half-fill a pan or deep-fryer with
oil. Heat slowly until the surface of the
oil appears to move.
3. Place shoestring potatoes, a few at
a time, into a wire basket and lower
into hot oil. Fry for a few minutes
until pale golden. Drain on absorbent
paper. Continue with remaining
shoestrings until all are parcooked.

4. When ready to serve, reheat oil.
Cook chips again in batches, until
crisp and golden. Drain well on
absorbent paper. Serve with mini
burgers (see recipe, page 90).

*Clockwise from left: Pecan Chocolate
Brownies, Shoestring Fries, American Hot
Dogs, Chilli Con Carne, Apple Pie,
Guacamole and Corn Chips, Disco Delights,
and Mini Burgers.*

Pecan Chocolate Brownies

3. In a mixing bowl, beat butter and vanilla, gradually adding sugar until mixture is light and fluffy. Beat in eggs, one at a time, then beat in chocolate until blended. Sift in flour and stir until combined. Fold in pecans.

4. Spread mixture evenly into prepared tin. Bake for 25–30 minutes or until cooked through and a crust forms on the surface. Cool slightly and cut into squares. Cool completely and remove from tin. To serve, dust top with icing sugar.

APPLE PIE

Preparation time: 45 minutes plus
   chilling time
Cooking time: 45 minutes
Makes 1
Medium

PASTRY
1½ cups wholemeal flour
1½ cups plain flour
1 teaspoon mixed spice
100g butter
3–4 tablespoons cold water

FILLING
6 green apples, cored
¼ cup sultanas
4 tablespoons sugar
extra sugar

1. Preheat oven to 180°C and grease a 23 cm pie dish.

2. To prepare pastry: sift flours and mixed spice into a bowl. Return bran from sifter to bowl. Mix well to combine. Rub butter into flour using fingertips until mixture resembles fine

Guacamole and Corn Chips

GUACAMOLE AND CORN CHIPS

Preparation time: 10 minutes
Cooking time: nil
Serves 10
Easy

2 ripe avocados
juice of 1 lemon
1 clove garlic, crushed
½ onion, finely grated
2 tomatoes, finely chopped
½ cup sour cream
few drops of tabasco sauce
100 g corn chips for serving

1. Mash avocados until smooth. Blend in lemon juice, garlic, onion, tomatoes, sour cream and sauce. Spoon into dip bowls and serve with corn chips.

PECAN CHOCOLATE BROWNIES

Preparation time: 35 minutes
Cooking time: 35 minutes
Makes 12
Easy

60 g dark cooking chocolate
125 g butter
½ teaspoon vanilla essence
1 cup sugar
2 eggs
1 cup plain flour
¾ cup chopped pecans
sifted icing sugar to garnish (optional)

1. Preheat oven to 180°C and grease a 20 cm square cake tin.

2. Melt chocolate in a heatproof bowl over simmering water. Set aside to cool.

breadcrumbs. Add water gradually to make a soft dough. Wrap in plastic or waxed paper. Chill in refrigerator for 20 minutes.

3. Roll out two-thirds of the pastry on a lightly floured surface or between two sheets of plastic wrap until pastry is 5 mm thick. Line prepared pie dish with pastry, trimming off excess. Roll out remaining pastry to cover pie. Set aside.

4. To prepare filling: cut apples into thin slices. Layer in pie dish. Sprinkle each layer of apples with sultanas and sugar. Cover with remaining pastry and seal edges with water. Brush pastry with water and sprinkle with sugar. Cover with rolled pastry. Bake for 45 minutes or until apples are tender and pastry is golden brown.

Disco Delight Biscuits

DISCO DELIGHT BISCUITS

Preparation time: 30 minutes plus
    30 minutes chilling time
Cooking time: 15 minutes
Makes 16
Easy

125 g butter
½ cup sugar
½ teaspoon vanilla essence
1 egg
1 cup plain flour
½ cup cornflour
½ cup self-raising flour
mock cream or jam
small red, green, yellow or orange
    unsugared jujubes

1. Beat together butter, sugar and vanilla essence until creamy. Add egg and beat well. Sift flours into mixture and work in to form a firm dough. Wrap and chill about 20 minutes.
2. Preheat oven to 180°C and grease an oven tray. Roll out into a sheet about 30 x 30 cm. Cut into strips 8 x 4 cm. Using a plain icing pipe or an essence bottle top, cut three holes in half the biscuits, leaving the rest whole.
3. Arrange on prepared tray and bake for 15 minutes, or until lightly browned. When cold, join together in pairs with mock cream or jam, plain biscuit underneath. Put jujubes in each round to represent lights — red, yellow or orange and green.

AMERICAN HOT DOGS

Preparation time: 15 minutes
Cooking time: 10 minutes
Serves 10
Easy

10 frankfurters
10 long hot dog rolls
American-style mustard (see note)
tomato sauce

1. Arrange frankfurters on a griller tray and pierce skin with a fork. Place under grill and cook, turning regularly for 10 minutes or until the frankfurters are cooked and skin appears blistered.
2. Split rolls lengthways without cutting all the way through. Spread lightly with a little mustard. Place

each frankfurter in a roll and top with tomato sauce. Serve hot.

NOTE
American-style mustard is very mild. It may be omitted if you prefer.

American Hot Dogs

Mini Burgers

CHILLI CON CARNE

Preparation time: 20 minutes
Cooking time: 55 minutes
Serves 10
Easy

2 tablespoons oil
1 kg minced beef
4 onions, chopped
1 clove garlic, crushed
1 teaspoon Mexican-style chilli powder
2 teaspoons paprika
1 teaspoon ground cumin
½ teaspoon ground coriander
1 x 800 g can peeled tomatoes
2 tablespoons tomato paste
1 beef stock cube, crumbled
1 x 750 g can red kidney beans
2 tablespoons cornflour blended with
    4 tablespoons water
bread rolls or steamed rice

Chilli Con Carne

MINI BURGERS

Preparation time: 40 minutes
Cooking time: 10 minutes
Serves 10
Easy

1 teaspoon vegetable oil
1 onion, finely diced
500 g minced beef
1 stick French bread or 10 small
    dinner rolls
butter
4 leaves lettuce, finely shredded
2 tomatoes, sliced thinly
1 carrot, finely grated
125 g cheese, finely shredded
tomato sauce

1. Heat oil in a pan and fry onion until soft. Combine with beef in a bowl. Divide mixture into 10 portions. Using wet hands, shape meat into flat patties a little larger than the diameter of the French bread or dinner rolls.

2. Place meat patties under a hot grill and cook 3–5 minutes each side, turning once until patties are browned and cooked on both sides. Slice French bread thinly into 20 slices or split dinner rolls in half. Toast bread or rolls lightly on one side. Spread with butter.
3. To serve: place each meat patty on bread and top with lettuce, tomato, carrot and cheese. Top with tomato sauce and bread. Insert a toothpick through the centre of the hamburger to hold it together.

HINT
Meat patties may be cooked in advance and reheated in the microwave at serving time, before assembling hamburgers; or the meat patties can be cooked in the oven at 200°C for 10–15 minutes or until cooked through.

1. Heat oil in a large pan and add mince, a little at a time. Cook until mince browns and separates into small pieces. Add onions, garlic and spices and cook 5 minutes. Add tomatoes, tomato paste and stock cube. Return to the boil, then reduce heat and simmer for 45–50 minutes.
2. Add undrained kidney beans, stir well and reheat. Add cornflour mixture a little at a time until mixture thickens. Return to the boil. Serve hot with fresh bread rolls or bowls of steamed rice.

GHETTO BLASTER

Preparation time: 1½ hours
Cooking time: 50 minutes
Advanced

2 x 350 g packets cake mix or
    2 quantities butter cake batter (see
    recipe page 96)
2 x 450 g packets soft white icing
orange food colouring
¾ cup seedless jam, warmed
black food colouring
1 cup icing sugar
2–3 tablespoons water
2 licorice allsorts
1 chocolate bar e.g. Flake

1. Preheat oven to 180°C. Grease
and line two 20 cm square cake tins.
Make the cakes according to the
directions on the packet or following
recipe. Divide the mixture between
prepared tins and bake for 40–50
minutes or until cooked. Cool.
2. Cut one cake in half vertically to
form the speakers. Roll the two
packets of soft white icing together
and colour orange. Cut off one-fifth of
the icing and set it aside for the
markings and finishing touches.
Divide the remaining icing in half and
cut one half in half again.
3. Roll out the larger piece of icing
until it is large enough to cover the
top and sides of the uncut cake with
about 1 cm extra on each side. Brush
the cake with warm jam and using a
rolling pin, roll the prepared icing
over the cake. Turn the cake over and
brush the edge of the underside with
warm jam. Bring the excess icing over
and press into the jam. Set the cake
upright (see diagrams 1 and 2).
Repeat this process with the two
smaller pieces of icing, covering the
two pieces of cake for speakers.
4. Roll out the reserved small piece
(one-fifth) of soft icing to about
16 x 22 cm. From it, cut two 4 cm
circles to form round speakers, and
two rectangles about 4 x 7 cm for the
longer speakers (see diagram 3). Use
the remainder to cut a rectangle,
18 x 2 cm, and another 18 x 4 cm.
Use these for the radio and for the
switch panel.
5. Cut five small squares, each
2 x 1.5 cm and use these for the
control buttons. Cut one last

The Ghetto Blaster

rectangle 8 x 4 cm for the cassette
itself. Mix a little black food colouring
with water to form a paste. Paint all
these small pieces with this.
6. Brush the positions for each of the
buttons with warm jam, and place the
buttons appropriately. Mix the icing
sugar and water together to form a
stiff paste of piping consistency. Pipe
in the numerals, lines and words as
shown. Place Smarties in position.
Stand the Ghetto Blaster on a cake
board. Put two licorice allsorts on top
of the main cake and balance the
chocolate bar between them securing
with icing if necessary.

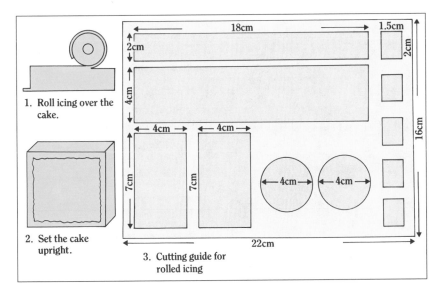

1. Roll icing over the cake.

2. Set the cake upright.

3. Cutting guide for rolled icing

Favourite Party Fare

SOMETIMES A THEME is not the order of the day and a simple party at home is what the young host or the parents want.

A variety of party food will make the event a special occasion. Included in this selection of recipes are Fairy Bread and Sausage Rolls, both perennial party favourites. Sandwiches cut into alphabet shapes, with the yummiest of fillings, are always welcome. Frozen Strawberry Pops are easy to make and should have the most pernickety eater coming back for more.

FRUITY MILK SHAKE

Preparation time: 5 minutes
Cooking time: nil
Serves 6
Easy

1 litre milk, chilled
1 cup fresh orange juice, chilled
4 passionfruit or granadillas
vanilla ice-cream

1. Put milk, orange juice and passionfruit pulp into the container of a blender. Cover and blend for about 15 seconds.
2. Pour into tumblers. Serve each with a scoop of ice-cream.

Clockwise from top left: Fruity Milkshake, Sausage Rolls, Alphabet Sandwiches, Fairy Bread, Frozen Strawberry Pops, Cream Cheese Shapes and Traffic Lights (centre)

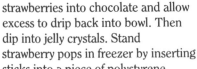
Frozen Strawberry Pops

FROZEN STRAWBERRY POPS

Preparation time: 30 minutes plus
  freezing time
Cooking time: 3 minutes
Makes about 20
Easy

1 x 250 g punnet strawberries
125 g white chocolate
½ x 85 g packet strawberry jelly
  crystals
lollipop sticks

1. Rinse strawberries under cold water and pat dry with absorbent paper. Remove green stems. Insert lollipop stick in the core end of each strawberry. Place in the refrigerator to chill.
2. Melt white chocolate in a bowl over hot water. Remove from the heat and cool slightly. Stir thoroughly. Dip strawberries into chocolate and allow excess to drip back into bowl. Then dip into jelly crystals. Stand strawberry pops in freezer by inserting sticks into a piece of polystyrene.
3. Freeze until firm.

FAIRY BREAD

Preparation time: 15 minutes
Cooking time: nil
Serves 10
Easy

10 slices bread
butter for spreading
1 cup hundreds and thousands

1. Spread bread thinly with butter. Sprinkle liberally with hundreds and thousands. Press down topping gently to make sprinkles adhere to bread.
2. To serve: remove crusts from bread and cut diagonally into quarters.

VARIATIONS
Instead of butter and hundreds and thousands use
*peanut butter and coloured sprinkles
*peanut-chocolate spread and toasted
  coconut
*honey and crushed chocolate-
  honeycomb bars

ALPHABET SANDWICHES

Preparation time: 45 minutes
Cooking time: nil
Serves 10
Easy

1 loaf sliced bread
butter for spreading

1. Spread slices of bread thinly with butter. Spread 10 slices or half the loaf with the filling of your choice, and top with slices of buttered bread.

2. Cut each sandwich into the shape of a different letter of the alphabet, using a sharp pointed knife. Skewer each sandwich with a toothpick or small flag with the individual child's name written on it.
3. Cover with plastic wrap, damp greaseproof paper or a lightly damp tea towel to prevent sandwiches from drying out.

FILLINGS
Tuna and Cress
Drain 1 x 425 g can tuna; mix together with 2 tablespoons mayonnaise and a squeeze of lemon juice. Divide between 10 slices bread. Top with cress or fresh mung bean sprouts.

Cheese, Date and Honey
Combine together 500 g softened cream cheese, 2 tablespoons honey and 5 tablespoons chopped walnuts. Beat together until light and fluffy. Spread over 10 slices bread and top with 250 g chopped pitted dates.

Peanut Butter and Jam
Spread 10 slices bread thickly with peanut butter. Spread remaining 10 slices with a little jam. Join each slice of peanut buttered bread with a slice of bread and jam

Alphabet Sandwiches

SAUSAGE ROLLS

Preparation time: 35 minutes
Cooking time: 25 minutes
Makes 48
Easy

1 onion, finely chopped
1 teaspoon vegetable oil
500 g sausage mince
1 cup soft white breadcrumbs
2 tablespoons tomato sauce
1 egg, lightly beaten
3 sheets frozen, ready rolled puff
   pastry, thawed
egg or milk for glazing

Sausage Rolls

1. Preheat oven to 220°C. Lightly
grease an oven tray.
2. Sauté onion in oil over low heat
until onion is soft and transparent. In
a bowl mix together onion, mince,
breadcrumbs, tomato sauce and egg.
3. Lay three sheets of pastry on a
lightly floured board and cut in thirds
horizontally. Divide the meat mixture
into six equal portions and spoon
across the long edge of the pastry.
Roll up to form a long sausage shape.
Brush lightly with a little beaten egg
or milk to glaze. Cut into 4 cm
lengths and place on prepared tray.

4. Bake for 10 minutes, reduce heat
to 180°C and bake a further
15 minutes until rolls are golden.
Serve warm with tomato sauce.

HINTS
Freeze uncooked sausage rolls and
bake as many as required directly
from the freezer.
   Bake sausage rolls ahead of time
and reheat at 150°C for 5–10 minutes
until heated through.
   If taking these on a picnic, place
the warm rolls in a covered
polystyrene container, with a hot-
water bottle filled with boiling water.

CREAM CHEESE SHAPES

Preparation time: 30 minutes
Cooking time: 20 minutes
Serves 10
Easy

10 slices bread
250 g cream cheese, softened
2 tablespoons sour cream
1 tablespoon icing sugar
spread e.g. jam, honey, lemon butter
topping e.g. Smarties, marshmallows,
   raisins or sultanas or shredded
   coconut

1. Preheat oven to 150°C. Cut out
shapes of bread using a variety of
biscuit cutters. Arrange bread shapes
on a flat oven tray and bake for 15–20
minutes until bread is crispy but still
pale. Remove from oven and cool.
2. Beat together cream cheese, sour
cream and icing sugar until light and
fluffy.
3. Fill a piping bag fitted with a small
star pipe with cheese mixture. Pipe
around the edge of the bread shapes.
Spoon a little spread into the centre
of the bread and decorate with your
choice of topping.

HINT
For a delicious variation, use fruit loaf
instead of plain bread. Spread dried
fruit loaf shapes with cream cheese
mixture and dust with cinnamon and
sugar.
   When drying the fruit loaf shapes
in the oven keep a close eye on them
— they could begin to brown due to
the high sugar content.

Cream Cheese Shapes

TRAFFIC LIGHTS

Preparation time: 30 minutes
Cooking time: nil
Makes 24
Easy

250 g processed or cheddar cheese
1 x 30 g packet of cheese flavoured
   biscuits
24 cherry tomatoes
6 gherkins, cut into quarters
small toothpicks or Twiglets

1. Cut cheese into 24 even-sized
cubes. Place biscuits in a bag and
crush. Add cheese to bag and toss
until coated with crumbs.
2. Onto a toothpick or Twiglet thread
one cherry tomato, one piece of
cheese and one piece of gherkin.
Repeat until all ingredients are used.
Chill until ready to serve.

Traffic Lights

Basic Beginnings

BUTTER CAKE

Preparation time: 45 minutes
Cooking time: 45 minutes
Easy

125 g butter
¾ cup caster sugar
1 teaspoon vanilla essence
3 eggs
3 cups self-raising flour, sifted
½ cup milk

1. Preheat oven to 180°C. Grease a 20 cm cake tin with melted butter, line with greaseproof paper and grease again.
    Alternatively, prepare cake tins as directed in novelty cake recipe.
2. Cream butter and sugar until pale, light and fluffy. Flavour with vanilla essence. Add eggs one at a time, beating well after each addition. Fold in flour and milk alternately beginning and finishing with flour.
3. Spoon mixture into prepared tin and bake for 40–45 minutes or until cooked when tested. Remove from oven. Stand in tin for 5 minutes before turning out onto a wire rack to cool.

OLD FASHIONED CHOCOLATE CAKE

Preparation time: 40 minutes
Cooking time: 45 minutes
Easy

60 g butter, softened
¾ cup caster sugar
1 egg
1 teaspoon vanilla essence
1½ cups self-raising flour
1 tablespoon cocoa
½ cup milk
¼ teaspoon bicarbonate of soda
¼ cup hot water

1. Preheat oven to 180°C. Grease and line a square 20 cm cake tin with greaseproof paper and grease again. Alternatively, prepare cake tins as directed in novelty cake recipe.
2. Cream butter and sugar together until blended (the mixture will not cream very well because of the high sugar to butter ratio). Add egg and vanilla and beat well.
3. Sift together flour and cocoa three times. Fold into butter mixture alternately with milk, beginning and ending with flour. Dissolve soda in hot water and fold into cake mixture.
4. Pour into tin. Bake for 40–45 minutes or until cooked when tested. Stand for 5 minutes in tin before turning out to cool on a wire rack.

BUTTER ICING

Preparation time: 10 minutes
Cooking time: nil
Makes sufficient to cover and fill a 23 cm cake
Easy

200 g butter
3 cups icing sugar
¼ teaspoon vanilla essence
1–2 tablespoons hot water

1. Cream butter until light and fluffy. Beat in sifted icing sugar and vanilla essence until smooth. If necessary, add a little hot water to get a smooth spreading consistency.

VARIATIONS
Chocolate: sift icing sugar with 3 tablespoons cocoa.
Orange: mix through the finely grated zest of 1 orange and substitute fresh orange juice for the water.
Peppermint: add peppermint essence in place of vanilla.
Coffee: dissolve 3 teaspoons coffee powder in the hot water.

BUTTERCREAM FROSTING

Preparation time: 20 minutes
Cooking time: nil
Makes sufficient to ice a 20 cm cake
Easy

This rich frosting is suitable to use as a filling as well as a cake covering. It is always best to use unsalted butter, which gives a sweeter, creamier frosting.

125 g softened butter
1 teaspoon vanilla essence
1½ cups icing sugar, sifted
2 tablespoons cream

1. Beat butter until pale and creamy. Add vanilla and half the icing sugar and beat until combined. Gradually add milk and remaining sugar, beating until smooth.

GLACÉ ICING

Preparation time: 10 minutes
Cooking time: 5 minutes
Makes sufficient to cover 1 x 23 cm cake
Easy

This is a very shiny icing that gives a smooth finish. The icing must be warmed first so that it becomes thin and runny. Pour over the cake immediately. To avoid cracking the smooth surface, try not to move the cake until the icing has set. This icing may also be used for piping but is then not warmed first.

2 cups icing sugar, sifted
2–3 tablespoons water
flavouring essence
food colouring

1. Place sugar in a bowl. Beat in water and essence to form a smooth thick paste. Colour with a little food

colouring, adding gradually until the desired colour is reached. The icing is now ready for piping.

2. To use as an icing, place bowl over a pan of simmering water and heat until mixture is runny and shiny. Pour immediately over the surface of the cake to be iced. Guide icing with a hot wet spatula. Allow icing to set before moving the iced cake.

TO COLOUR SUGAR

Place the required amount of crystal or caster sugar into a large strong bag or a large screwtop jar, add a few drops of food colouring and seal bag or replace lid of jar. Shake vigorously until colour is evenly dispersed and the desired colour is obtained. Add a little more food colouring if necessary.

TO COLOUR COCONUT

Place the required amount of shredded or desiccated coconut into a large jar or strong bag. Add a few drops of food colouring. If the food colouring is a very intense in colour, dilute it with a little cold water. Place lid on jar or seal bag firmly, and shake vigorously until colour is evenly dispersed. If colour does not disperse evenly, wear a clean pair of disposable gloves or wear a clean plastic bag on each hand, and work the colour through with your hands.

CUTTING SHAPES OF LICORICE AND ANGELICA

Lots of great shapes can be made from licorice and angelica. Cut these shapes using sharp scissors dipped in very hot water. Pinking shears will give a decorative edge. A sharp knife will work equally well but requires a little more care.

HOW TO MAKE A PIPING BAG

1. Cut a 20 cm square of heavy greaseproof paper. Fold in half diagonally to form a triangle. Run a sharp knife along the folded edge to cut cleanly.
2. Take corner (1) and roll it so it lies inside the corner (2).
3. Bring unfolded corner (3) around the outside of the rolled cone so the edges line up together.
4. Gently pull corner (3) upwards to give bag a tight, firm tip.
5. Secure with tape and fold over top of bag.
6. Fill bag with icing or other filling and snip a small piece off the tip.

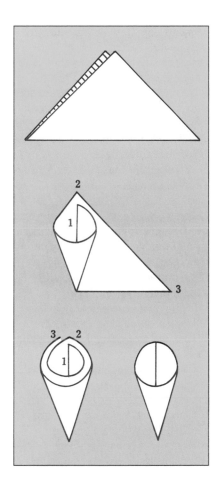

CAKE BOARDS

It can be difficult to find a suitable board or plate for children's birthday cakes. However, there is all sorts of equipment that can do the job. Generally, a board has to be fairly large to accommodate the size of the cake together with surrounding decorations. The board is usually covered to enhance the appearance of the cake, protect the board, and prevent oil or fat oozing through from the frostings and cakes.

Suitable boards include:
*pieces of masonite — ideal for cake boards; a hardware or timber shop will usually cut them to the required size;
*an up-turned dinner tray providing a flat surface; this is often large enough for the cake;
*a flat oven slide or baking tray;
*a large chopping board;
*the outside of a large cardboard box which has been used for packaging large electrical appliances;
*large pieces of polystyrene used in packaging.

Suitable board coverings include:
*coloured shiny wrapping paper;
*foil, smooth or scrunched to give an uneven surface;
*silver or gold cake paper available from icing specialist shops and health food shops;
*coloured fabric. (Often, however, fat will ooze out of the cake and frosting and stain the cloth);
*a board spread with a thin layer of icing and sprinkled with coconut, hundreds and thousands, chocolate sprinkles, silver cachous, a mixture of sweets or coloured popcorn;
*a board sprayed with gloss paint. Ensure that the board is thoroughly dry before putting the cake on it.

Sweets and Candy

Sweets make a delicious treat for children to take home after parties, and excellent prizes for party games. Commercially made sweets are a quick alternative for filling sweet bags, but home-made treats have an added charm and flavour. Some of these recipes can be made by the party host, others could be made with help from you.

Confectionery can be attractively presented in a variety of ways. Put some in a paper cup or a tiny basket, cover with cellophane and add a flourish of curly ribbon; or use paper serviettes or coloured paper, twisted into cones. Larger treats can be individually wrapped and tied with ribbon.

Children enjoy making their own sweet bags. Give them a good supply of paints, felt-tipped pens, coloured pencils and crayons, and an assortment of brown and white paper bags and let their imaginations run wild. Add a selection of scissors and glue (supervise younger children), tape, glitter, stars and stickers, used gift-wrap, old greeting cards, recycled boxes and containers.

Alternatively, make packaging from small lunch bags or cellophane packets. Make cardboard baskets decorated with hand-drawn patterns, or a collage of pictures cut from old magazines. Margarine tubs can be decorated with stickers and glitter. Try filling an ice-cream cone with sweets, then wrapping it in cellophane. If you have oddments of felt, fabric or tulle left over from sewing, use them to make pouches or small loot bags.

Filled sweet bags can be prepared well ahead of time. Toffee-based treats such as toffee apples, praline, sesame crunch and popcorn pearls should be stored in a dry place, particularly in humid weather. Alternatively, prepare them on the day of the party, or one day before.

Children enjoy helping in the preparation and cooking of sweets, but remember that hot sugar mixtures do reach very high temperatures, and can inflict serious burns if they are accidentally spilt or splashed. Young children, particularly, need help and a watchful eye if they volunteer as sweet-makers.

SECRETS FOR SUCCESS
Confectionery is not difficult to make provided a few rules are applied:

* Use heavy-based pans when making toffee or syrups.

* Choose wooden spoons for stirring sugar syrups as they do not transfer heat, nor do they discolour the pan.

* Prior to cooking, have utensils and ingredients ready. You will need to work very quickly before the mixture begins to set, so time is a crucial factor.

* A candy thermometer, although not essential, does take the guesswork out of cooking sugar syrups. If using one, place it in a saucepan of water and bring to the boil. Meanwhile, bring the sugar syrup to the boil in another pan. After the syrup has boiled, transfer the candy thermometer to the syrup; clip it to the side of the pan. Watch the temperature carefully, particularly as the mixture approaches the required heat.

*When making toffee-based sweets or boiling a sugar syrup it is essential to dissolve the sugar prior to the mixture boiling. Do this by bringing the syrup slowly to the boil, and stirring until the sugar is dissolved. Wash undissolved sugar crystals down the side of the pan with a pastry brush dipped in water.

*Unless the recipe advises otherwise, avoid stirring a sugar syrup after it has come to the boil.

*In humid weather, remember that sugar mixtures take longer to cook. After cooking, store in a dry place to prevent the confectionery from becoming syrupy.

DECORATIONS
When confectionery has been made, decorate it with hundreds and thousands, coconut, silver cachous, cherries, chopped nuts, licorice, melted or grated chocolate, sesame seeds, dried fruits or coloured sugar.

Clockwise from upper left: Frozen Moments, Toffee Apples, Speckled Bubble Bars, Fast Chocolate Fudge, Sesame Crunch, Toffees, Popcorn Pearls and Coconut Roughs. Centre: Coconut Ice, New Orleans Pralines.

Frozen Moments

1. Line a 28 x 18 cm shallow tin with greaseproof paper and brush lightly with oil. Place sesame seeds in a frypan and stir over low heat until lightly toasted. Cool.
2. Combine remaining ingredients in another pan. Cook over low heat, stirring until sugar dissolves and mixture boils. Boil for 2 minutes without stirring. Fold in sesame seeds and pour at once into prepared tin, spreading evenly. Cool 15–20 minutes.
3. Remove crunch from tin with paper attached. With a sharp knife, cut into small fingers or squares. Cool completely, then peel off paper. Wrap pieces individually.

SPECKLED BUBBLE BARS

Preparation time: 20 minutes
Cooking time: 5 minutes
Makes 24
Easy

1½ cups marshmallows
60 g butter
½ teaspoon peppermint essence
2½ cups Rice Crispies
½ cup hundreds and thousands

1. Line an 18 x 28 cm shallow tin with foil or baking paper and grease lightly. Place marshmallows and butter in a small pan. Stir over low heat until melted. Remove from heat.
2. Stir in essence. Place Rice Crispies and hundreds and thousands in a large bowl. Pour in marshmallow mixture and mix well.
3. Pour into prepared tin and spread out evenly with a spatula. Cool and cut into squares.

FROZEN MOMENTS

Preparation time: 35 minutes
Cooking time: 15 minutes
Makes 20
Easy

2 cups white sugar
2 tablespoons gelatine
2 cups cold water
vanilla essence
20 coloured ice cream cones
375 g mixed sweets

1. Place sugar, gelatine and water in a pan. Bring slowly to the boil stirring until sugar dissolves. Boil for 10 minutes, remove from heat and cool.
2. Stir in essence and beat with an electric mixer until mixture is thick and fluffy. Drop a few sweets into the base of each cone and fill with marshmallow mixture. Decorate with sweets and shredded coconut. When marshmallow cools it will set firm.

TOFFEE

Preparation time: 20 minutes
Cooking time: 15 minutes
Makes 24
Easy

1 cup water
4 cups sugar
1 tablespoon vinegar
hundreds and thousands or coconut
    for decoration

1. Heat water, sugar and vinegar in a pan, stirring until sugar dissolves. Brush any sugar crystals down sides of pan with a wet pastry brush.
2. Bring to the boil. Cook, without stirring, until mixture turns golden or reaches 132°C.
3. Pour into paper cake cases and allow to set. Decorate as desired.

COCONUT ROUGHS

Preparation time: 10 minutes
Cooking time: 1 minute
Makes 36
Easy

125 g copha
¾ cup icing sugar, sifted
½ cup cocoa
⅓ cup dried milk powder
1 cup desiccated coconut

1. Lightly brush a flat oven tray with oil. Melt copha over low heat. Mix together all remaining ingredients and pour in melted copha. Mix until well combined.
2. Place teaspoonfuls of mixture on prepared tray. Refrigerate until set.

SESAME CRUNCH

Preparation time: 20 minutes
Cooking time: 20 minutes
Makes 24
Easy

2 cups sesame seeds
½ cup honey
½ cup sugar
½ teaspoon ground ginger
½ teaspoon cinnamon

Toffee

NEW ORLEANS PRALINES

Preparation time: 25 minutes
Cooking time: 20 minutes
Makes 24
Medium

2 cups sugar
⅔ cup milk
⅓ cup dark corn syrup
½ teaspoon vanilla essence
1 cup pecan pieces

Speckled Bubble Bars

1. Combine sugar, milk and syrup in a heavy-based pan. Stir over low heat until sugar dissolves and mixture comes to the boil. Continue boiling until a teaspoonful of syrup dropped into cold water can be shaped into a soft ball or until mixture reaches 112°–118°C.
2. Remove from heat and cool to lukewarm. Add vanilla and beat with wooden spoon until mixture begins to thicken. Stir in pecans.
3. Spoon small portions onto greaseproof paper, flattening each slightly. Stand until set.

COCONUT ICE

Preparation time: 20 minutes
Cooking time: nil
Makes 20 pieces
Easy

1 x 410 g can condensed milk
1 tablespoon strawberry essence
3⅓ cups icing sugar, sifted
4 cups desiccated coconut
pink food colouring

1. Combine condensed milk, essence, icing sugar and coconut in a bowl and mix well.
2. Divide mixture into halves. Colour one half pale pink and press firmly into a lightly oiled bar tin. Top with remaining mixture and chill until firm. Cut into squares for serving.

TOFFEE APPLES

Preparation time: 50 minutes
Cooking time: 20 minutes
Makes 20
Medium

20 red apples
1 cup water
4 cups sugar
1 tablespoon vinegar
4 teaspoons powdered red food
    colouring or 2 tablespoons cochineal

1. Wash, dry and polish apples. Place a 15 cm skewer into the centre of each apple.
2. Combine remaining ingredients in a pan. Bring slowly to the boil, stirring until sugar dissolves. Boil, without stirring, until mixture becomes brittle when a little of it is dropped into iced water.
3. Dip apples into toffee and swirl around until coated. Drain. Cool on a sheet of greased foil until toffee sets.

POPCORN PEARLS

Preparation time: 1½ hours
Cooking time: 30 minutes
Makes 12 x 50 cm lengths
Medium

⅓ cup vegetable oil
1 cup uncooked popcorn
1 cup white sugar
1 tablespoon honey
1 tablespoon golden syrup
½ cup water
60 g butter

1. Heat oil in a large pan, add popcorn and cover pan with a lid. Place over moderate heat and cook, shaking pan occasionally. When popping stops, all the popcorn is cooked. Transfer to a large bowl, removing unpopped corn.
2. Combine remaining ingredients in a heavy-based pan and bring slowly to the boil, stirring until the sugar dissolves. Wash undissolved crystals down sides of pan with a wet pastry brush. Ensure all the sugar dissolves before mixture boils. Boil until mixture reaches 150°C. Test by dropping a small amount of mixture in iced water — it should turn hard and brittle.

3. Pour over popcorn and mix until well coated. Continue stirring until mixture sets and cools slightly. Place on large tray to cool.
4. Cut 12 x 50 cm lengths of heavy cotton. Using a thick needle, thread individual pieces of popcorn on cotton to make strings of popcorn, continuing until thread is completely covered. Tie ends together.

HINT
You can omit steps 2 and 3 and simply sprinkle the popcorn with a little icing sugar or garlic powder and then thread on cotton if you prefer.

FAST CHOCOLATE FUDGE

Preparation time: 15 minutes plus
    chilling time
Cooking time: 5 minutes
Makes about 49
Easy

125 g dark compound cooking
    chocolate, chopped
125 g copha, chopped
2 tablespoons icing sugar
1 tablespoon cocoa
½ x 420 g can sweetened condensed
    milk
½ teaspoon vanilla essence

1. Line the base of an 18 cm square cake tin with greaseproof paper or foil. Oil lightly.
2. Melt together chocolate and copha over a low heat, stirring until smooth.
3. Quickly stir in remaining ingredients until blended (mixture will begin to firm immediately).
4. Pour at once into prepared tin; smooth the surface. Chill until firm. Cut into squares to serve.

Fast Chocolate Fudge

Party Games

CHILDREN LOVE party games. Adults enjoy them too. For a successful party, have a varied programme of games prepared in advance. Keep things moving by having all necessary equipment to play the games — thimbles, counters or blindfolds — ready before guests arrive. When things get boisterous, introduce a few quiet games.

Remember to have lots of small prizes ready. One way of presenting these is to fill a deep bowl with assorted small items — fancy pencils and rubbers, small chocolate bars, whistles, candy canes — and let children choose their prizes with their eyes closed, on a lucky dip basis.

MUSICAL GAMES

Traditional musical games are familiar and popular, especially with pre-school children, and help break down the shyness barrier. Often, the same game is played repeatedly without any signs of boredom. Let them continue until they tire of it, then move on to the next game.

Ring-a-Ring-of-Roses

Players form a circle and join hands, then skip around singing the verse. At the words 'fall down' they all collapse on the floor. For older children, ring the changes by making the last player to fall be 'out'.

Ring-a-ring-of-roses
A pocketful of posies
A tishoo! A tishoo!
We all fall down.

Oranges and Lemons

One player elects to be an orange, the other a lemon. They form an arch by holding hands above head level. While all sing the rhyme, the other players file behind each other, continually passing under the arch. With the words 'chop off your head', the two children forming the arch move their arms down to capture the child who is walking through the arch at the time. That one selects a side — oranges or lemons — and stands behind the appropriate part of the arch. The pattern continues until all are captured. Oranges then have a tug-of-war with the lemons. The rhyme is:

'Oranges and lemons,'
Say the bells of St. Clements.
'You owe me five farthings,'
Say the bells of St. Martins.
'When will you pay me?'
Say the bells of Old Bailey.
'When I grow rich,'
Say the bells of Shoreditch.
'When will that be?'
Ask the bells of Stephney.
'I'm sure I don't know,'
Says the great bell of Bow.

Here comes a candle to light you
    to bed,
Here comes a chopper to chop off
    your head.

The Farmer in the Dell

There are several variations of this game, sometimes known as *The Farmer in his Den*. The farmer is chosen. The other children form a

circle and walk around the farmer singing:

The farmer's in the dell,
The farmer's in the dell,
Hey ho, the dairy-o,
The farmer's in the dell.

The farmer wants a wife,
The farmer wants a wife,
Hey ho, the dairy-o,
The farmer wants a wife.

The farmer in the centre then chooses a partner to stand inside the circle with him.

The verse is repeated with the following substitutions:

The wife wants a child;
The child wants a nurse;
The nurse wants a dog.

Each time, the last nominated child chooses another one to step into the circle. Finally everyone sings

We all pat the dog,
We all pat the dog,
Hey ho, the dairy-o,
We all pat the dog.

Everyone then proceeds to pat the dog on the back. The game starts all over again, usually with the dog becoming the farmer.

Here We Go Round the Mulberry Bush

This is a game in which the children mime the different actions as they sing about them. In a circle, they dance and sing:

Here we go round the mulberry bush,
The mulberry bush, the mulberry
*   bush,*
Here we go round the mulberry bush,
On a cold and frosty morning.

Then they stop, and as they sing they mime:

This is the way we wash our clothes
Wash our clothes, wash our clothes,
This is the way we wash our clothes
On a cold and frosty morning.

Each child or an adult then sings the first line of a new verse and as everyone sings the rest, the actions are mimed. Some suggestions are:

This is the way we polish our shoes.
This is the way we wash our hands.
This is the way we clean our teeth.
This is the way we iron our clothes.
This is the way we drink our tea.
This is the way we pat our cat.
This is the way we walk to school.

Keep the actions familiar and children will probably want to play the game for some time. When they run out of ideas, stop the game and start another.

Three Blind Mice

Children join hands to form a circle round a child in the centre, who is chosen to be the farmer's wife. The children skip or dance round singing:

Three blind mice,
Three blind mice,
See how they run,
See how they run,
They all run after the farmer's wife
Who cuts off their tails with a carving
*   knife.*
Did you ever see such a thing in your
*   life*
As three blind mice?

At the end of the last line, the farmer's wife tries to catch someone. The mouse then joins the farmer's wife in the centre and the game begins again until all the children have been caught. If the game starts over again, the first child caught becomes the farmer's wife.

When-the-Music-Stops Games

Ideally the person stopping and starting the music should be hidden from the players. However, a little judicious cheating ensures that every young child receives a prize.

Pass the Parcel

The players sit round in a circle. A prize, wrapped in several layers of paper, is passed round from player to player as music plays. When the music stops, the child holding the parcel unwraps one layer. Then the music starts again and the passing continues. Eventually the music stops for the last layer of wrapping, leaving the winner holding the prize. For very young children, place a sweet at every layer to hold their interest.

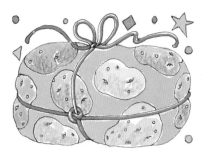

Hot Potato

Players sit in a circle. A smooth object such as a plastic ball is quickly passed round as the music plays. When the music stops the player holding the object is eliminated from the circle. Another variation of this is *Musical Torch*; lights are turned out, and as the music plays a torch is passed at just under chin level so that the face of each child is lit up. Whoever is left holding the torch when the music stops has to drop out. A stout plastic torch is best, as it may be dropped.

Musical Bumps

Players caper about as music plays. When it stops, all players must immediately sit down. Last one to sit is out. The game goes on until only the winner is left.

Musical Statues
This game is similar to *Musical Bumps*. When the music stops, the children have to 'freeze' in position and remain as still as statues. Anyone who twitches is out.

Musical Chairs
Two rows of chairs are placed back to back. The players march around the groups of chairs in the same direction in time to the music. When the music stops everyone must sit down, but there is one chair less. The person without a chair drops out. A chair is removed and the game starts again. The game continues until only two players are left competing for one chair.

Another variation of this is *Musical Cushions*. (Cushions are easier to move than chairs, too.)

Musical Hats
A funny game which is rather like *Musical Chairs*, but is played with a hat for each player, except one. Everyone stands or sits in a circle, facing in the same direction. When the music starts, each player takes the hat from the head of the person in front and puts it on. When the music stops the person without a hat is eliminated. Remove one hat and continue the game until only one person is left with a hat.

Jump the Broom
Put a broom on the ground. Play music as the children skip round in a circle, jumping over the broom each time they come to it. When the music stops, the child jumping over the broom, or the last child to jump the broom is out. Continue until there is one child left.

Musical Sets
All players skip round the room as the music plays. When the music stops a number is called and they scramble to form sets of that number. Call out a number that must leave one child out; for example, call 'four' for 17 children and four sets will form with one child remaining. That player drops out. With the number fifteen you could call out seven and one more player would be eliminated.

OTHER FAVOURITES

String Hunt
This is a good game to warm up a young party as it will keep the early arrivals occupied while waiting for the other guests to arrive. Allow a ball of string for each guest; tie one end of it to a small present and place the present where it can be seen. Unwind the ball of string, making a trail across chairs, under tables, around door knobs, under rugs and so on, making it tricky and moderately tangled, depending on the age group. As the guests arrive, each is given her ball of string and she starts to wind up the string. The string trail is followed until the present at the end is reached. It is a good idea to put breakables out of the way while the game is in progress.

Follow the Leader
A simple non-competitive game that delights young children and is a good one to get a young party moving. With some music playing, an adult leads the line of children around the house or garden either skipping, hopping or jogging and performing odd actions which the children copy. Crawl under tables, jump over benches and skip in and out of trees. The more varied, the better.

Froggy, Froggy, May We Cross Your Shining River?
One child is elected to be Froggy, and stands with back turned to the rest of the group. Two parallel lines are marked with a good space — about 4–5 metres — between them. Froggy stands behind the line on one side, and the rest of the group stands behind the line on the other side.

Together, the group chants, 'Froggy, Froggy, may we cross your shining river?'

Froggy responds, 'Not unless you wear the colour — BLUE!' or, 'Not unless you wear — GREEN SOCKS!' or whatever Froggy chooses. At the chosen word — 'BLUE!' or 'GREEN SOCKS!' — Froggy turns quickly to face the rest of the group, and the child or children wearing the nominated colour or clothing have to race across the river without being caught by Froggy. The child who is caught becomes the next Froggy, and the last frog returns to the group.

Pin the Tail on the Donkey
Draw an outline of a donkey without a tail on a large sheet of cardboard. Mark a spot where the tail should be. Place in a position where the children can reach. Each child in turn is given the donkey's tail with a drawing pin in one end. The child is blindfolded, spun round, steps forward and tries to pin the tail in the appropriate spot. The position is marked with the child's initial and the next child has a turn. The one who puts the tail on, or nearest to, the correct spot, wins.

What's the Time, Mr Wolf?
A chasing game that is best played outdoors. One player or an adult is chosen to be Mr Wolf. A den or safe place is chosen at the start. Mr Wolf prowls around followed by the rest of the children who keep calling, 'What's the time, Mr Wolf?' Mr Wolf must answer with a time of the day such as one o'clock, six o'clock, four o'clock and so on. When Mr Wolf, at his discretion, growls 'Dinner time' the children must dash for the den. If the wolf catches anyone before they reach the safety area, the victim becomes the next Mr Wolf. Alternatively, this game can be played by elimination. Each child caught sits down. The last player to be caught becomes the wolf for the next round.

Pass the Oranges
Arrange for two teams to stand in line with each person behind the other.

Each team is given an orange. The orange is to be passed down the line from one player to another without using hands. To do so, it is held by each player under the chin and transferred to the chin of the next player.

If at any point the orange is dropped, it must be returned to the front of the line and passing starts all over again.

The first team to complete passing the orange to all members, wins.

Sardines

An extremely popular hide and seek game that can be played indoors or outside. All players except one count to 100 together. The odd one out goes into hiding. All then hunt for the hidden player. When discovered, the finder does not shout out but joins the person in hiding. In the end, all seekers have become hiders, squashed into one hiding place with much hilarity. The first seeker to find the hiding place becomes the first hider in the next game.

Blowing Bubbles

Very young children are fascinated with bubbles. A supply of plastic bubble pipes and liquid can keep them amused for some time. Bubbles are best blown outdoors. It can be made competitive by seeing who can blow the biggest bubble, or whose bubble lasts the longest.

Guessing Competition

Place a number of small colourful sweets such as jelly beans in a glass jar. Ask each guest to guess how many sweets there are in the jar. The child with the nearest guess wins the jar.

On the Bank, In the River

A lively game for young children. Line them up behind a marked line. The side they are standing on is the bank, the other side is the river. Call out 'in the river' or 'on the bank', mixing up the commands. Children have to jump to the correct side. Those who do not are out.

Scavenger Chase

Depending on the age of the children, the game list can be made simple for very young children who have just begun to read, or quite complicated for older children. The idea of the game is to give each player (or pair of players) a list of objects to collect within a determined length of time. A good idea is to write the list on a paper bag, which can be used for collecting. The first to collect all the items on their list wins. A simple list might include a piece of string, a

flower, a gum leaf, a round stone, a feather and so on.

A variation of this game is an Alphabet Hunt; each player is given or chooses a letter of the alphabet, and has to collect things beginning with that letter.

Trains and Stations

One person is chosen to sit in the middle of a circle of players who are holding hands with their arms crossed. Another person in the circle is chosen as the leader who sets the train off. Two people in the circle are 'stations'. The train is sent around the circle by a squeeze of the hand and every time it passes a station the person says, 'toot toot'. The train can be sent in the same direction or sent back by squeezing the hand on the side where the train just came from. The aim of the person in the middle is to guess which person has the train at any particular moment. If their guess is correct, then the person caught with the train has to go into the middle. Stations should be changed at changeover of players.

Fishing Competition

You will need an assortment of coloured fish cut out from light cardboard. The host will enjoy making these before the party. Attach

a safety pin to the nose of each fish. Write a number on the back of each fish to represent its weight and arrange them all in a large shallow dish which represents the lake. Turn them over so that the numbers cannot be seen. Give each player a fishing rod, made by tying a small magnet on to the end of a pencil with a piece of cotton or light string. On the starting signal, all the players take their rods and try to catch as many fish as they can. When they are all caught, everyone adds up the total weight of the fish they have caught. The player with the highest score wins.

Wobbling Bunnies

A fun game for very young children. Players make their hands into ears at the sides of their heads and bunny-hop about, pretending to be rabbits. At the call of 'Danger', they freeze, and must keep absolutely still for the count of five. Any player who twitches a whisker during the count, is out.

QUIET GAMES

When things get rowdy, your nerves are fraying and a change of pace is needed, these quieter games can be introduced to vary the activities and keep the children's interest. They can also be played for a short period after the meal on wet days. Some of these games will also come in handy during school holidays, when travelling or on weekends.

I Spy

A child starts the game by silently choosing an object that can be seen in the room, then saying the first letter of its name. For example, if it's the clock, the child will say, 'I spy with my little eye something beginning with C'. The first player to guess the correct answer chooses the next object and starts the next round.

Alternatively, the game can be played with pencil and paper. All players are asked to write down as many things as can be seen all beginning with a certain letter. This can be played several times, finding a winner each time.

O'Grady Says

Also known as *Simon Says*. All players face O'Grady (or Simon) who performs various actions and gives an instruction that should begin with 'O'Grady says'. Some instructions deliberately omit the phrase, for example, 'O'Grady says touch your toes' or 'Hold your nose'. The children must only copy instructions prefaced by 'O'Grady says'. Players who perform an action that does not begin with 'O'Grady says' are out. The last child remaining is the winner.

Memory Test

Make a selection of about twenty common objects such as a spoon, key, button, book, sweet, pen, paperclip, safety pin etc. Place them on a tray and cover them with a cloth. Give each player a pencil and paper. The players gather round and the cloth is removed for two minutes. Then the tray is taken away. The players have to write down as many objects as they can remember. The player who makes the longest correct list within a set time limit is the winner.

Hangman

Pin a big piece of paper on a board. Think of a word of more than seven letters that the children will recognise, such as *kangaroo* or *elephant*. Draw dashes at the top of the paper to represent the number of letters making up the word. As each player calls out a letter, and provided it is correct, write it in the appropriate place. If it is not correct, start drawing a hangman, one line for each wrong call. If the correct word is completed before the hangman is finished, the group wins and you lose.

Paddy's Black Pig

This is great fun for a small group of children, or for playing one-to-one with a child.

The child, or group, are asked questions, to which they may only give one answer: 'Paddy's Black Pig.' Any child who smiles or giggles is out. Carefully framed questions form traps for the unwary;
'Who did you see when you looked in the mirror this morning?'
'Paddy's Black Pig'.
'Who's your best friend?'
'Paddy's Black Pig'.

Another version of this game is *Sausage*: instead of Paddy's Black Pig, the only answer that may be given is 'Sausage'.

Hat Making

A quiet game for a small number of children, this works very well when played in pairs. Give each pair one newspaper, three sheets of coloured paper, twelve pins, a roll of sticky tape and a pair of scissors. The pairs are asked to produce a fancy hat in fifteen minutes, using only the given material. The winning hat is the one voted best by all the players.

Feeling and Remembering

Fill a leg of a long thick sock with an assortment of about fifteen familiar objects such as a marble, cotton wool, matchbox, spoon, thimble, a walnut, a pencil and so on. In turn, the children are each given about a minute in which to feel the objects. Players then begin to write down as many objects as they could identify. The winner is the one who correctly identifies the most objects.

What's Wrong?

This is best played with a small number of children in a fairly uncluttered room. Tell all the players to take careful notice of all the details in the room. Explain to them that you will make some alteration to the room. Then send all the players outside and make your change, such as changing the chairs around, reversing the position of the vases, putting on a lamp light and so on. Call in the players and ask them to tell you what is wrong. The winner is the one with the first correct answer.

Making Words

The players are given a reasonably long (but comprehensible) word, which they write at the top of their sheets of paper. They are then given a set time of about ten minutes in which to make up as many words as they can from the letters of the given word. Score by giving a point for each word. No word made must contain less than three letters. Determine before the game if scoring will be allowed for plural words which are formed by the addition of the letter 's'. Some useful words for this type of game are:
alternative, Australian, chrys-anthemum, curiosity, combination, consequence, dictionary, dishwasher, enormous, fantastic, grammatical, monumental, maximum, necessarily, observatory, procrastinate, rigmarole and *theatrical*.

Mystery Matchboxes

Fill each of eight matchboxes with the following or other materials of your choice:

1. nails
2. rice
3. matches
4. pins
5. peanuts
6. lentils
7. gravel
8. sugar crystals

Write the number on each box. Tell the players what the contents of the boxes are, but not which box contains which objects. Let the children make a note of the objects. They then shake the boxes and try to match the correct box number with the contents.

GAMES WITH BALLOONS

Balloon Fight

Every child is given a balloon. They have to throw their balloon into the air and keep it up there, while at the same time trying to knock other players' balloons to the ground. The winner is the last player with a balloon in the air.

Whizzing Balloons

Each player stands behind a line and blows up a balloon of a different colour, or one marked with a player's name. The balloon is held at the neck to keep it inflated until the word 'Go' is called out. The balloons are then released to whiz forward. The balloon which travels the furthest wins.

Blow the Balloon Race

Divide the children into two teams, each team with a round balloon and each child with a straw. Each team has a starting line. On their hands and knees, and blowing through the straw, each child chases the balloon along the ground from the starting line to a turning point and back again. The first team to finish wins.

Broomstick Relay

Mark two parallel lines approximately three metres apart, and call one the starting line. Divide the children into pairs, then line them up opposite each other behind the line. Each child at the head of a starting line has a broom and a balloon. Each must sweep the balloon towards their opposite number, who must then sweep it back again. Bursting balloons disqualify sweepers, and the first pair to successfully complete the relay are the winners.

Hop and Pop

Tie a balloon to one ankle of each player. Children have to burst each other's balloons while keeping their own intact. A player is disqualified once his or her balloon is burst.

Knee Balloon Race

Players each have a book and a balloon. With the book balanced on their heads and the balloon held between their knees, they must race from starting point to finishing line. If

balloon or book are dropped, they must start again. If a balloon bursts, the player is disqualified or must start again. For a large party the players can be divided into teams and a normal relay procedure used.

Bat the Balloon

Divide the children into two teams and seat them, crossed legged on the floor and facing each other. The players must remain seated. The balloon is tossed between them and each team tries to tap the balloon over the heads of the opposite team, onto the ground behind their backs.

Balloon Dress-ups

Everyone, including the onlookers, enjoys this funny game. Each child is provided with an uninflated balloon, a chair and a basket containing an old hat, gloves, socks, scarf, coat and an old nightie. There must be similar items of clothing in each basket. The baskets are placed opposite the players some distance away. The players are lined up at their chairs with the balloon. On the starting signal they must blow up the balloon and secure the end. Then, taking the balloon with them, they run to their basket and put on all the clothes. When completely dressed, they must run back to their chair and sit on their balloon until it bursts. The first player to burst the balloon is the winner. A tip for the children: the more inflated the balloon, the easier it is to burst.

BLINDFOLD GAMES

After the age of four, most children enjoy blindfold games. Younger children can become quite frightened by them.

Blind Man's Bluff

One player is blindfolded, spun

around three times and left to catch one of the other players. The child must then guess, by feeling, who she has caught. If she guesses correctly, the caught child takes over as the Blind Man.

Taste and Guess

Players are asked to go out of the room while six or more dishes of different things are laid out. They are then led in blindfolded, and asked to taste the different things. They have to guess what they think they've eaten. Only a small amount should be given to each player. Suitable substances are grated cheese, mint leaf, cold pasta, tiny pieces of orange, desiccated coconut, sliced tomato, a cocktail onion and so on. Each player who has finished can stay in the room and quietly watch the others. The person who correctly identifies the most dishes is the winner.

Blindfold Drawing

Give each blindfolded player a piece of paper and a pencil, and a subject to draw, such as a house or a vase. When the players think they have completed their drawing, ask for some additions to be made, for example, 'Put a letterbox on the house' or 'Draw in the garden'. The winning picture is the one voted the most amusing or the best by the other players.

Find the Bell-Ringer

One child is given a bell, and all the others are blindfolded. The sighted child then mingles among the blindfolded children, occasionally ringing the bell. Players do their best to catch the bell-ringer. The one who succeeds is the next bell-ringer, while the last bell-ringer joins the group of blindfolded children.

GAMES FOR THE UNDER TWELVES

The following party games are enjoyed by the pre-teens and can be organised by the children themselves.

Wrap the Mummy

Divide the players into two teams and choose a child of equal size for each team. This child is to be the Mummy. Get the players to stand in a row, behind a line about two metres from their mummy. The object of the game is for each team to completely wrap their mummy in toilet paper, until no clothes or skin show. The mummy must stand perfectly still, with arms close to the body and legs straight and closed.

On a starting signal, the first player of each team has two minutes to start wrapping the mummy. When the time is up, the roll of toilet paper is handed to the next player and the first wrapper must go to the end of the line. No helping is allowed. The team who first completes the wrapping of their mummy is the winner.

Doughnut-Eating Race

Hang short lengths of string from the clothes line, one for each player. On each string tie a doughnut. The height of each doughnut must be adjusted so that the player has to stand on tiptoe to reach it with his mouth only. Hands must not be used. The first one to finish eating the whole doughnut wins.

Chopsticks and Marbles

A game best played by small numbers of children. Place about thirty marbles in a large bowl with water in it. Each child is given a turn of two minutes' duration. Using the chopsticks, and only one hand, they have to pick out the marbles and transfer them to a smaller bowl. Write down the total number of marbles moved after each child's turn, before returning the marbles to the large

bowl. The player who moves the most marbles is the winner.

Wooden chopsticks are the easiest to use.

Consequence Drawing

Give each child a pencil and a long sheet of paper that has been folded into three sections. Ask them all to draw the head of a person on the top third. The paper is folded once, then passed to the next player, who draws a body on the middle third. This is then folded over, passed on, and they all draw the legs and feet. The paper is passed on for a final time and then opened out, with hilarious results.

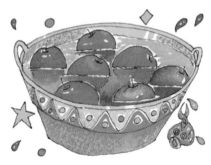

Apple Bobbing

Fill a large basin with water and float apples in it. Players kneel down and attempt to catch an apple using only their mouth. Each player who successfully removes an apple from the water may eat the apple. The winner is the player who first catches the apple. (This game must be supervised in case of accidental water inhalation.)

Postman's Holiday

You will need ten boxes, each with a posting slot and labelled with a different town or street name. The boxes are hidden around the house or garden. Each player gets ten envelopes with the same ten place names. Starting from a common central point, players pick up one envelope at a time, write their initials on the back, then run off to post it in the right box. They then run back for another envelope. They must post their ten envelopes as fast as possible. When they have all done so, open the boxes and check the envelopes inside. The one with the most posted correctly, wins.

The Chocolate Game

A hat, scarf and gloves, a knife, fork and plate, a bar of chocolate and a dice are needed for this game.

All players sit in a circle on the floor. In the centre of the circle is the hat, scarf and gloves with the bar of chocolate, and the knife and fork on the plate. In turn, each player throws a dice and when they throw a six, they rush to put on the hat, scarf and gloves. Then they try to both unwrap and eat the chocolate using only the knife and fork (no hands allowed). In the meantime, the other players are still taking turns to throw the dice. As soon as another player throws a six, they rush to remove the hat, scarf and gloves from the first player, put them on and continue to try to eat the chocolate. The first player rejoins the others. The game continues until all the chocolate has been eaten.

The Ring Game

Arrange the players in a circle with one player in the middle. Players hold a circle of string, onto which is threaded a ring. At a signal to start, the centre player closes his eyes tightly and counts silently up to twenty. While this is being done, the players in the circle are sliding the ring from hand to hand round the string, all the time trying to conceal it under their hands. When the centre player has reached twenty, he opens his eyes and tries to spot which player is holding the ring. If guessed correctly, the player holding the ring changes places. If not, the player stays in the centre.

Guess in the Dark

Another 'in the dark' game which is enjoyed by children aged about nine or ten.

All the players sit round a table and are provided with a pencil and paper. The lights are switched off, and an object is passed round the table from player to player. The lights are then switched on and the players write down what they think the object was. Provide about twelve very different and unusual objects, such as a hair conditioner sachet, an apricot, a plastic house fly, a bulb of garlic, a piece of pumice stone, a piece of sandpaper, a wrinkled passionfruit, or a large sinker. The person who correctly lists the most objects is the winner.

Murder in the Dark

You will need pieces of paper, one for each player. Mark one with a 'D', another with an 'M', and leave the others blank. Fold the pieces of paper and put them in a hat. Each player draws one and looks at it without showing or telling anyone else what is on their piece of paper. Only the detective, who drew the D, takes position at the light switch. All lights are turned out. The room or house must be very dark. Other players move about the room. The murderer, who drew the M, approaches a player, grasps their arm and whispers 'You're dead'. The victim obligingly screams and falls down. All players must freeze, except the murderer, who tries to move away from the 'corpse'. At the count of five, the detective restores the light and tries to discover the murderer's identity. The detective can ask anyone as many questions as she likes. No players except the murderer may lie about their actions. Only the murderer can lie, but he must confess if the detective correctly solves the crime and asks, 'Are you the murderer?'

Magpies

This is a miniature scavenger hunt that can be played throughout the duration of the party, whenever a player spots something to add to their collection.

At the very start of the party, each child is given a matchbox with their name on it. The object of the game is for each player to collect as many tiny things as they can fit into their matchbox. Grains of sand or sugar are not counted. At the end of the party the matchboxes are collected and the contents counted. The player who has collected the highest number of objects is the winner.

The Flour Game

Tightly pack a kitchen bowl with flour and turn it out onto a plate so that there is a flour mountain. Stand the plate on some newspaper and put a blunt knife beside it. On top of the mountain place a sweet. Players take turns to cut away tiny slices of the mountain without making it collapse. When the mountain collapses and the sweet falls, the player responsible has to put his hands behind his back, bend over the place and eat the sweet from the flour.

Hedgehogs

This is a funny game for all ages, and is especially useful at small parties.

Give each player a fairly large potato, a saucer of pins and a pair of gloves. Each player, wearing the gloves, is then required to pick up the pins one at a time and stick them into the potato. The one who has given the hedgehog the most spines in three minutes wins the competition.

Charades

Charades is a popular miming game enjoyed by children of all ages. The idea is for one player to act out a word or a title, in mime, while onlookers try to guess the word. Having decided upon a word, the player acts or mimes a little sketch to illustrate each syllable of the word. For example with the word 'jigsaw' the player could dance a little jig for the first syllable, and pretend to saw for the second.

More than one person can take part in a charade. With young children it is often better to have at least two. A small party could also be divided into two teams, with each person on one team acting out one clue to the identity of the charade. The team guessing the correct identity in the shortest time wins.

Instead of words, a theme for charades could be chosen, such as nursery rhymes, book titles, films, pop songs or characters from a popular television series.

OUTDOOR GAMES

Overpass, Underpass

Divide the players into teams and get each team to form a row. Team members must pass a selection of objects over their heads from the first player to the last in the row. When the object reaches the last player, he returns the objects back between the legs of the players until it reaches the front. For extra fun and confusion, do not wait for one object to return to the front of the line. The object of the game is to get all the objects back to the beginning of the line as fast as possible. Balloons add an extra fun factor, as they float away out of reach.

Water Race

Divide the players into teams and get each team to form a row. At the head of each row is an empty bucket, with a full bucket of water some distance away. The first member of each team has a plastic mug. Using this, the team must transfer water from the full bucket to the empty one, by running in turn up to the full bucket and bringing back a mug of water. The first team to fill their bucket is the winning one.

Back To Back Race

All the players are to run in pairs. Each pair faces back to back with arms locked at the elbows. In this way, they have to run to a line and back again, so that one player runs forwards and the other backwards. On the way back, the pair returns with the player who last ran backwards now facing forwards.

Brick Race

A start and finish line are drawn. At the start line, players line up with two house bricks each. They must stand with one foot on one brick and put the next brick in front of them, then move onto the second brick while balancing, picking up the first and moving that ahead, and so on to the finishing line.

Tissue and Straw Race

Each team arranges itself in a line. Each team member is given a straw. The team leaders place a tissue over the end of their straw. One end of the straw is in the child's mouth. The child inhales to hold the tissue on the other end of the straw. The child transfers the tissue to the next player, who must inhale through his straw to take the tissue. In the same manner, it is passed along the row. Except at the start of the game, the tissue must not be touched by hand. If the tissue is dropped, the passing must recommence at the front of the line. The first team to finish is the winner.

Slow Tortoise Race

Bicycles can be used for this race. A start and finish line are drawn. The slowest person in this race is the winner. The children must be well spaced on their bikes so as not to wobble into each other. Everyone starts to ride their bicycle as slowly as possible. The last rider to reach the finishing line is the winner.

This slow-motion race can also be played without bikes, with the children crawling, hopping or skipping instead.

Tug of War

This is a popular game of strength. You will need a strong rope, at least four metres long. Divide the players equally into two teams. The sturdiest person of each team is chosen to be the 'anchor' at each end of the rope. Draw a line on the ground between each team holding onto the rope and tie a handkerchief to the middle of the rope. The handkerchief should be hanging over the ground line when the tug starts. At the starting signal each team tries to pull the other team across to their side of the line.

Hot Potato Relay

Divide the players into two equal teams. Each team is given a spoon and a basket. Make two rows of potatoes in front of each team. They should be very well spaced and there should be the same number of

potatoes as there are team members. On the starting signal, the first player runs to the first potato, picks it up with the spoon (no hands are to be used), and carries it back to drop in the basket at the starting line. She then gives the spoon to the next player who runs, picks up the next potato and brings it back to the basket. The first team to get all the potatoes into the basket wins the game.

Sack Race

Always lots of fun. Each player climbs into a hessian sack and, holding the top of the sack by the hands, must jump, without falling, from the start line to the finish line.

Drop the Handkerchief

All the players except one form a well-spaced circle facing inwards. The remaining player runs around outside the circle and drops a handkerchief behind one of the players in the circle. Immediately the player discovering the handkerchief must pick up the handkerchief and chase the player who dropped it. If the player who dropped the handkerchief beats the other player back to their place in the circle, then the one who is chasing becomes the next one to drop the handkerchief.

This is a variation of a traditional game called *A Tisket, A Tasket*, in which the player outside calls:

'A tisket, a tasket, a green and yellow basket.
I wrote a letter to my love and on the way I dropped it.
I dropped it once, I dropped it twice, I dropped it three times over.
One of you has picked it up and put it in your pocket.
It wasn't you, it wasn't you, it wasn't you . . . it was YOU!'

At the last shout of 'YOU!', the chase begins.

Egg and Spoon Race

An old-time favourite. Each player is given a hard-boiled egg and a spoon. They must hold the egg balanced on the spoon, while running from the starting line to the finishing line. To make this game more complicated for

older children, make it a rule that if they drop their egg they must put it back on the spoon, go back to the starting line and start again.

A variation of this race can be played with each runner holding two spoons, each containing an egg. Potatoes could be substituted for hard-boiled eggs.

Three-Legged Race

Players are divided into pairs. The right leg of one person is tied with a scarf to the left leg of another runner. A little practice period should be allowed before this race.

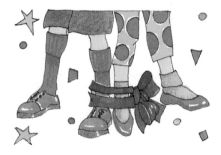

Wheelbarrow Race

Two lines are drawn, a distance apart. The players are divided into pairs. One player gets down on all fours and his partner picks up his feet, making him into a wheelbarrow. The pair run in this way from the start line to the other line; then players reverse positions for the return trip. The fastest pair wins.

Grandmother's Footsteps

All the players, except one, stand in line with the one chosen to be Grandmother standing some distance away with her back towards them. The players creep forward, but whenever Grandmother quickly turns round they must stand still. If she sees any of them moving, they must return to the starting line again. The first to reach Grandmother becomes the next Grandmother.

Another version of this game is *K-I-N-G Spells KING*. The player who is King calls out:

'K-I-N-G spells KING!' and at the word KING she spins round to look at the advancing children. Any who are seen moving are out, and the first child to successfully reach the King becomes the next King.

List of Recipes and Games

GAMES

This edition published in 1995 by Leopard Books
Random House, 20 Vauxhall Bridge Road, London SW1V 2SA

First published in 1990 by Murdoch Books®, a division of Murdoch Magazines Pty Ltd

© Murdoch Books®, 1990

ISBN 0 7529 0088 9

Food stylist: Wendy Berecry
Illustrations: Gaye Chapman
Designer: Robin James
Finished art: Ivy Hansen

Typeset by Savage Type Pty Ltd, Brisbane
Produced by Mandarin Offset, Hong Kong

The publisher thanks Hide 'n' Seek, Military Road, Mosman and Toy World, Oxford Street, Bondi
Junction for their assistance in the photography of the Picnic Party (page 63).

USEFUL INFORMATION

All recipes are thoroughly tested
using standard metric measuring cups and
spoons. All cup and spoon measurements are
level. We have used eggs with an average weight
of 55 g each in all recipes.

WEIGHTS AND MEASURES

In this book, metric measures and their imperial equivalents have been rounded out to the nearest figure that is easy to use. Different charts from different authorities vary slightly; the following are the measures we have used consistently throughout our recipes.

LENGTHS

Metric	Imperial
5 mm	¼ in
1 cm	½ in
2 cm	¾ in
2.5 cm	1 in
5 cm	2 in
6 cm	2½ in
8 cm	3 in
10 cm	4 in
12 cm	5 in
15 cm	6 in
18 cm	7 in
20 cm	8 in
23 cm	9 in
25 cm	10 in
28 cm	11 in
30 cm	12 in
46 cm	18 in
50 cm	20 in
61 cm	24 in
77 cm	30 in

OVEN TEMPERATURE CHART

	C	F	Gas Mark
Very slow	120	250	½
Slow	150	300	1–2
Mod. slow	160	325	3
Moderate	180	350	4
Mod. hot	190	375	5–6
Hot	200	400	6–7
Very hot	230	450	8–9

CUP & SPOON MEASURES

A basic metric cup set consists of 1 cup, ½ cup, ⅓ cup and ¼ cup sizes.
  The basic spoon set comprises 1 tablespoon, 1 teaspoon, ½ teaspoon and ¼ teaspoon.

1 cup	250 mL / 8 fl oz
½ cup	125 mL / 4 fl oz
⅓ cup	80 mL / 2½ fl oz
(4 tablespoons)	
¼ cup	60 mL / 2 fl oz
(3 tablespoons)	
1 tablespoon	20 mL
1 teaspoon	5 mL
½ teaspoon	2.5 mL
¼ teaspoon	1.25 mL

LIQUIDS

Metric	Imperial
30 mL	1 fl oz
60 mL	2 fl oz
90 mL	3 fl oz
100 mL	3½ fl oz
125 mL	4 fl oz (½ cup)
155 mL	5 fl oz
170 mL	5½ fl oz (⅔ cup)
185 mL	6 fl oz
200 mL	6½ fl oz
220 mL	7 fl oz
250 mL	8 fl oz (1 cup)
280 mL	9 fl oz
300 mL	9½ fl oz
315 mL	10 fl oz
350 mL	11 fl oz
375 mL	12 fl oz
410 mL	13 fl oz
440 mL	14 fl oz
470 mL	15 fl oz
500 mL	16 fl oz (2 cups)
600 mL	1 pt (20 fl oz)
750 mL	1 pt 5 fl oz (3 cups)
1 litre	1 pt 12 fl oz (4 cups)
(1000 mL)	
1.5 litres	2 pt 8 fl oz (6 cups)

DRY INGREDIENTS

Metric	Imperial
15 g	½ oz
30 g	1 oz
45 g	1½ oz
60 g	2 oz
75 g	2½ oz
90 g	3 oz
100 g	3½ oz
125 g	4 oz
140 g	4½ oz
155 g	5 oz
170 g	5½ oz
185 g	6 oz
200 g	6½ oz
220 g	7 oz
235 g	7½ oz
250 g	8 oz
265 g	8½ oz
280 g	9 oz
300 g	9½ oz
315 g	10 oz
330 g	10½ oz
350 g	11 oz
360 g	11½ oz
375 g	12 oz
400 g	12½ oz
410 g	13 oz
425 g	13½ oz
440 g	14 oz
455 g	14½ oz
470 g	15 oz
485 g	15½ oz
500 g	1 lb (16 oz)
750 g	1 lb 8 oz
1 kg (1000 g)	2 lb
1.5 kg	3 lb
2 kg	4 lb
2.5 kg	5 lb